News from Somewhen

Visions of a fragile utopia

Hugh Barton

Illustrations by Val Kirby

First published in the United Kingdom in 2026 by
The Cloister House Press

ISBN 978-1-913460-98-3

Contents

Foreword   1

Prologue   3

PART I: **Transition and initiation**   7

    1   I left my body on a distant shore   8

    2   The unknown, remembered gate   13

    3   The lady of situations   20

    4   An erstwhile home   29

    5   Conflicting messages   41

    6   The moot   49

PART II: **The future of land and place**   61

    7   Vale and Wold   62

    8   The farmer   73

    9   The urbanist   84

    10   Local-global planning   97

PART III: **Exploring a strange society**   113

    11   Greek Games   114

    12   Off the leash, maybe …   125

    13   Health equity   139

14 Diktat v democracy   150

15 Mountains and microchips   155

16 The path of Ubuntu   165

17 Cultural exchange   174

18 Identity and sexual politics   182

PART IV: **Synthesis and revelation**   195

19 Delving deeper   196

20 Housing and habit   204

21 Can you hear the future weeping?   211

22 Beer and Bristol   223

23 If all time is eternally present   232

Epilogue: **Tiger Spirit**   247

Thanks   254

Foreword

A young woman called Robyn Ghorra, recently lost to this world in a coma, finds herself transported as if by magic to a future era. She discovers much to surprise her – causes for both despond and delight. The new age has made remarkable strides towards a more sustainable and nature-friendly environment. Society appears to value equity, conviviality and individual freedom. People are healthy and happy. Gradually she uncovers what has happened to enable these advances. They have been triggered by a reaction to multiple mid-century crises – climate, ecological, economic and technological. She also comes to suspect that the new utopia is only possible through long-term democratic autocracy. The future remains uncertain, the issues complex. When, later, she is abruptly returned to her own time, Robyn finds she has retained amazingly precise and detailed memories of what she saw and did and felt. She is determined to pursue her newfound idealism in her own work and life, and asked me to write up her story, an account of her experiences. I was hugely flattered to be trusted by her. In the process I learnt more about humankind's future history than I ever could have imagined. We both hope that you will be inspired by her story.

Hugh Barton

Prologue

Friday was supposedly my day off. I'd been looking forward to it: a morning session helping out at a local Stroud foodbank; then a stone wall-building workshop, with a social lunch; later a good walk along the canal towpath and over the Common in the spring sunshine. Altogether a very satisfying agenda.

Working at the foodbank had been a revelation. There were still so many families, after financial meltdown in 2008, austerity and then the pandemic, who were really hard up and needed our services. Most of those coming for sustenance were regulars, some sad and despondent, others stalwart copers – parents with hungry kids showing a level of courage and positivity which humbled me. I helped by filling food boxes, talking congenially to clients, serving tea.

By contrast the workshop involved hard, creative labour. As usual I would be muttering under my breath at the inert lumps of stone which would not fit in their allotted positions, then gleeful when I solved the problems, joking and laughing with my companions. Then the walk.

I am besotted with the glorious landscape around Stroud, modified over millennia by humankind: the incised river valleys draining to the Severn, haunt of dippers and otters; the bold, old, stone mills, giving a powerful sense of local identity; the high meadows of the Commons, with skylarks, cowslips and orchids. I think of the five richly vegetated industrial valleys that meet in Stroud as the 'forgotten' Cotswolds – so different from the picturesque villages and softer landscape of the dip-slope draining east – the whole area a delight for walkers, full of surprise and intricacy.

However, my walking idyll was not to be. I had been summoned the night before by the boss of the consultancy I worked with, for an apparently vital early meeting with an important client, to try to clinch some aspects of a big housing scheme. Making an early start, my trusty folding e-bike took me the eight miles cross-country from Stroud to Cam & Dursley station on the main line down to Bristol. The train journey was a pleasure, meeting with others in the cycle/train fraternity – I was the token woman amongst them!

The cycle ride from Bristol Parkway to my office a couple of miles away should, in retrospect, have been a warning. Danger lurked at every congested junction. At one big roundabout a huge pantechnicon turned left across my line of travel, not noticing me down by his side. There were no bike lanes to protect me and I couldn't see his indicator – if indeed he had used it at all. He practically crushed my little Brompton. I had to swerve violently to avoid collision, then slewed to an almost catastrophic halt as the bike escaped from under me. Luckily, on this occasion, the bike and I both survived. When I got to the office I was able to cool my fevered brow with a cold shower, thankful for this thoughtful perk my employers offered.

The meeting involved some of the top people in our planning and design consultancy – plus me, as a mid-level urban designer. We met with key decision-makers in the development company, together with a couple of junior planners from the local authority. I felt chuffed to be party to big decisions, even more so as my layout for the scheme, which prioritised the needs of pedestrians, children and older people, was given the green light. Other aspects of the scheme, including its location, were far from ideal, but were not, I considered, my business.

The meeting over, I returned to Stroud for what remained of my day off. My place is in upper Stroud, a two-bedroom rented flat off Bisley Road, which I share with a young woman in her mid-twenties (at thirty-one I feel much more mature!). She works from home, as I do some days, so the coffee machine has a big job to do keeping up with our demands. This particular morning, to my chagrin, she had her boyfriend with her. They were considerate enough, moving from the living room to her modest bedroom. The irony is I have a king size bed in my room, with no-one to share it, while she has a single bed and a succession of sharers. I try not to be jealous. Indeed, often quite the reverse – thankful her latest partner had not been somehow foisted on me! Life is quite full enough without romantic entanglements. I devote myself to job, community choir and charitable activity.

By now my stint at the food bank would be over, and the morning session of the stone-walling workshop would be wrapping up. So I aimed to catch the others at the lunch break. I changed into my rough-tough walling gear and got out the sports bike – such fun down the hill! My hair blew wild in the breeze. It was exhilarating.

What happened subsequently is etched on my mind with alarming and unnatural clarity. Despite being many months ago, it feels like yesterday. I barely escaped with my life.

It was partly my own fault. As I cycled down the hill from the upper town – freewheeling without a care in the world, enjoying the sunshine, eyes looking skywards for the swifts I thought I'd heard screeching – a car approached, travelling up the hill, way over the speed limit. A red-faced, middle-aged bloke, driving a big, wide, silver gas-guzzler as if he owned the road, was hogging the single lane allowed by parked cars. I swerved violently but he caught me a glancing blow. A large woman in the passenger seat shouted at him, 'go on, go on, don't stop, it's only a bloody cyclist. He'll (sic) be fine!'

I was on the ground, my bike sprawled over me, conscious of no pain, but bleeding from hands and head. The monster car sped off up the hill. I picked myself up, dazed and shaken. A passerby, walking up the hill, offered encouragement and TLC, partially restoring my faith in human nature. What a blessing! He'd seen the accident, reported the woman's words to me, noting her built-in gender presumption, but sadly failed to take the number plate of the vehicle. He bundled the bike, with its bent front wheel, into a side entrance, and took me gently down the road, round the corner, where, as luck would have it, the town's small hospital was located. He stayed with me for the initial formalities, assisting with the explanation of what had happened, then gave me his mobile number and waited while I was seen by the nurse. She patched me up, and with the duty doctor observed my physical and mental state for a while, before allowing me home – actually at my insistence. In retrospect that was probably foolish.

Walking slowly back up the hill, I felt strange and woozy. But I made it to my flat and let myself in. Drank some water. Collapsed in the armchair. Couldn't face the idea of food. Told my flatmate what had happened and watched some dumb programme on TV. Images on the screen swam in front of my eyes. I rang my Mum, who lived on the other side of town.

She was in one of her more confused states. I realised that sharing my plight with her was pointless. Conversely, I had nothing to offer her.

After that I took stock: no bones broken; bandages on head and hand; cycle waiting to be rescued; rip-roaring headache. Took painkillers and went early to bed. Miracle of miracles, I slept.

Part I
Transition and initiation

This waterlily, from the North Pembrokeshire coast, represents purity, rebirth and strength.
The magical transfer from our time to the distant future is like a new beginning

1
I left my body on a distant shore

After what seemed like a long, dreamless sleep I drowsily surfaced, coming slowly to consciousness. I felt a gentle rhythmic motion, side to side. There was a low drone. My eyes wouldn't open, apparently sticky with sleep, but I sensed light and dark. I realised the light was very local, immediately around me. The world beyond, out there, was dark. The gentle rocking lulled me back over the edge of sleep, dreaming. I was riding down the hill again, carefree and enjoying life, my hair (long as it had once been) blowing in the wind, and the swifts screaming overhead. There was no big beast of a car. I came almost to the end of the road. But then was at the top again, careering down the hill – look, no hands! – faster and faster, not a care in the world, until a sudden, alarming emptiness below catapulted me back to the start, repeating the same wild ride, down, down, down, but not getting anywhere. Blackness loomed ahead. An ominous cloud of darkness, blocking out the light, threatening. The bike was gone. I seemed to be hurtling down a black chasm, orchestral music screeching, discordant glissandi plunging to the depths of sound, falling, falling, about to crash into a hard black vacancy.

I started awake. Just the quiet hum and gentle movement. My eyes refused to open but I sensed there was forward momentum. I was travelling, and through a black tunnel. It went on and on. The feeling of imminent overwhelming threat evaporated but my heart was racing, ears blocked, head dizzy and befuddled. What was going on? Mad ideas flicked through my mind … the darkness of the birth canal, had I regressed to the womb? Or was I like Alice, transitioning from one world to the next down the rabbit hole, or in a railway carriage from one chess square to the next, with a bespectacled sheep, knitting …

That final whimsy was a clue. I was in a train, travelling through an endless tunnel. The low drone was the engine. I felt the seat I was sitting on. My eyes flickered. Blurred vision of an old-fashioned train compartment, two cushioned benches facing each other, mirrors and luggage racks, sliding door to the carriage passageway. No-one else in the compartment. No sheep knitting. Just me. And the darkness sliding past outside.

Suddenly – blazing light! We'd erupted out of the tunnel. Dazzled, I closed my eyes tight, wanting to retreat back into what seemed a safe dark place. Thoughts flashed through my mind. I could not engage with where I was. Was I in a time-warp? On a train from an earlier age? The accident was vague and distant in my mind. I seemed still to be in dream territory. I tried to take note of myself. Body tense, heart pounding, head completely befuddled, eyes resolutely closed. With a conscious effort of will, I gave myself rescue instructions: deep, slow breaths. Sit upright. Imagine how tall I can be. Relax hands. Reduce eyelid pressure. Allow colour to come through the eyelids. Catch the fleeting range of blue and green and yellow and red. Enjoy those sensations.

My racing heart slowed. My mind became calm. Then, drawn to the bright light on one side, I realised it was time. I opened my eyes, opened them wide.

Blinking in the brightness, I found myself looking out of the window. A magical green valley with woods, clearings, occasional stone cottages, sliding past. I blinked hard and looked again. My heart warmed. I knew this valley! The river flowed down to my home town. I was travelling back home! The scene was perfect, the time-shaped landscape of wool and water. But my reverie was short-lived. I became aware I was not alone.

I turned to face the opposite bench. A man was looking straight at me, openly, blatantly. Surely he'd not been there before! Instinctively I averted my eyes and pulled my flimsy dress down over my thighs. 'Hi, hello, welcome!' The man spoke with a friendly voice, a slightly odd accent I didn't recognise. 'You're so welcome. I think and hope your transition is complete. But you must have been anxious, over the last few minutes, and puzzled I guess.' I found my voice, one word at least: 'Shocked!' I said, looking aslant at him, trying not to engage. He clearly sensed my unease. 'It must have been very strange indeed,' he said warmly, his necklace jangling. 'Let me introduce myself. I'm Rufus, appointed to look after you and guide you.'

Something in his voice and manner gave me confidence. I began to relax and looked at him. He was young, white, average height and slim, dressed in a brightly coloured shirt and shorts and sporting glittering necklaces. His body language was relaxed, almost laid back, his mien totally unthreatening. He was speaking again: 'First things first. I'm ignoring your plight! You've got practically nothing on! Here's a set of clothes and footwear not too different from your time. Quickly please, before we reach the next stop. I'll wait outside.' Rufus went out into the passageway and pulled the blind down.

For the first time I took in my appearance. Clothed in – not very much! All I had on was a short, cotton nightshirt, not a dress at all. And bare feet. It flashed across my mind that my state of undress made me dangerously vulnerable. No wonder other people were steering clear of my compartment; any normal person would wonder what on earth I was doing there. I stood up, struggled out of my nightshirt and got dressed. He had provided quite conventional, lightweight summer clothing. I knocked on the dividing glass. Rufus came in. 'Thank you,' I said, 'I feel much better now!' In fact I was flummoxed – astonished – how my mind had come back to me. No headache. I was feeling much more poised.

The train was gliding steadily down its long slope into the valley. Rufus pointed out of the window. 'I expect you recognise some of this – but look over there – something new to you I'm sure.' The view did rather confuse me. Cresting the valley side above the woodland, brilliantly sunlit, were fields planted in regular strips, each field angled differently. 'Vineyards? ' I queried. Rufus nodded, smiling. I couldn't remember them at all. They reminded me of the south of France.

Then the landscape started to change. Stone cottages grew in number, all higgledy-piggledy up the sides of the valley, hanging precariously in the pattern created – as I knew – by wool workers centuries earlier. Then grander buildings appeared. The train slowed and came to a halt. To my surprise we'd reached a station. Stroud was the first station, further on down the valley. But it wasn't Stroud. I couldn't quite take in the situation, except the name: Chalford Station, it announced. But there was no station at Chalford – the line went right through! My unease grew again. 'Excuse me,' I said, 'that station does not exist. What's happened?' Then I remembered that it had existed once upon a time. I looked again at the retro decor of the coach compartment. 'I'm gobsmacked!' I said, 'have I travelled back … back in time?' Rufus looked at me sympathetically. 'No, not back. Forward. You are now living in a later age.' I let his words sink in a moment, 'How much later?' I asked, heart in mouth. 'It's not really for me to say, but quite a long time.' replied Rufus. 'It is all rather complex. I'll try to explain later. We're on the half-hourly shuttle service between Swindon and Cheltenham.'

I heard the words. My brain refused to process them. Was I still in dreamtime? And yet... a beautiful, almost familiar landscape; frequent train service; very personable, civilised young man. It was all alarmingly coherent.

Rufus seemed to comprehend my confusion, gently opening his palms towards me, talking in quietly rational tones: 'Yes, it must be difficult to grasp,' he said. 'But you are in the future not the past. And this compartment is simply modelled on a 1950s design, it's completely misleading. They provide it for difficult, vulnerable or very special passengers, and I booked it for you and me. The rest of the carriage is totally different.' And which am I, I wondered, difficult or vulnerable – or very special? Then the significance of his words suddenly struck me like a clash of cymbals. I was in the future, dreamworld or not. The accident was still fuzzy in my head, but I thought...coma! I'm in a coma! Somehow that thought settled me. If I was dreaming, I thought, it was a good dream. Rufus was nice, the train comfortable, the sun shining, the valley beautiful. What's not to like? So – engage with it, accept it, enter into it.

As my brain tried to catch up with the new reality, the train arrived at the next station: Brimscombe, it said. Another new one! And a huge transformation had occurred all round it: lots of new buildings, somehow foreign in style – and I glimpsed the canal. 'We'll show you this area some time. Really interesting what has happened here,' said Rufus. We move off again, following the canal. Rufus pointed: 'There's my favourite walking destination,' he said, casually. It was Stroud Brewery, more or less as I remembered it, though now brightly painted and more open to the towpath, lots of boats crowded around, a narrow bridge spanning the canal. 'It seems you're not the only one to like it!' I commented, then really surprised at what I'd said, because it was gently ironic and conversational, not stressed out. 'The canal is great,' said Rufus. 'You can boat right over the top these days, if you're willing to negotiate God knows how many locks. Plenty of intervening hospitality opportunities, of course.' I was, to my surprise, taking things in. 'You mean right over the Cotswolds to the Thames?' 'Absolutely. That only happened a decade or so ago. Planned way back at the beginning of the century, of course. Wow! Things sometimes go so slowly! Now the people of the Thames valley drink water from the Severn, greedy lot! That's also how we get the water up to the top of the hills, to feed the canal. Pumped up from the Severn, then down the canal to Cricklade.' I vaguely remembered that plan.

The train was approaching Stroud. I looked up and there was the spire of the Cemetery Chapels – an iconic landmark in the town, not far from my home territory. I was comforted to see it there.

We slid almost silently into Stroud station, and I was abruptly wrenched out of my sense of the familiar. The whole feeling of the place was different. Strange-looking buildings had sprouted everywhere; the multi-storey car park had vanished; there was a long, stationary goods train, rather tatty; new bridges spanned the railway. But there was no time to ponder. Rufus gathered me up and ushered me out of the compartment into the corridor. I realised that the rest of the carriage was all one space, thronged with people, some making to get off. I felt suddenly vulnerable, but Rufus shepherded me onto the platform, somehow protecting me from the crowd. The people were taller and very diverse. No-one was seriously overweight. Women and men were smartly dressed. We waited on the platform until there were fewer people around. My pounding heart slowed. I took a deep breath, almost a sigh, trying to come more fully into myself, trying to arrive at the place that had been home. For some reason fragments of poetry echoed in my mind: *suspended in time … I left my body on a distant shore …* T.S. Eliot! Was I really here? It was like home. It had been home. But it had changed.

2
The unknown, remembered gate

We walked off the platform. Rufus was watching my reactions with interest. 'Yes, it's all changed. The people must seem different. Not very wealthy, but it's a pretty healthy and happy community. We'll have a chance to observe a bit later. And I saw you looking at the bridges – both made since your time. That elegant pedestrian bridge, with lifts and the spiral gives wheelchair access across the station. Constructed in the thirties, I think. Before that, as you know, getting from one side of the station to the other was impossible for people with mobility problems, buggies or heavy bags. Shocking how long it took to put that right! And the big bridge slanting across over there is the bus bridge.' I was beginning to see things more clearly, trying to put my cool professional hat on. 'What happened to the multi-storey car park?' I asked. 'Oh! We didn't need that anymore,' said Rufus with a dismissive laugh. 'What we did need was a transfer station.' I looked puzzled. 'For all the goods coming and going by rail,' he explained. 'There's the train now. The goods arrive, are unpacked and sorted, ready for distribution. I'll show you later.'

A bus was waiting outside the station. Going to New Stonehouse, it said. I noticed the electronic information board. Rufus tapped his large wristwatch: 'All on here too,' he said. I thought, Ah! Gloucestershire has come into the twenty-first century. At last! We walked on and looked at all the new development – new to me anyway. The old car park south of the railway was now full of European-looking blocks of houses and flats, three or four storeys high, with what looked like solar roofs, and a semi-basement level below with a garden above. I had the oddest sensation of déjà vu. It looked like something I might almost have designed myself. With a shock I realised it was quite old, now, and showing its age. Attractive, though. What gave it a continental impression was external shutters on every window, and lots of balconies. 'All those homes paid for the bridge,' Rufus told me. It seemed he knew my design background, because he went on: 'This was one of the first local developments to be pretty well carbon neutral, and the first with shutters too – more to exclude summer heat than winter cold. The basement used to be for cars, but most people can't afford them now. Now it's for bikes, storage, recycling, a few shared vehicles, and a marvellous, if incredibly noisy, racetrack for kids.' We climbed the few steps up to the garden level, and looked over the gate: lawn, benches, flowers, bushes, trees coming up through the basement light wells, well-maintained raised beds for produce – a delightful scene. All good, I thought! I relaxed my shoulders in pleasure, thinking if this is all a dream, I may as well enjoy it.

Rufus encouraged me back down, into the public space. I saw that the pedestrian way over the railway spiralled to ground level and continued across the space to the cliff wall above the canal, becoming an elegant curved steel bridge over canal and road, with people coming and going. I could see it linked up with the arches of a defunct railway and, I presumed, the cycleway to the neighbouring town of Nailsworth. It was uncanny. My mouth fell open in mixed disbelief and delight. Turning to Rufus, still shy of spontaneous expression, I said: 'You know, Rufus, that's almost unnerving. Brilliant, though! This route was dreamed up back in the teens – my time. It's actually happened!' 'Yes, well, about time,' said Rufus coolly. 'It's all part of the strategy to make Stroud much more walkable, despite all the hills. But that bridge to Rodborough only appeared a decade ago, when the area below was redeveloped. Already, though, it's been an absolute boon. And wait until you see the other bridge conceived back then, on the other side of town. We're getting known as the town of bridges.' My heart leapt, but I tried to hide my enthusiasm. 'I know the one you mean! I'd like to walk over it, see how it feels.'

'Yes! It was all about opening up sites close to the town centre, packing 'em in close by... people I mean,' said Rufus, then raised his eyes to the sky and put mock ennui into his voice. 'But god! They weren't exactly in a hurry, were they. From conception to birth, sixty years! The longest gestation known.'

My mind went into overdrive. That was a bombshell. Not the weak joke. The time elapsed! My face must have dropped a mile. Rufus looked at me with concern. 'Sixty years?' I almost whispered, incredulous. 'So that means ... the year is now ...?' Rufus was crestfallen. 'Ah! Yes. Sorry. So sorry! I didn't mean for it to come out like that. I was supposed to let you down gently. Too late now. I'll have to tell you.' He paused. 'The year is twenty-ninety. Two thousand and ninety.' I gulped, not really believing it. 'Fuck!' I said, very deliberately, breathing deeply, then gave an inane laugh.

Despite the shock, I was really surprised how my mind reacted. The me that I was used to would have lurched into ultra-angst mode, been nervy as hell since arrival. But instead I wanted to treat the situation as an outlandish game. I thought to myself, I've been beamed, as in Star Trek, across space and time – from hospital bed to train carriage, from the twenties to the nineties, and I'm going to take it as though it's just a normal flight from Heathrow to Rome, or Rome to Rio. My voice piped up, a sort of trained rational response: 'Rufus, could we please sit down and have a nice chat about what on earth has happened?'

There was a kiosk between the two pedestrian bridges, and a seat nearby facing sunwards. 'Let's sit here,' said Rufus. 'Just have a look around, take stock a bit, while I get refreshments.' He produced water bottles from a knapsack I hadn't noticed before, filled them at a water fountain, handed me one, and went to the kiosk. I looked at the people passing by, properly, for the first time. Men and women, girls and boys, black, brown, yellow and white, with quite a lot looking a bit like me – mixed heritage. Whether laughing or frowning, hastening or dawdling, everyone looked positive, alert and alive. And their clothes full of rich textures and inventive variety – for the most part quite smart – unconventional but smart – the Stroud inclination for shabby chic no longer so much in evidence. Some of the men reminded me of seventeenth century dandies, with tights, doublet and hose, all very colourful. The women were often more reserved in style and colour, with less flesh on show than the men. However, it was difficult to generalise. Sometimes I found it difficult to tell the men and women apart; they seemed more of a height than I remembered, with most women taller than me – a new experience for me! The younger girls and boys seemed almost unisex. I looked in vain for people who were seriously overweight, or dejected or self-obsessed. Like many places, Stroud had always had its share of such people. I realised another sharp contrast – phones were not in evidence. I wondered if radio communication was into eye pieces or some other wizardry I could not dream of. Everyone looked ridiculously healthy and friendly. The future seemed benign!

Rufus had come back with two Mars bars. 'I chose the vegan ones,' he said, 'not being sure of your tastes. They're just as good.' I bit enthusiastically into the bar. 'Oh wow, I said, very nice, but …' 'Fig and honey,' said Rufus, 'both English in origin. The chocolate is a bit of a treat, naughty really. It's quite pricy now, all fair trade and carbon taxed, with local oat milk.' We sat in silence for a little, chomping our new-style Mars bars, then I turned to my companion, and, rather deliberately, asked, 'Rufus, what has happened? How come I'm here? What's going on?'

He looked seriously at me. 'That is a very appropriate question, and one which I can't answer properly at all.' He sounded suddenly a bit pompous. I looked askance at him. He went on, 'I'll try to explain insofar as I can. You'll know from twentieth century theories – especially Einstein's theory of relativity – that time is not a steady, ever-flowing stream. It can go very fast or very slow. Scientists have been investigating the nature of time, the relationship to speed and space and mind, the possibility of time travel. Maybe somehow you jumped in time – or rather, were jumped. Someone knew it was going to happen. I was given training and told to mug up on the early century years. Then this morning I was contacted, on an old-fashioned mobile phone, and told I must meet you on the train, befriend you and act as your guide for as long as you choose to stay.'

I was impatient at this. 'For as long as I choose to stay! As long as I choose! That implies I decided to come in the first place. And I didn't! Anyway, who instructed you? For that matter, how did I get onto the train, dressed in a nightshirt?' Rufus reacted with calm friendliness, 'My line manager, Professor McCanlis. He told me I'd find you in a state of undress, and to provide suitable clothes to help gain your trust. But who instructed him, and what he knows, and how you arrived on that train, at that time, I haven't a clue. It's way above my pay-scale! But you know, the subconscious works in mysterious ways. We don't really understand 'mind' or 'spirit', even now. In fact, in some ways we're more fully aware of our ignorance now than ever before. The more we try to mimic mind with smart robots, the more we discover there is a lot more to it than a memory bank, a body-minder and a calculator. You might have chosen to come.' He smiled in apparent sympathy and shrugged.

I realised that was it. I wasn't going to get much more out of him. He was in the dark too. Or more likely had been told to play it cool. As we stood to go, I asked, 'and will I get to meet your prof?'

'I profoundly trust so,' he said. 'That decision is rather out of my hands. Come on, we're going down to the canal.'

We walked round a huge old block of flats – once upon a time a busy cloth factory – then down a broad flight of steps between buildings. At the bottom, a small square by the canal, a nineteenth century stone warehouse, extended in glass, and a bustling cafe. The canal was busy with narrowboats and canoes, some negotiating the lock that I remembered so well. People milled around, chatting, boat-watching. All so strange, familiar but strange. The phrase 'the unknown, remembered gate' flashed into my mind. T. S. Eliot again maybe. Somehow the reflection calmed my spirit. I would try to engage positively with this unintended experience. Looking around, I said: 'This, this is great! Just how I always imagined it, only better!' 'Stroud's been a thriving canal town for over fifty years now,' said Rufus. Done wonders for the local economy, kept us going through the devil years – people and businesses wanting to be here. They've had to expand the town. Mind you, they had to anyway.' 'Really?' I said, 'that must have been difficult, with the hills hemming in the town.' 'Well, I'm no expert,' he said, 'we'll get hold of one of the urbanists, hopefully they can explain.'

We went back up the graceful stepped way to the station, through the bus station, where small driverless buses were coming and going, and cars – mostly taxis, Rufus informed me, all robotic – and then on over the original station footbridge. It had been dilapidated when I last saw it, back in 2023. Now all spick and span, gleaming, with clear-glazed viewing possible over the tracks – lovely! We emerged into the station square. It had been transformed: new buildings on two sides, beautiful paving with a maze and intermittent fountains; e-bikes and trikes along one side, cafe tables spilling out in front of the old hotel. Two young kids were jumping in and out of the waterspouts, tempting fate.

This was a dream come true! A beautiful civic square by the classic station building, people walking, kids playing in safety. I insisted we linger for a moment to drink it all in. If this were a dream, I wanted to stay in it! Rufus told me the new design was a very recent investment by the local authority, very controversial, because funds were short. A special Provincial grant had eased the reservations. We sat and absorbed the atmosphere. Then Rufus became re-energised. 'Come on Robyn, there's lots to see, let's move on.'

He led me out of the square, along the side of the tracks, into what I remembered as the back side of the town centre, all ugly shop backs and random parking. But there were no vehicles now. A series of stalls, small workshops and colourful container pods; people bustling along or idling past the stalls, gossiping; the old Goods Shed alive with artistic activity. 'The nickname for this area is Diagon Alley,' said Rufus with a laugh. 'You know, after that classic children's story you must have been brought up on … Because all this was a dead area, magically transformed. And what's more,' he said, 'you can get almost anything here – wands, hats, rabbits … ' I smiled awkwardly, but appreciated his casual humour.

We walked up the slanting path on the side wall of the square beyond the Goods Shed, and there, out in the open air where the multi-storey car park had been, was an absolute hive of activity, stretching alongside the tracks on two levels. Any number of contraptions were manipulating boxes and stuff down below, while elegant bridges swept overhead with carts and vans parading demurely along them. 'Watch,' said my companion. I watched, astonished. The vans lacked both cabs and drivers. The carts had no horses. They would stop at various points and boxes surfaced from below and were placed onto or into them. No hands, no humans visible. I saw the lift structures that managed the transfers. The whole process was meticulous, seamless, completely odourless and almost silent – just a gentle whir of machinery. I stared in amazement. Rufus smiled with pleasure. 'It's not rocket science,' he said, 'just clever engineering and electronic tagging. The big containers come in by train,' (I glanced across at the goods train in the adjacent siding) 'and everything in them has a destination code, which allows sorting and onward travel to factories, shops, services, workshops and homes. Though actually people often collect things for home by trailer bike – it's much cheaper!' Indeed, I then noticed, over on the town side of the Sorting Station, several cyclists packing and chatting. It all seemed to be working like clockwork.

'Almost time for lunch,' said Rufus, 'I think you'll recognise the cafe we're booked into. What do you fancy? Vegan, veggie, fishy, meaty, beery, coffee?' I was still transfixed by the scene in front of me, but turned to him, smiling, despite my general sense of dislocation. 'Vegetarian and then strong coffee would be great,' I said. We strolled past the edge of the sorting station and into the heart of the town. No vehicles, it seemed. People milling around, shops and cafes and workshops, personal services of all kinds. Some establishments I recognised, though almost invariably in the 'wrong' place. I was struck by the number of second-hand and repair shops, selling all kinds of things. Some shops were offering services that were completely mysterious. One that puzzled me had a rather suggestive window display and was simply called Hedonism. I filed this away in my mind for later query, because we'd reached the central square of the town: no traffic, but loads of people, bikes and small driverless carts weaving their way. Seeing my gaze, Rufus told me that cycles and robocarts are restricted automatically to 15 kph here. Not mph, kph! I noted.

At that moment a blaze of sound erupted from the balcony of the old town hall. A band playing Beatles songs! We stopped. I listened, entranced, and looked around the public square, where a crowd had gathered. There had been judicious demolition since my time. It was bigger and much better, with superb decorative paving and a strange fountain reminding me of Hundertwasser, the twentieth century Viennese designer. The memorial clock tower had been moved to a more central spot, and was now a key feature.

We enjoyed the band for a few minutes. It moved on from the Beatles to a more contemporary work, I was informed, with a rock beat backing a kind of raunchy, syncopated, eastern-sounding song. Then Rufus dragged me away. Walking up the street away from the Town Hall I saw that the long Edwardian terrace with shops below, which I'd loved in my own time despite the lack of love bestowed on it by some owners – had been renovated a while back, with all the stylish detail picked out in brilliant colours, though now beginning to peel. Rufus was more interested in people. He kept on meeting people he knew. I saw how engaging he was, warmly embracing one man, while effortlessly sheltering me from potentially awkward introductions. To my delight we went into Withey's Yard, tucked away off the High Street. The cafe I had been to so many times was still there! I told Rufus that I happened to know this was the very first coffee shop in town, before my time, back in the 1980s. 'And here it is still,' he said. 'It's a lovely, secluded, sunny corner of the town. My favourite! We're meeting someone special here.'

3
The lady of situations

We sat down opposite a sharply dressed, middle-aged woman who greeted us with loud earnestness, and the kind of conscientious concern which I thought was that of a professional therapist. I was immediately on my guard. Rufus noticed this at once – as a contrast to the increasingly easy, chatty relationship we had already developed. He introduced the woman as Edith Lord, but before we could talk further a young waiter demanded our attention. 'What would you like?' he asked. To my surprise Edith ordered a half pint of locally brewed beer; she didn't look like a beer drinker. We had water. 'Would the set veggie meal be OK?' she asked. 'Fine,' said Rufus, and I nodded. I wondered why we had sat down with her. Edith looked at me. 'So, Robyn Ghorra, how are we doing?' she said, friendly but brusque. 'We're doing fine,' I said guardedly, with an unintentional slight over-emphasis on the 'we're' – I was trying not to react to her manner.

Rufus explained briefly what we had done that morning. 'Well – how does it feel, to be thus transplanted?' asked Edith, 'I just can't begin to imagine it!' I couldn't look her in the eye. 'It feels very odd,' I said, 'I don't know at all what's going on.' She waited for me to elaborate, but when I didn't, she went on, more gently than before, 'Yes, it must be quite extraordinary. Like being born again, thrown into a new world. What a shock!' 'Yes, well, you know, I half recognise …' I stumbled over my words. 'And, and … the oddest thing was when I woke up … in a … a tunnel, which seemed to go on for ever and ever. Before I was rescued by Rufus.' I looked up and smiled at him archly. He rescued me again.

'Edith is actually here to welcome you. She's co-mayor of Stroud Valleys Authority. Has been for many years. She and her partner have worked miracles, bringing the area back after the doldrums, the Bad Years, in the middle of the century.' I was puzzled by the references: the Stroud Valleys Authority was new to me, and Rufus spoke of the Bad Years, another mystery, with audible capitals. But no explanation was forthcoming.

'Thank you Rufus,' she said. 'I was forgetting protocol – never my strong point! Robyn ... may I call you that? You are so welcome to Stroud. We are really privileged to welcome a time-traveller – one of the first. I really hope that you have a positive experience here, and when you return take back salutary lessons – inspiration perhaps, but also learning from us what not to do. And my god, there are plenty of those. I'll want to get a debrief from you before you go. We hope to learn a lot from you about your time – the lost years. You will help us plug the knowledge gap. Understand more about how people thought and behaved, stuff erased by solar and electric overkill.

'Now, we do have to talk about some necessary rules: about Protocols, Press and Profile – the three Ps'. Before you do anything that might threaten your ...' She trailed off, becoming conscious that Rufus was trying to signal to her. I was really disturbed. My face and body language betrayed me. Edith asked with genuine concern if I was alright.

I was like a deer caught in the headlights. The mayor had brought my existential plight back into focus. It had somehow been sidelined, become hazy even, when I was just with Rufus; he was so empathic and reassuring. I gulped and spluttered, and in rather a small voice: 'Madam Mayor ... can you help me? What ... what am I doing here? I've no clue. I didn't choose to be a time traveller! Am I? Am I really? A time traveller? I just feel ...' My voice died in confusion and uncertainty.

'I'm so sorry,' said Ms Lord, 'for my overbearing approach.' She looked contrite. Rufus said: 'It's alright Robyn, I know Edith was not intending to alarm you. Let's start again. It's actually good to let it out now. Just tell us what you want to, after these first hours in a new world. No rush. Take it easy.'

He was looking at me with such simple trust and empathy that I calmed down, took a deep breath, and gathered myself a bit more together. 'Well ... well, when I first woke up in the train I was completely discombobulated. It was all so strange. I thought I was in the past. Lost in time. But now, now it's kind of magical, coming to a place I know well and yet all different. Fascinating on one level, terrifying on another. I feel almost like I'm in a dream world, but everything is tangible, real, living, logical, making a kind of sense. And I'm just a participant observer, just ... just

… absorbing all these impressions. But … am I really here?' I found myself waving my hands around uncertainly.

'So do you feel detached from reality?' asked Rufus. 'No, not really, not at all, not detached.' I paused. 'Through a glass darkly, a child here, trying to work it out …' I was looking at Rufus, giving me confidence. 'You've been marvellous, Rufus – fending off unwanted people, helping me to arrive, and I do want to know more, to see face to face. But no responsibility. No protocols. No press, please! You may be welcoming me... Edith... but I'm not a celebrity. I'm just a girl, a woman, living in a mind-warp. I just want to be inconspicuously living in this time-mind-warp – until I can return safely.' I almost laughed inanely at this thought. How could I, from another time, another world, be inconspicuous? How ridiculous! And what hope was there of returning home?

Edith picked up where I left off. 'Hah! That's exactly what we want you to do. To live inconspicuously.' She tried to soften her rather abrasive manner. 'It should be obvious to you that your presence here is not accidental. You were carefully chosen, and your transition from your own time has been meticulously planned. We need to learn more about your time, the twenties, given the loss of so many records. We want to show you everything, to respond to your needs and queries, to meet people face-to-face who can explain our world and how we got here, while all the time you have a low profile, being almost invisible, not attracting attention or raising questions about your origin in people's minds – except for those people privileged and trusted to be in the know. Rufus here, his job is to keep you unnoticed.' Her direct gaze appraised me. 'Mmm … looking at you, being invisible is not entirely … well, to be frank, you are an attractive young woman.'

I squirmed inwardly but maintained decorum. Rufus leapt in: 'You'd be amazed, Edith, she's done so well so far. There are plenty of other attractive women – and men – around, especially more twenty-somethings since the Communiversity got started. That's the local branch of the University of the West of England, Robyn, started in the seventies. And you do blend in well, with just a median skin colour, neither black nor white. Nor mottled!' He added with a grin.

'Thanks,' I said, with what I hoped was a tinge of irony. In fact, I was bemused and embarrassed by the personal directness of both Edith and

Rufus, no beating about the bush, and treating ethnicity so casually. Later I came to appreciate it. A frank, unbottled, Yorkshire-style approach: no offence intended and none taken. People did not stand on ceremony or pussyfoot around sensitive matters. Rufus was trying his best to put me at my ease. Edith, though, was not one to recognise any awkwardness. She steamed on: 'That's good, then. What we need is for you to be just commonplace, an ordinary visitor, really interested in what's going on here. You're an architect, aren't you?' 'An urban designer,' I said. 'Yes, excellent. It gives you a particular angle. And I have to say, we do consider ourselves in the vanguard. Lots of cutting-edge activity and policy. Nowhere better in the whole West Country, and the province leads the way nationally. Of course, places like The Netherlands and Kerala in India are ahead of us. But we are proud of our Valleys.' She smiled beatifically.

Rufus chipped in: 'So that deals with the question of profile. In a word, low! That chimes very well with your instinct, does it not, Robyn?' I nodded assent. 'But I have a question,' I added, 'please explain about the province?' 'Ah, sorry. The West Country is one of a dozen provinces in England, with quite a lot of powers delegated from central government. It includes Gloucestershire, Bristol and Bath, Somerset and parts of Wiltshire. We'll learn more about it another time.' He looked at Edith. 'So now, you also mentioned protocols and the media – what about those?'

'Quite,' said Edith, addressing me. 'Protocols. Umph. That simply means working through and with the formal channels. Avoid rocking any boats. Don't get yourself into trouble. Don't get us into trouble.' 'What formal channels?' I asked, trying to stop my stomach sinking. 'Oh! No worries,' she said, dismissively, 'I mean Rufus, Rufus! That's all. He is your guide and protector – at least for the moment. With Sam as backup. All that's out of my hands; but what I say to you, very clearly, is that you must listen to what he says. In particular about who you are. Conceal your true identity from everyone, except those few that Rufus OKs. He's a good lad, good lad!'

I baulked a little at what I felt was her patronising tone, said without any twinkle in her eye. But Rufus simply accepted it as a compliment. 'Thanks Edith,' he said. He seemed so tolerant, non-judgemental, immune to a potential slight. I realised I was not quite in that space myself, but endeavoured to lighten up my response: 'Oh, if that's what protocol means, no problem. Rufus has been great. I just hope the power of protocol does not go to his head.' I almost grinned at my comment, surprised that I was capable, after such trauma, of any levity. Rufus smiled benignly. The mayor ignored it and steamed on. 'Now, when it comes to the press, the media, social media especially, you have to be ultra careful. Beware of strangers who ingratiate themselves with you; no interviews; no hint to the world at large that you are a stranger to this era; no contact through social media. There are so many channels of communication available, I'm afraid you'll have to be ruthlessly restricted, especially electronically. We'll give you a false identity, which you'll have to fully adopt so you don't betray yourself. All contact has to be through Rufus or others he specifically identifies to you.

She paused. 'This may all seem very draconian, but the risks to you, and to this time travel experiment, are imponderable. There's the potential for huge historic havoc. I must admit to having severe doubts about the wisdom of the whole thing. However, here you are, and here you behave!'

'That's all fine,' I said. 'I much prefer it that way – I just want a quiet life here. In my time, the twenties, it was becoming almost impossible to avoid being linked into many groups. Not for my grandparents, they were offline and private. But for my Mum and me, and my friends, so many networks, so many connections, adverts sprouting up everywhere all the time, lots of false news, strangers sending death threats to celebs and politicos, teenage suicides, it was really difficult to focus on anything.'

'Not quite the same now,' said Rufus, 'this country went over the social media hump about forty years ago – and after the Bad Times (I could hear his capitalisation again!) it's not nearly as mad as it was. The novelty has worn off. A bit like the love affair with cars. It's over now! We're not going back – it's too risky. However …' he paused, 'we've got to be careful, and rumour-mongering is inevitable. They don't want rumours even beginning.' I wondered again who 'they' were – the people behind Rufus. The people behind the people behind Rufus. I wanted to delve into the mystery of my transition and magical appearance in 2090. I also thought that keeping me secret for long was crying for the moon. It was bound to get out.

'That's right,' said Edith Lord, 'take no risks, tell white lies!' She got up, her food finished, impatient to get on. 'Sorry to have to leave you so soon.

Delightful meeting you. So glad we see eye to eye. I've got to knock heads together. Not for real, unfortunately, just on Beam. It's about funding the direct rail link to Bristol. So important! So delayed! Enjoy the coffee. Goodbye!' And she was gone.

Rufus looked at me as we went on eating. 'She's quite a whirlwind, isn't she?' he said, 'and she gets things done, breaking down barriers – even if some heads do have to roll. She won't stand for any obfuscation or messing around.' 'I can quite see that,' I nodded. 'But Rufus, something you said about a crisis – the Bad Times. What crisis?' Rufus looked at me with a calculating eye. 'It's complex. I can't really go into it now. We'll have to come back to it in due course, I'm afraid.'

'OK, OK. So, a couple of things the mayor said.' I was feeling almost myself. 'What on earth is 'on Beam'?' 'Oh, that's the modern equivalent of Zoom, so indispensable in your time during the pandemic. Zoom and Beam have been essential helps to our zero-carbon strategy, reducing the need for travel. The Communiversity is part of that too. Local higher education opportunity.' 'Yes, I see. The other thing was this railway she mentioned. Did I gather correctly? A route from the Valleys looping down to join the Bristol line? You know, that line existed until about 1962; closed by the dreaded ... oh! I can't remember his name now ... Beeching! That was it. Seems like another world! We had to do a student project imagining its reopening – how we would design it. And it still hasn't happened!' 'For a while there's been an indirect and slow tram route,' said Rufus. 'But the proposed railway would be much better.'

At that moment the coffee arrived in a cafetière and with elegant cups and milk jug. It smelt just as good as ever, I thought, but what riveted my attention was not the coffee, it was the waiter who brought it: the same one as before, but now I saw him: a lissom lad, maybe about twenty, very personable and alert, dressed in purple tights and short crimson tunic decorated with Celtic motifs, with earrings, startling eye shadow, flamboyant hair and a lovely, exuberant smile. Quite irresistible! I tried to hide my emotions but must have failed, for Rufus was alert to my every glance. I was oh so casually – I thought – watching the boy as he moved away. Rufus leant towards me and said quietly, 'He's gorgeous, isn't he? One of the good reasons for frequenting this place!'

Once again I was taken aback by his directness. My face must have betrayed me, for Rufus laughed away any embarrassment, twinkling as he said, 'I'm thinking about his great sense of style, of course!' He told me that styles of dress had evolved over the century, and gender stereotypes had broken down so that these days men often dressed up and showed off more than the women. 'You know the images we have from the eighteenth century? Well, we men have apparently reverted to type! Though I gather Stroud was quite well known for whacky dressing in your day too. Now, men consider it a matter of obligation to be, well, stylish, colourful.'

I thought of what one male friend had said to me: men's clothes were so boringly conventional, all in black and brown and denim blue, with little variation in style. Meanwhile – he said and I concurred – there were women's and girls' clothes in every style, fashions triggered by celebrity culture, advertising, magazines, packed with the latest throwaway fashions, full of ridiculously long-legged austere beauties encouraging young women and girls to spend, spend, spend. With huge environmental impacts.

I volunteered, 'Yes, well, we didn't have it all right in my day. I didn't really understand the girls around me. I suppose they loved dressing up; it seemed to me they were just out to impress each other, being fashionmongers, changing for each party. But then, I was brought up as a puritan really, and not just about clothes.' 'Uh-huh, I think I know what you mean,' said Rufus. 'Puritan – in the sense of narrow-mindedness – is the last thing we are nowadays. Some people like one thing, others like another, tolerance of difference is a fundamental value.' 'Yes, it was in my time too – but more rhetoric than reality I think.' I quite liked this new freedom of men's dress – sneaking another look at the winsome young man.

Rufus went on: 'I should say that I'm dressed in this relatively sober garb, a bit retro, because I didn't want to alarm you at all at our first meeting. Hey, Robyn, there's been a much more important change in clothing. Have you noticed the fabrics and the quality?' 'Not really,' I said, 'it's all a bit new.' 'Yeah, of course,' he said. 'Feel my jeans and jerkin. See if you can guess the materials, and my T-shirt, too.' This took me aback, much more intimate than I thought appropriate, or even wise. I hesitated, looked at the man who was my guide and supposed protector. There was absolutely no sexual suggestiveness in his expression or body language. He was just being straightforward. Maybe touching was not so taboo amongst mere acquaintances as it had been.

I felt the jerkin, which was a simple, elegant design. 'It's wool,' I said, in surprise. He realised I was going no further, not touching his thigh. 'Yes, absolutely, you're right! Good Welsh wool. And my trousers are linen. My T-shirt is basically hemp, and practically indestructible.' 'Well, I understand nylon and so on going off the agenda,' I said, 'because they depend on oil. But what happened to king cotton?' 'I'm not really sure of the detail,' said Rufus. 'All I know is that way back in the century, there were real concerns about cotton – being so thirsty, demanding so much water, particularly so much irrigation from the rivers of central Asia that the Aral Sea was being killed. Then along came climate change and made it even worse, and now it's carbon- and water-taxed. Internationally, with a local top-up. You can still get cotton clothes, and artificial fibres for that matter – including re-used nylon. But both are expensive, so I choose not to. We've rediscovered the alternatives! The change in wool production has been stunning. All those sheep in Wales are producing wool. And here in the Cotswolds too, you'll see, producing wool as well as meat. Long overdue! Forward to the Middle Ages! Back to the future!'

'Anyway,' he went on, 'really the biggest shift has been our behaviour: away from fast fashion, as they used to call it. Fast fashion – the primrose path to the everlasting bonfire. Clothes now are made to last. The sweatshops of India and Bangladesh have gone. Now their skills are valued for quality as well as speed, and people are much better paid.' 'Wow, it's good, isn't it?' I said. 'Things have changed, and for the better I see!'

Rufus looked chuffed, and promptly changed the subject. 'Hey! It's time for a move. You're staying with me in the Cohousing in Woodchester. Have you finished your coffee?' 'Er … not quite … it's excellent coffee,' I said, and Rufus continued, 'Yup, we must thank Edith. It's very expensive these days because of the tax on it, but the chicoffee substitutes are often not worth having!' 'Er … what's the point of taxing it if it doesn't change your behaviour?' I queried. 'Good question! As I understand it, which isn't much, consumption has gone down a good bit, and it's also changing the behaviour of the fairtrade producers, so the tax can be cut as they reduce their greenhouse footprint. We could find an eco-economist for you to talk to. Sounds like you'd have some good discussions.'

We chatted idly for a few minutes while I drank down to the dregs. 'Is your car close by?' I asked. Rufus looked at me with mild surprise. 'Oh, no car for me! Being hale and hearty and where I live, I don't qualify. Anyway, what would be the point? Just an expense. A big expense. Plenty of taxis round here, waiting for our call. However,' he said with an element of drama, 'I think you deserve a treat, given what you've been through. So I've just summoned a rickshaw, powered in part by a real person.' 'A rickshaw?' I said in surprise. 'I'm trying to picture one. And when did you do that anyway? I didn't see you on your mobile.'

'A mobile phone, do you mean? I've never had one of those old things. But I do have this.' He showed me his wrist. There was a kind of watch on it, perhaps more of a wrist band, not as chunky as my sports watch, but broader right round. 'It's all I need. Does everything! But actually I pre-arranged the rickshaw – you know, the kind of velocipede they use in India – and just confirmed it timewise a moment ago.'

We went out of Withey's Yard onto the High Street. There, sure enough, was a splendid rickshaw, seating two, with a collapsible hood for rain or sun, and a woman, all ready to pedal. The woman introduced herself as Sacha. 'Sacha's a neighbour of mine, originally from Bangladesh. Moved here twenty-five years ago as a teenager,' said Rufus. 'Yes,' she said, in a rather deliberate, inflected voice, 'it was after disastrous floods in my home country. What a contrast, from cosmopolitan Dhaka to sleepy old Stroud; from blazing tropics to bloody English weather!' She laughed. 'Actually, I love it. The weather I mean. Not so cold as I expected and great for growing veg! Do get on and we'll be off. I'll tell you about some of the places as we pass them.' 'That'd be lovely!' I said, immediately warming to her friendly manner. I was determined to enjoy the ride.

4
An erstwhile home

We threaded our way discreetly through the pedestrians to the town square, down and under the railway arch to the canal bridge, in the company of assorted bikes, trikes, and a self-driving bus. Narrowboats, looking much the same as ever, were negotiating their way through the lock. To one side was Wallbridge Green, now attractively planted and with elegant new buildings arranged harmoniously around it.

'I must tell you something about this,' said Sacha, pausing the rickshaw. 'We're so proud of all the volunteer effort that went into this canal, way back, before my time – it really shows the strength of community that existed here. The Stroudwater Canal was finished down to the Sharpness-Gloucester Canal in 2029, and then over the hills to the Thames in 2047, transforming the nature of the town. There had been so much dereliction along it in the late twentieth century – shocking really. Development, if it happened, turned its back on the canal – until, that is, the whole thing was reopened and boats started plying their way up and down, and the canal became the new focus of the town. People love water and love watching boats! And just look at the bustling waterfront, the square over there, and the housing on the south side – really attractive I think. And that beautiful curving steel bridge above.' She looked at me, to gauge my reaction to the scene in front of us.

It wasn't difficult for me to act the stranger – I felt a stranger. This was a new world. 'Yes, it's awesome! I do hope we'll be able to find the time to boat along the canal another day.' I was looking hopefully at Rufus.

Then off we went, along the old Bath Road. Almost immediately Sacha held forth again – telling us about the factory on the right. 'It's very special, unique! A survival of the first industrial age. A woollen factory specialising in cloth for tennis balls and billiard tables, still operating after all these years; they have a worldwide reputation! They do guided tours to show how processes have changed over the centuries, and how the energy source has evolved from water, to coal, to renewable electricity now.'

As she spoke I kept on being brought up short by cars passing with four people in facing each other and no driver ('social taxis' I was later told), and other cars with no-one in at all. Really weird! And I was noticing something else – the changes to the street we were in, the main road going south. Many buildings renewed, pavements wider and very well used, the cycleway we were on and a separate carriageway for buses and taxis. Auto electronic sensing, Sacha said, meant there were no collisions. More shops had sprung up, which was surprising, given the online trend I assumed was still happening. Sacha was a mine of information. She had lived in one of those big old Edwardian villas we had passed – a brilliant home for a three-generation family like hers, and right on the main bus route, ten-minute service as regular as clockwork, cheap standard fare to anywhere in the Valleys – couldn't be better! Apparently the houses were highly prized now. Indeed, the street had the feeling of an attractive neighbourhood boulevard, where previously it had been a noisy, smelly traffic channel, intimidating for cyclists, risky for pedestrians, though offering some of the cheapest housing in town.

We reached more open country. There were woods and vineyards up the sides of the valley. I was surprised by signs to the Roman Villa – only a mark on the map in my day. There were coaches turning towards it. Sacha told me it was the biggest tourist attraction in the Valleys. 'There's this amazing Roman pavement, the best in Northern Europe, with gorgeous mosaics that had been covered up for ever to preserve it.' Clearly not for ever! As far as I was concerned it had completely vanished from consciousness. Now resurrected at last! Immediately after that, we passed a big old pub I recognised – that was a comfort! – and we were into the small town of Woodchester. 'My homeplace,' said Rufus, with obvious pride. I glimpsed some of the new development and facilities as we passed. The journey of about 4 km from the canal had taken us little more than ten minutes – at a pretty steady 25 kph courtesy of the combination of pedal and e-power. We came to a new square, by the main road, with a cafe and outdoor seating giving it a relaxed air. What a transformation! I thought.

'Here we are, up this street to the left of the cafe,' said Rufus. A few hundred metres along we halted. 'This is where I live. Welcome to Woodchester Cohousing!'

I thanked Sacha, very genuinely. I felt at home with her. Rufus had earlier intimated she was one of the cognoscenti – those in the know about me. That was interesting in itself, and I imagined this would not be our only meeting. I didn't want to lose touch with her, and suspected her life had been devastated by climate change. I asked her to tell me more about why she had to come to England.

She looked at me very seriously, with sadness in her voice. 'After the catastrophic floods, millions of us were homeless, literally millions. It was the second inundation, worse than the first. The sea took over whole swathes of the Ganges-Brahmaputra delta. There was little space or opportunity in the rest of Bangladesh, already densely populated and the economy in shreds after the disaster. The UN got an international response together, resettling people. The West of England province was marvellous, so welcoming! My family, all of us, and three thousand others from our neighbourhood, were all settled in the Nailsworth Valley.'

She was looking at us both intently, not moving. 'I'm told it was very controversial, and there were battles royal. But I'm profoundly grateful that it happened. The urbanism department worked with us and with local people to create this small new town out of the two Woodchester villages. It was very moving. Luckily, we had some richer, entrepreneurial people in our community, and as part of the agreement they started a woollen factory, getting wool from Cotswold farmers, and some cottage industries around it. We all had skills and could retrain fast. The English lessons were excellent, and everyone had to do them. So, although some of us had lost everything, our homes and livelihoods, what with UN grants and open arms from people locally, we made a go of it. I used a small grant to start this rickshaw business about eight years ago. There are now a dozen of us in the co-op. We feel really at home here, it's amazing. I feel so proud to be part of the Valleys community. It's just great!'

The hair on the back of my neck was prickling, my eyes were watering, I could barely speak. It was the human tale of complete disaster transformed to hope and life, and also the paradox of unexpected wool revival in the Cotswolds. 'Wow,' I said, 'what a story. That's … that's fantastic!'

She looked at me with warmth and appreciation, nodding gently. 'Yes, it is,' she said seriously. We said our goodbyes and Sacha pedalled off.

Rufus took me through an arch in an imposing four-storey house (the common house, I discovered later) and into a large inner courtyard formed by three- or four-storey houses and apartments with large balconies. There was a lawn and raised flowerbeds, a toddlers' play area and a kind of sculptural structure clearly made for adventurous clambering. 'Most people are still at work or school,' said Rufus, 'which is good timing! Not too many people around.' He looked at me seriously. 'We have to be discreet. Most of my co-mates do not know your origin, and it's best that way, or the rumour engine will be unstoppable. So ... I hope you are happy to be just a visiting friend from another part of the country.' I told him of my newly minted cover story, that I was on a study tour from Manchester. He seemed pleased, saying, 'I'll tell you explicitly if and when we meet a person you can be open with. Meanwhile, I'm afraid, you are going to have to ration your social contacts, at least initially, until you are really comfortable with your double life.' I thought this was eminently sensible. The last thing I wanted was to become a time-travelling celebrity, part of a freak show. But I did want to find out much more about the era I'd been transplanted to via some kind of wormhole in space/time. I really needed to understand what had happened to me.

Rufus took me around the courtyard, warmly greeting an elderly couple who were planting out a raised bed, helped by a machine Rufus called a plantbot. He didn't introduce me to the people or the bot – sheltering me, I felt. We doubled back to one end of the common house and went upstairs to the top floor. He unlocked the door into a big living space. 'Our best guest suite,' said Rufus, with obvious pleasure. I looked around. 'Awesome!' I said. It was too. Just beautiful. The way the light flooding from windows played on angled surfaces. The feeling of the space. Distinctive wooden, practical-feeling furniture. To my eyes, used to student accommodation and 'neat' flats, it was sumptuous, sophisticated. 'It's lovely, thank you,' I said. 'I really like the bold colours and the way a screen doesn't dominate the space, and all the natural light.'

'Ah ha!' said Rufus. 'Just you wait!' He murmured a few words. A whole section of wall sprang to life. There were suddenly people in the room, around them a woodland glade, young children playing. The sense of being right there, in the scene, was tangible. 'This is live,' said Rufus, 'at the local Forest School. I haven't turned on the surround-sound, obviously.

What would you like to see? Provincial parliament in session? Local wildlife? A 3D animated film? Football match?'

'No, no, turn it off! It's too real!' I remonstrated. In truth it was as if things were actually happening in the space, children gambolling right around me. 'Ah, I guess holography has come a long way since your day. He turned it all off with a word. The room reasserted itself. 'Actually, we are currently restricted in how much we can watch, it's very energy intensive and expensive. I'm not allowed one at all – I have to watch in the Common House. You're very privileged! I'm quite surprised this one is working.' He consulted his watch. 'Ah. It was supposed to be turned off. It is, now. Sorry. Failing that, we should try to expose you to some of our other filmic innovations, like feelies and smellies.'

Feelies! Shades of Aldous Huxley's Brave New World. I shivered involuntarily. Brave New World was a dystopian vision. I felt an alarming suspicion: 'All this marvellous entertainment – what's it for? Is it like bread and circuses – to keep the Roman masses under sedation? You know what I mean?' In my mind I was alarmed that all this technical witchery might just be a cover, just the seductive surface of an authoritarian society. I'd already had hints of this. I didn't want to be rude to my hosts ... or were they really my captors? Was Rufus my ever-so-charming jailor? I looked at him. Was he discomforted by my accusation? He had a glint in his eye, but was smiling broadly, and almost nodding. 'There are some authoritarian elements,' he said, with an open gesture, palm up, 'but we pride ourselves on our democratic credentials. Democratic authoritarianism. Robyn, you will have to make your own mind up, it'll be very interesting to see what you think, coming from a different age. I'll show you as many facets of our society as I can. We'll meet some really special people, but please don't rush to conclusions. In fact, I wanted to say, we'd be very grateful if you could record your impressions and thoughts as they happen. Your perspective could be illuminating for us. Don't be awkward about negative thoughts. Put 'em in! We want it warts and all, not a false positivity. Your real responses. And ... we want to know everything about your own time.'

'You want me to write a diary?' I was slightly nonplussed. If Rufus was my prison warder he was devilishly plausible. 'Yes, exactly! Would you be happy to dictate it? The machine will correct grammar and infelicities without losing your distinctive voice. Or I can find you an old laptop with a keyboard if you prefer.' 'Um … neither,' I said. 'I've had a graphics training, so I love hand-written material. I'll write it.' In the back of my suspicious mind was the thought that written stuff could not be tampered with so easily as electronic material.

Another thought struck me. 'Don't tell me writing is dead.' 'No, I won't tell you that!' said Rufus. 'But I have to admit it is on life-support. Young children do have to learn to write with pen and pencil. The kids here in the Cohousing say they have to start right back with Egyptian hieroglyphics, and later illuminate modern letters and stories as if they were medieval monks. Very creative; they say they enjoy it, illuminating with dinosaurs and spacecraft, and I've seen beautiful examples using Celtic and Aboriginal patterns. I'm told it frees their minds to help grapple later with Chinese. But adults simply don't bother. What's the point?'

'It was just beginning to go that way, even in my day,' I said. 'I'd love to meet some school-children, when it's convenient.' 'Um, yes,' he said, 'that could be awkward – too exposing. Maybe a carefully chosen teacher.' Alarm bells rang again – my every contact was to be vetted. 'Anyway,' Rupert went on, 'beautiful pens and paper will be yours. We'll ask Cyla. She can get almost anything.' 'Cyla?' I queried.

'Oh, I'm so sorry, said Rupert, 'Cyla' is short for encyclopedia. It's now the standard source of information in most countries. The old commercial systems of your day became more and more driven by vested interests and advertising and at the beck and call of specific governments, especially China and America. Then it all fell apart in the Bad Times. Now Cyla is run by a UN agency based in Kenya. Some advertising revenue still, aimed at businesses, but also some support from member states. Privileged access – meaning the buying of top slots in search engines – is outlawed. Then there is 'Cylahome', which is our household manager, managing heating (very rarely needed!), ventilation, lighting, entertainment, cleaning, drainage systems, basic household supplies and all that sort of thing. She keeps the buildings and processes in some kind of equilibrium, tied to sustainability criteria, and she sure lets us know if things are going awry.' I nodded, more or less understanding.

'You can activate Cyla very easily – like the systems I believe you already had back in the twenties – just by saying her name clearly and then asking a question or giving a command.' He asked Cyla the time, she responded in a cool female voice, very well modulated, 'fifteen forty-eight'. Rufus went on, businesslike: 'Your terminal is linked to me, so any special request which Cyla can't fulfil herself comes to me, wherever I am. If you want me, just ask Cyla and she'll find me.' He tapped his wrist. 'And in the interests of research and safety, all your conversations with Cyla or with real people, and your choice of music or entertainment, are all monitored. You are unique! You are a time-traveller, and we want to understand you and your own time and your reactions to here and now. My research colleagues are listening in!'

Alarm was growing on my face. I was well and truly bugged!

'Please don't be alarmed, Robyn. Here in this flat you can ask for privacy and Cyla will oblige, until you reactivate her or speak to someone or use the radio or screen. But immediately you're outside, I would become aware of you, and have backup. All for safety's sake. Anyway, Cyla is the most straightforward creature you can imagine. You can't turn her off, but it's you that activates her. She has a world of knowledge at her beck and call, and she is incapable of telling an intentional lie. So if you want to deceive me or someone else, you'll have to do it yourself!'

I was barely comforted by his assurances: no real guarantee of privacy, but I focussed on the practical. 'I can't see any terminal. Where is Cyla?' I asked. Well, he said, that's quite a difficult question. She has ears and mouths and noses everywhere, in each room. Then through Cylahome she has physical assistants, for cleaning and delivery, and she manages your micro kitchen, makes tea and superb chicoffee, almost as good as the real thing, and stocks that tiny fridge with juice and savoury nibbles. You can ask for specific things and she'll provide if the community has it in stock. 'That sounds good,' I said cautiously. Then an incautious thought occurred to me. 'What about booze?' 'Ah, yes, that too, but strictly rationed I'm afraid. That's our own policy, we came up with it a while back, primarily on cost grounds. There's probably enough, depending on your tastes.' 'Don't worry,' I said, 'Cyla couldn't possibly be as mean as my mother!'

Rufus was still on a mission: 'Your choice how much you use Cyla. My advice is to use her a lot, whenever you want. She's so informative and unbiased. She's not allowed to express her own opinion or promote any political views, but can report what others think or do, giving precise weight in terms of how many think it, giving comparisons. You can display things on the screen when needed. Look, I'll show you how it works. Cyla, show me a 2D map of Woodchester.' Part of the huge screen came alive. It was impressive. I knew the 2020 pattern of North and South Woodchester quite well, and could see how radically it had changed, integrating the two parts, expanding into a small town.

Rufus told Cyla to turn off the map, and a thought struck me – ricocheting back into my consciousness like a boomerang. 'Cyla,' I said, almost thinking of her as human ... I need to ask you something. Lots of things. What has happened to the Earth? To the climate? Sea-levels? How hot is it now? Has the Amazon rainforest survived? Has the Greenland icecap? Survived, that is?' My voice had risen in pitch, rather alarmingly. Cyla, calm as ever, asked me to focus my questions, saying she could deal with them in sequence, but that would take some time. Would I like to prioritise? I gathered myself. Then, more focussed: 'Cyla, first tell me how the average global temperature has changed since 1850; then tell me how much sea-level has risen, say since 2000; then show me on the screen how the English coastline has changed, if at all, since 2020. Concentrate on the area of the Wash and the Fens.'

I was rather pleased with this last question! I knew something about the problems of the Fens and the East Anglian coast: the idea of managed retreat as sea levels slowly rose and more violent storms battered the fragile coastline. I'd seen apocalyptic forecasts of land loss around the Wash, with the sea inundating parts of Lincolnshire, Cambridgeshire and Norfolk.

But first things first. Cyla told me the temperature rise since 1850, when industrialisation took off across parts of Europe and America, was 2.5 degrees C, and likely to rise significantly further. So the 1.5 and 2.0 degree target of the 2020s had been comprehensively missed. Sea level since 2000, she said, had risen by sixty centimetres, or about two feet. Early in the century it was rising at around five millimetres per year, but that rate had increased alarmingly and was now over ten millimetres per year. I took in the figures without shock, though with a kind of resigned disappointment and some horror. When the wall-screen then showed me the shift of coastline after ninety years I was not surprised either – in fact obscurely disappointed, which was ridiculous! It was much less than the prophets of doom suggested back in the twenties, though they were probably working to a much longer timescale. Cyla explained: 'The process of planned loss of prime farmland to the sea, together with some settlements, has been continuing for about fifty years. So far three hundred and thirty square kilometres have been given up to the sea, and over seven hundred to saltmarsh. The management plan involves very extensive salt marshes and willow swamps. The willows have been genetically engineered to tolerate salt water, and act much like a mangrove swamp, absorbing the force of the sea, creating new habitats and protecting lands behind. Some settlements, built on slightly higher land since the Middle Ages, have effectively become islands, with access channels through marshes and swamps. It is anticipated that further retreat is likely in the quite near future if the pace of the Greenland ice-melt increases. I can give you further information on request.' The screen faded.

My instinctive reaction altered as Cyla spoke, and as I absorbed the seriousness of the changes. My stomach grew heavy with dread, thinking about how much further it might go. At the same time I recognised that the coping strategy was coherent, it seemed impressive, and I wanted to know more. But Rufus cut across my thoughts: 'What pertinent questions you asked! We must talk to someone in the know about these things. That's something we can discuss tomorrow. What I suggest for now is that you make yourself at home. Have a rest after the ordeal of your transition. Then at 19 I'll come and fetch you and take you across to my pad, where we can have dinner and talk. I'll introduce you to my buddy, Sam, and to our local poet. He lives over there.' He pointed through the window at a whackily painted ground floor flat across the courtyard. 'He knows everybody. Can get us introductions and ...' He stopped, looking at me.

As he was talking, I'd sunk deep into an armchair, suddenly washed out, exhausted. The transition to this new age, the experiences of the day, the realisation that climate and sea-level trends represented complete failure of my own era, completely sapped my reserves. My eyelids drooped. 'Rufus, I'm sorry. I've got no energy. I can't concentrate any more. I just need a good rest.'

Rufus looked at me, slumped in the chair, smiled his warm smile, and spoke more gently. 'Of course. Stupid of me. I'll tell you what, you just hunker down here for the remainder of the day, get some sleep. Lots of sleep. I'm sure you need it. Ask Cyla for any food or drink, and you can call me, as I say, if you need to. We can postpone the social supper until tomorrow, I'm sure that'll work out fine. Anyway – I had thought that tomorrow should be a very relaxed day, just being here, letting you acclimatise...' '...and sleep!' I said, closing my eyes involuntarily and allowing a grimace of postponed stress. I don't know how long that moment lasted. It was interrupted by Rufus saying something about me and exhaustion, but he needed to give me something. I struggled to sit up and be alert. 'Here's a wristy for you which doubles as a phone and GPS too. Keep it on. If you need me, just say 'contact Rufus' and it puts you straight through, or to Sam, my backup, if I'm not available. You always get to a real person. Quite privileged you are! But you can't call anybody else, I'm afraid. Anything else, ask Cyla. She's a marvel!' 'Well, thanks,' I said, 'see you later – tomorrow?'

'Today! I'll drop in about 20.30, after you've had a good rest. There are one or two things to sort out for tomorrow,' Rufus added. I won't actually lock you in, but please don't wander around and bump into people until you've been more fully inducted. It would be very risky.' And Rufus was gone.

With the relief of his leaving, at last on my own, I struggled up and looked out of the window. Children, playing, full of raucous enjoyment. A cheerful sight. As I watched I realised my eyes had glazed over again. I took off my shoes, collapsed onto the settee, and had just enough wit left to ask Cyla to make the room darker, and wake me at 7 pm. Cyla replied: 'I will wake you at 19.' The room was cast into twilight. I thought that I'd better be careful what I wished for. But then thought no more, pulling the soft woollen throw over me.

*****

A soft burring woke me. Slowly coming to, still half asleep, my mind was in a dream world, with an earworm, *brave new world* going round and round to a kind of tune. The dream was confusing – in part a disaster movie and in part the vision of a magical place. As my conscious mind gradually took over, I wondered was I like Miranda (a part I'd actually acted at Uni) in Shakespeare's Tempest, after the storm, seeing 'a brave new world that had such people in it', or was it something quite different. Not the innocent paradise of Miranda but the dystopian future imagined by Aldous Huxley. That led to a further thought: was the beauty and good sense of the new Stroud just a cover for a much darker underlying reality?

With a big sigh I parked that worry and began to take in my surroundings properly for the first time. The room was spacious and elegant, a generous living/working/sleeping space, full height windows opening in two directions, one onto a balcony lit by the evening sun; storage built into the walls, all beautifully decorated with wooden furnishings and earthy tones. There was a desk and adjustable chair, a piano-style keyboard, a small table and comfy chairs, and a double bed in an alcove. To one side there was a sink and what I took to be the cooker, with cupboards around. Experimentally I pushed a button on the wall by the desk. Out slid a beautiful drawing board. It was uncanny. It was almost as though I had designed the whole room myself.

Cyla piped up: 'Good evening Robyn, I hope you had a refreshing rest. We have tried to provide you with things you might have had at home. The drawing board and laptop are modelled on early century examples. In the drawers of the desk you will find paper, card, pens, pencils, the laptop and other equipment you may find useful. The drawers in the wall contain a wide range of clothes. The hanging space is rather disguised – at the far end of the bed alcove.'

'Thank you Cyla,' I said, simultaneously realising that I was treating Cyla like an adult, while I rather sensed that I was being treated like a child. Or a pet. Or maybe the prized specimen of a species thought extinct. 'Would you like the shower room?' asked Cyla. 'Why yes! How did you know?' I responded, feeling even more that I was being managed. 'My training included observation of human behaviour, enabling me to respond more effectively to people's needs. The shower room is behind you. I'll open the door. The style may not be familiar to you, it is in the latest retro fashion.' I swung round as a door I'd not noticed before opened. The shower room was actually rather basic, except that auto responses cut in alarmingly. There was nowhere to put clothes, so I backed out quickly and nervously stripped off, aware that Cyla was watching me all the time. Only a machine, I said to myself. Then I luxuriated in a delicious long hot shower, while in the full-length mirror I saw the signs of tension wash away. I smiled at my paranoia and fear of this strange new world and its people, determined instead to welcome the unexpected, unprecedented experience, enter into it with an open-minded sense of enquiry, determined to get what I could out of it and enjoy myself. I might be a pet, but I was being treated with consideration and respect. Maybe it was all a huge charade, but the only way to find out was to adopt an open, engaged and enquiring approach; and anyway, I had to admit that despite all my reservations, I liked Rufus. My puzzled smile grew broad, an inane grin, laughing at my fears. I would embrace the moment!

Returning to the main room, I asked Cyla about young women's clothes – what styles were fashionable. The screen flashed into life with a confusing array of images. Not needing to impress anyone, I decided to put back on the clothes Rufus had given me. I requested a cup of redbush tea, scrambled egg on brown toast with a green salad. I went out onto the balcony, the evening still mild, and watched the young children playing on the swings and the formidable climbing frame – they were so adept and agile, for kids so young, and I was impressed.

Back inside I found good quality paper and pens, and started making notes about what had happened during the day since the terrifying transition in the dark tunnel. Those notes didn't make it back to my own time but did help me remember everything. In fact my memory puzzled me greatly. It seemed like a new ability, almost photographic – so detailed, so specific.

Rufus briefly dropped by again at 20.40. He went through tomorrow's highlights: sharing breakfast in his pad and meeting his partner; going into Stroud to the identification office; looking all round the Cohousing buildings and grounds. Not a packed day, so leaving time for me to rest and adjust. After he left, I returned to writing up the day. It all seemed good, and for a moment I felt a positive presentiment hovering in my heart.

5
Conflicting messages

Rufus's invitation to breakfast was very welcome – something I needed to help ground me. He lived in a fourth floor flat on the far side of the Cohousing square, with a spacious living room and a separate bedroom, though I didn't really take in any details on this initial visit, because he immediately introduced me to his partner, Samantha. She was gorgeous and very young, as I thought. She greeted me very warmly, inviting me to call her Sam, and said straight off, quite matter of fact, that she and Rufus were sex-buddies. I blinked in surprise at her language. I was beginning to realise that my middle-class reserve in such matters was not the fashion of the times.

Sam said how good it was to meet Rufus's new time-travelling companion. 'I'm not only Rufus's girlfriend,' she said, with a smile, 'I have several other strings to my bow. I've just finished the five-year training in Spatial Health, and now I'm working for the provincial public health authority in Bristol on healthy, sustainable environments, liaising with local authorities and community planning groups.' Great, I thought. But listening to her, watching her eye contact with Rufus, I was not prepared for my own reaction, which I profoundly hoped did not show – a pang of jealousy – instantly dismissed as illicit by my cultured self. I covered it up, recognising that in my vulnerable state, having lost my own world, my sense of identity in this new world had prematurely fused with Rufus. As I told Sam everything that had happened the previous day, I found myself praising her partner for the way he had handled the situation. Maybe over-praising.

Any awkwardness was swept away by the arrival of breakfast. Not by Cyla and some mysterious automated system, but by Rufus, who had been busy while we were talking. It was an absolutely delicious concoction of honey and yogurt and fresh peaches, the latter apparently from Spain – so early in the season, I thought – the honey and yogurt from local producers. We were also treated to real coffee – one small cup each, Italian style – and superb croissants. Our conversation blossomed, bubbling with bonhomie.

Watching Sam and Rufus together, their body language, their relationship was clearly more than purely sensual – they were in love with each other.

By the time Rufus and I needed to leave for town, I felt positively mellow, enjoying their company. 'No time to hang around, I'm afraid,' said Rufus. 'The appointment's at nine.' 'God, that's pushing it in rush hour!' I said, as we walked down the stairs. 'No, no,' said Rufus, 'you're forgetting, we have conquered congestion!' We strolled three hundred metres in hazy sun, down to the main road. The tram stopped nearby, regular as clockwork, every ten minutes. It appeared just a minute after we arrived. To all appearances it was free. A public transport system that worked! I felt as though I were in a rural version of Amsterdam or Zurich. The valley views of vineyards and woods from the rickshaw had piqued my curiosity, so now I hoped to see more. But the tram was quite full. Gazing at the view was not so easy. It made its way to Stroud, taking us to Merrywalks, which was clearly the tram centre, dropping us off close to where it seemed everything was happening. The street had originally been constructed mid-twentieth century over the culverted Slad Stream. In my time it was a noisy, smelly, traffic bottleneck with a multi-storey car park, bus station, cinema, McDonald's and vacant site by the railway arches … but now it had been transformed! No car parks any more, no carriageway, no ugly cinema building, but crowds of people coming and going to activities in the newish six-storey buildings on the town side, and through the parkland on the west side. I saw that the stream had been revealed in places, with seats overlooking, and opposite in the park the Old Convent's gothic buildings now revealed and resplendent. Crowning it all a beautiful pedestrian bridge in gleaming metal and elegantly carved wood sailing right across the valley from town centre to parkland. It quite took my breath away.

We went into one of the office buildings. 'I've booked you in and explained the context to the unit head,' said Rufus. 'She's the one person here in the know about you. She's dealt with the others too.' I looked at him sharply. 'From earlier centuries,' he said. 'But look, we've got a couple of minutes to spare. I'll tell you about that bridge you were looking at.' He launched off, telling me how it had been conceived aeons ago (I knew this well – 2017 to be precise!) leading from the upper town and the centre across to the linear park, schools, homes, Leisure Centre and Museum in Stratford

Park. "It's been a huge success, an absolute boon for children and cyclists and frail people, keeping people on the level and short-circuiting the distance between key destinations.'

'Is Tesco still there?' I asked. Rufus was momentarily thrown. 'Oh, Tesco!' he said. 'Yes, I remember ... I'm pretty sure it went bust in the Bad Years. Its business model just couldn't adapt to the straitened circumstances people found themselves in – along with some other supermarkets.'

A moment later we were ushered into a medical consulting room and welcomed by a middle-aged doctor of rather indeterminate gender ('she' according to Rufus). She said the process would take only ten minutes, as she used a simple swab to numb my lower left arm. I was startled: 'What's that for? I thought I'm here for an identity card!' Rufus caught my eye, looking embarrassed. 'I'm so sorry, I should have explained. You'll have an identity mote grafted onto your bone. It's so small it's almost invisible, and goes in through a fine wire, hence the anaesthetic.' I looked at him open-mouthed. In my head I responded with an emotional rant: Fuck! That's not on! It's not fair, not in my contract at all, messing with my body! Giving God knows what power over me! What my voice said, though, was 'Oh! I didn't know about that! Is it absolutely necessary? It does strike me as a bit of an infringement of my individual rights.'

The good doctor was looking at me, nonplussed, perceiving the emotion behind the words. She shook her head quite vehemently: 'No, no, no, it's not like that at all. I'll try to explain, and quite honestly, you must have been living on another planet to avoid this mote for so long – most kids have it at ten years old. Why you're here is not my business, and I do understand you're a special case. Look, put this mote in context. We once had paper identity checks – passports and driving licenses. Then we moved to machine readable cards and mobile phones. But they could be lost or stolen. Then this technique was developed until it's now quite refined and not really invasive at all. It's grafted onto the bone rather than just under the skin. Much more robust. And very secure! No more worries. Check with friends or family or anyone. Just basic identity info, with the rider that it can be triggered by family members or carers to tell them where you are, and this has proved amazingly helpful for lost kids or dementia sufferers.' I had almost calmed down while she spoke. Rufus took up the story: 'Yes, and a key reason for introducing it was robots. Society needed a foolproof way for machines to distinguish between human and robot.'

The doctor was looking quizzically at me, disbelieving my apparent ignorance. 'Sorry, I had a very sheltered upbringing,' I said – which was quite true! Anyway, after that they went ahead with the injection. No blood, no pain, barely any discomfort. As we left, Rufus breathed a deep sigh of relief. 'Whew! That was a close one. I'm really sorry. I hadn't allowed for the cultural and technological shift between your time and now. I didn't want to have to reveal who you really were. The fewer who know, the safer we are.' 'I didn't feel safe in there at all!' I ventured. It was actually more than that. I began to suspect that this new society was manipulated and controlled. By whom was the question.

We took the tram back to Woodchester town. There was a range of small businesses and shops close by the tram stop, a number of people milling around. As we walked back to the Cohousing, I sensed the different atmosphere on the street. In my own time, most people, including me, normally avoided eye-contact. We are either absorbed in our social media world through phones, or plugged in to music, or consciously distancing ourselves from strangers; some are depressed and demotivated, which is not exactly surprising given the Covid blues. When people did look at me, in my own time, I was carefully non-responsive, maybe just a whisper of a smile. Some older Stroudy people even gave a cheery greeting, to which I have to admit I gave only a cool though polite rejoinder.

But now, maybe because of who I was with – though it seemed more than that – almost everyone greeted us, making a point of being friendly to both of us. Following Rufus's lead, I tried to be warm and friendly in response. People seemed much more demonstrative and outgoing, more like I imagined Italians were. Could we put that down to the warmer climate? Or a strong sense of local community, helped by the South Asian influx? Or greater safety on the streets?

When we were back in my room and being regaled with drinks, courtesy of Cyla, I pointed out this contrasting behaviour to Rufus. 'Well, as it happens, I have made a bit of a study of this,' said Rufus. 'The psychology of neighbourliness, people's perception of safety and conviviality on-street. And you're right. There's been a really significant change over the years. Back in the twenties, as I've read, the awareness of misogynistic behaviour became very high, and quite a lot of women were shy or afraid of going out in unknown places or at night. And the police weren't trusted to do their job either. Even more to the point, the actual level of violence, not only to women, but amongst boys and young men, gang membership, drug dealing and knife crime, was much higher than today. I believe the critical factor which led to change was the sense of social solidarity as a result of shared trauma – the mid-century Bad Times. And our social policies are now so much more relevant and effective than they were, and cheaper too! The level of inequality in society peaked in the thirties and forties. It's been going down ever since, and it really affects perceptions and behaviours. Then of course, Robyn, there are the more prosaic explanations. The streets are much less noisy. Vehicles are almost completely safe and never hit pedestrians. The current conventions surrounding wristies and earplugs mean people are more alert to where they are and who they meet. You'll be amazed – people can be fined if they bump into others while walking down the road buried in their own private world. It's quite draconian, I feel, but has helped to increase awareness. Then there's a quite alarming degree of surveillance.' He looked up and out of the window. 'Violent or unlawful actions can often be spotted by robo-detectives, and they are allowed in certain circumstances, with human oversight, to identify you via your mini-implant.'

Remembering my earlier inner rant as he talked, I now felt more able to express myself directly, just with Rufus. 'Bloody hell! This *is* a police state!' I exclaimed. 'Big Brother is actually watching you! State control is here! Or are the big tech firms in command, with their robot detectives? Nothing is private, just mind your behaviour!'

'No, no, it's not like that at all! I must have said it all wrong. The implant has given us much greater freedom.' I looked at him in disbelief. 'It's freedom from crime in particular. Knife crime, theft and burglary, rape and other unwanted sexual behaviours – all are now a fraction of what they were. Even murder and manslaughter are less common. Road accidents almost abolished. From my perspective, I cannot imagine why identity cards were so politically toxic a century back. Only those with malign intent would want to be invisible. Now there's nowhere to hide, and that makes everything more comfortable. Look, please, suspend any judgement until you have met some more people – people who know things. Just hold on to the questions and uncertainties you have now, so you can pursue them over the next few days.'

My sense of shock and disbelief remained. 'Yes. That's exactly what I'll do! I'm not at all convinced, but thanks for trying to explain.' I paused. 'However ... I just want to come back to something else: thinking about my own behaviour in the 2020s, with your training you may have insight. Cos the image of a reserved girl, keeping herself to herself, is not the full truth. I may have been like that in private life, but when I was in role, being an urban designer, at meetings, going round asking people questions on the street, observing how people behaved in different places, I'd be really confident. Not a timid mouse at all. Where did that come from? Why the difference?' 'You've said it,' said Rufus, 'you were playing a role; you had a job to do. It gave you a clear position in society. So while in normal life you were intimidated by strangers, when in your role, like being in a uniform, you might even have been a bit intimidating to others, or more likely a sympathetic ear people could confide in. It's all quite natural!' 'I'll choose the sympathetic ear,' I said.

A little later we went on an explore. We descended the elegant, spacious stairs, four floors worth of staircase. I was surprised at apparently no lift. Rufus explained there was one, a good big size for furniture, serving several staircases. 'We make the assumption that almost everyone will want to use the stairs. When I was studying your time I was shocked at the level of dependence on lifts and escalators: hotels and shopping centres where the lifts are right there in front of you, but the stairs are hidden away. Even fitness centres – how ironic! When we know that climbing stairs is really good for keeping muscles fit and flexible and postponing arthritis.' He was quite adamant! I heartily agreed with him.

Going outside I admired the community space again: raised beds with mixed vegetables and flowers; a splendid all-age play area; a lawn with seats, some shaded by semi-mature trees. It was lovely.

Rufus showed me the community room, large enough for everyone to gather, the shared carpentry workshop, the bike repair place, the 3D construction shop, with varied materials available. We sat down in the community room. There were a number of people there and Rufus introduced me. They were very cordial, studiously not prying, as if forewarned. I was intrigued by a couple of women, probably a bit older than me. They were breastfeeding a baby. While we were there, they swopped the baby from one to the other, and the infant immediately latched on, looking very happy. It was apparent the infant had two mums – they were quite lovey-dovey with each other. From my perspective inappropriately so, but I tried to hide my reactions. This was a different world.

Outside again, looking at the roof, Rufus explained the water collection and purification system – roof water and grey water; the solar roofs which made more electricity than the co-operative needed, the battery water tower built into the hillside; then a bit further afield, a tennis court, croquet and badminton lawn, a swimming pool, a climbing wall, plus large greenhouse and extensive allotment area. 'Some of these facilities are open to the town, paid for by the parish,' said Rufus. I was fascinated – the technology was streets ahead in some respects, just like ours in others. I asked Rufus about the battery tower and about sewage. He laughed! 'Oh, the tower is full of water, gravity power, as deep into the ground as above; pumped up when we have surplus electricity, generating as it falls at times of peak demand. Rather old-fashioned now, but we keep it until the price of the new-fangled mini-batteries comes down. They are super-efficient, and don't rely on rare metals, but I'm not sure how they work. And sewage – well, we're part of the Woodchester system, down in the valley, an extensive reed-bed system. But you know, on everything like water, sewage, electricity, we are interlinked to the wider district system, and that to the region. We just have to pay if we import services, and we get paid when we export. Woodchester is big enough now to be pretty self-sufficient.

I was all agog, wanting to ask more. 'This is brilliant, I said, you really seem to have sorted the carbon issues. Though at what cost? At the cost of individual or family autonomy? Everything seems controlled. If it weren't for that, I could really enjoy living here.' 'Well, you are – living here. So enjoy!' said Rufus and made to move us on. His rejoinder gave me a jolt, suddenly reminding me of my lost world. I went quiet. I noticed a troop of children going to the swimming pool, chatting happily.

For the rest of the morning and the afternoon I was left to my own devices – recuperation time. Rufus stressed that it was best if I stayed local, in the Cohousing estate. Everyone there knew he had a guest, and to be friendly but not inquisitive. In my cover story, I was based in Manchester, but on study leave, and also recovering from some kind of unspecified trauma, so my privacy should be respected. It was a fine day, quite warm, spring was sprung, the may was out, the leaves were coming out on the old oak trees. I had a lovely time mooching around, particularly in the garden areas, sitting watching, sitting drawing, sitting musing, sometimes just sitting. I needed this time. Acclimatising, if that's the right word. Pondering the problems of the society I'd left behind. Both disturbed and impressed by my impressions so far of the country I'd come to. The bird life was fantastic. I could not remember so many species in one area. I decided my favourites were the goldfinches – always going about in chattery groups, flitting to and fro – and perhaps the bullfinches, bigger, blousier and bossy with it.

Resting quietly in a far corner of the garden, a wooded area, I was startled by two totally unexpected creatures: a red squirrel, bold as brass, hanging upside down stealing the bird-food, its prehensile tale wrapped round a branch. And then hearing a distinctive song I'd last heard in New Zealand. No! It couldn't be! Yes, there he was: a tui! Looking almost black, but with an iridescent sheen flashing blue, and all resplendent with his white neck tufts. Quite extraordinary! I could just about account for the red squirrel – all the campaigns of my time must have born fruit at last. But the tui … that was a puzzle! Cyla later told me that just as British settlers had introduced blackbirds to New Zealand long ago, so some mischievous Kiwis had smuggled into England a couple of tui. And they had flourished.

I had a relaxed lunch in my room, then afterwards found there was only one thing I wanted to do. I stripped off, lurched onto the bed, snuggled down under the duvet, and apparently fell fast asleep. Three hours later I woke up feeling refreshed but conscious I'd just escaped from a dire situation. Dreaming again! In my waking-up dream I was looking down on a land full of smiling people, young, good-looking and brightly dressed, moving jerkily around. I became conscious that their movements were choreographed, structured, and then glimpsed through the land surface the dark machinery below, that made everything above function like clockwork. The people were automatons. I was drawn down amongst them and myself became a puppet with no will of my own. Then I awoke fully and breathed a sigh of relief. I still had agency! The dream image seemed to have echoed the freight Sorting Station, though triggered by my fears of Big Brother.

I had a drink and looked around in appreciation of my space. I spent the rest of the time before going out for supper drawing the view from the balcony, making notes about my experiences and jotting down questions which I hoped to be able to answer eventually. I greatly enjoyed making use of my skills with pen and ink, in a sense reaffirming who I was. What again surprised me was my ability to recall everything almost perfectly – an attribute I had not experienced in my previous life. I was more used to confusing people's faces and names, misrepresenting timescales, sometimes forgetting just the word I wanted. I'd always prayed not to be a witness to crime, because I'd be the most hopeless giver of evidence. But now ... crystal clarity.

6
The Moot

At nineteen on the dot (I was acclimatising to the local timekeeping!) I went over to Rufus and Sam's flat. It was good to see them, and to inhale the delicious smells pervading their space. I immediately asked about the red squirrel. Apparently, the greys had been subject to birth control. I was fascinated by this. Sam told me that already in my own time, a combination of landscape management and culling of grey squirrels had been effective in Scotland, allowing reds to revive. Then a devilish plan was trialled habituating greys to the use of food hoppers that only they could access because of their heavier weight, lacing the food with oral contraceptives. It proved remarkably successful only requiring occasional management. Culling became unnecessary, greys gradually reduced in numbers and reds flourished in their stead. Now red squirrels were seen right across England and Wales as well as Scotland. I wondered if similar techniques were now being employed to control possums, stoats and weasels in New Zealand, where I had spent some years. It seemed much more humane than poisoned bait and traps. Yes, said Sam, absolutely.

I mentioned the tui as well. Apparently, Sam said, much to ornithologists' surprise, it was doing rather well in urbanised areas with plenty of tree cover. And people were loving the sound and sight of them.

I was really intrigued by all this, but further exploration of local wildlife was curtailed by the arrival of the fourth member of the dinner party: Able Cranston. Despite his venerable years and unusually sober dress he was a live wire, with flowing locks and a luxurious beard, an ample waistline and an alert, vital directness. He was probably the first person I had seen who clearly overindulged – as his subsequent freedom with the wine bottle confirmed.

'A delight to meet you, lass from the past, you take me back to my youth, an absolute privilege. Bravo, Rufus, what a catch!' He spoke with a northern twang and for a moment I thought he was being patronising, with words like 'lass' and 'catch', but his double handshake was firm, his expression direct and genuine. I told myself it was vital not to judge people, when language conventions can change so much, and anyway I immediately liked him – he reminded me of someone I knew, but couldn't think who.

After more pleasantries Rufus called us to order and sat us down, smiling genially at me. 'Now I'm going to introduce a degree of formality into the proceedings. I think it would be helpful to us as well as to you, Robyn, if we each said a little about ourselves. So we have a clearer idea of where we are coming from. There are nibbles on the table, and local wine when you want it. If everyone is happy, we'll introduce ourselves, and then ask you, Robyn, to say something about yourself and your time. Then after eating we can discuss a programme to illuminate our world for you.' The others nodded agreement. I just looked at them then helped myself to nibbles.

'OK, I'll start,' said Rufus. 'As you know, Robyn, I'm part of a team working on time travel theories and possibilities from the past to the present. We have had some partial successes and some unmitigated disasters up to now, which has led to restrictions on our freedom. Previous trials have all been from centuries ago, trying to avoid direct contamination with the present. It seems that time is progressively less predictable and constant the further back we try to go. So, you are our first 'experiment' – I must be blunt about it! – from the more recent past, and the transfer at least has gone beautifully. I profoundly hope you are fully here, body and mind, and that's what you feel too. You must tell us a bit later what you think.

'My role in this project is the psychologist on the team, delegated to be your guide and your protector. I've been trained – in theory anyway – to understand where people are coming from, you know, their context, their personal values and so on. I know little about the physics of transfer, or the psycho-physics, except to say that all the most successful transfers have occurred when the person's in a coma, like you. Some tie to specific space and time seems loosened then, and we can reach out and try to create an opening to this world and time. You're the first from this century. Before you came, I did a crash course in early century conditions and lifestyles, and it's so illuminating now to meet you in the flesh. I'm so glad you were able to transfer.' He paused, looked warmly at me. 'There! I hope that's enough from me.' I nodded in response, drawn to him more. He glanced significantly at Sam: 'Samantha?'

'Oh do call me Sam – I can't stand Samantha, you wretch!' she said, flashing her eyes. I realised immediately that she was no bimbo. She was a dark beauty, mysterious, though perhaps enigmatic and unpredictable are better words. Her accent vaguely southern European (but then, I couldn't quite place Rufus, either). She was dressed for summer: crop top, mini skirt and translucent tights (echoing your time, she said), head crowned with a foxy frizz. She looked at me appraisingly: 'Well, OK, I'm here, privileged to know about you, because I'm Rufus's friend, and he couldn't have kept it all from me!' She laughed, bright eyes looking at her mate. I felt awkward, but tried not to show it. She said more seriously: 'I hope to be helpful and useful to you, with my knowledge of the research into social behaviour, climate and ecology, and healthy urban environments. I'm really passionate about spatial planning and landscape design – such powerful tools for wellbeing!'

I papered over any residual embarrassment. 'That's great, you're right in my line of work. In my day there was lots of research, almost totally ignored in practice, and people spent all the time arguing whether nature or nurture was more important, you know, in determining behaviour –

and health.' 'Yup,' said Sam, 'both of course; but now we know that the social and physical environment has the edge. And the good news is we can manipulate the physical environment, over time. The bad news is we manipulated it in all the wrong ways in the first part of this century, so my job now is to advise policy-makers how to do better, and we are! It's so complex – thinking about how places and housing and transport and so on affect all the social and economic and ecological variables, and vice versa. I find it all fascinating! I spend most of my time out there in the field, observing, asking, evaluating social and market responses to interventions, trying to understand how people behave and what they feel, then recommending any improvements to design principles, etc. I know it's all very different from your time, if I've grasped it right. Your spatial decisions, I understand, were made on political and market grounds, not scientific evidence and observation.' She looked at me quizzically.

'An awful lot of the time, yes, you're right,' I said. She carried on: 'So now urbanists and designers are required to be like doctors, knowing how to improve health and sustainability all based on exhaustive research and experimentation. I believe it's working, and so does the body politic and most of the people. Anyway, that's my field. Be really interesting to see what you will find and think about us.'

Rufus was leaning back in his seat, smiling broadly. I couldn't work out whether it was in admiration or amusement. 'That's great, thanks Sam.' 'OK,' she said, mock humble. I thought her work was fascinating, right up my street. I said to her how great it would be to get together. 'No worries about that,' said Rufus, 'we can discuss it later. But now, all yours, Able.'

Able needed no further prompt. His voice was mellow and casual. 'Talking of ethnicity and culture,' he said, 'we've actually become quite a mongrel society. Sam here is a four-way mongrel, with Maori blood in her, plus Devonian, black Columbian and French, though not necessarily in that order. You yourself look a bit of a mix, with some middle-eastern genes, am I right? And as for me,' he chuckled, 'I'm Welsh, Norse and Middle English, with a little Scottish mixed in. And all to the good I say. Mongrel dogs are brighter than purebreds. The same goes for the human species. Though I have to be careful who I say that to. Incidentally, I'm not actually an unadulterated man. Nor woman for that matter. I went through a gender re-assignment programme at quite a tender age, barely an adult, at a time when it was in the news a lot. It was difficult initially, but I've no regrets now, I'm glad to say – unlike a few others of my generation – and I'm still enjoying life!' 'And how!' said Sam. Rufus raised his eyes in mock shock. These guys were very direct, I thought – they seemed to be able to say anything to each other, even with a stranger present; political correctness gone AWOL. Or maybe, I added to myself, it's taking a different form.

Able resumed: 'Now, what do I do? I'm a poet, a composer, a socialite and bon vivant. That's about it.' Rufus chipped in, 'Able Cranston, you are a rogue. Let me tell you, Robyn, Able is one of the leading poets in the country – poems all about nature, the Earth, our relationship to it, our inner selves. He's been called the twenty-first century Wordsworth. In music he's been at the forefront of the revival of twentieth century composers I'd never heard of, like Britten, Janacek, Messiaen and Stravinsky, through his programmes and media presence. I thought they were not at all my cup of tea until he twisted my arm and exposed me to live orchestral music. Now I know they're fantastic!'

'Though that is not,' said Able, turning back to me, 'the reason why he invited me here tonight. He invited me because of who I know – almost everyone who is anyone, and quite a lot who aren't. Generally I prefer the latter.' 'That's because they don't dare interrupt you,' said Sam, winking. 'Got me in one,' said Able, chuckling, 'however … I don't really like talking about me. Robyn, tell us something about yourself. I'm dying to know something about your life and times. I was in a skirt and blazer at school when you were whisked away here. I'll be very interested to see how false my early memories are … were … are!'

There was an expectant pause. My brain went into overdrive, and calculated that if Able had been a teenager in the early twenties he could be mid-eighties now. He didn't look it! I coloured, suddenly tongue-tied, confused by my sudden instant maths. Seeing this, Rufus handed me a glass of wine. Able looked mischievous, a twinkle in his eye. He saw I was looking confused. 'Hey Robyn,' he said. 'We have childhood memories in common. Try this! "Courage," he said, 'there's always hope! Bring me a thinnish piece of rope, or if there isn't any,"' he paused and looked at me, and I abruptly relaxed at his irrelevance and chorused in, '"bring a thickish piece of string. Then to the letter box he rose, while Pooh and Owl cried Ooh and Aah, and through the letter box he squoze ..." '

We stopped. Sam was looking puzzled. 'Great to have shared childhood memories!' I said, laughing my embarrassment away. 'Or second childhood memories,' added Able as an aside. 'Well,' I went on, 'I'm Georgie Robyn Ghorra, but I prefer to be called Robyn. At school the initials GG led to me being mercilessly mocked as a horse. Though ironically Ghorra means horse, in Arabic I think. I was born in 1992. Doesn't that sound strange now! To an English mum and Iranian-Syrian father, both studying French in Paris. My dad dutifully married Mum 'to give her a name,' he said, but soon after he went back to the Middle East, to Lebanon in fact. My mum said he told her that the last thing he wanted was to foist himself on her for the rest of her life. Mum brought me up as a single parent, in quite a strict puritan style – partly her Quaker background, and she'd also shared with my dad an interest in Islam, with its traditionally very sheltered view of girl children. We lived in Gloucester, then later in Stroud, and I went to the girls' grammar school in Stroud.'

'I thought grammars had been abolished way before that,' said Rufus. 'Not in Gloucestershire, my dear, said Able, 'or Essex for that matter.' 'Well, I enjoyed the education, it did me some good,' I said. 'Turned me into a bit of a culture vulture, not really at one with the zeitgeist of the time.' Able smiled benignly: 'The benefits of privilege,' he said. 'But go on Robyn.' I looked at Able, slightly annoyed by his assumption of privilege, and surprised then at my forthright response: 'If I'd been privileged, and my mum had had more money than she did on a teacher's salary, she'd have sent me to one of those so-called public schools. Plenty of them in Gloucestershire. She wanted to. She was really protective. So, no TV (do you know what I mean by that?). Not till my teens. No mobile till I was fourteen. That really cut me off from my school mates. And from boys too. I became really shy. At the time I just accepted my hermit lot and devoted myself to my studies. But now, looking back, I'm shocked and actually a bit angry. I had to be all demure and pure, unsullied by the world, no short skirts or bare midriffs, no parties, no friends. Well, some, actually, because I have to say, I loved sport, and excelled at athletics. I was in school, county and regional teams, and that brought me respect and friends, which I really needed.'

The others listened with rapt attention. I looked at them in what might have seemed an aggressive way – as if they were to blame – then took a deep breath and sighed. Sam smiled sympathetically and asked me what else interested me. I told them of my love of history. Not the kind of history they taught in school, but world history. I think because my dad was from the Middle East, and I discovered that the so-called dark ages were anything but dark. They were bright and brilliant over in the east, in Byzantium and the Islamic cultures. Lots of wars, but wow, the art and architecture! 'When I was twenty Dad managed – I don't know how he wangled it – to take me to Iran, where there was something called the Islamic Republic. Women were pretty repressed – oppressed – at the time, but he took me to some of the really special places. Esfahan! That's what I remember most. They say when you've seen Esfahan, you've seen half the world. It was magic.'

'So you did meet up with your dad?' queried Sam. 'Oh yes, but, like, only once a year,' I said. 'He would come at Easter and take me walking and climbing. North Wales, the Lakes, the Alps too, while I was still at school. The trip to Iran and Syria, which he arranged amid all the awful violence of the time, was like his signing off. He wanted to share his rich, rich heritage with me. Before I went my own way.' I felt tears welling in my eyes, suddenly sad at the tragedy of Iran, Syria, Lebanon and the Palestinians – and, I suppose, at the loss of my father.

Rufus said, quite gently, 'things aren't so bad in the Middle East now. We'll be able to tell you something of that another time, the political and the ecological situation. Tell us about the direction you took after school.'

'Straight to uni in Bristol, studying human geography, and a bit of ancient history. I became fascinated by the origin and planning of towns. Worked as a trainee planner for a bit, then got a place on the Oxford Brookes urban design course. Completed that in 2020 – despite the onset of the pandemic. Now working for a planning consultancy in Bristol, living here in Stroud.' 'What about friends?' said Rufus. 'Ah, like, all my friends were hobby friends: music, mountains, sporting friends. I didn't seem to make friends just as friends, and no real romance either, with boys – or with girls for that matter, which would have shocked my mum.

'But that all seems so far away. I don't know where I am. Really, this is all so strange, I'm just suspending disbelief, waiting to surface into reality.

Maybe I'm, like, locked into a coma reality. The last thing I remember is being knocked down by a car, and going to hospital, and, like, being put to bed.' I looked at the others, conscious that my speech was deteriorating; I'd consciously stopped using the word 'like' as a spacer after leaving school. 'Sorry, I don't mean to be rude. I don't mean I think you are all unreal. In fact that's what I don't understand. You are so real and, um, nice and welcoming, and Rufus has explained the situation, as far as he can, which is very helpful. I'm just, um, discombobulated. It's all mad. And I don't understand how I'm coping.'

'We all appreciate your situation,' said Rufus, 'and for myself, I'm really impressed by your coping ability. And what you've told us is very helpful. Revealing! I'm beginning to understand why it is you, not someone else, who is here. I'd like to know a little more about you. For example, what kind of work were you doing?' 'Oh,' I said. 'I was quite a small cog in the development machine, but interesting work, fun in fact: producing masterplans and designs for housing estates and regen projects. Problem solving through design. Though it was sometimes frustrating – working with developers especially. They ruled the roost – always brought their own very conservative, conventional assumptions to the table. They just wanted to reproduce what had sold well the year before last. And they believed the traffic engineers, often, rather than me. So my beautiful pedestrian-friendly, low-carbon schemes got watered down. Diluted almost to extinction. And the local planners weren't strong enough. Full of good intentions but undermined by arbitrary government planning rules. It was a difficult time.'

'Yes, I've picked that up – true enough,' said Sam. 'It's quite difficult, because of the loss of much electronic data, but from my reading of history, catastrophic mistakes were being made, especially in the period 2010 to 2030. Settlements were all car-based, except in the big cities, housing impossibly expensive, more and more people on the breadline and half the population living shorter, less healthy lives. Did it feel like that to you?'

I was slightly nonplussed at her outright condemnation of my own time – even though it was accurate enough. 'Well, yes, it did a bit, there were some dark times, but seeds of hope too!' I said, in my best bridge-building mode. 'Indeed, indeed,' said Sam, 'and the 2021 Glasgow climate conference was one of them, it really began to shift attitudes, but then it took us another fifty years to really turn everything around!' I thought of the places I'd seen since my arrival and laughed out loud, suddenly aglow: 'Yes, but you have! It's all brilliant now. I love this new world, I love it – what I've seen of it!' The others smiled broadly.

When Able came to ask a question, it was on a different plane altogether. He wanted to know what I thought about gender politics – more particularly how I perceived gender roles and attitudes in my own day. This was awkward. As a young woman he had made critical gender decisions. 'Well, ummm, that's … slightly out of my comfort zone,' I said, surprised again at my ability to refocus my thoughts. 'I don't – I didn't I mean – actually know any people who came out as trans. I couldn't make my mind up about all the debates at the time. They could get quite nasty, it seemed to me. I did know people who were gay or bisexual, though that wasn't a big deal really, just natural I thought. But I didn't agree at all with younger teenagers being allowed to change gender or sex. And all those sagas about sport and women's washrooms being invaded by trans women, I had a lot of worries all round that. Anyway, we were designing out part of the problem, making all loos unisex. And no pissoirs any more! That's about it.'

'Well, thanks,' said Abel. 'I actually remember some of that. Very interesting! You were ahead of the game! The de-gendering of space seems to me a positive and very necessary move. Equals out the toilet queues for men and women, for a start, and gives trans people a place to go that they feel safe and comfortable using. It took its time to work through everywhere, though. We have taken it a bit further, as you'll discover. But tell me, Robyn, were you ever tempted by the thought of gender re-assignment as a teenager?'

'Oh no! I wasn't.' I replied. 'However …' I wondered how far confessions should go, to these people who I barely knew. Somehow, I didn't seem to care. I took another swig of delicious local wine. 'In my later teens I was really attracted to other girls – so beautiful, though I didn't connect that with sex. But then, an all-girls school, no real social life, Mum policing my internet use like an ultra-zealous Jesuit…!' I saw the others listening, attentive, very warmly accepting me, as a person, not just a professional. 'I'll tell you what happened once, which really shocked me. I was in a mixed age interschool athletics competition. In fact I was the captain of our team. I was sharing the printed programme with a brilliant young sprinter, and our hands kept touching, and WOW! The electricity! I made it happen several times, just for the excitement, reaching parts of my body I barely knew existed. So after that I defined myself as a lesbian ... Of course, nothing happened – I was much too reserved and inhibited. I've never told anyone this before! The unrequited attraction to other girls lasted for several years; it was very intense at the time, but then after I went to uni and started mixing with boys, I defined myself as bisexual. I had a very rich sexual life – although all in the imagination! Since then it's really only been men.' Sam interposed, eyes bright. 'You should try a bit of both, I say. Nothing like variety!' I wasn't sure if she was being serious, so hesitated to speak, suppressing an illicit tingle of anticipation.

'That's fantastic, Robyn, said Rufus. 'You're so open with us, it's really helpful. You know, variety, diversity, acceptance of difference, that's built into our culture now. And not just in relationships – diversity in almost everything! You're filling the huge gaps in knowledge about early in the century – vital! But ... if you don't mind, we must come to the main business of the evening. We need a plan for you, Robyn. The question is, what do you want to see? What do you want to know? And what do we think you ought to know?!' There was a pregnant pause. The change in conversation was a bit abrupt for me. But I already had a few thoughts: 'OK ... I want to see and understand the countryside, it's all so altered, and then the towns, and transport, and housing and buildings and energy and the whole economic system. I want to understand all the social changes and what's happened to robots and things, and, and ... I want to meet people.' My mind was in a bit of a whirl, the new world opening up to me.

'Hey, that's more than enough to be going on with! We'll try to satisfy you as far as possible. However, you have to recognise that there are limits because of your unique origin.'

Rufus explained, carefully and in some detail, what those limits were. Initially at least I could not roam free or meet people casually. It all had to be managed. There would be a few people who would be fully taken into confidence, knowing who I was. They had to be primed, and the soul of discretion, bound to secrecy except to others in the know. Otherwise the risk of one era contaminating another was too great. I felt like I was in quarantine. It reminded me of lockdown, stuck at home, in the COVID-19 pandemic. Or maybe I was actually the virus itself, imported into this idyllic age from a problematic past, which had to be isolated, cut off from people.

However, the secrecy was just something I had to accept. My planned itinerary was exciting. Somehow I was managing to suspend existential angst and rustle up an enthusiastic sense of enquiry and curiosity, wanting to know things, to understand, to grapple with the mysteries of the future. Abel was a miracle! He seemed to have a finger in every pie, always knew the best person to speak to, whatever the field. The others acted as a break on his ebullience, particularly Sam, who was cool as a cucumber. Eventually we settled on the priorities and Rufus set about organising at least the next couple of days. Tomorrow, he and I would go out into the countryside, travel round to see the pattern of land use and settlement, have a walk in the woods, then visit an innovative farmer. The following day I would go with Sam to meet the chief urbanist of the Stroud Valleys, who apparently had a superb overview of social and economic as well as environmental change. I'd be able to see the magical models of the town and area. Beyond that we kept options open. The first two days' experience would help shape further visits and meetings.

I had a host of questions – to do with wildlife, energy, buildings, transport, technology, lifestyles, social media, belief systems, politics and so on. Tech questions were buzzing in my mind. Walking through the town, people didn't seem to be glued to phone screens at all, in the way they were in my own time. My three companions were clearly not fixated on their wristies, I was barely conscious of the electronic technology at all. I thought that somehow it must now be all so sophisticated, maybe direct brain-to-brain connections? Or was that pie in the sci-fi sky? It made me really interested in the social changes that had happened, how that related to education and work practices as well as technology. Abel and the others stressed that politics had altered beyond recognition (which couldn't be a bad thing, I thought!). It was all local now, so the trends in the West Country might be different from surrounding regions.

I was exhausted by it all. The day's experiences made me lethargic. After exchanging warm goodbyes, Rufus took me back across the green to my staircase.

I climbed the stairs to my fourth floor pad. As I undressed and washed, Cyla offered me herbal tea, which I gratefully accepted. It was delivered almost instantaneously. Then she asked if I needed any sex toys. I was taken aback and, shocked into being quite sharp with her, requested pyjamas. None available apparently; out of fashion! A nightshirt or fresh knickers and T-shirt were available if I wanted. A few minutes later, dressed in the proffered nightshirt I'd opted for, I fell into bed. Very comfortable and cosy! In no time, I drifted into sleep, apparently unphased by the extraordinary change in my life. Music floated into my head: the violin spiralling ever higher at the end of The Lark Ascending. I was transported into the heavens.

Part II
The future of land and place

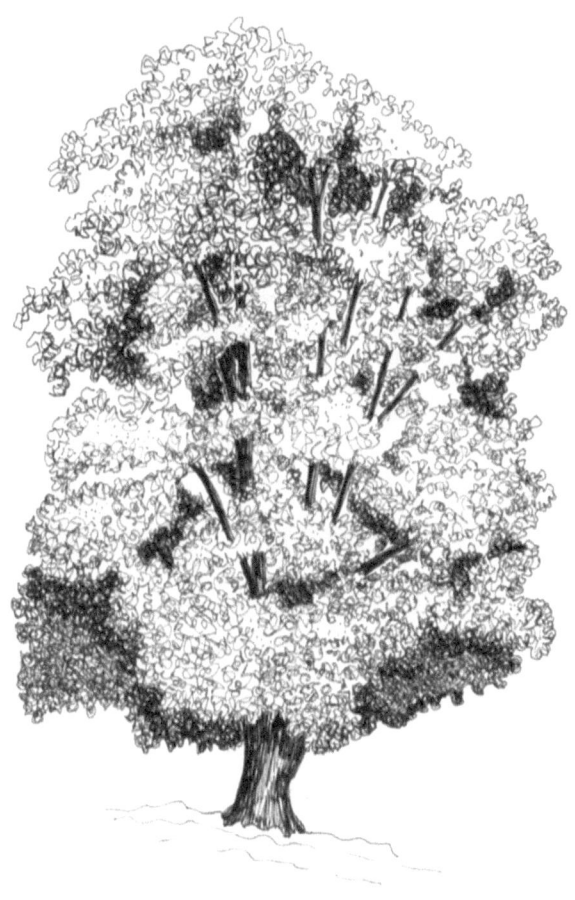

The English Oak, drawn in Stroud, Gloucestershire, home to an amazing diversity of creatures. The oak signifies wisdom, strength and endurance, all of which are vital to the realization of a healthy, sustainable environment

7
Vale and Wold

Heavenly sleep, deep into the night. Woke up with a start, sweat pouring off me, arms and legs flailing outside the duvet. Ripped off my nightshirt. The nightmare was still vivid, though difficult to recall later: an endless staircase, spiralling up, Escher-style; and a tall, thin, shadowy figure, which I instinctively thought was the figure of Death, parading in multiple dimensions, round and through the staircases, going somewhere, getting nowhere. Rapid mouth-breaths, heart racing and arms aching. No pain in the chest, but still fear grabbed me: a heart attack? My critical mind said nonsense! I lay still and made an effort to relax, consciously slowing my breathing, taking deep breaths, imagining a tumbling sunlit stream. Then I glimpsed the cool pre-dawn light through a slit in the curtains, taking the edge off darkness and fear. I felt my pulse. Not quite so histrionic but still throbbing in my neck. I willed it to go steady.

I moved to get out of bed. The bedside lamp came on automatically. In the en suite I washed myself all over with a cold, wet flannel. The air dryer sprang to life unbidden. Looking at myself in the mirror, I told myself to stretch up, stand firm, be calm, breathe deeply. The discomfort had gone, my pulse had steadied, and I saw that my wrist band was displaying the rate: 72 was still a bit high for me. Suddenly a strange tinkling sound rang out from my wristband. 'Doctor' glowed at me from the display. This was more than uncanny, it was unnerving. I hesitated, then pressed 'accept voice call'; I didn't want visuals in my state of undress.

A man's voice with a slight West African accent said 'Ah! Hello! I'm Dr. Aguta, I'm monitoring your health, and fully in the know about your origin. I'm glad to see your pulse is steady again. The attack must have been really uncomfortable, and a real shock for you.' 'Er … yeah … absolutely. Out of the blue, after a nightmare,' I said. 'How do you feel now?' 'Much more myself. Thank you.' 'Good. Well, I think you deserve some explanation.' This is a first, I thought. 'There are a couple of things. As you may imagine, whatever your conscious coping abilities (which are amazing, given your recent time transfer), your subconscious needs time to adapt, and is flailing around a bit. Also – and this is more conjecture than absolute knowledge – your body, back in the hospital, back in time, may have had something of a crisis, and you got the ripples from it here. I'm not at all sure about that. We don't really understand how it works, how you can be in two places at once. Your conscious self is in this age, but at the level of the unconscious there could be some residual interaction.'

'Oh … thank you,' I said, 'that is helpful.' 'OK, then I'll let you get back to sleep. I think you'll be alright now. Goodbye.' 'Bye.'

I felt disturbed – that I was under constant surveillance: Cyla, the chip, the phone, the doctor. To get a call like that! But actually, I was also oddly comforted – someone was caring for me. I relaxed, but couldn't immediately re-enter sleep, so put on a dressing gown, picked up an art book on Byzantine Ravenna, and sat on the bed. Engrossed in the three-dimensional images which sprang out of the page, and the transformative beauty of San Vitale with its green-gold mosaics, I read until my eyes drooped. Before flopping into bed I felt my pulse; back to normal, a nice slow 58, an athlete's rate.

*****

The next thing I remember was sunlight pouring through the window, bright and warm on my eyelids. I lay still and listened. Birdsong! A rich tapestry of song. Blackbirds, chaffinches, great tits, swifts screeching, a medley, one repeated glissando I couldn't place – a very pure, clean sound. The curtains and window must have opened a bit by themselves. I was relaxed, snuggling under the duvet, but listening intently, bathed in the sheer pleasure of morning sun and the unadorned sounds of nature. A sense of wonder suffused my being. The night fears had evaporated as if they had never been.

Eventually I got up, showered and dressed. Just in time, for my wristy told me Rufus was on his way over. I signalled OK, ready. Cyla unlocked the door and he came in. Cyla revealed the breakfast options, made tea for me and chicoffee for Rufus. As we breakfasted together, Rufus explained, 'this is our Severn Vale and Cotswold explore day. We'll have the chance of a walk and end up with tea at a lovely farmhouse.'

After a leisurely repast Rufus called a taxi, which appeared in less than five minutes. 'Not cheap,' he said, 'but essential for this outing – we're going all over the place.' He instructed the vehicle to head up to Selsley Common.

It was quite slow in the built-up area. The taxi was clearly low in the street pecking order, giving way to pedestrians, cyclists and e-scooters. But we were able to relax and enjoy the view. As we purred our way around the streets of Woodchester I noticed that some of the old mid-to-late century (twentieth century!) detached and semi-detached houses had been replaced by colourful half-timbered three and four storey terraces. Seeing my interest, Rufus told me these were carbon-neutral solar dwellings, with reused bricks and timber. The newer buildings, apparently, were carbon positive, over their lifetime exporting more energy than they import, taking more carbon out of the atmosphere than they put in, even allowing for the construction costs. I was duly impressed, though not surprised. Even in the twenties architects were working towards such buildings, and the Tory government had been intending to legislate for zero carbon but had chickened out. 'Sam will be able to tell you more when you go to Gloucester, where they really are making progress, said Rufus. 'This town's pretty good overall in the carbon stakes. The only real problem that I'm aware of is allotments and smallholdings. Demand is huge, and we are struggling to find land which is suitable and available.' I was struck how Rufus was using 'we' not 'they'. He clearly felt part of the decision process, not estranged from it as I remember so often feeling.

We soon broke free of the buildings and gardens and went steeply up through woodlands. The Common was still the Common. The taxi (in its studiously genderless voice) asked if we wanted to walk across to the view and look. We did! The taxi drove off. 'Hey!' I almost shouted, 'where are you going?' – conscious that I was anthropomorphising the vehicle, which was ridiculous. Rufus explained he'd let the taxi go off on another mission for forty minutes.

Selsley Common was looking comfortingly familiar, with the ancient barrows at the highest point. Cows and people alike were out and about. It was part covered in cowslips, with orchids coming. It threw my sense of time out of kilter. I was back in my own era. However, when we got to the edge and looked out across the Severn Vale, I gasped in surprise. The changes were obvious, and startling: the woodland coming up to meet us, trying to take over the open common; vineyards on the lower slopes; scattered woods and croplands all over the Vale; the line of the motorway, once so prominent, now not visible. Where the motorway junction had been there was an extensive area of confused grey and green – huge blocky buildings, with trees around, rather an ugly scar on the land. It extended back into the more ordered green townscape of Stonehouse, which had expanded to absorb neighbouring settlements, all camouflaged by an urban forest. I listened ... no traffic sound. And there, beyond all that, was the River Severn, huge and wide, glistening in the sun.

'It's high tide right now,' said Rufus. 'But it's so big!' I exclaimed. 'Yes, well, way back, in the forties I think, they decided to open up some floodlands for the spring tides. Actually, the river decided. It would not be refused! There were some really bad floods with the more violent storms. And when storm flood coming downstream meets the surge of the tidal bore in its pomp coming upstream ...' I interrupted: 'Yes, we had all kinds of strategies for trying to manage that, I know 'cos I was advising landowners to change agricultural practices, make permeable surfaces and sustainable drainage systems and so on.' 'Yes, all that happened, eventually. But ...' (he paused rather dramatically) 'the fury of the weather gods as the climate changed was not to be mollified! So all kinds of action were taken up and down the river. In the sixties the Welsh government became very radical and took dramatic action, compelling rewilding upstream in the Severn, slowing the runoff, but we still had to admit defeat – if that's what it is – and give the river everything it wanted in the Vale. The climate geographers say we're geared up now for at least a generation, before more is needed again.'

I gazed at the view before me. It all felt like a foreign land. I asked Rufus about the confusion of development by the old junction. 'Derelict' he told me. 'Old commercial and industrial properties and warehousing, made obsolete in the Bad Times – the wrong answer to the wrong question. Now left as a warning and being gradually reclaimed by nature. Like the remnants of a lost empire.' I looked and pondered. The name Ozymandias sprang into my mind: *I am Ozymandias, King of Kings. Look on my works, ye mighty, and despair.* We turned and walked past the old overgrown quarry where I remembered childhood picnics and a falteringly romantic tryst when I was twenty. Then we were in the woods. Despite telling myself not to be so silly, I felt shy and awkward wandering into this enclosed landscape with a man who was still basically a stranger. Rufus was alive to my unease: 'Turn on your safeguard,' he instructed, 'it'll record everything and is being tracked.' I immediately did so, but worried, who is tracking me? It felt again like I was being managed. And of course, I was. Nevertheless, I was impressed by my companion's awareness.

The woods had changed. I remembered the escarpment woods as mature and big in scale, dominated by beech, almost gloomy in summer leaf, but now they were young, the canopy intermittent and spring-transparent, emerald-bright leaves and diverse species – oaks, chestnuts, maples, lindens, beech, the occasional ilex, even the odd olive, which was a surprise. There was the faint pungency of garlic, the white flowers just emerging, and glades gilded with woodland flowers, some strange to me.

'These woods,' said Rufus, 'planted thirty years ago, were intentionally more diverse than the woods that were blasted back in the fifties storms; we were essentially hedging our bets. The beech trees were from southern France, better adapted than native varieties to our summer droughts. Down in the Vale there's lots of Tuscan oak. But now of course we wouldn't dream of importing live trees from overseas! Aotearoa – or New Zealand, as you may still know it – has shown us the biosecurity way. Even for cut wood. We've got our own nurseries experimenting with selective breeding, and finding what species are best.' I wasn't so interested in the beech. A glade of quite mature elm had seized my attention. 'No way!' I said, mouth open. Rufus laughed: 'elm,' he said, 'yes, completely immune!' He meant immune from Dutch elm disease which had ravaged the English countryside in the late twentieth century. 'No more imports!' he repeated adamantly.

He explained more about timber strategy: how high wood demand early in the century had been very substantially reduced through reuse and recycling, how little timber was now imported, how extensive were the forests of soft and hardwoods, how temperate 'Celtic' rainforests with their complex ecosystems were reviving in Wales, the Southwest, and especially on the west coast of Ireland. 'And we've had to cut our coat according to our cloth,' he said. 'Things are designed to last. No more new kitchens every house move when the ones already in place will do very well! Anyway, we can't afford them!'

It was lovely and cool in the woods. We came through a fence to a steep, rugged area of much older trees, with more mosses, lichens and ferns over rock and trunk. Rufus told me that a woodland charity was trying to manage (or unmanage, he said) this woodland as a temperate rainforest. 'It's much wetter here than down in the Vale, catching the westerlies,' he said. 'But it's a bit of a struggle to sustain rainforest habitats, given our pretty dry summers.'

I wanted to linger there – in the complex, richly textured forest, trees weirdly shaped and draped with foliage, full of strange smells and buzzing insect life, with sudden hidden movements in the undergrowth and fallen trees and rocks furry green with moss. It felt like a prelapsarian world.

But there was no chance to linger! Rufus said, 'Right, we need the find our taxi. It's buzzed me.' We made our way up towards the top road through the woodland, greeting a couple of old people striding purposefully along. Suddenly I saw something running half hidden in the oaken undergrowth. 'Keep your eyes peeled,' said Rufus quietly. As luck would have it, we didn't have to. In a clearing just ahead of us, there they were, wild boar, a whole troupe of them, feeding peacefully. 'Not really wild, whispered Rufus, 'very much farmed. They are so well adapted to this terrain, roaming free in the woods, and actually helping biodiversity.'

'Farmed for what? 'You mean you eat them?' I don't know why I was shocked. 'Of course!' he said. 'When we meet the farmer it will all be explained, I'm sure.' I took a while to absorb this, what seemed like a contradiction. I'd become a vegetarian, almost vegan, in the fond belief it was good for the planet. It had taken some time to learn how to maintain a balanced diet, but I'd done it. Now I found in this future world my assumptions challenged. I remained to be convinced!

Soon after, we came out near the top of the scarp and found the taxi waiting for us. The road seemed alive with cyclists. The taxi gently negotiated its way along, until we dived off the edge and down through the forest and vineyards. Before long, we were meandering through the orchards, farms, woods and hamlets of the vale.

We paused by a pond where a group of youngsters – in their late teens or early twenties, I thought – were at work. 'They're doing their National Service,' said Rufus. I looked askance. 'What do you mean? National

Service? They don't look like soldiers to me.' 'Oh, they're not! Sorry, I forgot. This system has been going all my life, so I kind of just take it for granted. Some people do go into army training, but the vast majority choose social and environmental activities; there are so many options. It's normally called National Community Service now – NCS. I planned this stop so we could see what they get up to – wetland and wildlife enhancement, I was told. Helping the beavers!' He laughed. 'I had to do it, of course – I asked to be attached to a mental wellbeing centre. That helped me decide to study psychology.'

'Do you mean everyone has to do this? Why do you have it at all? It takes freedom away from people, just when they are spreading their wings.' 'Yes, everyone!' said Rufus. 'Though I must admit there is political debate about this. I'll explain the context. It was introduced late in the forties after the most violent riots in living memory. My parents say they were awful – the riots, I mean. Not restricted to the big cities, but in many small towns too. Triggered by the climate catastrophe really, and mass immigration and youth unemployment. The government decided that a national service year was going to be one way of cutting unemployment, integrating different cultures, helping people to get along together, and at the same time compensating for the appalling low level of public services after a period of austerity. Very controversial as you can imagine – with many making the argument you made about freedom. The unions complained about scab labour, displacement of real jobs. But amazingly it worked, we've got it now, and it's more than paid for itself in a whole host of ways. Actually, I did my thesis about this initiative. I looked at the impact on mental health, both short- and long-term. It was stunning! Really positive! It helped to create a sense of belonging to society, building shared identity beyond tribal identities if you like – whether those were related to football, race, gender, education or whatever. For immigrants there was the obligation to learn spoken and written English as part of their social year, which transformed their prospects. That was open to indigenous youngsters too, those who hadn't done so well at school. It all helped. Hey! I could bore for Britain on all this!'

I was rather conscious of intruding on the team's domain. However, a cheery wave from someone who appeared to be in charge reduced my worries. 'I forewarned them we might drop in,' said Rupert.

We engaged with the leader, who herself was maybe only twenty, and she introduced us to her motley crew, who explained what they were doing, both practical work and scientific monitoring, as well as artistic activity, and everyone having a go at all aspects. I was surprised by the holistic approach. They clustered around us, chatting, gave us chicoffee (any excuse for a break!), and boasted enthusiastically that eels had now reached the pond, up from the Severn along the stream they'd been working on. While they spoke I pondered the way my own assumptions about education were being challenged. Apparently the age sixteen to twenty-one was not a matter of A-levels and then university or job, but a multi-faceted experience developing useful physical, intellectual and social skills, creative problem-solving and disciplined responsibility. There was a lot of choice how each person shaped these five years, with a mentor guiding and facilitating them. I was fascinated, wanting to know more, but before long Rufus whisked me away.

Back in the taxi, I said, 'Wow! That was such a breath of fresh air. Rufus, just explain further how – er – NCS works.' 'Well, it's all about young people and wellbeing!' He said with a laugh. I laughed with him, feeling relaxed. 'They are given a choice when to take their service year, and whether full time or part time over two years. The range of ages gives leadership opportunities for the older ones and role models for the younger ones. Always mixed gender and of course mixed race. They get paid the basic living wage. They volunteer for an official body, charity or not-for-profit company – a wide range of projects and schemes are on offer. They're monitored by the National Service Agency. It's amazing, the whole thing is very cheap to run and just light touch controls. And it's worked miracles for social cohesion and the sense of identity, reduced substance abuse, and significantly reduced crime.'

Rufus went on, 'the sixteen- to twenty-one-year-olds were once two groups. Social scientists and lawyers, and eventually the government, decided that the legal child/adult distinction – a vulnerable child up to eighteen, then abruptly a fully responsible adult – was artificial in the extreme, leading to many unfair situations and decisions. The alternative was to define a new breed of young people who had more rights than children – like the right to vote – but still needing guidance to achieve full maturity. Well, the arguments raged about what to call them: youths and maidens? Young adults? Proto-adults? Pre-adults?'

While Rufus had been speaking we'd been travelling in our uncannily quiet vehicle, passing farm hamlets which seemed to be hives of activity, and villages which were a far cry from the commuter and retirement villages of my own era. There was a lot going on. Lots of local facilities. I wondered how that was achieved. We also passed one village which was apparently dying, with many of the cottages derelict and a complete lack of visible services. Then we turned back into the hills up narrow meandering lanes, where I rapidly became completely lost. I had by now realised the great change that had come to the countryside: more woodland, more rewilding, interspersed with more market-gardening and vineyards. As we went around and about through the incised valleys and plateaus of the Cotswolds, something else was revealed. Where once ploughed fields for grains had been dominant on the tops, there were now pastures. And grazing these pastures were sheep and lambs, in places coexisting with wind turbines or raised-up solar panels, so the animals could wander underneath – double-cropping in a sense.

This was altogether a bit of a puzzle – the Cotswolds reclaiming their ancient role as sheep-wolds. How, I wondered, did this achieve zero carbon and biodiversity? I held my tongue ... just carefully observed and noted. But Rufus sensed my reserve. He was not to be deterred. 'I know, it's sheep not grain. I suggest you ask the taxi about it.' I thought I would go straight to the heart of my concern for nature and wildlife generally – which the return to sheep farming, on the face of it, undermined. 'Has wildlife increased at all since the beginning of the century?' The pleasant voice replied: 'According to some measures, insect life has recovered to pre-world-war levels, and wild bird and mammal life has increased threefold.' 'How has this happened?' I asked. 'Land use change, and the abolition of almost all fertiliser, insecticides and herbicides,' came the answer. Rufus almost intervened, implying I should go no further. But I persisted: 'Taxi, explain what has happened to hedgehogs, for example.' Hedgehogs had always been a favourite of mine, almost vanished without trace in parts of England. 'Hedgehogs have revived in number and are now common,' our transport said. 'The main reason is the change in agricultural practice so that worms and insect bugs are plentiful and suitable habitats both more prevalent and connected.' I was surprised, indeed delighted, though scarcely believing what I heard.

Rufus cut across my thoughts: 'Robyn, do have a look around, now we've stopped for a moment.' The taxi had slid to a halt. I saw we were in a wide village street. It was clearly a thriving settlement, with old and new houses clustered around the village centre, a primary school, several shops and workshops, solar panels on every roof, including on the old Cotswold stone cottages. I exclaimed in surprise that listed buildings with stone roofs had been allowed to be compromised in this way. We began moving on slowly, as Rufus said that the eco-farmer he'd arranged for us to meet would be ready and waiting. As we wended our way out of the village, he told me, 'yes, apparently that was quite a battle, way, way back – I mean persuading the owners and the powers that be that all buildings, listed or not, should eventually become solar-powered. Re-roofing had to incorporate solar collection. That was an essential part of the bargain.' I was intrigued. I had been cultured into assuming the bijou Cotswold rows were sacrosanct.

'Really – tell me more,' I said. 'What bargain?' 'Oh well, you know ...' he said. I waited. 'It's quite complex, and the guy we meet tomorrow, the chief urbanist, will give a better explanation. Basically, every village or town has to be as self-sufficient as it can be. Only then are places allowed to grow.' 'Even in a protected landscape?' I said. 'Especially then,' said Rufus. He pointed back to the crest of a hill above the village we'd left. 'See those?' I did see! A couple of large wind turbines. 'This was a key village, I guess, allowed to expand,' said Rufus. 'Allowed!' I said, 'That's a revolution! In my day in the Cotswolds the policy was village preservation, no expansion. It didn't work, mind you. And another thing: key village! That's an old planning policy term, from back in the sixties.' 'You mean the nineteen sixties? I didn't know that!' said Rufus, 'Great! I need to know more. You can teach me for a change!'

But not now, I thought. There's too much going on. We travelled several kilometres along tortuous, potholed lanes. Some things don't change, I thought. We had to slow down as we approached a straight, well-surfaced track crossing the road, as a cyclist whizzed across. 'Ah, yes,' said Rufus. 'Cycleways have been created, a while back now, to link directly between villages, for e-bikes, scooters and small e-carts – not for us or bigger vehicles though, let alone those huge, heavy old tractors, which are now banned anyway. The old lanes our taxi has to use are rather left to go to wrack and ruin – a sign of straitened times.

A little later we passed through another village, a stark contrast to the last one, with no obvious facilities, not even a pub, and most buildings and gardens tatty, like in the declining village we'd seen earlier. I was rather shocked to see it again. 'This is sad, what's happening here?' 'It is sad,' said my companion. 'I expect this is what we call, with typical half-truth, a transition village. Transitioning towards sustainability, is what it's supposed to be. But I think it's transitioning towards death.' 'Yes, look at those empty houses,' I remonstrated. 'They could be used to house all those migrants you've talked about.' 'The provincial government won't allow it,' said Rufus. 'Settlements like this are unsustainable, they import all their needs and export all their poisons, they're a drain on the planet. They always were. The landowners and house owners have done bugger all for years and years, so they have a huge ecological footprint. I do understand the policy, we can't afford – the wider community can't afford – to support them.' 'Yes, but what about the people still living here? Put on the scrap heap of history?' 'No, no, no! Some people like it here, they just get on with their lives. But it's kind of mothballed. One day something will happen, someone will take action and things will change.'

'Really?' I said, suspicious of his relentless optimism. 'And I'll bet the people who are still here are the poor – those with no option to get out.' 'OK, you may have a point. Tomorrow we will ask Mr Kleiner. Actually, thinking about tomorrow, it won't be me. If you remember, you'll be going with Sam, she's more into all this – the human built environment.'

Rufus was silent for a moment, checking the way the taxi was taking us. A moment later we were gliding gently down a smooth farm drive towards a farmstead. Rufus became ebullient again: 'Ah! We're here! Now we'll meet our eco-farmer – very innovative and influential, who's been told all about you – your origin I mean. I think you'll find this very interesting.'

8
The farmer

Our 'eco-farmer' lived in a traditional Cotswold farmhouse nestling in a dell with woods around, a big farmyard and a delightful garden to one side, alive with tulips and wallflowers. A woman opened the heavy oak front door with a beaming smile of welcome. Rufus introduced her as Sarah Beard, the farmer we had come to see. I did a double take, silently berating myself for expecting the farmer to be a man. The porch, full of coats and boots, led into a large farmhouse kitchen, centred on a massive, rough-hewn table for at least eight people where a feast of cold meat, cheeses, pâtés, breads and salads was laid out on it. A cluttered old dresser took up one wall; pots and pans hung from the ceiling. It almost felt as if I had abruptly gone right back in time. Then I saw there was no range in the large old fireplace, no Aga, while the kitchen units were unconventional and – to my eyes – futuristic.

Sarah busied herself making a pot of tea. 'I'm giving the bot time off,' she said, with a tone of dismissal in her voice. 'I get a much better cuppa if I do it myself! The bot can stay in its cupboard!' Sarah was a robust, down-to-earth woman in dungarees, with her long auburn hair tied in a bun. Middle-aged, but which side of fifty I couldn't initially guess. She chattered while bustling around the kitchen, asking shrewd questions about my own background and how I came to be here, and sharing jokes with Rufus, whom she clearly liked a lot.

Settling down at table, she declared, with obvious relish, 'Well, now you can tuck in! Just tuck in. You know, you and I have so much in common, by comparison with this whippersnapper here.' Rufus seemed delighted with his label. I looked puzzled. 'Well, love, I was born in twenty twenty, so we overlapped a year or two. It's grand to see someone from my era!' My head couldn't quite do the maths at that moment, but I gazed at Sarah with fresh respect, seeing now the signs of wrinkles round her neck, hair greying in places, then rejoining with warmth, 'And you don't look a day over fifty!' Sarah smiled back: 'Sixty-nine, my dear, been that for a year or two! All down to diet, exercise, good work and sex!' I forced a smile. Rufus guffawed. 'Still at it, then?' he said. Sarah responded with mock afront, 'What cheek! You rude boy! Take a new husband every seven years, that's my motto. My current husband is doing stalwart work online, up in the study. I'm not sure if he'll make an appearance. Anyway, let's get down to business.'

Sarah was quite something. Despite her brusque manner and her bravado, I warmed to her. 'Tell me,' she said, 'what you expected our countryside to be like?' 'More woods, more wilderness, more vineyards, and the Cotswolds dominated by organically farmed grains, very few livestock, maybe,' I said. 'Ah, good,' she said. 'Right on several counts. Almost half my farm is woodland, some old and mature, much of it more recent. Quite open woodland, with plenty of woodland edge and overgrown hedgerows, all encouraging wildlife diversity and allowing grazing animals below.' 'Oh yes,' I said, 'this morning we saw small wild boar in the woods near Selsley.' 'Indeed,' she said, 'I have pigs and deer and a few bullocks. All strictly controlled in number – we undertake extensive woodland farming, so that the animals maintain ecological equilibrium. Plenty of foraging for them. If they breed indiscriminately, they can destroy the very environment they love. My animals have rights to a good life and isn't it their choice when they breed? Of course they love it – far better than a boring old field of monoculture grass. And they can shag to their hearts content, but I control which offspring are allowed to mature, and which we slaughter and eat.'

I remembered reading about something similar, back in my day, so said: 'Sounds OK, but how do you make it pay? Don't you get very low returns per hectare?' 'Well,' Sarah responded, more serious for a moment, 'agricultural land prices have moderated over the years – more realism and less spurious investment value – so land productivity can be lower too; but, more to the point, we are devilish clever!' 'How's that?' I asked. She explained about their policy of diversifying income – the orchards, vineyards, vegetable fields, vertical greenhouses, grazing fields for the sheep, as well as the woodland for other livestock, all contributing to viability, together with training and school courses. And as far as the woodland itself was concerned, they judiciously harvested mature trees, supplying craft micro-businesses on the farm. She said it was quite a community, more a hamlet than a farm. Then she turned to how they manage the woodland livestock: 'Animals roam widely and do need monitoring. We keep a close eye. You may not like the thought of it, but we mark each animal with a tiny implant, so we can track their movements, train them to respond to trigger stimuli and call them back to the ranch when we need them. They become obedient. Just like I like my men!' Her dark eyes twinkled wickedly.

I smiled weakly, being untutored in responding to risqué jokes, especially when in bad taste. But then my mind focussed on the matter in hand, frowning. 'Come on, spit it out!' said Sarah. 'It's not the implant that worries me,' I said, 'but, well, I'm a vegetarian, and believe eating meat is essentially …' I hesitated. I'd been about to say evil. 'It's essentially bad for the environment, for the climate, and inhumane for the animals.'

'Alright,' she said, glancing at Rufus, who nodded as if confirming we had reached the nub of the issue. 'You're absolutely correct, back in the dark ages, early this century, things were bad, from what I've heard. There was intensive meat production, heavily dependent on grain from overseas, allowing us to claim greater sustainability; our cattle and sheep were farting away, and their methane was contributing alarmingly to global warming, their slurry was polluting water courses, killing life in streams. And I'll tell you something more! The resulting ammonia was mixing with other pollutants to generate very fine particle matter – PM2.5s – more than from all diesel engines in the country. And you know the COVID-19 pandemic?' 'How could I not?' I said. 'Oh, sorry, stupid of me, said Sarah. 'You've lived through it. Well, the belief is that the death toll was worsened by all the fine particulates in the atmosphere, many ascribed to cattle pollution.' She changed tack, almost without drawing breath. 'Look, I respect people who don't eat meat, though for me vegans go too far. If you want a non-meat diet, the meat substitutes are really good now, and no longer rely on cash crops from overseas. We have artificial meat production: using enzymes that make flesh by consuming carbon dioxide and nitrogen from the air. Real meat is more of a high quality, organic, free-range niche product – tasty, textured and varied – and of course more pricey.'

I took a moment to process this. Rufus cut in: 'So tell us, Sarah, how come it's alright to grow animals for slaughter now, but for many people wasn't back then?' She gave a bit of sigh, saying she still had to fight these battles. 'And the answer is three words, extensive, local, organic.' She paused, then explained each in turn: extensive meant husbandry at the density that the environment can cope with - indeed benefit from - indefinitely, like her animals in the woods and her sheep on the topland fields. She told me that there were fewer farm animals overall in Britain now, and people were eating less animal meat, specifically much less of the prime and pricey cuts which determine overall demand. Artificial meat was attractive in quality and price. 'But,' she declared, 'in the Cotswold Hills many more animals are farmed now than used to be, and that's what the toplands are good for. ' Apparently the very early farmers, a couple of thousand years before the Romans, had cleared the woodland, and animal husbandry had created the grasslands. She castigated the farmers of the twentieth century for growing grain, right across the Cotswolds, relying on big annual inputs of fertiliser, weedkillers and pesticides to maintain production, undermining the long-term fertility of the shallow, stony soils. Literally costing the earth.

Sarah went on: 'Anyway, my livestock more or less look after themselves. The woodland animals are bred to survive winter in the open. No slurry! If we do have to have some animals in sheds, we add iron sulphate or other substitutes which cuts slurry methane almost to zero. Their diet is so diverse and healthy I quite envy them! Selective breeding and judicious gene manipulation help a lot. So overall there is less belching methane, negligible slurry methane, and no carbon from artificial fertiliser, tractors or field buggies. And let me tell you something else – absolutely critical – that official calculations seemed to ignore early in the century.'

Sarah leant forward and spoke quite intensely. 'Methane! It's gradually absorbed and transformed by soil and plants, so its average life in the atmosphere is about a decade. It's not at all like carbon dioxide, which persists much longer, like over a hundred years – more than that if there is deforestation. As the farming and food industries have gradually decreased the number of herbivores farmed, and progressively breed and feed better, then the atmospheric level of methane from farming has gone down quite fast – this has already happened.' She continued, explaining that the effect on greenhouse gas levels had been positive, helping to compensate for the huge longevity of high carbon emissions, which are still driving global heating. She said it was reckoned that now, in this country at least, animal methane levels were well below pre-industrial farming levels, and not so very far above the pre-farming methane levels from wild herds.

Sarah could be persuasive. I was impressed – and said so, sharing with her that I'd gone WOOFing (sorry! Working on organic farms) in the university holidays, and had a grasp of all this. I knew something of the issues.

'Now, moving on,' said Sarah. 'let's add in the local. We are no longer, in England, allowed to buy fodder grain from overseas, exporting our carbon footprint to countries like Argentina and Ukraine. That's been salutary! And we charge for imported meat through the nose – by tariffs, I mean. The whole world is moving slowly in this direction, but we're ahead of the game. Some market fundamentalists see it as anti-trade and anti-globalisation. Maybe it is! But I see it simply as pro eco-globalisation, pro the Earth, our habitat. The carbon tax is a major factor.'

'Yes, and it's not all good,' said Rufus. 'World trade in cash crops has slumped and that's hit some countries hard.' 'OK, yes,' said Sarah, still on her high horse. 'But who suffered? Mainly the big landowners who, a century ago, with the help of the World Bank and their own governments, dispossessed the small farmers and made them wage slaves instead. And often poor wages at that, like in Africa. The answer is localisation there as well as here! Power to the producers, not the profit mongers! Anyway, let's not get into all that. I'll agree there are some vexed issues, especially where climate change has made food production more problematic. Can we leave that one? I want to talk about the third factor: organic and regenerative principles.'

From my WOOFing experience, I could predict what she would emphasise: no artificial fertiliser, no herbicides or insecticides, judicious rewilding, letting the weeds grow rampant. I asked her about the sheep pastures on the hills.

She smiled. 'Well, for any herd there are normally three fields in rotation, sheep on one, nitrogen-fixing on a second, and the third fallow. Sheep love a varied diet, so not just grass but lovage, clover, all kinds of tasty herbs. They flourish on it. You know, there were experiments on this in the Cotswolds back in the twenties. We've learnt a lot. For so many decades, wheat, maize and rapeseed exhausted the soil, and farmers relied on ridiculous quantities of nitrogen to maintain fertility; on top of that climate change did its worst. But now we are at last really regenerating the soils. The herbivores are critical to this. They complete the organic cycle. And we've banned all heavyweight machinery which compressed the soil and speeded up water runoff. So now more moisture is retained in the soil, erosion is reduced and flood risk managed better. Grain can be grown elsewhere in the country. Not here – it's completely the wrong place for it!' She looked almost triumphant.

I was beginning to understand; just needed a while for it all to sink in. I wasn't ready to abandon my vegetarianism just yet. Rufus saw that I'd had enough – enough argumentation and enough food. We'd all finished a delicious lunch. 'At the risk of cutting you off in your prime, Sarah, let's have a break,' he said. 'That was really helpful, and there's more to tell I'm sure. Shall we go and look round the farm?'

Sarah jumped up with alacrity. We donned wellies and headed out – through the farmyard with hens scrabbling, across to the stream and lake, where Sarah pointed out the water turbine which was busily generating. 'Just enough fall to make a real difference, at least in winter – It keeps us going through darker months.'

My attention was elsewhere. The lake was enfolded in the woodland – the leaves of willow, beech, sessile oak and robinia fresh and bright in the dappled sunlight. There were swans and tiny cygnets out on the lake. The cygnets were in a perfect line, strung out between the parents. 'If only all children were like that!' said Sarah. I was sighing with delight. It was all so beautiful. 'You know,' I said, 'this all seems like a dream. A dream of Elysian fields and wonder-woods and a sustainable, biodiverse food system, just as we might have imagined it in my time, only better.' I looked pointedly at them. 'Makes me suspicious that there's a dark side to all this.'

Rufus turned to face me and responded with unusual seriousness. 'The dark side is behind us … and could well be in front of us too. We – the country and the world – went through incredible trauma mid-century. We had to learn or perish. And learn fast, because we had not planned for crises that really had been well predicted. This, now, is a blessed time historically speaking, because in the aftermath of overwhelming crisis people become socially minded and pull together; the forces of reaction and selfishness have not yet reasserted themselves. The psycho-historians say it's a bit like after the Second World War, when there was such a sense of communal endeavour, and society worked towards social inclusion in health, education and employment, the United Nations was founded, and so on. That mood only really lasted thirty or forty years, before the rot started to set in. Some parts of the world are in eco-crisis right now, the climate is still warming. We can already see what is round the corner for us too, as Atlantic currents begin to alter. Robyn, there's a lot to tell. Let's leave it for the moment, and just enjoy the farm.

I nodded. His words had put a dampener on my mood. We walked past the lake and came upon a large, glazed ziggurat rearing up in a wide clearing at the bottom of a valley. 'The vertical farm,' said Sarah. 'Did you have them in your day?' 'No!' I said. 'At least, not this big. It looks totally out of scale. And vertical farming didn't really take off, I think because of the energy needed.' 'Well, farming had to adapt, you know. Renewable energy is so cheap now. This is an experimental project, we're monitoring it carefully, or rather our university partner is. It's a controlled environment, powered by stored solar and wind, with a huge range of vegetables and salads layered within it, very efficient in water, winter warmth and land use, giving us all-season food. And it's so accessible! The residents in the farm hamlet just pop out and pick what they want. Brilliant!' I had to take her word for it. Despite its scale, the structure was actually rather elegant.

As we walked on up the wooded sides of the valley, with an orchard blended into the woodland, the beauty of the managed and productive natural world rescued me from any despondency. A couple of roe deer grazed nearby, seeming remarkably tame. 'They do eat nice fresh leaves off the trees,' said Sarah, 'so we keep their numbers low, and protect the young trees. More pigs. Some cattle.' Towards the top of the slope there were vineyards, sheltered by tree belts which stretched up to the sheep pastures. It was all so attractive, rich in texture and birdsong, and refreshing to see theories I'd heard propounded in my own time realised here. Sarah told me about the ferocious hot winds they sometimes got in summer, when the woods acted as invaluable windbreaks, moderating the temperature. 'On the top I've even planted some conifers now, because they're better windbreaks.'

When we got back to the farmhouse, a postprandial chicoffee triggered a more casual conversation. Sarah and I started reminiscing about our shared past. Initially I was really uncomfortable; I didn't want to link my lost past, my roots, to the new present. But as she talked of her schooldays, I shook off the feeling, as if programmed to live in the moment. If she were actually sixty-nine now, (or had she meant she was really seventy-plus?) then I worked out that in 2023 she was two, and would have started school a couple of years later. She remembered the 2020s with surprising clarity. I started talking freely about my life. It was very odd, we were like two girls together. I liked my older companion – not just her knowledge, but her brave, can-do attitude, her warmth and engagement with me. As we talked, her lack of respect for convention became obvious. I really admired that, finding it so difficult myself. I wanted to ask her about her husbands. I wanted the insight of a feisty, aware woman into the social mores and behaviour in this strange new world. I needed a mentor. Subconsciously, I worried, I wanted a mother-figure to hold my lonely hand.

Rufus was listening very carefully, not interrupting. Later he admitted that he'd recorded the whole conversation, for historic social psychology research, he said, swearing not to share it. We were interrupted, though, by one of the farm workers, a large man with a small moustache and a big smile. Apparently he was going to feed the house pets over the weekend. 'Here's the key,' said Sarah. 'You're my back door man.' He responded with quick wit: 'I hope you have a front door man as well.' 'I should be so lucky!' she said. They both guffawed, laughing loud and long. Rufus joined in. I was a bit slow on the uptake. As Sarah came down to earth, she said, 'sorry love, we nineties folk, you know, we're pretty earthy.' I managed a small smile, then laughed too, tensions falling off me. It all confirmed my sense of Sarah's warm, freedom-loving nature.

After that we got down to business again. She elaborated on agroforestry, which is clearly commonplace, creating open woodland for grazing animals – the trees for carbon sequestration, clean air and biodiversity, mixed in with early crop patches of grains and vegetables maturing before the full leaf canopy, so sunlight reaches them. She said that trees can actually increase crop productivity by providing shade in high summer when temperatures can be crippling, reducing water evaporation from the soil, and by deep roots accessing water and nutrients from way down.

Then when they shed their leaves the soil is improved. She talked a lot about regenerative farming – a phrase I'd often heard bandied around in my own time – seeing soil microbiology as the basis of healthy living soil and the foundation for productive pasture and livestock, stressing the role of subsurface fungi filaments and networks linking diverse plant species, and the vital importance of minimal soil disturbance and careful grazing regimes for all kind of reasons: the stability and quality of humus, water retention, carbon capture, biodiversity …

I asked Sarah about the sheep. Were they mainly kept for high price meat? 'Goodness me, no!' she said, chortling. 'No, no! It's their wool and their milk. Some are slaughtered young for meat, mainly the boys, but most go on have long, productive lives. We produce sheep cheese, butter and yoghurt. And the fleece … well years ago there was very sophisticated research into how to make sheep's wool useful for many purposes – it's comfortable to wear next to the skin and so on – and how to breed better. And that coincided with the cost of artificial fibres made from oil going through the roof – mainly because of the water crisis in many cotton-growing areas of the world. That was so bad, rivers seasonally drying up, irrigation impossible and so on. So natural, locally sourced fibres have taken over. It was a revolution! Back to the Middle Ages! Now we – meaning we the British sheep farmers – supply wool for a host of different products: clothing, carpets, soft furnishings, insulation, lanolin in cosmetics, packaging, and also mixed with corn starch for injection moulding for household goods. You name it! And when the quality is poor, there are other uses – like daggy wool for fertiliser – organic fertiliser. It's all great, and quite profitable. We've begun using the bones too, processing them to replace hard plastics. So the whole sheep is used. All those hill farmers in Wales have come back after decades of rewilding. You can imagine that is quite controversial, given the powerful nature lobby. But we need the raw material. One of the old mills in the Valleys – Stanley Mill – is a new model factory. Society needs …' she paused with a dramatic flourish, 'WOOL!'

I laughed in delight at her enthusiasm – such a land transformation! Such an economic transformation. A bit later she showed us a plan of the farm. It was bigger than I had imagined. I could see the intricate patchwork of field and wood. There were sheep shelters and a milking parlour on the topland. Workshops were clustered round the farmhouse – people working in small businesses making use of the farm's products. In my mind I listed the crafts, from wool scouring, carding and spinning to honey, cheese and wine-making to furniture, that were going on.

'Co-operation is the secret,' said Sarah. We work collaboratively – they're not all employed by me. Each craftsperson pursues their own markets, but all work together for the benefit of the farm community, with open-book accounting; and … we thrive! We have shared social and environmental auditing and budgeting. And in some spheres, like energy, we are part of the parish. We create a surplus from our water and wind turbines, and solar electric, and that contributes to the parish supplies. When and if you come back, I'll get my husband to explain all that. He's an expert!'

Rufus and I left a little later in a different taxi. I dozed on the way back to Woodchester. It had been a rather full-on day. That evening, after a stroll round the housing co-op's grounds, just nodding to people I met, I ate in my room, lazily accepting the menu offered by the system, and started writing the diary of my experiences in what seemed like a utopian world. For the moment I was happy to remain ignorant of the dark side.

But something very worrying occurred to me while I was writing. I can't imagine why it hadn't occurred to me before. I must have been so intrigued by my new life that I had forgotten about my old, real, life. My mother and father would be long gone, but what about me? If I was living two thirds of a century in the future, then it was not impossible that I was still alive – very old, it is true, but alive. I worked it out: ninety-eight! Old to me, but not so very old in this new world. What about children I may have had? Any children I'd had might be in their late middle-age prime. I might have grandchildren. Even great grandchildren. I was sweating with anxiety. Nobody had even touched on this issue.

Violent shivering shook my body. What would happen if I met myself? Met my mature offspring before they had been born? It was a terrifying thought.

In distress I called Rufus and he came round at once. I tried to explain my existential fear, though it came out all garbled. Rufus understood. He asked Cyla for a whisky, looking concerned. He handed the whisky to me. I was shaking so much it almost fell through my hands. 'No, your older self is dead,' he said calmly, 'and you have no children. You were chosen for transition to this time partly because of this.' 'Did I die young? Did I achieve nothing in life?' I was not comforted, but my shakes reduced to an intermittent spasm. 'On the contrary, I believe you achieved quite a lot,' said Rufus. 'However, so much data, so many records and publications were lost mid-century. Everything was online, electronically stored, just digital. A fatal mistake. The Cloud more or less evaporated in the crisis, and with it much of human history from earlier in the century. We don't know how things happened. That's part of the reason for you being here, you can tell us what it was like. But I can't tell you in any detail what you did in later life. 'You mean,' I said, almost choking with fear, 'I've been whitewashed, erased, deleted? Fucking hell! Who can do that? They didn't ask me! It's totally illegal!'

Rufus was very good. He pointed out that ignorance of my own life since transference was a prerequisite for time travel, for my autonomy. We were getting into deep mysteries here: pre-destination versus free will, choice versus fate. Time travel was not like just choosing a destination and going there. Rufus stressed that even the top scientists had barely begun to plumb the depths of space-time reality. He himself was at a complete loss. Except he knew that she, Robyn, was a free agent, not fulfilling a set script. And so was he.

It took me a long time to calm down, despite whisky and rooibos tea, chocolate biscuits and a sympathetic hug from Rufus. After he left, I took paracetamol (thank goodness that was still around!) and went to bed, sleeping fitfully. Waking early, listening to the birds, I carefully took control of my emotions, trying to avoid rationalising the situation. It was not rational. Instead, I tried to build a sense of acceptance of where I was, and what opportunities that offered – live for today, for tomorrow we … Well, tomorrow we haven't a clue, so take no thought for it. The real future, not yet lived, will have to take care of itself.

9
The urbanist

Tomorrow had arrived. When he came over, Rufus was gentle with me. I was rather brusque back. He picked up on my new determined mood and capitalised on it, first piquing my interest, then really enthusing me with the mission for the day. This was to be our 'place day' – human places and spaces. Place was my territory: the way places are, the way they evolve, their design, use and abuse, the way they affect people for better or worse. Do they make for healthy, stimulating lives and plenty of opportunities for all – especially children and old people? Do they use scarce resources wisely and have a small eco-footprint?

I was to meet the chief 'urbanist', who was clearly equivalent of our chief planner, though with a broader remit. By repute, he had been influential in shaping the Valleys for nearly two decades, making positive things happen, selling a healthy agenda to the politicians, businesses, civil society and local people that everyone seemed to have bought into. Rufus told me that the co-mayor had briefed him about my background and sworn him to secrecy. Far from being a stuffy bureaucrat, he was, said Rufus, a live wire and an inspiration. I couldn't wait!

I found myself suddenly thinking about the work meeting I'd attended before the accident, before the extraordinary transition to this new age. My mind was wrenched back in time. I had a sense of guilt about the scheme we had discussed, my conscience triggered by the imminent challenge of meeting the chief urbanist. I had let the inadequacies of the proposal just be accepted, without demur. Yet my training told me the scheme would be very car dependant, an outlying commuter settlement for Bristol, reinforcing social inequality and with a large carbon footprint. The development was in the wrong place, wrong in relation to bus routes, services, flood risk and biodiversity, wrong in having no social housing, only so-called 'affordable' housing. Overall it prioritised profit, not people. The council planners had lacked authority, pulled their punches, just accepting the developer's arguments. I had said nothing. I felt profoundly embarrassed that my firm, and I as designer, had accepted the brief for what, from the outset, was clearly going to be an unsustainable development.

Abruptly I came back to the present, in my room. Rufus was looking at me quizzically. I realised that even before I'd been exposed to end-of-century principles, my suppressed ideals were being released. Phrases like healthy cities, sustainable development, humane and equitable places, were not to be treated as convenient rhetoric, but given real, tangible and precise value. I hoped the chief urbanist would speak, as Quakers might say, to my condition. To my professional condition.

Rufus handed me over to Sam for the day. She had a training not too different from mine and was eager to hear what the chief urbanist would say. We decided to cycle. Not on the ubiquitous e-bikes but person-powered – quite a challenge. Twenty minutes, she said, at the outside. The bikes were excellent, very lightweight, with auto gear change (though that could be overridden), and alarmingly efficient brakes. Invisible sensors on the bike scanned the cycle tracks for risks and impediments (including pedestrians!) and would apply those brakes if necessary. It took some getting used to but I soon learnt their ways and got ahead of them. We went via the old cycle/walkway along the long-dead railway. Now transformed, beautifully surfaced, and with priority at road junctions, it was much better linked into its surroundings. As we approached the town centre I saw a dream had been realised. The cycle route spanned across old railway arches, bridged boldly over river, road and canal to reach the higher town level close to the station, via the elegant curving bridge I'd seen on my first day. It was just brilliant!

We parked the bikes and I saw that the high canal embankment on the town side had been hidden. In its place was a six storey, linear building, stretching along the canalside – all wood construction with solar roof and walls – apparently the Stroud Valleys council offices. Looking down I could see the wharf where narrowboats and leisure craft were moored, just at the base of the building. The main entrance was next to us, at the upper level. We went in and immediately had to stop by a checkpoint. No reception, which I thought a little unfriendly. 'Don't worry,' said Sam, 'it's all automatic, courtesy of your mote and facial recognition technology.' The green light came on and allowed us entry. I was immediately struck by the full height atrium of the building, floors below and above, with plants hanging over the balconies, so the effect was almost as though we were in a shaft of brightness in the forest.

The stairs spiralled up and down. I saw a man coming up the stairs, waving genially. He was middle-aged, black, and with the warmest, most engaging manner. His stylish suit surprised me; I'd not seen many of them out and about. Not the usual institutional blue or black but a foxy orange, and his broad white tie had musical notes on it. He introduced himself as Wulf O'Leary. His voice betrayed a slight German accent – or was it Irish? 2090's accents were all puzzling to me. Sam gave him a big smile –she clearly knew and trusted him. I smiled politely, and he responded with twinkling eyes: 'Amazing, amazing, great to meet you. A real privilege. What a remarkably strange situation. It must have been very tricky, frightening, for you. You are so welcome here.'

I responded cautiously, 'it's a privilege for me too. I'm really looking forward to today. But I've not yet fully come to terms with the whole situation at all.' 'Well, I'm delighted you're here, and I gather you have urban design skills, so I'll try to explain where we are now, clearly, and satisfy your curiosity. I hope to learn something from you too – what the situation was really like back in the twenties. At that time distance things often become more rumour and conjecture than fact, romanticised or denigrated. Now, do come this way.'

He led us into a well-lit meeting room. 'And real coffee is served. A special privilege!' Over coffee, Wulf emphasised that we should have a completely open discussion – no holding back. He would not be offended, indeed he relished challenge and debate. I surprised myself by boldly asking about the building itself. 'This new building. Back in my time this side of the canal was completely different – a thickly vegetated embankment, rather valued as a green wildlife corridor. So what changed?' 'Well may you ask,' said Wulf. 'What changed was the level of risk. Years after the new housing was built on the old car park – I gather you saw this on your first day – increasing evidence of potential slippage started to show, and cracks began to open on the big wall. This was probably due to the increase in torrential downpours, tropical in their ferocity. The embankment, with its buildings above, was reckoned to be in danger of collapse. We decided, just eight years ago, to make a virtue of necessity. Always sensible! Instead of simply reconstructing a big retaining wall, which would anyway have destroyed all the vegetation, we built these carbon neutral offices, with the wall at its back, using the space to good advantage. And I hope you agree – the building is a treat.' 'I love it!' said Sam.

A bit later Wulf took us into a large public room flooded with natural light. A number of people were chatting and pointing. In the middle was a model of the centre of Stroud, going out to the inner neighbourhoods and commons. Very impressive, with hills and valleys to scale, buildings beautifully modelled, and even a trickling river Frome. It reminded me of the vastly bigger model I had seen of central Shanghai. 'This is our not-so-secret weapon,' said Wulf. 'People love it! They can see what is happening to the town – we update it regularly with an AI 3D printer linked to architects' drawings. It makes it far easier to persuade investors, civic groups and especially councillors what is right to do. This gives them a grasp on reality. Sadly most people don't understand maps now, and digital options never quite match the lived experience. The trickling water – just a trick of course – is the pièce de résistance, but children are fascinated. They become more engaged in the future of their urban habitat. There are a few other tricks too.' 'Like what?' said Sam before I could.

'Oh, an artificial sun tracking winter and summer arcs – though it's too bright for that right now. And even sound: wind rustling leaves, and birdsong. Not the ubiquitous pigeons, I hasten to say. More to the point, we can show alternative schemes as if real – pop-up designs if you like, courtesy of holography. Very useful! Downstairs we've got another big model of the whole Stroud Valleys, all the smaller towns and the commons, which is absolutely indispensable when discussing what, where and how things should happen.'

We returned to the smaller space. I asked Wulf why he was called an urbanist, and what the implications were, though I had an inkling already. 'Ah, there's been quite a revolution,' he said. 'It happened in the forties and fifties, at the time of crises. The tectonic plates of professional silos – mixing my metaphors – were split asunder and reformed. And about time too! So I'm an urbanist, which means I have an amazingly wide brief to achieve 'sustainable development', essentially to integrate social, economic and environmental facets of settlements – holistic thinking, if you like. The central focus of urbanists is spatial and development decisions. The problem with the town planners of old was that they had become more focussed on procedures and processes than outcomes – often slaves to changing government prejudices. Almost forgetting the idealistic vision of the early twentieth century planners, or that of classical designers. The political system and planning laws were a disaster, and unlike doctors, with their Hippocratic Oath, planners' and designers' moral stance was weak – honoured more in the breach than in the observance. They found themselves highly compromised, not in a position to speak truth to power – neither commercial nor political power. It was quite understandable given the overall political and economic set-up, and actually they were more compromised here than in some other European countries. - Decisions were driven by landowner profit and political expediency rather than the needs of the community as a whole, let alone the needs of the global eco-system. The professionals were trapped into enabling unhealthy, unsustainable environmental decisions, even though many of them knew what they ought to be doing – struggling against all the odds.'

He told us that there had been many attempts in universities, even a hundred years ago, to break down professional silos and jealousies by joint teaching in early years, understanding the environment holistically, with real-life projects. They'd proved hugely popular with students. But governments and institutions were always behind the curve – way behind. Eventually, when the world stared imploding, fundamental shift happened at last. Town planning became subsumed within the new urbanist profession, rediscovering its health and wellbeing roots. The great bonus was that urbanists were charged with taking the overview, trying to understand the whole system of town and city regions, how everything is interdependent and related. 'As an urbanist,' said Wulf, 'I have much more authority, and a heavy responsibility. I can knock heads together in both public and private sectors. Community development, population health, equity, transport, housing, green infrastructure and economic development, they all come within my remit. A huge privilege! My Department of Urbanism is co-ordinating, working collaboratively across all those fields. It's of course a matter of persuasion, but the goals are held in common. It's good! For the most part, it's working!'

He paused, seeing my quizzical expression. 'You mean,' I said, thinking of the uncoordinated reality in my own time, 'that transport engineers, housing surveyors and associations, asset management people and so on, are all pulling together now?' 'Yes, yes, yes and mostly!' he said. 'Surprising, isn't it!' 'What about the design professions?' I asked, 'I'm an urban designer. Has that profession changed like the planners?' 'Aha,' he said, there's been much evolution there as well. For a start, the architects have adapted. Back in your day architectural training was rather dominated by aesthetic values and the grand vision thing. Great buildings were indeed created, but mundane housing and service buildings were often, well, mundane. The builders were often going their own way anyway. It was just the way the market operated. Then back in mid-century a novel idea was borrowed from ancient times – that of the master-builder, like in gothic cathedrals. So now we have a profession that is really expert at the structural engineering and building technology as well as architectural design, putting together those old professions. All major projects now have to be led by a master-builder – actually there are plenty of women in this role, despite the name!'

'As for urban design, the problem was that the architects and engineers tended to design local environments, but both had rather narrow perspectives – the building plot or the road layout respectively. Urban designers and landscape architects were different breeds, but often brought in too late. Then society demanded places that planned for conviviality, inclusion, active travel, sustainable water management, biodiversity and climate resilience. All these came roaring up the agenda. So now we've got an integrated profession called place design, which really complements the urbanists and the master builders. All three have a common first year of training, so they learn how to talk to each other, and find it easy to scale up or down. It's vital that town planners, urbanists, understand the skills of healthy urban design. And the system is, well, not bad – much better than it was!'

I was suitably impressed and asked what was it that broke up those long-standing professional and institutional silos, what changed governments' minds? Wulf paused and thought for a moment. He looked at me and turned the question round: 'That's quite a complex story. You may have more handle on it than you think. Looking at your own time, what were the real tensions for your profession and for society at large?'

Transported suddenly back to the twenties, a whole raft of issues flooded my mind. Hesitantly at first, but with increasing conviction and a sense of release, I set out the situation as I perceived it. First in relation to British society in the wake of long years of austerity after the 2008 financial crash, later reinforced by the pandemic. I told Wulf and Sam how inequality had grown, how the rich were living longer, healthier lives but the poor were living shorter lives, with more of those shorter lives in bad health – mental or physical or both. This was after a century of gradual improvement in both measures – and I could date the reversal precisely: 2012. It was the direct result of drastic cuts in services for all age-groups – from midwifery to youth clubs to public health to social care – which had come in a couple of years earlier. And also the evolution of a regressive housing system and car-oriented urban structure that penalised the less well off by forcing households to spend a high proportion of their income on accommodation and transport, increasing financial stress. I said there was immense frustration in the built environment professions, because many people realised that the policies imposed by successive governments fundamentally conflicted with professional ethics of sustainability and healthy environments – and gave the lie to government's own rhetoric.

I was on a roll by this time. The mention of healthy environments sent me off on a new tack – that there were countervailing forces, the seeds of hope. Going right back to the beginning of the century, I was aware of a new movement stimulated by the World Health Organization, called 'healthy urban planning'. Scarcely a new idea, since once upon a time town planning and public health had been bedfellows, and healthy environments had been seen as the purpose of planning. But in the noughties the idea caught on again amongst academics and the evidence base became more and more impressive, so that the WHO felt justified in calling for human health to be put at the heart of spatial policy making. I stressed how climate resilience was part of this, because it was considered the biggest threat to health and wellbeing. Also how planning for natural habitats was part of it, because of the evidence that people need nature – they are part of it. But despite this, things just went backwards in Britain, except for some superb city centre renewal projects.

I paused, about to wax lyrical about some cities I'd visited in Europe. Wulf was smiling broadly. 'Thank you! You've set it out very clearly, and hit the nail on the head. I can carry on the story. Over the following decade or so it eventually came to boiling point, triggered by a series of climate and migration crises, and a complete hiatus in housing, health and social care. It was in Wales that it happened first. Built environment professionals went on strike, as they realised they were betraying both themselves and the wider community. They had been mouthing platitudinous, earth-friendly rhetoric while supervising a remorseless path in the opposite direction. Almost but not quite deceiving themselves and the politicians and the public at large! However, the really crucial changes came later, not through the proto-urbanists, but the economists. Very powerful people, economists. God knows why, but governments tend to believe them. When the great meltdown happened, the world was in agony with communications down and coastal storms flooding people out of home and land (you'll learn much more about that I'm sure). Anyway, a huge international gathering of economists, confronting the abject failure of all their models, threw out the traditional measure of progress – GDP – lock, stock and barrel. They declared that measuring progress by financial turnover was redundant. Not fit for purpose, counterproductive. They were right! If only they'd listened before! Instead they adopted an integrated measure of social and environmental health, devised some years before by city planners, health economists and ecologists, under the auspices of the UN. Wales and then the other governments in these islands bought into it, following the lead of the Netherlands and Sweden. It was a game-changer. Tell her, Sam!'

Sam put on a kind of catechism-reciting voice, smiling broadly. 'Instead of measuring progress by how much money we spent on making pollution and then cleaning it up, we measure progress by how unpolluted we are, and the reduction in pollution-related disease. Instead of measuring the turnover of fast-food outlets, we measure changes in obesity of different population groups. Instead of measuring general income levels in pounds, dollars and so on, we measure how much real purchasing power poorer groups have with their disposable income. Accountants developed new skills: carbon footprints, biodiversity measures, inequality assessments, circular economy audits. In planning, we were at last allowed to value real things above spurious, market-orientated government targets. Things like accessibility, travel choice, housing affordability, work, greenspace, beauty, wildlife, carbon, climate resilience. All the things we had preached for generations but which been undermined by the warped vision of politicians and the Treasury. Planning and design decisions were eventually taken out of direct political control by the politicians. It was their own choice – it relieved them of a hell of a lot of aggro. Urbanists and designers are now treated more like environmental doctors, or maybe midwives and surgeons. We have to consult appropriately, especially local people, and there are plenty of safeguards, through appeals and regulatory bodies, keeping us up to the mark, assessing if wellbeing and environmental progress are being achieved.' Sam looked at both of us, rather pleased with herself.

'Exactly,' declared Wulf. 'And lo and behold, things have improved! The long-running housing crisis is in retreat; towns and cities are functioning much more efficiently, offering people more freedom and choice than ever before; air pollution is practically non-existent, water pollution rare; longevity is on the rise for all income groups and ethnicities, and environmental inequality minimal; biodiversity is rapidly improving in town and country, despite climate change; energy costs are right down. And, what is more,' he gave a flamboyant flourish, 'greenhouse gas emissions are net zero; indeed in Stroud Valleys District we absorb more than we emit!'

I was smiling so broadly I thought I must look like an idiot. It was the sheer bravado and buoyant optimism of the others. Intoxicating at one level – though triggering a certain suspicion of wishful thinking on another. The triumph of sense over prejudice! Could it really be so? I wanted to dig deeper. Where were the flaws in this miraculous transformation?

'Thank you, both. That's very inspiring. Fantastic. But I saw something yesterday that really disturbed me – on my trip through the countryside. I saw villages that were dying – not the majority, which were beautiful, but a few seemed under-occupied, with derelict buildings, no facilities, nothing at all, just some abandoned people. I even saw a church with the roof fallen in. How does this fit your glowing picture? What's going on?' I was surprised how outspoken I'd become, a guest of only two days in this world. But my bluntness didn't faze Wulf. He looked at me with a benign expression, as if I were a good student making a salient point.

'Ah, you noticed that. Yes, you might think it a sign of deprivation, maybe the result of exclusion or arbitrary rule. But ironically dying villages reflect the choice of local people – people of the parish. One has to recognise that democracy at the parish level can be more autocratic than equal, often just a few people forming a self-perpetuating cabal. Be that as it may, freedom of policy choice has for better or worse been pushed down to the lowest viable level. Rural parishes have for a long time had significant powers and responsibilities, as of right, a bit like French communes. They can marry and divorce people, they can subsidise local facilities, they maintain local route networks, they're responsible for local churches and chapels. So local people have choices, but of course those choices are framed by wider policies that attempt to plan for everybody, and for the planet too. Higher tier authorities set the ends but not the means of those local decisions, if you understand me.' I nodded. 'Well, two of the crucial goals set on high are carbon neutrality and water neutrality. Every town, urban quarter, parish or parish cluster has to achieve these. At least that's the way it works in the West of England. The lowest tier can deliver energy self-sufficiency how they like – by all kinds of community projects, depending on local resources. Round here it's normally a combination of wind turbines and solar plus some storage, and occasionally water power. There is potential for trading with neighbouring places, though the finances are stacked to encourage local autonomy.'

'Now, you asked why are some villages dying? That happens when the local parishioners can't agree on a good strategy, and the parish fails the carbon-neutral test. When we ask why, it often seems to be that they've been heavily influenced by landed interests. They are relying on grid electricity and effectively exporting their pollution. Others are paying for their excess consumption, so the parish is taxed at least an equivalent amount, and no community fund grants are available. So very little happens. People move out. Houses are left empty. Any residual services leave because their custom has gone. Eventually something gives, or a new broom arrives and sweeps out the dust, and a plan is made. Then the place suddenly becomes attractive again.'

I was shocked. 'It all seems very draconian,' I said, 'dictatorial in fact.' 'Yes, I guess you're right,' said Wulf. 'At one level. Draconian and absolutely necessary. It all comes down from global UN commitments. We have no option. The worldwide carbon and other emissions from earlier centuries, and the first fifty years of this century, have landed us in one hell of a mess. And we in this country bear a heavy responsibility for the historic emissions now devastating poorer countries. Energy dependence is a crime like theft. We don't imprison or cut off recalcitrant parishes, or big businesses for that matter – they're critical in all this too – but we bear down on them by means of tax and regulation. We are really fighting for human survival. That's a real motivator. We're all in it together, and together we've got to conquer climate heating and live with it too. It's all about solidarity.

'The other thing I should say, is that it's not just energy. Every town or rural parish has to demonstrate every five years how it is performing in relation to water, air quality, soils, wildlife, housing affordability and accessibility to key facilities. Often parishes form partnerships to do all this, creating parish clusters. So: are the farms biodiverse and regenerating soils? Can people, including children, get to shops, schools, community centres? Can poorer households afford housing? What about local jobs? And let me tell you. It is working! There aren't many parishes now on the worst grade. Communities and businesses have for the most part come round to their socio-environmental responsibilities. It makes good sense. It makes for new opportunities. It makes for healthier, more productive, people.'

What a complete turnaround! I thought. In my day, (gosh, it feels odd to say that!) in the 2020s, Cotswold villages are sanctuaries of the rich, with huge carbon footprints, three gas guzzlers per household, rural services subsidised by the towns. Things like electricity, water, schools, postal services – they are all much more expensive to deliver to dispersed places but priced the same as in the urban areas: poor towns subsidising rich villages, where most of the poor had been excluded by house prices and the loss of social housing.

'I see the logic, absolutely,' I said to Wulf. 'But what do you mean by opportunities?'

'Think about it, he said. 'A cluster of parishes, with quite a number of villages, hamlets, farms and rural businesses, can take control of their own future: their local food, water, sewerage, energy, wildlife and landscape, schooling, shops and community facilities, their whole quality of life. All very satisfying. The cluster will build a sense of community and generate local jobs, bringing cash into local coffers. We support them, if they are hitting socio-environmental targets, with judicious investment, for example in community schools with shared recreational facilities and bikeways linking between the villages. Of course the same thing goes for our bigger settlements: our towns of Stroud, Woodchester, Nailsworth, Stonehouse, Minchinhampton, Eastcombe, Brimscombe and Painswick. The basic rules of building local autonomy are the same. Larger companies have equivalent obligations, like generating their own electricity, managing all the water supply, runoff and treatment in situ. It works up the scale too. Our authority, Stroud Valleys, is the amalgamation of all the parishes and town councils, and we are obliged to be as self-sufficient as is reasonably possible. Same for Severn Vale, Gloucester, and so on. We have to show that we are doing our bit across all the key social, economic and environmental criteria. It's a decentralised system. The West Country provincial government has given us the powers and the responsibility to be good global citizens.' He paused, looking rather gently at me, almost apologetic for the intensity of his statement.

I took more than a moment to absorb it all. 'But surely, I said, people still have to travel around, and many things you need come from far away, trade is important, and not everywhere has the resources to allow autonomy. What happens if a parish or a city is poor, with no money to invest? ' I was beginning to suspect that huge inequities could result from this system, and then whole communities would be squeezed and even killed off.

Sam chipped in quickly: 'Perhaps I can help by looking at our Woodchester Town Parish. We're far from self-sufficient in jobs or higher services, so of course people commute or shop or visit elsewhere. The bus shuttle and bikeways give very efficient connection to Nailsworth and in particular Stroud, where we can get fast trains direct to Gloucester, Cheltenham, Swindon and London. At the same time, we, as a parish, generate more electricity than we use, so export it to the grid. Trade is still critical, we can't make everything here, so rely on imports, while our farms and linked businesses produce lots of fruit and veg and jams and wines and so on, and market them regionally or even internationally. An automatic tally is kept by the local authority, and I'm told it's a really simple system. So … we're not an island, we're not cut off from our neighbours. Far from it!'

Wulf added, 'there's a legal obligation to achieve a balance of inputs and outputs at the district level including all the private sector and community sector trade. The system isn't perfect by any means. And we have to be practical, so actually we are pretty lenient with individual parishes in terms of trade and work patterns – you can't control everything. But we are ultra strict on energy! We have to be!

'That's all very impressive,' I said. 'Really, I mean, it's incredible. From where I stand – stood! – it's amazing. All so logical and well organised. It must rely on excellent levels of co-operation. And cross-party agreements – none of the traditional bickering and polarisation.'

'Absolutely! Too true!' said my host. With a winning laugh, he added 'Mostly!'

I went on: 'I've so many questions. I want to know more. What is happening elsewhere in the world? How are other countries coping? And here, I don't understand the housing situation, with millions of immigrants, how you can cope?' I noticed a frown on Sam's face. She told me that the perspective has had to change, often in the face of difficult politics; that most of the immigrants over the past half century had arrived out of desperation – that they were climate and conflict refugees. She emphasised international agreements under the UN, forging partnerships between countries devastated by climate change and those able to offer help and a new home. 'Woodchester is evidence that it can work. The refugees are welcomed and integrated.'

Wulf looked at his watch. 'Look, in a short while I've got to give a wide-ranging lunchtime briefing to officers, using our Strategic Model. I think you'll be impressed with it, and your timing, coming here, is immaculate. Maybe not accidental! We don't use this model all the time – it's much too costly in energy terms. Today I'm using it with all the more recent appointees across the whole authority – all departments. It will set the scene more broadly. It may not answer all your questions, but it could help. Why don't you join with us? Would that be OK, Sam?' Sam didn't need to consider. 'Yup, absolutely, of course. We just need to make sure we adopt a low profile, as visitors, as it were, so no prying questions.' 'Naturally,' said Wulf, 'I'll make sure you are well insulated.'

Ten minutes later we got up and followed him along to a much bigger room – more like a lecture theatre, with seats arranged in a crescent, facing a tall blank white wall. We came in at the top, and Wulf sat us down at one side. There were some people already dotted around the amphitheatre. A few minutes later the place erupted with people, coming in from all quarters, mainly young women and men, filling up the seats and chatting. It was somehow both a very familiar sight and foreign – dress and mannerisms and accents all varied and often different from my own time.

Wulf was down at a console in the front, fiddling with controls. He stood up, a charismatic figure, looking around at everyone in the tiered seats. Silence descended.

ை⋞

10
Local-global planning

'Welcome everyone,' said Wulf. 'It's marvellous to see people from all the departments of Stroud Valleys Council. And a special welcome to our two guests, a visiting research fellow from Manchester and her local guide, come to evaluate our progress.' (There was a ripple of applause). 'Before I show you anything at all, in the interests of interdepartmental interchange, I need to manipulate you! There will be buzz groups later, so please shuffle around so that you are next to someone from a different department. Leave your predictable, friendly colleagues, leave your comfort zone, and risk sitting next to people you don't really know, who might have altogether contrary views. They won't eat you! See this special egg timer? I'm starting it right now. You have two minutes. Move NOW!'

There were shufflings and mutterings in the audience, rising to a crescendo of noise and activity, some scampering with laughter from one side to the other, just at the last moment. They seemed like teenagers, temporarily let loose from the daily grind of lessons.

'Thank you, that was fun to watch,' said Wulf. 'Now, I know most of you have not seen this magical holographic display before. We do have to ration its operation because of its energy demand.' He described the technical nature of the beast in words which completely baffled me, but I did gather that the base level of display was the result of the amalgamation of many aerial photographs, taken on sunny, summer days in the early afternoon, so as to give a reasonably consistent shadowing effect. Then digitally altered to illustrate varied scenarios.

The magic happened. The blank wall we were facing became alive, and a huge 3D aerial image of the Cotswolds and the Severn Vale occupied the space in front of us. It was so tangible, I felt I was there in a hot air balloon, looking down and across. I could see Gloucester Cathedral at the top, the river estuary winding down towards us, Wotton and Dursley and the Cotswold scarp, all rather close and large, at the bottom. The view shifted as I gazed at it, gradually homing in on the Stroud Valleys. My jaw had dropped, my mind was transfixed by the sense of being there, in the image. So much so that I did not take in a lot of what Wulf said. He was outlining the unique characteristics of the landscape, its evolution and current value in terms of geology, water, air quality, soils, biodiversity, climate, food production and natural energy potential.

Then, quite abruptly he changed tack, asking: 'What, then, can this beautiful, adapted landscape contribute to human wellbeing, locally – and globally?' The all-enveloping hologram faded, giving way to a 3D image of the slowly revolving globe. Picked out in varied tones and colours were countries suffering severely from climate change – flooding, land loss, drought, soil erosion, excessive heat – resulting in huge refugee exodus; and in solid green those cool regions which were able to increase food production and population because of warmer temperatures. Amongst the former were many tropical countries. Amongst the latter were, for example, Canada and Scandinavia. Next to the globe was a chart showing historic carbon emissions and global temperatures. To my surprise and alarm it showed that coal, gas and oil exploitation peaked only in 2038. While temperatures rose from the relative stability of the pre-industrial age, to one degree above that in 2018, 1.5 degrees consistently by 2030, 2.0 degrees by 2050, nearly 2.5 degrees now, in 2090. There were a range of futures beyond that, with a central prediction of a 2.8 degree peak in

2120, then very slowly falling thereafter. He stressed these figures were rounded averages, given the varied experience of different world regions, then pointed out the recent slowdown in the pace of warming as global greenhouse gas emissions began to decline, partly as a result of the mid-century economic depression. He reminded us of the slowness of natural carbon sequestration, and the unpredictability of world ecology, especially ocean ecology. He also mentioned the inevitable approximation of past estimates, due to year-on-year climate variability, which is affected especially by El Niño and La Niña in the Pacific Ocean. Then he changed tack again.

'Now I want to give a bit of a historical perspective, which they may or may not have taught you at school and college,' he said. 'You might've thought that the problem of climate change was only properly recognised at the seminal Abuja World Summit of 2059, thirty-one years ago. Ancient history for some of you here today! But in fact it was recognised by the world community way, way before that, almost a century ago – at the 1992 Rio Summit. It took that long – two-thirds of a century – for decision-makers in government and commerce to fully engage with the issue and take effective action. Meanwhile, as you know, the world was falling apart. A self-inflicted tragedy not just for the human race but also for so many other species, with extinctions this century at a level not seen since the end of the Mesozoic age.'

'In the post-Abuja era we have at last taken major steps to right our wrongs, and you may feel cautiously optimistic as a result, especially living in this green and pleasant province. The vast majority of countries started taking co-ordinated mutually supportive action under the aegis of the UN, by way of drastic and long overdue adaptation and greenhouse gas zero measures. The 2062 UN Earthplan was, historically speaking, an extraordinary achievement. However, curb your optimism, we are not out of the woods by a long way. I'll demonstrate the global issues by looking at some of the countries highlighted in front of you in blue (for flooding problems), red (for aridity and heat problems), and purple (for both, and other critical issues). Let's look first at the most populous country of all, India. The total number of people has at last begun to fall, thank goodness. That brings its own issues, but the environmental problems are legion.'

Wulf carried on, in his lively and persuasive manner, but my mind was elsewhere. I was distressed and frustrated. His historical perspective had skipped – leapt is more like it – right over my period and what had happened earlier in the century. He'd barely mentioned the Bad Times. Just took them for granted, assuming his audience would know about them. Of course, he was not lecturing to me, but the sense of the world having shifted on its axis since 2023 – I couldn't work out why – was disorientating and alarming. I temporarily allowed myself to wallow in angst, wrestling with the possibilities, going round and round with things in my head. Eventually I recognised that the effort was foolish, indeed pointless, and I felt then as if I'd emerged from the mud and the sun had poked his nose out from behind the clouds. My attention was suddenly drawn back into the room. Wulf was still talking: '... so the Dutch, with their long tradition of water management and land reclamation, have coped far better than other countries I've looked at. The sea has taken back some of what it might have considered its rights, but the Netherlands has carefully controlled the process, protecting the urban and rural populations.

'What then, does the future hold, and can we plan for it? The World Summit last year, as you know, expected heating to peak, or plateau, early next century, around 2.8 degrees. This is far higher than the hopes expressed early this century, but far lower than the doomsters predicted. We believe that we are within reach of a sustainable earth ecology. There are, though, some riders – conditions we must fulfil – if land and sea temperatures are to moderate. The first is to maintain the rate of increase in our global carbon sinks. Re-afforestation is the most obvious aspect of this. Several of the countries I've been talking about have, as you can see, made considerable progress on this front, with biodiversity, water management and local climatic benefits. The second is to speed technological innovation in some of the poorest countries of the world, enabling local wealth creation with zero carbon impact. The third is to pray that Siberian permafrost melting does not speed up unexpectedly, releasing the stored methane. And the fourth – and this is the big one! – is that we take extraordinary measures to try to slow right down the progressive melting of the Greenland icecap. The last thing in the world that we want is for Greenland to live up its name!'

An insistent hand in the audience interrupted his flow. Wulf welcomed the questioner, who asked how was it – given that carbon dioxide emitted into the atmosphere from fossil fuel burning took about a century to be absorbed by sea, land and flora, and current levels of global emissions were a fraction of those 100 years ago – that temperatures were not now falling rapidly?

'Great question,' said Wulf. 'The answer is convoluted! There are what I think of as inertia factors. We've started a ball rolling, rolling downhill, and it's difficult to catch it up and slow it down. First, you'll realise of course that carbon emissions are not the only gases heating the atmosphere. Methane is another. We've significantly cut anthropogenic methane emissions by changing our energy sources and adapting agriculture, but the slow defrosting of northern Siberia and Canada is releasing more year on year. So that is a rider to our 2.8 max hopes. Then, probably more significant, the ocean has warmed alarmingly this century and its capacity to absorb yet more carbon dioxide has reduced. It holds its heat much more than the land and affects both climate and weather profoundly. There are other feedback loops reinforcing heating. The warming seas and atmosphere have the effect of progressively reducing sea ice coverage in Arctic and Antarctic oceans, and also cut the seasonal length of snow cover on land. Snow and ice reflect sunlight, while earth and open water absorb it. The Earth's albedo is reduced, so we retain a higher proportion of solar radiation. These feedback loops reinforce the warming trend, and, as I suggested, are not entirely predictable. We need to watch our step!'

Wulf then homed in on the English West Country. He said the province was relatively fortunate in relation to climate change, having water security, good energy and food-producing potential. So as part of UN-brokered agreements made at Lagos, the region had agreed to accept major immigration, climate refugees from Southern Asia especially. Other parts of the British Isles were accepting other groups. Ireland for example, with its relatively low population and extensive agricultural land, was accepting dispossessed farmers from tropical East Africa, who were transforming agricultural productivity, as well as re-foresting huge swathes of land. Wulf went on to outline the political and social tensions and pressures that needed managing in the West Country: how to strike a deal between the needs and cultures of the indigenous population and the newcomers. He suggested that the relatively new science of psycho-history had provided much evidence on the way societies evolve and adapt, and had helped smooth the paths of immigrant groups.

Then he turned to the spatial planning of the Stroud Valleys, examining population increase and change, housing, health, jobs, services, movement, leisure, greenspace, water, energy, food production, trees, biodiversity ... As he layered each of these factors on top of each other, complexity onto complexity, I got a sense of what it meant to tackle strategic planning, and I have to admit, it was awesome. Wulf's grasp of all the issues was formidable. However, I became more and more puzzled about implementation – knowing the way decisions tend to be actually taken in practice, very disjointedly, with politics, pragmatism and profit determining actions.

Luckily one of the young professionals asked a relevant question: 'Wulf, thanks for this overview, but how does it work in practice? I mean, each company looking for its profit, each agency geared to its own remit ... why isn't there chaos?' 'Well, there was,' answered Wulf, 'and look where it led us! Go back early this century and there was a gaping policy-action gulf. On the one hand the policies of government and local authorities, and even some businesses, were pretty good. They reflected public concerns and scientific analysis. But on the other hand, the actual decisions, about investment, resources, locations and development, tended to reflect vested interests – financial and political and bureaucratic vested interests – silo thinking. It's vital to understand what happens when those vested interests are in control, as you suggest they could be, so let me give you an example. Back in the century new housing developments were ostensibly determined by the Local Plan, which was a land use plan for the whole of the local authority, like the old Stroud District. The theory was that new housing should be located so as to reduce the need for travel and facilitate healthy walking and cycling access to local facilities and open space. But the reality was that the local authority was obliged by government to ask landowners and house builders where they would like to develop. The local authority would then choose the best sites from the list offered. Given the vagaries of the market – who wants to sell land for example – it was really all a lottery. The sites which came forward were usually not the most healthy or sustainable at all – not the best for people. In this area they were typically car-dependent, forcing households to buy cars just to live. The system led us down to hell. Escaping back out of hell has been the shared motivation of the last forty years. We have progressively changed investment patterns, behaviours and lifestyles. Of course, some changes were already happening piecemeal, showing the way. Theories of human ecology have been critical, providing the necessary coherent framework for decision-making, encompassing and entwining all the relevant sciences and policy areas. Every agency can see how it relates to the whole. My job, and the Strategic Urbanism Unit's job, is to tie things together and keep everyone up to the mark – in the common interest: healthy people, healthy places, healthy planet.'

'And are we winning?' someone shouted out. Wulf was pretty measured on this one. 'Well, I wish I could just say yes! Our local human habitat of the Stroud Valleys is in pretty good shape now. My number one criterion – to absorb more greenhouse emissions than we emit – is achieved. We are playing our part, though admittedly it's easier for us than the cities. My number two criterion – more people living healthily for longer, without mental or physical illness – that's doing well too. But Gaia, Mother Earth, is still reacting to our sustained abuse of her, and some major countries are dragging their feet, so at a global level the uncertainties remain.'

Wulf gestured to the huge image behind him, which obligingly homed in on the Stroud Valleys. 'Each of you will know a part of the picture, your field. I'll try to explain the logic of the whole spatial strategy. Forgive me if some of it is boringly familiar. It all starts from the time of crisis mid-century. Our newly created province decided to develop an integrated plan: urban and rural, social, economic, cultural, environmental, spatial. A real tall order. But the need for it was blindingly obvious. Some politicians and some businesses were nevertheless keeping their eyes tight shut. We learnt from the Netherlands – as usual they were ahead of the game. And we – I should say they, as I was in nappies – really started to understand the meaning of 'sustainable development', not as a rhetorical battlecry or greenwash, but for real.

'The question was, how to engage everyone in this project? Well, at the philosophical level it means casting aside the millennium-old tradition of dualism and 'divide and rule'. Them and us. God and the Devil. Man and nature. Male and female. First-past-the-post democracy. The adversarial legal system. No! We realised it meant working together creatively, searching for solutions that tackled the whole panoply of problems, not just the one currently top of the agenda, or the one that's the most profitable. Sometimes those solutions were quite ridiculously simple and had been recognised by many before the end of last century: promoting walking and cycling, for example – a win-win-win policy in terms of the three strands of sustainable development. Yet it was only in the thirties that Britain really started addressing the urban form, locational and development decisions that could make that policy work for all. Another no-brainer was for energy-efficient, carbon-neutral buildings: retrofit of all existing buildings being a key part of that – reducing emissions, cutting fuel poverty and creating jobs. And related to that, using all roofs for solar power – actually a principle initiated in the late twenties. Such an obvious solution when combined with energy storage. Obvious to us. But early in the century old habits of thinking in the building industry and in building conservation ruled the roost. The integrated strategy knocked heads together. It was the vehicle for effective co-operation. We've built consensus between the major political parties, and actively involved universities and industry and civil society, so the spatial strategy is broadly agreed. It is no longer a political football and it manages market pressures so that many firms benefit. And it is ruthlessly supported on appeal by the provincial regulators.

'But that's all history. What about now? Well, you may be surprised to know that my other general point is about rhetoric. Having denigrated rhetoric earlier, it nevertheless remains important, and it's vital to get it right, because people latch onto it. It can engage emotions and motivate action. It needs to reach the parts that arid policy statements will never reach.'

Wulf looked challengingly around at his audience. 'Right. Time to wake you from your slumbers! Here's a question. What words or phrases can motivate people to support good spatial decisions? Shout them out!'

I looked at the faces and dress of the staff: men and women in equal degree; all skin colours; wide age range, though mostly younger. A bold young woman volunteered an answer: Local autonomy! Another followed on with User control! Someone else Save the planet, save people! Then came Diversity of people, economy and nature! Then, tongue in cheek, Save the hedgehogs! Followed by a wag shouting out Liberty, equality, fraternity! Oops, sorry sisters.

'Yes, yes, thank you!' said Wulf. All good thoughts. Let's pick on liberty, but I'll reword it – FREEDOM. It's a great battle cry, and used to be perceived as politically right wing, at least by the right wing. But when it applies to everyone, particularly those with fewer resources at their disposal, it cuts right across privilege and becomes more left wing. We now, in 2090, have a degree of non-partisan recognition that it means freedom for everyone, every family, to be able to choose a home to suit their needs, and to have safe travel options, educational and wellbeing opportunities, a sufficient basic income. That plays right into our spatial strategy. Let's look at one part of our district to see how it plays out.'

He highlighted the lower Frome valley, and it grew to dominate the space. I became aware how the main town of Stonehouse had evolved. Indeed, I'd noticed from the top of Selsley Common how Stonehouse was now a big town. Wolf went on 'Contrary to some beliefs, size matters. So does distance. Size, to be able to support a good range of urban facilities. Distance, to ensure everyone can access those facilities without motorisation – relying on human energy. That is one of the key tenets of our freedom principle. Real choice of movement mode. The old town of Stonehouse gave us a good start, but the late twentieth and early twenty-first centuries were disastrous, spawning new developments that were unintegrated and relied on high car ownership and use, cultivating sedentary behaviour. The towns across the old Stroud District were dissolving. Historic character was destroyed. Quite extraordinary, given all the official policy statements. All driven by land and market interests, not efficiency, public health or global sustainability. It was only in the thirties that that trend was effectively challenged – a critical moment.

'So … what we have been trying to do now for half a century is pull it all together – from unconnected patches to a rich sewn-together quilt. Every town needs an economic rationale, and Stonehouse has it in spades: flat land close to the old motorway freight terminal and on a junction of the national rail network. Mind you the potential of that junction was strangely ignored for generations. But now the 2070 intercity station at the main line junction is the busiest by far in historic Stroud District. The town grew around it – so much so that the old Stonehouse is now just a neighbourhood and has gone rather up-market, a mixed blessing. Through expansion we've been able to accommodate a considerable number of migrants. Their social and cultural integration, initially problematic, has been what I believe is one of the triumphs of the strategy.'

'If you look at the image, I'll show you some of the planning principles we've incorporated. First, a belief in local neighbourhoods. These are what we call twelve-minute neighbourhoods. Everyone lives within twelve minutes' walk of most local facilities. The neighbourhoods are fuzzy, overlapping, complementing each other. The catchments of facilities tend to vary, so neighbourhoods are quite fluid. Your neighbourhood may be quite different from that of people living round the corner. Each person has their own perspective. Just like when sunlight shines through rain each person sees their own rainbow, depending on where they are. Now, look at the pattern of local facilities. Here you can see the schools, parks, community centres, shops and services. At 4 kph walking speed (slower than you, maybe, but bear in mind older people and parents with young kids), twelve minutes means a maximum distance on flat land of 800 metres. This is not circles drawn on a map, but actual distance, along safe and attractive routes. Entirely walkable for the vast majority of people, and a far cry from the unrealistic twenty-minute neighbourhoods promoted by some in the twenties. Fifteen minutes was better, but still too long.

'I want to look now at how places should be spatially planned. First to emphasise the greenspace system. You'll see…' He struggled momentarily to reveal all the water courses, open spaces, parks, fields and woods. 'You can see how all the greenspaces are interlinked, creating a network connected to open country, ideal for recreational walks and also for wildlife. And for water and flood management too. Here,' he paused a moment, highlighting, 'are the main habitat areas – with the water-based habitats along the canal especially important. To that we add the safe pedestrian, pedal and e-bike routes. Look – a great network! A connected town! The vast majority can now choose to walk or cycle to the town centre, station, leisure, secondary school and other facilities. Incidentally, we use the same time standards for cycling: the 12 minute bike-town. At a modest 15 kph average that means the maximum distance to the beating heart of the town is three kilometres. Actual distance, not as the crow flies. We're following the same principles elsewhere in the valleys, though it's not always as simple as for greater Stonehouse.

'The wider structure of towns is determined by public transport. Bus and tram systems link places together, and any new major developments, like retail and office centres, leisure or cultural centres and secondary schools have to be within easy walking distance of the core ten-minute-frequency public transport network. To tell the truth, there haven't been many such investments in the last few decades – there's little spare money around – so the reality is we've been trying to ensure our public transport improvements tie in earlier developments to the network. The Forest Green Rovers stadium by the old motorway junction is a case in point, on the old tram route from Stroud to Cam Station.'

I was studying the model, noticing the new routes, bridges and connections, when a voice piped up from the audience: 'It all looks hunky-dory, Wulf, but I'm at a loss to know why these particular standards were adopted, given the range of users. Aren't such criteria both arbitrary and really inflexible? I mean, I cycle faster and am quite prepared to go at least six kilometres each way on a daily basis. So aren't you artificially restricting development?'

'Interesting point, but are you a typical resident, do you think?' asked Wulf. 'We're working with all types and sizes of people, trying to be inclusive. People make their own choices, given their situation so some can and do cycle or walk much more than our standards. We know that the fall-off in cycle use becomes quite significant at longer distances, especially for older people and young children. We can't control where people live, the housing market is another issue, so we're attempting to cater for all, wherever they end up. As part of that we are working towards a constellation of towns – strings of towns in the five valleys, drawing together all those disconnected commuter villages and urban fragments. You can bus between them or cycle on excellent cycleways, to access a very wide range of facilities and jobs. If I pan out in scale a bit ...thus ... you can see how the linked towns of the Five Valleys – Stroud, Stonehouse, Nailsworth, Painswick, Brimscombe, Eastcombe and Woodchester – also share efficient bus, tram and rail links to the big cities for high level facilities. Our analyses show that the vast majority of people now have real choice and opportunity and freedom of activity, association and access. There is that word – FREEDOM – again. Freedom for everyone.

'However, our Stroud valleys are not perfect. I'll admit this! I'd like you now to cluster into small buzz groups, and from your varied perspectives think of problems that need addressing, or policies that you feel are not working well. Feel free to range right across the remit of local and regional government. Within fifteen minutes identify three priorities for review or action, as you see it. Speak them into the numbered recorders by your seats. Your words will appear on the wall screen by number, then you can edit. Keep them brief or we'll run out of wall! You'll be able to glance through them today, and see them online later today, then they'll provide starters for next week's meeting and valuable feedback to me and colleagues.' Wulf left it at that, and chatting commenced in the hall, tepid at first but soon warming up – voices raised in discussion.

I was in two minds about it all, and turned to Sam to share my thoughts. Intellectually I was impressed. All kinds of principles that I'd learnt at college, but rarely seen implemented, were coming together here. The images that Wulf flashed up all looked very seductive, very attractive. But in parallel I had an instinctive revulsion. Under the pressure of migration, my beautiful valleys had been overdeveloped, losing some of the open prospects. My cynical self wondered to what degree he was gilding the lily. I'd worked in the private sector, and knew how to massage the message, select the best but atypical views of new development. I had a deeper worry too. Given the vagaries of the land and development markets, and the power of vested interests, how was this level of clarity, logic and co-ordination achieved? In Britain?! It was so improbable that I was driven to suspect autocratic powers were necessary. Just as everyone had to accept identity implants, so land ownership was controlled by the state.

I reminded myself, and told Sam, that back in my own time, I'd seen great presentations about certain European cities, especially in Scandinavia, and my favourite city, Freiburg in Germany, which seemed to have got their act together. Thinking about it, they did control land ownership to a degree, so I wondered how it worked in England now. However, I also recalled that some of the much-praised 'compact' and 'sustainable' cities, like Milan and Barcelona, actually had extensive low-density settlement penumbras dispersed all across their region, relying on high car ownership and use, undermining the ideal of active travel. There were no powers to prevent this. I needed to find out the secret of Wulf's apparent success.

The buzz session had been carrying on while I pondered. The wall was packed with ideas. Wulf said, 'OK, we'll reconvene now. Thanks for all your contributions. They look quite thought-provoking. Do look through them, see whether they echo what you said or put forward different ideas. AI has already categorised and grouped them, though I'll just check the results before releasing them on the website. Now, any general questions before we finish?'

The question that almost erupted from one noisy buzz-group (they seemed like keen students!) drew me back to basics. They declared that they were alarmed at what Wulf had said about the rolling ball. They'd spent the time arguing about to what extent the world was now on a safe trajectory, since official and scientific sources put varying gloss on the situation and it was difficult to interpret the data. They wanted to know, for real, what Wulf really thought.

The chief urbanist beamed. 'Yes! The acid test! Well, given the uncertainty of both the natural processes and human responses, we remain on a knife-edge. While we are avoiding the worst scenarios of scientists early in the century, runaway global heating is still an alarming possibility. Not a probability, I hasten to say, but a possibility. The probable future – our central forecast – suggests that peak temperature, as I said, will be within the next thirty years, and thereafter, given continuing decline in anthropogenic greenhouse emissions which we can now confidently forecast, temperatures and climatic events will moderate. If that is the case, then the current ecological recovery should continue. However, I come back to Greenland – and parts of Antarctica for that matter. So much water is stored in those icecaps that we can predict with certainty that if it melts faster than it has so far – and the signs have not been entirely reassuring – then sea-level rise would be sufficient to drown some of the great cities of the world, and much productive land. Which is why I say we have to take very expensive concerted international action to insulate Greenland, southern Greenland in particular, from the summer sun. Experimental techniques to do just that are being co-ordinated by the UN. We are not out of the woods!

Now, climate impacts vary across countries. Here in the British Isles the risks are complex to unravel. We have a mild temperate climate thanks to the Gulf Stream, a huge conveyor belt, if you like, flowing northeast across the Atlantic, redistributing warmth and essential nutrients, nourishing marine life and keeping north-western Europe ideal for human habitation. It is part of an interwoven pattern of ocean circulation which includes the cold Labrador Current from the Arctic. Two variables lead to real concerns. One is the general warming of the ocean. The other is the increasing strength and reducing salinity of the Labrador Current, as it is fed by more icy melt waters from Greenland. The Doomsday scenario is that the Gulf Stream is cut off by the Labrador Current and plunges northwest Europe, including these sceptred isles, into bitterly cold winters and cool summers. However, the timescale is unknown; we have been lucky so far, and it might just be a modest change that counteracts the effects of the warming climate. We have to try to plan for all eventualities.'

My mind was in a turmoil, not sure I was taking in what he said – especially about the Labrador Current and its implications. My oceanic knowledge failed me. I vowed to find out more later on. Meanwhile Wulf was continuing. 'In the West Country we fondly believe we are in the vanguard of learning how to cope with these possible eventualities. The local universities and innovative entrepreneurs have been really key in pushing things forward in human health and wellbeing, natural ecology, farming, food, water, energy and emissions. And what I haven't mentioned before – the circular economy. Business has really bought into our catchphrase, 'Make it local!'. In other words, a lot of our products and services and financial exchanges are within the West Country or near neighbours. More wealth shared locally, not being lost to external investors and producers.

'Now, in formal partnership with the Netherlands, Scandinavia, Tamil Nadu, Chile, Vietnam and Aotearoa, we are exporting good practice to the world, even the USA! This is because if people want to sell to the partnership, they have to pass quite rigorous social and ecological tests. And they do want to sell, because as a group we're relatively rich. This is quite a new initiative, using trade not as exploitation but as co-operation. Other countries are looking to join the group.

'Ah! I see time's up. I'll stop there. The follow-up seminar will happen at the same time next week. Cue for some voluntary homework! Please do engage with this – it won't take long, but can get you thinking. Review all the problems listed on the wall and in no more than two hundred words summarise the key issues as you see them. Preferably in elegant hand-writing! Then upload to the website for all to read. I look forward to the different professional insights in discussion next week. If you fancy a chat this evening, I'll be at the Crown and Sceptre at 18.00. It would be great to get to know more of you. One pint of best for first comers! It's great beer, locally brewed. It would be good to see you. Far end of Horns Road. Just before the old cemetery. OK. That's it! Thanks for your attention.'

The audience gave him a warm round of applause and started to disperse, a few hanging around to have a quick personal word. I didn't move – I felt a bit bamboozled. It was as if he'd been talking to me, rather than the assembled staff. He'd been castigating my own time – more than fair, I thought – but I also felt a little defensive, which was ridiculous. And I knew the Crown and Sceptre, was delighted it was still there, wondered if we – Sam and I – could join Wulf for a pint later. I looked at her. 'Could we go to the pub this evening to chat more with Wulf, if he's up for it?' I asked.

She hesitated. 'That would be pretty risky,' she said, 'so better not. Anyway, we've got a treat in store for you late afternoon. We're going to the Greek Games in New Stonehouse. We won't get away until about 20. Come on, Robyn, I'm famished. And I've got to leap long jumps later. Let's find some lunch.'

Part III
Exploring a strange society

Drawn in a garden in Stroud, these three herbs represent the diversity of society: more specifically Bay is for courage, Rosemary for love and Oregano for joy. The principle of Ubuntu is about drawing all people together: 'I am because you are'

11
Greek Games

What happened later could not have been more of a contrast with the studied seriousness of the morning meeting and lecture. The Greek Games were a revelation! Shocking, in a way, but enjoyable and exciting too. Since athletics was one of my favourite sports, I was really looking forward to the competition. Sam had her small sports bag with her, so after lunch we spent the early afternoon walking along the canal, then chatting and busy in a coffee shop – Sam using something a bit like an iPad, me writing long-hand notes about the morning. Sam was fascinated and curious. 'Your choice!' she said. 'I love your handwriting.'

Rufus joined us later at Stroud station. The sleek, bright red shuttle train arrived like clockwork. No driver! I thought of all those union campaigns in my own time to keep train drivers and managers, and the lack of a reliable service. I remembered the problems I had once had at this same station, when helping a wheelchair-bound relative into a carriage – rushing from one end of the platform to the other in search of the ramp, and no-one apparently there to assist. On that occasion a rather stolid train manager had eventually rescued us. Here, now, the passengers looked quite self-sufficient. But yes! There was a uniformed middle-aged woman available on the platform, giving advice when asked, keeping a watchful eye on proceedings.

Onto the train we got. It left precisely on time. We stopped briefly at a 'new' halt at Ebley and an old one at Stonehouse, before reaching a much bigger station, named New Stonehouse, north of the old town, where our line from London met the line up from Bristol and went on to Birmingham. A good location! Getting off there, we were in the heart of the significant settlement which Wulf had illustrated. An elegant central square, lots of facilities, bustling pedestrian streets, four- to six-storey multi-use buildings, a convivial and purposeful atmosphere.

Sam explained that after some early-century, car-based developments had gone to the west of the town, across the railway barrier, a new plan had been drawn up in 2040. Gloucestershire County Council capitalised on its swathe of county-owned agricultural land holdings to the north of Stonehouse to create a connected, integrated Greater Stonehouse centred on the new railway station, at the nexus of cycle routes and accessible to green parkland that we were now approaching. Commercial activities in business parks nearby, dependent on motorised transport, were taxed so highly, via the carbon and health taxes, that they all moved to the new centre. The old town was now a rather upmarket neighbourhood within Greater Stonehouse. Rufus emphasised that accommodating the tide of climate refugees was a powerful motivation for expansion, as well as being the source of much political conflict. The scheme was a radical response. But to my eyes, looking around, it had led to a thriving town.

A few hundred metres down a tree-lined street and we were in parkland, on a broad track through the trees, with crowds of other people. We emerged into a wide open space harbouring a substantial wooden building, very idiosyncratic in its design, sporting huge laminated arches. There were tables outside, people drinking and conversing. I noticed there were no children. Rufus explained that the Games were not deemed child-appropriate by the current council. 'Would you like a beer?' he asked. Then seeing my doubtful face: 'Quite in order you know. This is entertainment, we're here to support Sam, not work!' 'Nothing for me,' said Sam, smiling. 'Just hard graft! Can't imagine why I do it. I'll go and get ready.' She vanished. Rufus and I bought half-pints – still in pints! I thought – and sat in the sun. 'No rush,' he said. I had leisure to look around. Mainly younger people. A wide range of dress, including Asian styles, all very colourful, and very 'Stroudy' too, I thought; there seemed to be no single convention.

I had a rather equivocal response to one of the male fashions –tights and short jacket showing off shapely legs and pubic bulges like ballet dancers. My logical brain queried my reaction – given that girls' and women's fashions were often designed to show off their bodies, why should I find it mildly disturbing that men were doing the same? But I did!

I was pressing Rufus to tell me what 'Greek Games' were. He'd expressly asked me not to ask Cyla or my wristy, so the experience would be a surprise. Now all he would say is that these games were about athletic prowess, inspired by the games of ancient Greece, but not entirely like the Olympics as I knew it. Greek Games were not yet fully international – just a handful of European and East Asian countries so far. The event we were to see was the Gloucestershire championships. The top performers would then go to the Provincial Championships in Bristol.

Having drained our beer, we moved through the wooden structure. On the far side was not the track and stadium I'd been expecting, but a large grass amphitheatre. A track was marked out on the grass. Around it were grass slopes, some with a series of tiers incorporated, reminding me of ancient Greek stadia. People were already disporting themselves on the slopes. But what riveted my attention was something else altogether: the athletes warming up in the arena were all naked! I realised abruptly why these were called Greek Games – I thought of all the Greek and Roman statues and images on ancient pots, the classical enjoyment of the naked male form. But here there were women too! My austere upbringing kicked in and I was quite taken aback, though my rational self immediately chastised me for prejudice, or at least narrow-mindedness. I tried to observe without judgement. Rufus was watching my reactions with interest.

I noticed that not all athletes were completely starkers. There were a number of men with discreet pouches and women with sports bras. Rufus explained that while everyone signed up to the principle of nudity, some who were more well-endowed found it uncomfortable, inhibiting their performance.

Looking at all the athletes, I began to get over my initial reaction. I worked hard to sense the underlying values that motivated these games. Were they part of a 'back to nature' movement? Young women and men celebrating their bodies' beauty and grace, not embarrassed, not acting with provocative sensuality, not trying to titillate, just enjoying the sense of being naked in the fresh air, their bare feet on the grass, in contact with the natural environment. Right now they were warming up, fine-tuning their athletic abilities, while keeping minds cool and unclouded, getting ready for the thrill and tension of race or jump or throw, without artificial aids of track or running shoes, just the unadorned human.

As if reading my mind, Rufus told me that in the first part of the century there had been progressive refinement of technological athletic aids, to the point where it ceased to be possible to compare the performances of one generation with another. Eventually there had been a strong reaction against all the sporting technology. People wanted to get back to basics and feel the cool grass between their toes. Hence the invention, in Holland originally ('as you might expect,' he said) of the Greek Games.

The competition started. I found the sight of naked people running on the green grass, of beautiful young bodies striving for perfect performance, very exciting, completely unexpected. It was all so innocent! Even my conservative self could not deny the sheer exhilaration of the experience. It brought back fleeting memories of my young childhood, being allowed to play and run with friends barefoot in the meadow; and even younger, playing naked in rock pools on the beach during our holidays in West Wales. I was surprised at those memories – they were vivid – yet I'd not recalled them for many, many years.

As the Games progressed I gradually came to terms with my own reactions, not so much besotted with bare bodies but rather enjoying their athletic prowess and competitiveness, willing certain athletes to win, enjoying the alertness and energy it gave, like when I had watched the England women in the 2023 football World Cup final. It was a new feeling for me in this era. I found the whole experience very moving, so real, and something approaching a sense of joy swept over me. 'It's beautiful; quite extraordinary; not like anything I'd imagined,' I said to Rufus. 'And they're all so gorgeous!' He smiled broadly. I went on: 'Nothing like this could ever happen in my own time, 'it wouldn't be allowed – not even contemplated – much too open and explicit and risqué; it would have been assumed to be sexualising sport!'

'Are you sure?' Rufus rejoined. 'When I looked at your time, the visual records that have survived, it seemed that so much in women's fashions, the music industry and the cult of celebrities, was about titillation. Consider, even, the female athletes in the Olympics. They weren't acting suggestively of course, but their sports clothes were absolutely minimal, designed, quite incidentally, to be tantalising to the male and lesbian gaze.' 'That was just the fashion!' I said, rather taken aback by what he had said. 'Exactly!' he rejoined. 'Sexualisation of everything, that was the fashion, young children's clothes too, the girls anyway. OK, I'm exaggerating, but not much.' 'It was about reducing air resistance – for the athletes I mean,' I countered. 'So why did the men wear more then?' 'Did they?' I asked. 'Yup; longer shorts and running vests.' He was almost laughing at my discomfort! I saw the point of his comments. 'Well, men are hairier! I said, tongue in cheek. Rufus guffawed. 'I think now we are much more honest and straightforward,' he said.

At that moment our attention was drawn back to the arena. Sam was doing the long jump right under our noses. 'God, look at that!' said Rufus. 'She's good!' I noticed all the long-jumpers were wearing briefs. Rufus explained 'You don't want sand up your ...' He left the sentence hanging. Crude, I thought! On second thoughts, practical.

I was transfixed by the power and grace of the leaping athletes. Then our eyes were drawn up to a hologram which was hovering above the arena. The final stages of the marathon, coming down over Doverow Hill, were on view. The race was close. The cheering from the crowd grew intense. We had to suspend conversation until a few minutes later the first runners came into the stadium, ran round the track and completed the race.

In the gaps between these and other events Rufus and I went deeper into what had happened to trigger the shift in social and political attitudes that now allowed naked games. He did admit that acceptance was not universal. There was rejection of the initiative in most of the USA, Africa and the Middle East, primarily for religious reasons. However, in Europe there had been a rediscovery (not for the first time, I thought) of ancient Greece, Rome and Byzantium. This heritage had become central to education and cultural development – partly as an attempt, Rufus thought, to reinforce European identity in the face of an ever more multicultural society, partly in reaction to the conspicuous failure of neoliberal capitalist economics and politics during the century.

I reserved judgement, instinctively believing that the racial medley and cultural diversity I observed could, or should, lead to a new synthesis, not retrenchment. I was more convinced when Rufus elaborated the capitalist point in relation to sporting activity. Earlier in the century, he said, the commercialisation of sport had reached such a pitch, with astronomical wages for some footballers, cricketers, rugby players and tennis stars; football teams and players were bought and sold for exorbitant sums by oil states and private equity holdings; a great divide had opened up between the grassroots and top professionals. The time was ripe for a more inclusive and ethical sporting structure. Hence the Greek Games and other initiatives, part of a movement growing up in parallel to commercial sport and gradually supplanting it when so many billionaires had gone bust in the Bad Times. These Games, Rufus informed me, were amateur and not-for-profit, the prizes modest. Yet many top performers were choosing to participate. It was the taking part that mattered.

He went on, 'Anyway, another point. When the movement for Greek Games gained momentum, in the sixties, it found fertile ground in many countries, as a means of promoting inclusion, enabling a sense of acceptance of all, whatever people's bodies were like.' I pointed out that almost all the bodies on view were beautiful, many skin colours and probably varied genders and sexualities for all I knew, but all were comely and lissom. Where were the fat and the ugly? (I was surprised – coming as I had from an age of language sensitivity – at the directness of my language). Rufus laughed. 'Ah,' he said, 'that's what you see now. But if we came tomorrow there's much more variety – disabled athletes and also non-athletic sports like darts, chess, e-footy, snooker, ringlord (that's an electronic game), whist and rummy – all added into the mix, some played inside of course, but still having to be naked! Many competitors are not very pretty to look at. Really odd, even! That's inclusivity for you!' 'No chance of hiding your cards up your sleeve then!' I said. 'Quite! And most of those games are open equally to men and women, and anyone in between.' 'Do men and women ever compete equally in more physical sports?' I asked, thinking of horse racing and dressage in my own day. 'Not in the very physical sports, no,' said Rufus, 'but it's happening more, even in Olympic sports like bowls and bobsleigh, quite a cultural change really. Oh, and an odd one: croquet.' 'Croquet!' I said. 'I don't believe it! Has that made its way into the Olympics?' 'Spread around the world!' said Rufus. 'Possibly the most vicious sport alive, but once its British upper-crust image had worn away, people came to love its unpredictability.'

We were missing out on the games in front of us. To our delight Sam was doing well – in the later stages of the long jump. And the 5,000 metres was just reaching its climax. I recognised one of the competitors – the beautiful boy from the Withey's Yard cafe. He looked so young, though the programme assured me he was in the adult category. I couldn't take my eyes off him! His running was so graceful, like a gazelle. Rufus saw my looks and said, 'He's quite a lad isn't he? Very handsome. And quite insatiable with it – his appetites I mean. Or so they say.' He grinned mischievously. I looked askance at him, for such inappropriate comments. This level of directness seemed quite un-English.

The boy did well, but not well enough to quality for the regional games. 'Interesting,' said Rufus. 'Last year he won the young adult competition; but now he must be twenty-one, and in with the big boys. Men peak for 5,000 metres at about twenty-eight.'

At that moment we saw Sam was just completing her last jump. Our conversation veered back to her impressive performance. She came second and was through to the regional games. I was really glad for her, and realised I loved the elegance of her body, not in a sexual way but with pure aesthetic delight.

She vanished into the building, and when she reappeared, having showered and donned clothes, I gave her a congratulatory hug and we celebrated with cups of tea. A little later as we were going out, we bumped into the boy-man there, now in shorts and T-shirt (thank goodness!). He immediately recognised me and introduced himself as Bob, a somehow unexpected name, but Bob he was. He said he'd remembered me from the coffee shop, my meeting with the mayor. 'I couldn't forget you! You were clearly both important and different!' I smiled warily, making conversation: 'Yes. Visiting from Manchester. On a study tour. I was impressed with your performance earlier. Your running, so stylish and economical. Do you work full time at the cafe?' He told me he was studying part time for a higher degree in linguistics and ecology at the Communiversity. I was immediately interested, both in his degree and the place – if the Communiversity was a place. I asked him to tell me more. He eyes lit up and he said he'd be delighted; but had to rush off now because he was on duty at the cafe. Rufus negotiated a time we could meet a few days hence, in the evening. I suddenly wondered, was it wise?

Later we took the train to Ebley, walked across the river and up through fields to Selsley village where we had a celebratory dinner at the pub. My mind was still buzzing with Wulf's lecture. For me there were so many gaps in the story. He had used the 2062 UN Earthplan as his kicking off point. What had led up to that? Rufus had frequently referred to the Bad Times, but neither he, nor Cyla, in my room, nor my wristy, had been willing to elaborate. After his second glass of wine, I thought the time might be ripe, and said, 'Look, I've got a real problem. All that you are showing me, the amazing people like Wulf and Sarah that we've met, it's all fantastic, the games were glorious, a revelation, and you are being wonderful guides, both of you. But I feel like I'm floating in space – enjoying the beautiful panorama below, but with a feeling of total unreality, not believing it, not believing that I can stay suspended – I may come crashing down. My world of the twenties is so different. All the futuristic books and films are dystopian, anticipating a totally inhumane political and technological future. I haven't a clue how we got here, now. How you got here. There's just this reference to the Bad Times, clearly with capital letters. I need to have an inkling, more than an inkling, a real understanding of what turned things around – what happened to enable this utopian world?'

It was clear that I'd had a few drinks too! I looked quite challengingly at my companions. Rufus smiled sympathetically at me and knowingly at Sam. 'Far from utopian,' was all he said. I just carried on, in retrospect rather a rant, saying that I'd been frustrated at every turn. It wasn't just people who had kept the truth from me, it was artificial intelligences as well. Cyla just skated over the surface when I asked her – generalisations, no specifics, waffle really. And my wristy seemed to have swallowed the same textbook. I was in the dark.

I stopped, eventually. Rufus was looking thoughtful. 'I think it's time to come clean,' he said. 'It is absolutely true that you've been insulated from the full horror of what has happened this century. We thought it best to protect you in the first days of your visit. Cyla and your wristy have been programmed accordingly. A rather paternalistic attitude, I grant you. That's the nature of the world we now live in – though actually we've adopted the term maternalistic to imply a caring, enabling approach, not authoritarian, we hope.' Rufus paused. 'So, if Sam's in agreement ...' He looked at her for confirmation. She said, 'Absolutely, go for it Rufus. I was never really happy withholding information anyway, as you know. I should tell you, Robyn, he's been glued to early century history modules for weeks, in preparation for this moment. Best if you hear it first in person, not as a podcast or something.'

I was mute. 'I'll try to give a potted history, starting in your era,' said Rufus. 'Back in 2015, at the international meeting in Paris called COP 21, the world's nations agreed to limit temperature rise to 1.5 degrees, reckoning that was the maximum that would still give us a good chance of avoiding global disaster and runaway warming. 2050 was set as the date by which the world needed to achieve net zero greenhouse emissions. That didn't mean no fossil fuel extraction at all, but that any residual carbon and other emissions would be completely matched by absorption, especially by trees. Many countries then made targets for the reduction of greenhouse gas emissions for 2030, as a staging post. There were impressive technological advances being made, but hard policy lagged behind. Almost without exception, those targets for 2030 and 2050 were missed. Implementation failed. Indeed, some policies and investment decisions continued to go the wrong way, exacerbating the problem. The most obvious example, evident in both rich and poor countries, was transport: increasing air travel and dependence on motorised movement, while the lack of adequate infrastructure impeded the transition to electric vehicles, including in many low and medium income countries. Heating was another problem. And cooling. In Britain in your decade, the twenties, there was almost blind faith in the potential of heat pumps, ignoring the fact that many urban properties were not suitable, and sidelining the obvious need to retrofit all the leaky old houses for energy efficiency. Part of the problem was simply a lack of skilled engineers and builders, despite in-migration.

'Anyway, the result, as you heard from Wulf, was that the key 1.5 degree heating limit was breached, even some years in the twenties, then comprehensively in the thirties. Progress was being made, but much too slowly. Glaciers went on retreating. The sea warmed. Loss of Arctic and Antarctic sea ice left polar bears and penguins stranded. The net loss of tropical rainforests was eventually halted, but there was not enough overall tree-planting gain to compensate for continued fossil fuel burning. Weather became more extreme in many parts of the globe, more storms, more severe storms, coastal flooding, droughts and heatwaves and wildfires. The amount of forced climate migration was increasing alarmingly. The contrast between the fate of the rich and the fate of the poor within many countries, and between countries, led to increasing civil unrest. In the Middle East and Africa there were water and migration wars. There were private armies commandeered by billionaire industrialists fighting autocratic regimes, often about rare metal mineral reserves. All this was then compounded by disastrous tech failures at the end of the thirties and then again at the end of the forties, courtesy of peak solar activity. Then the partial collapse of the internet and bankruptcy of some multinational tech firms undermined all the assumptions of the early century. It was obvious from ecological and technical and human perspectives that the old neoliberal economic model was failing. Comprehensively. It was simply outmoded, incapable of coping with the multifold crises, if it ever had been.'

Rufus paused for breath. 'That sets the scene for change, I think!' I was sitting almost rigid in my chair. Sam gave her lover a little clap, then said: 'Let's have pudding, and risk another bottle too, before you give the next instalment.' He nodded enthusiastically. They started chatting about the games, the results and those now going forward to the provincial competition. I breathed deeply, not entirely shocked by what I'd heard, but quite disturbed nonetheless. Most of it, apart from the tech crisis, had been foreseen by environmentalists and the risks discussed at the COPs. I stayed quiet, reflecting.

A little later Rufus continued the story, back in his pulpit. 'In 2049, the very year before we were supposed to hit net zero and everything would be hunky-dory, there were storms and coastal flooding round the world on a scale never seen before. Several low-lying island states, and a number of big capital cities, were inundated, with massive emergency rescue operations undertaken. Some polders in Holland, and parts of the Somerset levels, were lost to the sea. The previous few years had also seen famine after long droughts and rivers drying up in parts of Africa, and even China. All this coincided with another pandemic on the scale of COVID-19. The climate scientists were forecasting a hellish future, with temperature increases of 3 or 4 degrees. Some smaller countries had actually been taking pretty effective action over the previous decades, but major countries, notably the USA, China, India, Brazil, Russia and Nigeria, had been sluggish to adapt. The 2049-50 crises at last led to a profound shift in thinking. There was worldwide recognition that for a century and more we had been following false gods; that disjointed incremental action was no good at all; that the likelihood of runaway global heating, and far more catastrophic sea-level rise than the 0.4 metres already seen by 2050, was becoming more and more inevitable if we continued on the path of conspicuous consumption and the capitalist dream. What really changed minds was the economy, of course! The signs had been threatening since the internet debacle a couple of years earlier, and now there were major banking failures as companies and countries defaulted; the insurance industry went into meltdown, many firms going bust, cancelling agreements and fighting shy of supporting new investments. The impossibility or very high expense of insurance put a huge dampener on economic growth. The world went into a recessionary spiral.

'Riding to the rescue came the United Nations. It had been comprehensively reformed and strengthened, at long last, in '45, a hundred years to the day after the original constitution was established in San Francisco after the Second World War. Countries round the world, faced with galloping economic disaster, demanded concerted action. The interdependence of all countries of the world, the commitment to greater equality within and between nations, and the sense that humankind was part of a global ecological system, had been written into the revised constitution – mirroring the amazing idealism of the original charter. The UN commandeered the nations of the world to work together in preparation for the World Summit of 2056. In some ways that was the real turning point, leading to the '62 Earthplan that Wolf mentioned. And the rest, as they say, is history!'

'Gosh!' said Sam, 'that was impressive! A brilliant résumé! And quite enough to be going on with! You know, you looked so different while delivering that.' She turned to me and asked: 'Did all that come as a surprise? Or was it what you might have expected?' I pondered a moment, then said, 'it's alarming – and riveting! My heart is racing. But it does begin to help me understand how we got here. Sometime, not now, I'd like to know more about the way the UN was reorganised, and also about the technological crises … which were not really anticipated by people in my time. I'd like to know more. Also to find out more about how individual countries have fared. That would be interesting.'

It was quite dark outside, and time to leave. As we got up to go, Rufus said that Cyla could help with some questions. He would take the blocks off. Allow me freer access to the Euronet. We walked back by torchlight along a well-made gravel track through woods and orchards and vineyards to Woodchester. I was subdued and thoughtful, reflecting on the Bad Times.

Then the mild exercise, clear sky and cool fresh breeze released me from that malign spell.

What a crowded day it had been! On my eventual return to my pad, I was pondering contradictory thoughts – first trying to join the dots of global history between my time and this time, then wrestling with the Wulf's spatial strategy, while my heart was bursting with vivid, sensuous impressions from the Games. But even with all these things going round and round in my head, as my body snuggled into bed I drifted soon enough into sleep.

$$\wp\!\sim\!\wp$$

12
Off the leash, maybe ...

I woke early, with a kind of heaviness in my heart, or a sense of unease – odd after the stimuli of the previous day. At first I could not work out what was causing these feelings. I lay in bed, despondent and glum, hoping my mind would reveal why. There was a patter of raindrops on the window. I got out of bed to draw back the curtains. They opened of their own accord before I got there. The cloudscape was dark and gloomy, though there was one shaft of brilliant sunlight across the valley. The raindrops were running down the windowpane, chasing each other, wriggling striations glinting tepidly in the dull light, distorting the world beyond. For a while I was mesmerised, forgetting my night fears.

Not for long. They came back with a vengeance, my subconscious buzzing with worry. With a rising sense of dread I searched my mind for the cause. It was very personal, nothing to do with the fate of the world. It seemed I was in a haze of unknowing, being carried willy-nilly down a path not of my choosing. Trying to focus, I realised what it might be ... I was still worrying about what had happened to my real self, what I had done in life. What had happened to all the people I knew? A further thought struck me, with force: am I really the same person now as before – mind and body? The transfer through time of a real person seemed pure science fiction. More likely this, now, was a kind of afterlife – I'd always been agnostic about that, keeping an open mind. If I had actually died, never emerging from the coma, this could be a dream world, battening on to my own experience of life, a kind of tarnished, wish-fulfilment heaven.

The more I dwelt on these uncertainties the more agitated I became. The rain came on harder in sympathy. It hammered on the window, coming and going with gusts. It was the first time I'd experienced rain in this era. It had a strange effect on my mood, bridging the time-gulf, making me feel I was back home, in fact back in the family home when I was a kid. Rain … torrential rain … nothing quite like it, while being safe inside the house, somehow more secure because of the rain.

As I dressed, looking in the mirror at my furrowed expression, the memory of those fears crowded back on me. By the time Rufus arrived to share breakfast in my room, I was almost paranoid. I don't know what I said to him, I think it was pretty histrionic. He was calmness personified, recognising the reality of my worries, saying he had been half expecting them, but thought it better not to anticipate. He said, 'honestly, Robyn, rely on what you feel in yourself. Do you feel like a cyborg or a ghost? I know you for what you are, a real, live, warm, here-and-now woman.' He made to take my hand in reassurance, but I reacted: 'Yes! No! Rufus, how can I trust you? Every new revelation has to be dragged out of you! I don't know. I feel manipulated! Am I real? Am I dead? What about family? You haven't told me!' Tears were starting in my eyes.

He sat down on an upright chair, leaning slightly forward, with a concerned look, arms hanging down between his thighs. He gestured me to sit too, but I was pacing around, head wagging like a startled hen. 'As I told you, yes, you've died,' he said, baldly, spelling it out slowly, following me with his eyes. 'What the surviving records tell us about your life in real time, without time-travel, is that you died at the age of 88. A decade ago. You had several long-term relationships – not clear how many – but didn't have any children. You dedicated yourself to your mission in life. You've no partner or close relation now alive, at least not in Britain. I believe this situation, the lack of family, made you a suitable candidate for transfer, when you were in the coma. As for the mystery of that transfer – how you can be here in body and mind – I will leave explanation to my boss when you meet him in a few days.'

I sagged, stopped pacing, sat down. 'And what was my mission? What did I do?!' He responded gently, 'I'm sorry, all I know is that it involved your professional field of design and planning for health. Apparently you made quite a contribution, working with the UN. More than that I don't know. There may be more out there about you, waiting to be discovered, but the wisdom of my elders is that more detailed information would not help you, or me for that matter, and could confuse the issue. Much of your history, like everyone's, was lost when the internet collapsed.'

I felt deflated, and comprehensively confused. No history, no children, no partner, or at least none living, no known achievements. A non-person! All those lost years. I looked sideways at Rufus: 'I need to spend some time alone, just exploring.' 'Point taken,' he said. 'Let's have some breakfast. What do you fancy? I'll just have muesli and toast. Could you order, please?' That suggestion pulled me back into myself. I talked to Cyla, then Rufus responded to my request: 'As it happens, you could have free time this morning. I thought you might need it after the intensity of yesterday. You may well discover all kinds of things when by yourself, rather than spending the whole time with me. I suggest you ramble round this town – find out how it works.' 'I'll do exactly that,' I said, a little aggressively. Then I'll walk up to the Common. Get a wider perspective on things.' 'Good idea,' said Rufus mildly. 'Do you want a preview of the town, a hologram? And of Rodborough?' 'No I don't!' then, as an afterthought, 'thank you.'

The cup of tea and bowl of cereal settled me down, worked wonders, drawing me back into the moment. I was quite surprised at myself. I determined to take control of my own moods, and to find out more about my past-future history, my Mum and Dad, my relationships. They, my minders – whoever they were – were not going to tell me unless I forced them. I carefully explained my worries again to Rufus, trying to be objective and logical, looking him in the eye, apologising – kind of – for my behaviour. He told me all that he said he knew, and I didn't press him: that I had not died in 2023, that my mind was my own, and my body reconstituted here while I still lay in a coma back in the hospital. That I would be returned safely before 'waking'. He held out his hand. I shook it rather formally, then said, to my surprise, 'Actually, Rufus, I've changed my mind. I need a hug.' We hugged. Quite demurely at first, but then more warmly. I breathed out, deep sighs, relaxing at last. Then sprang away, smiling awkwardly, needing separation but glad of the brief communion. 'Thank you, Rufus … Really, I don't want to go out alone today. It's too soon. Tomorrow would be better, but today, there are so many things around Stroud I want you to show me. The canal and so on. Would that be OK?'

Rufus looked at me with a sympathetic eye – or was it a calculating eye? I couldn't quite interpret. Anyway, he said, 'Ah! Good! Just what I hoped. I have a nice itinerary already forming in my head. We'll walk from here, once the weather improves. Then tomorrow maybe you'll be ready to ramble by yourself. The only fixed event tomorrow is a meeting late afternoon about health and equity, so you would have most of the day to explore, get your personal take on things and places, unsullied by me. That'll be refreshing, and I look forward to hearing your perspective afterwards.'

Later, mid-morning, the rainclouds cleared. Rufus and I took an interesting route through the town, rising gently, contouring up through woods to the Bear Inn at the top of the hill. It was a bit of a route march, no time to dawdle, so I determined to revisit the Common, more at leisure, the following day. Then we went steeply down the far side of the Common to the canal, which was alive with paddle-boaters and canoeists. 'Most people only work three days a week,' said my companion. 'Plenty of spare time. Their physical activity is monitored of course.' 'Monitored?' I said in surprise. 'Yes, naturally, by their wristy, so they can see how well they are doing, while the info is registered and analysed by the RM who can alert both bod and boot.' Rufus cocked his head, saucily.

I laughed at his descent into colloquialisms. 'Rufus, you are talking riddles. Again! What do you mean by RM? Bod and boot?' 'Oh dear! Sorry! Falling into slang! How wicked of me! RM is the Robotic Monitor, normally in your wristy, linked to Cyla. Don't know why it has such a big name. You are the bod. The boot is your AA – activity advisor, a real person, who can try to boot you into action. I guess these shorthand names were all part of a marketing exercise years ago.

We bridged the canal and watched all the activity by the landing stages near the old Stroud Brewery. Some things change very little. Boats and boating, for example. It's quite surreal to sense the timelessness of the canal scene. We had a spot of lunch in the Brewery, then walked along the canal towards Stroud. The towpath had grown much wider, so that cyclists could thread their way through without intimidating pedestrians or falling off into the water, and the buildings had changed – some revamped industrial units, some housing, the latter fronting attractively onto the towpath. Eventually we reached the point where the Great Western Railway slanted across high above the canal and the river, found our way over the canal on a 'new' bridge and then down to the river. It was all very relaxing. I temporarily forgot my existential angst. We took a diversion down and along the river, suddenly into the deep cleft wooded valley of the Frome. The hum of the town was gone. Just the rippling stream, the rustle of leaves and occasional bird song. A few people. 'Often frequented by lovers, I'm told,' said Rufus. The dipper was busy on the rocks. We watched him for a while. Time seemed to have stopped here, in this magic place. Rufus pointed to evidence of water voles in the banks. He was disappointed, though, that the kingfisher did not flash past and the otter failed to make an appearance. I had seen both once in an earlier life.

We retraced our steps, crossed the river by the rapids on a very old bridge, then up the slope, and reached the area I knew as Rodborough Fields. Before my day there had been a battle royal to preserve them from housing development, to keep them as open fields. The clinching argument on appeal had been the amount of traffic generated, which would overload the narrow access roads.

I was not entirely surprised to see things had changed. The new development was elegantly done, with terraced houses, generously proportioned, and some four-storey flats, grouped around green spaces with play facilities, mini-allotments, trees, and, in one case, a gravel area for boules. Streets were like linear play areas for young children. Rufus got Sam – via his speaker-phone – to explain the estate: all affordable housing, a net exporter of solar power, and boasting the latest very efficient battery storage, shared water collection, a special bee and butterfly garden, and a selection of shared electric vehicles – bikes, rickshaws, and robocarts. I asked Sam how it was the precious fields had been lost. She said, 'It's not lost at all – this is a brilliant living area, and there's a lovely park further on. But to put it bluntly, as the population increased with migration, there was a desperate need to house people in accessible places, where they could get to things by foot and bike. Rodborough Fields was an ideal spot, so close to the centre of the town, and the development links to that stunning footbridge over river, road and canal. You know – the one you went across yesterday with Rufus. You'll see! You go across the beautiful community-run park first.

A little later I did indeed see. The park was part nature reserve, part recreational – it felt like a place for kids to go wild, back to nature. Then we crossed the elegant vaulted steel bridge, and some way over we looked down on what had once been an industrial estate. The area had been redeveloped at some point. Now, apparently, it was partly housing, but mainly acted as a warehouse, linked to the Sorting Station. I could see building materials in the outside space and there were robocarts coming and going along the old bypass, some quite large. Then we passed the Council Offices and station, and into town.

Time for lunch. Very tasty. Vegetarian. I was surprised at the number of small food shops and diversity of goods available, and no vacancies, when in my day it had been all booming hospitality but retail decline. After a bit of a wander we crossed the other big pedestrian bridge over Merrywalks, past old school and new housing to the huge superstore site. Tesco no longer! The building was still there, covered in solar collectors and repurposed as another warehouse – for non-perishable foodstuffs. The robocarts made deliveries to each neighbourhood in the Valleys at particular times of week. It was all designed to maximise efficiency and minimise electricity use. We reached Stratford Park. Beautiful as ever. The redwoods, planted over two centuries before, were touching the sky.

I found the kaleidoscope of images from the walk fascinating but discombobulating. I knew the whole area so well that I was finding it difficult to separate old from new in my head. It was like there were two realities competing. Rufus, trained in therapeutic psychology, saw my inner confusion and gently took me back 'home'. Some of the larger delivery robocarts had seats at the back, not very comfortable but serviceable. We hitched a lift on one going to Nailsworth, which dropped us on the main road in Woodchester.

I chilled out for the rest of the day, showering, making notes, drawing, resting, reading, then spent a social evening with the couple. Very relaxing.

*****

The plan for the following day, before an arranged meeting with two mystery guests to talk about health and social issues, gave me the opportunity I wanted just to mooch around, acclimatising, seeing how the place – this new town of Woodchester – worked, able to meet people without my guides. Space was exactly what I needed. I wanted just to be for a while, observing, chatting idly to local people. A shower of rain delayed my departure. Rufus insisted on displaying the hologram of the area, pointing out some of the key features of the town, then showing me how to use GPS on my wristband, but I also wanted a proper map. Cyla told me that paper maps no longer existed, except for professional use. It shouldn't really have been a surprise. Already in my day fewer and fewer people could read a map, instead just using their phones and blindly following routes that their app showed them. They would get lost if the phone lost connection or ran out of juice. My own training had made me a map addict. Cyla came to my rescue and provided an ultra-slim A4 pad that did have a map on it, easily scalable, with photo-images at will and real-time information available. Quite a nice toy!

I went out later, once the rain had washed the world anew, so the air was crystal clear and the sunlight glistened off wet surfaces. I felt reborn, ready for whatever fate next had in store. I wandered down to the square, the local centre I'd seen before. People were friendly but non-invasive; I really liked the atmosphere. There was a fair-sized Co-op, together with specialist food and convenience shops, a Bangladeshi restaurant, several reuse, repair or swap-shops and a large post office. Amazing! Post offices, along with banks, had been vanishing in my 'youth'. This post office was offering everything: not simply postal but the full range of financial services, including all the old banking services it seemed, as well as information and personal contact with loads of social and community services. A one-stop shop! It also had a coffee corner. I resisted temptation.

A big sign informed me the post office was a state-run corporation, sharing space with a joint West Country province and Stroud Valleys local authority advice centre. It seemed strange that it was still called the Post Office. Three people who I took to be of Bangladeshi origin were deep in discussion, one clearly an advisor at the centre. I noticed with some surprise that all the notices were in English, none in Bengali – thinking about all the effort Bristol made in my own time to be inclusive and multicultural.

A young man asked me if I was OK, could he help at all? Maybe I was looking a little uncertain, like a stranger. I said thank you, could he tell me the way to the community centre, thinking it was nice to ask someone, even though I had the pad. He looked at me oddly, maybe puzzled by my accent, but in a friendly manner gave me directions to what he very deliberately called the town hall. 'It's only five or so minutes' walk away,' he said. Then I asked him about the lack of notices in any language other than English. Again he looked oddly at me, and speaking slightly as it were to a child, or a person of little brain, he said, 'Well, of course, it's not necessary, everyone has wristies or mobiles that can do instant translation. I think there is also the belief of some people that it provides an incentive to learn English. I'm not sure about that myself. Everyone here speaks good English anyway, the learning requirement is universal and the provision for learning so engaging. '

I thanked him and made my way to the 'town hall', recognising the old village streets. I was shocked to discover that the town hall had a steeple. It was the Victorian gothic parish church I'd once sung in! Repurposed. The churchyard seemed now less a cemetery, more of a park. The south roof was glinting black, not the normal Cotswold buff. Made of solar panels, I thought. I went into the building with some trepidation, to be assailed by toddler noise – a preschool group at the back of the church. Actually it was well screened from the main space, and under a kind of balcony, very elegantly done. The main space, despite the pillars and vaulted ceiling, no longer felt like a church. There was a stage and wall hiding the chancel area, and refreshments in one of the aisles where some older people were chatting.

I found my way to the east end, beyond the wall. What had been the holy of holies, with high altar and choir stalls, now had a mezzanine, supported independently of the outside walls. I couldn't immediately gather what happened up there, but down below it was clearly a kind of library, a few people studying at screens. Some books were lovingly displayed on a stand, as if ultra-precious, and rather to my surprise I recognised many of them:

Shakespeare's Tempest, Pilgrim's Progress, Gulliver's Travels, The Time Machine, News from Nowhere, Brave New World, 1984, The Chrysalids, The Handmaid's Tale, and others not known to me … all utopian or dystopian tracts. The germ of an idea formed in my head. Maybe I should write up this future world.

There was a young lad sorting documents at a desk, no more than a boy. I asked him about this place. 'Oh, this is the History Centre,' he said, as if it were obvious, and went on, clearly on a mission. 'The old books and maps are very precious now, as you know. Upstairs is amazing. There's quite a collection but we have to restrict access. Then we have special displays down here every month. Last month it was Woodchester history, right back to the Roman times, even pre-Roman. We were completely packed out. Everybody seemed to want to know about it. This week it's imagined futures. Then over there's a more permanent exhibition about the new town plan, interactive maps and explanations, really good, even I can understand it! Then in that corner we've got living history – you know, recordings of what old people can remember, before the Bad Times, early on.'

'So when was all this started?' I asked. 'When was the church converted?' 'Oh, ages ago, at least ten or twenty years ago. They told me that when the climate refugee influx happened and the new plan was made, the town council decided to rescue the semi-derelict church. And they wanted to tell all the newcomers about the history of the villages.' 'So as to kind of ground them in their new home?' I asked. 'Er, yes, I guess so.'

He then volunteered his own situation: 'I'm just here two days a week, keeping an eye on everything and you know, helping along.' He saw my slightly puzzled expression, 'Let off the Bacca grind actually. Well, sent off here, it's part of my Community Service. I'm doing it over two years – something different next year, outdoors I think. It's very strict! But so interesting too, meeting people, having to be organised!' 'What? No-one here to guide you?' He looked oddly at me again. 'Of course there is! She's in touch all the time. Has her beady eye on me. There whenever I need her.' I realised with a jolt – remote management was commonplace.

I was keen to know more about the design of the town, but thought my ignorance was getting too obvious – and risky. I thanked the guy and found my way into the elegantly screened north aisle. To my surprise it had retained its religious function: altar, crucifix, communion rail, seats in serried ranks. I thought I even detected incense in the air, but that might have been just the power of suggestion. So traditional religion, Church of England style, has not been banned, I thought, simply hived off into a corner.

I went back into the main space and across to the chatzone and cafe. There was a big notice advertising a grand event on Sunday morning, under the heading ONE EARTH COMMUNITY – apparently involving music, dramatic readings, global environment sharing and communal songs. I asked the elderly woman who was serving refreshments, about the event. 'Oh, are you new here?' she said, with a definite Cotswold twang. 'Well, it's every Sunday, very welcoming to people of any religion and none, very enjoyable, so artistic, lovely socially, really inspiring. And, it does what's on the tin. All these ongoing crises around the world, it helps us understand all about them.' I was impressed. I ordered a flat white and asked about joining in. 'Just turn up, dear. Now, we always make a point of being personal here! Trying to be inclusive. My name is Lily. What's yours?' I was a little abashed and felt myself blushing, momentarily tongue-tied. 'Er … Robyn. I'm er … er... new here.'

I realised I was in danger of getting out of my depth and looked at the time, but my wristy was instead saying 'back off!' Rufus! He was watching me! 'Oh, so sorry,' I said, 'I've got to get on, thanks so much for telling me about the event. I'd better swig down my coffee and go.'

A little later I headed for the new secondary school, following the map, passing a primary school as I went. It was clearly break time. The older kids were noisily erupting into the adjacent public park. There seemed to be rather a dearth of responsible adults – I did spot one eventually. The children, all sizes, colours and temperaments, started games and random socialising. As I walked past them a few of the older ones came over, bold but very friendly, and asked me where I was from. I was astonished at their lack of caution, also surprised that they immediately spotted me as a stranger. In my time children were taught to avoid eye contact with strangers, and anyway would have been corralled within the school grounds. No-one allowed in or out. Fortress schools! I responded to the kids that I was a time traveller from Manchester. They liked that. They wanted to know about the Mancunian climate, 'in your time' – was it as wet and miserable as rumour has it? I confirmed their worst suspicions, and avowed that Gloucestershire was much nicer. Then it was the question I'd hoped to avoid: which team did I support? Seeing the teacher looking quite sharply at me, I made to move smartly on, saying, 'Oh, you mean in Rugby League?' The kids laughed and went away happy. I reflected it was like déjà vu. Stroud was now like the Netherlands in my own time. My urban design course had included a trip to Rotterdam, and I'd been amazed at the direct and open way children treated us students, asking about why we were there. They had been really curious, and I loved meeting them. However, thinking about the exchange with these children now, I chastised myself for reinforcing stereotypes of the north.

The secondary school, when I got there, was a quite different animal from my expectations. It was called Woodchester Gymnasium and seemed to have everything going on in it. The young people were mostly invisible in classes, but as I explored – to my surprise it was completely open – I could see there were also adults in social groups, a resource centre where young and old mixed, physical activities galore going on. I was impressed to see a doctors' surgery as part of a healthy living centre, with trainee kitchen and organic cafe linked in. There were beautiful green spaces, including a productive garden with mini-allotments and a community farm rich in wildlife. Trees framed the facilities, offering shade and diverse habitats. People were everywhere, doing things: it was a fantastic social, educational and health hub. I talked to one of the gardeners. She lived locally, a writer, and spent two hours a day either growing things or going on long runs with the club based there. She told me that Woodchester had been so lucky to get the investment in this integrated facility, courtesy of the Bangladeshi and Bengali influx.

One of the bigger allotments was being managed by children. I talked briefly to their teacher, who said the class 'owned' this patch, and they were experimenting with salad veg, beans, wheat and oats. I could see that the tomatoes were already doing well, despite it being only spring. The children (about twelve years old maybe) prepared the ground, planted, grew, picked, ate, saved seed for next year. There were hens in the corner. Some of the children were keen to tell me all about them, their names and characters and what they ate (waste food included). No artificial fertiliser was allowed so chicken manure, they said, was essential for soil productivity. The droppings were added to a huge compost heap. The teacher told me they will harvest the wheat and oats later, in a couple of months, and go through the whole process of winnowing, making flour, making bread. Then eating their own-grown lunch of salad, eggs and bread – and biscuits and flapjacks too. Fantastic, I thought!

He went on: 'The trick is to make it also a real scientific experiment. For example, growing some lettuce in soil with compost added, by comparison with just soil. Do they grow differently? How much? Kids are naturally curious. Then also I have to admit competition comes into it, they love competing with other classes. Who can grow the biggest cucumbers? And they're tremendously concerned about the future of the planet, and how to feed ourselves sustainably is a big part of that.' He smiled broadly. 'I just love this lesson! I can introduce learning about horticulture, diet, cooking, health, science, maths, human and physical geography out of it, basing it all on their own experience.'

Aren't you hidebound by the official curriculum?' I asked. 'Good Lord no! Where were you brought up? A core principle of national guidance is learning by doing, so this subject plays right into it. Didn't you experience things like this? Maybe you were in some inner city school struggling to find space? Not that it's my business.' I laughed off his disbelief. 'Just looking for the logic,' I said. 'I've not really got to grips with educational theory. You've been so helpful! Thanks a million!'

My mind and heart were filled to the brim with the morning's experiences. At one level it all seemed like commonsense – straightforward, obvious – but at another level I found it extraordinary that England had grown so community-oriented, so socially together. My knowledge of twentieth century history was poor, but my mentor, Able, later compared what I found with the period after the Second World War, when there was a short-lived era, maybe a couple of decades, when social freedoms were valued above individual freedoms. Maybe the existential global crises, which I did not yet properly comprehend, had engendered the same shared awareness a century later.

Time was passing. My rendezvous with Rufus and the doctor was not until 16.00. I really wanted to visit the Common again – Rodborough Common – where I'd spent so much time in my youth, enjoying the fresh air, walking Mum's dog and slurping ice cream. I found an alternative path up the hill to the one Rufus had taken me the previous day. Very civilised it was, beautifully designed, though steep and needing maintenance. My professional hat came on rather sharply: where do the pushchairs and wheelchairs go? Looking at the map-pad, I saw the answer: an alternative, much longer, easily graded route. How bountiful is that!

The steep path wended through woods. The people I met were friendly, greeting me in a rather clipped way. Sounded like either 'low' or 'more'. It took me a while to work out – short for 'hello' and 'morning'. Instinctively, being a well brought up gal, it felt lazy to me.

When I reached the open grassland at the top, the sun was shining. The Common was alive with hawthorn bushes, the may in profusion. Orchids were just beginning to go over and the cows were already out – very early, I considered, it was still April. The seasons seemed rather out of joint. However, the overpowering sense for me was one of comfort and familiarity, the timelessness of the place. I wandered past the clump of pine trees, some clearly young replacements, full of nostalgia. That was where we had often picnicked, when I was younger, playing 'sporting croquet' on Dad's rare visits. 'Sporting' because of uneven ground and cowpats. I felt quite emotional, but the usual tears refused to come. That was puzzling – such a powerful tug back to my previous reality could have had me bursting with loss. Yet I was keeping my cool. Right, time for an ice cream! I thought. I wonder if the ice cream factory is still there, at the edge of the Common? I made my way over, delighted at the paucity of traffic. In the small quarry car park there were two taxis and a line of e-bikes with neat trailers. Not for kids, by the look of them. Dogs! The dog-walkers were still at it!

I arrived at the ice cream factory. It had grown! My internal policy bureaucrat was affronted. It was completely against conservation rules! However, my reaction moderated when I realised it now offered lunch as well as ice cream. I munched through a delicious goat cheese and salad sandwich, with a Stroud Brewery beer, then rum and raisin ice cream. I didn't seem to need to pay – just waived my wristband, and the robot serving me seemed happy. It was distinctly odd. The bot had stylised movements, rather angular, but with a well-modulated voice, a beautiful face, and clearly trained to manage sales.

I sat outside on the grass gazing at the view of Stroud, reflecting on all the changes in everyday, mundane life, and in social organisation. I felt there were worrying autocratic elements all too evident, but otherwise there was a very socially aware, civilised feel. I was struck, for example, that teachers seemed to be less hamstrung by national policy than in my day, and Woodchester Town Council had been able to take creative initiatives. It was confusing. I wondered if all the positive things could only be sustained by sensitive centralised control – 'maternalistic', Rufus had called it. The attendant risk was that if a populist demagogue or market fundamentalist gained power then the sensitivity would be sacrificed. Were there safeguards perhaps? The local government structure in the West Country Province and Stroud Valleys suggested that local control was to an extent embedded.

Something else puzzled me. People talked about financial difficulties since the Bad Times, and there were signs of that in the environment (though less than I'd experienced in the twenty-teens and twenties). But the overall quality of life seemed far better than could have been expected. How to square that circle? My brain could not engage with all the complexities. I started musing, wondering how my old world could possibly transition to this.

My wristy beeped. Rufus had sent me a message. Time to return to base. He added that the robo-police had contacted him, not to worry, but someone I'd met or seen that morning had expressed concern at a seeming stranger wondering round at large, and unfamiliar with commonplace things of modern life. Of course, I was immediately worried and rang Rufus. 'Ah!' he said, 'it's the Town Hall. Your identity is automatically screened when you go in and is checked against a database. Maybe the AI monitor found something in your artificially constructed history less than convincing. Don't worry, we'll sort it. See you soon.'

That was it. It rather took the gloss off my overall warm feeling about the day's explorations. I wended my way back down into the valley by the easily graded route. If I met people, I greeted them, which seemed expected, but was cautious, not getting into conversation.

13
Health Equity

I was a little late for the meeting with Rufus and the medical people, so arrived at the meeting room in the Cohousing apologising profusely. 'No worries at all,' said Rufus. 'I've been following your progress all round about and up and down. Looks like you've had a really good explore. Now, tea?'

I should not have been shocked. I knew I was under surveillance. But nonetheless I was taken off guard, so failed to see immediately who was sitting at the table.

It was Sacha. Sacha who had peddled us from Stroud on my first day. I smiled and shook her hand warmly. She volunteered that she was a part-time taxi-rider and part-time health doctor – in fact, part of the small health unit based at the Woodchester Gymnasium. 'So you're a doctor, you prescribe medicines and so on!' I said. 'Fuck, no!' she said. Don't come to me with your scarlet fever or flu. No, if you're ill, go to my medical colleagues. And then only if you really need to. Self-treatment is all the rage these days – so much sound diagnosis and treatment is available on-line. No! The whole emphasis of the NHS nowadays is about keeping healthy in body and mind – public health as it used to be known. And that's where the health doctors come in.' She stopped and looked at Rufus. He nodded and laughed. 'You have started, so you'd better finish,' he said. Sacha obliged: 'I don't mean to be rude – I'm sure you're not personally defensive about it – but back then, early in the century – you didn't have a National Health Service at all. It was a National Illness Service! OK, the curative services were often impressive, but other than an immunisation programme, prevention of illness was sidelined and lots of official decisions made things worse, not better. The population grew progressively less healthy in the teens and twenties, their needs kept on growing – like their bodies! – all the funding went into acute care, into hospitals. Absolutely tragic. Life expectancy and years of healthy life were actually falling for poorer people. So shocking! You probably know much more about this than me. They only started the long process of correction in the later twenties. With so many built-in assumptions and vested interests it was like turning the Titanic. But they did! Radical change happened. A minor miracle.'

I looked at her with a mixture of astonishment and admiration. I hadn't listened to such a tirade, to such vehemence, since arrival. What she said resonated with my own training, trying to design 'healthy urban environments' in the face of contrary market pressures and a government which seemed wilfully blind – or maybe in the pockets of big pharma. At best trapped in its own bubble. And I had noted, in my own time, the rise in the death rate, and studied it.

'I'm afraid I'm all too conscious of the trends back then,' I said. 'Indeed, I remember that one of my lecturers in 2015 pointed to the appalling state of health in deprived city suburbs, and the fact that 2012 was the high point of longevity. It was downhill after that. It sticks in my mind that in some poorer neighbourhoods, men had an average of only fifty-five or so healthy life years, before becoming physically or mentally disabled. The women a bit longer. A quarter or a third of life was lived with a disability of some kind, preventing fulltime work or active retirement. And costing the 'NIS' – meaning us, the tax-payers – the earth.' I said 'NIS' with deliberate irony.

Having calmed down a bit, Sacha continued, 'I gather you've discovered our Gymnasium – our integrated education, health and activity centre? Yes? Well, it's all happening there. Children learn about food and exercise and healthy living, and dance and music and art as well – and some global issues – at a tender age, poor things! And adults are attracted in by all kinds of devious means to understand the mantra: healthy people, healthy places, healthy planet. People, place and planet! New residents are particularly drawn in, by personal invitation from the town mayor, so they get to know the ropes, the rules, and the people in a convivial environment. That's been really helpful for my compatriots. The women, the mothers, we give them special attention, because of traditional Muslim gender roles, and they learn good English really fast. No indulging the language barrier. We make sure it fades away. And they learn how to cook healthy Bangladeshi meals with British ingredients – cheaper and local. Quite tricky, but it's amazing what you can grow here, now, in this slightly warmer clime.'

'That's amazing!' I said, with enthusiasm. She went on: 'Yes, that's the situation, and it's born fruit. Most people live to seventy-five or eighty before they become seriously hampered by problems. And that's not because of anything sophisticated like brain or organ transplants. It's about living and loving and laughing healthily, and not being skint. Jesus! Some people seem to go on for ever! Anyway, that's my job. All about wellbeing!'

Sacha paused. Rufus seized the moment. 'We're so lucky to have Sacha here! She's a live wire. In a moment we'll have Edith too. You know – the mayor who welcomed you on your first day. She's a doughty campaigner for equality and has the ear of the bigwigs down in Bristol – in the provincial parliament. But before she comes, Robyn, anything that occurs to you? Questions for Sacha, comments on what she's just told you?'

I hesitated. There was so much in my head. 'Well … in my day the public health officials I met seemed mostly to be concerned with drugs, drink, food – and sex.' I laughed. 'I suppose you've banned all those now?' Rufus was kind enough to grin at my joke – though in my mind it was a barbed reference to the increased state control that I perceived. Sacha guffawed, maybe delighted at my bravado, then steamed on: 'Not at all, not at all! Quite the reverse!' She told me that all the more common addictive drugs were now legal, some available only on prescription, and drug addiction was treated as an illness not a sin, so the petty crimes that once fed the drug habit had largely gone. There were still issues because new lethal drugs did appear from time to time but the authorities were quick to act.

'Not so good on booze, though,' she said. 'There's still some alcoholism and occasional alcohol-fuelled violence. It's so deeply embedded in the culture. Actually, the high number of Muslims here in this town has begun to shift social mores away from drink. And we've made big strides in treating alcoholism. We're also working on a form of gene therapy – though after two or three generations it's still a work in progress. Healthy diet – yes, that's improving. Some old American fads have been abolished. Almost. As for sex – well, we encourage it! It's good for you.' She claimed that some of the risks related to sexually transmitted diseases, unwanted pregnancy, sexual abuse and even rape, had been eradicated.

I was just about to ask how the risks have been managed so successfully, when, to my frustration, Edith burst into the room. 'So sorry I'm late! I've just been told there's a crisis. We may need a change of plan. But I don't want to interrupt!' She pressed her lips together, pantomime style, and waggled her head. Rufus smiled broadly: 'Don't worry! You've interrupted comprehensively, we were just getting into sex! But Edith, what's the crisis?'

Edith was looking at her wristy, said something into it, took a moment to answer him. 'I'm afraid I've been called back to the Council Chamber in Ebley. My co-mayor is holding the fort but would like backup. There's a crowd of libertarians making a racket about the latest parish energy guidelines. Would you like to come with me? I'll probably not get directly involved – I'm much too sharp-tongued, while my colleague is silver-tongued. There should be time to have our discussion.'

Rufus said: 'Yes, fine, let's do that, if it's alright with you both, I'll call a taxi?' Sacha and I nodded. The taxi must have been close by. It was just outside the Cohousing when we reached the entrance – a social taxi, with seats facing each other. As we travelled, Edith explained more: 'Really odd alliance, this libertarian group – between extreme left-wing anarchists and extreme right-wing capitalists. At least that's my take on them. What they share is a total distrust of government and top-down diktat. We've recently tightened up the energy self-sufficiency requirements for parishes and town councils, which I tell you, is absolutely necessary if we are to be carbon neutral and avoid overloading the grid with all this decentralised electricity generation. OK, it is top-down, but I argue it also gives more power to localities. Each community has to work things out for itself – in terms of building and transport and commercial efficiency and how best to make electricity. It empowers communities to take control of their own eco-footprint. That's what I would say to these anarcho-capitalists!' Sacha chipped in: 'Yes, Edith. I'm convinced about your strategy, but not about your tactics. More could be achieved by voluntary co-operation, I'm sure. The latest rules are pretty draconian.' Edith came right back at her, and they continued their discussion for the rest of the journey. Rufus said nothing.

I was fascinated. It was the first time I'd heard any hint of political conflict. The fact that it was happening, live, here and now, gave me an obscure sense of hope. Despite the compulsory identity motes and so on, protest movements were alive and well. Maybe democracy had survived after all.

*****

When Edith had had a quick look at the ongoing protest, and we were safely ensconced in one of the Council committee rooms, Rufus brought us back to the issues of health and equality. He suggested an agenda: first mental and social wellbeing, then physical health and wellbeing, then the huge question of inequality. 'We've already touched on mental health issues a bit. Is there anything else you'd like to say about this, Robyn, before these women take the floor, and you can't get a word in edgeways? Britain in the 2020s maybe? I'd be very interested in getting your perspective. So will the psycho-history team.'

'Um ... OK,' I said. 'Bearing in mind I'm no expert. It's just what I pick up from news programmes and talking with members of what we call the chattering classes – which includes me of course!'

I launched off into some of the problems of the early twenties as I saw them: the pandemic and lockdowns; continuing austerity; loss of services like buses, youth clubs and road maintenance (which meant cycling was dangerous, and vehicles were getting damaged and scrapped earlier than they should have been); homelessness, fuel poverty, and housing stress as costs escalated but incomes didn't; mental and emotional distress (especially among poorer households, which I'd experienced when volunteering at the food hub), combined with totally inadequate mental health services; empty shops and the chaos of strikes; a sense of frustration and powerlessness and being trapped, fake news everywhere, and a feeling that one could no longer trust those in authority. And all this against the terrifying global backdrop of wars in Ukraine and Sudan and Palestine and existential worries about the climate. It took me quite a while to illustrate all that. They listened intently.

I stopped, suddenly conscious I was going on rather. 'Yes, all that is more or less what I'd heard,' said Sacha quietly. 'It must have been a difficult time.' I nodded, then thought of another issue I'd become very conscious of. 'Then there was social media,' I said. 'It seemed to compound all the other problems. When I was younger I experienced the huge pressure to conform, especially in body shape, face, hair, clothes. Then lockdown happened, education went online, no-one was allowed to visit friends. Kids and teenagers were abruptly isolated and social media became a lifeline, even more important, and mental health suffered.

'I think one real difficulty was the question of gender. Suddenly it seemed many teens were – more consciously and at a younger age than before – considering their sexual orientation and gender identity, with some deciding they were not comfortable with the bodies they had landed up in. As well as there being more information and more opinions available than in pre-internet days, I think it was all part of there being more tolerance, acceptance even, of difference, promoted by social media.

'Mind you, Facebook, Instagram and TikTok were all so addictive, and designed to hook people in and ultimately make profits from adverts. So kids were bamboozled by rumour, fake information and horror stories, anything to keep them online, often reinforcing their own fears and prejudices. Then there were computer games too. Many kids were stuck in their bedrooms, not going out. Teenagers seemed to have become addicts to me. It was a kind of atomisation of society, increasingly fragmented and sedentary, cut off from earthy reality. Social media was both good and bad. It enabled friendships and exchange even through lockdown. But also mockery and bullying any time of day or night. If you were hooked, you couldn't escape. I had a friend back then, in my teens, who was so worried about being thought unattractive that she stopped eating. She became almost just skin and bone, and wouldn't go out. A few unkind comments on Instagram sent her into a spiral of depression.' I paused, remembering her destructive state of mind.

'Christ!' said Sacha. You've given us quite an agenda there. What about physical health? What are your perceptions about that?' I realised to my surprise that I had less to say about physical health – despite all the political and media hype about COVID-19, cancer and so on. 'Well, all that sedentary lifestyle didn't do any good. People seemed to be getting more overweight and more obese. We talked about it as an epidemic, in fact. I read something about there being two tribes of people: the active and the inactive. The active played sports, did Parkrun, went to the gym, walked and cycled everywhere. Those who were inactive drove everywhere and slobbed about in armchairs. For active types like me it was a relief in the pandemic, there were hardly any cars on the road – we could walk down the middle of the road, kind of take ownership of the street. Though after lockdown the cars returned, and despite the increasing awareness of climate change, they were bigger than ever. One ran me down, and now

I'm here. It was odd, because at the same time there was a real upsurge in some sports, such as women's football and running clubs.'

I carried on. 'Oh, I must tell you about my experience in the States. I went to Birmingham, Alabama (I put on a mock American accent – very naughty!) for a conference, sent by my firm. It was shocking: nobody walked anywhere and everybody was fat. In some suburbs you actually couldn't walk anywhere because there were no pavements. Shops next door to each other had huge car parks, but there was no way for pedestrians to get from one shop to another. We were shown one big church with a massive car park, and there were a couple of four-seat buggies going round collecting people to go the hundred metres or so to the building. And even at the university in the centre of the city – where there were no shops at all! – they asked us, the English group, if we wanted a taxi to take us to the hotel, which was a five-minute walk away! Quite extraordinary!'

'That's very interesting,' said Sacha. 'I've been very much aware of the problem of obesity back then, especially in America, and their dietary habits and size of helpings, but it's fascinating to hear your Alabama experience on their total car dependence.'

'The thing in Britain,' I went on, 'it seemed to be very much a cultural thing. You had the fast food tribe and the organic cafe tribe, which more or less equated to working class culture and middle class culture, though it was a bit controversial to say that and of course it was not a rule, just a tendency. Professional people were less likely to be obese. When I was working from home I'd often pop into the Stroud town centre for a coffee or something, and really noticed it, looking in at the different cafes. The other thing I noticed, on weekdays, was the number of people who were clearly down on their luck, looking downcast, depressed, just shuffling around because maybe they had no money, a few begging. Totally different on Friday and Saturday when rich people came in from all the villages around for the markets. The contrasts were very striking. And worrying.'

'That's fascinating,' said Sacha and Edith together, as I paused. They laughed and Edith nodded to Sacha, so she continued. 'Well, Robyn, we've done research into past trends, albeit hampered by the loss of so much data in the Bad Times, and it all confirms your observations. We often have to rely just on printed reports and books that have survived. I'll try to summarize what we know.

'After a century of progressively longer and healthier lives, it all went into reverse in the teens and early twenties – most especially and disastrously for poor people, who bore the brunt of the financial squeeze, and felt disenfranchised and powerless. Household income was and is an absolutely critical determinant of health. I've read quite a lot about this. Poverty was caused by three major factors: economic decline, austerity and a housing crisis. After the financial crash of 2008 the economy flatlined; in fact GDP per capita actually went down, because at the same time the population was increasing with high immigration. People were getting poorer, and that was exacerbated by years of austerity which drastically cut local services and generally reduced public sector pay levels. Meanwhile the housing sector was broken, in the sense that people were having to pay more and more for housing while their real income went down, often being forced to find accommodation far from their work or family connections, then needing to buy one car per adult in order to reach places they needed to. At the same time they could see a small but significant minority of people raking in huge bonuses, buying up lavish second homes, driving expensive vehicles, flying in private jets. It was clear after the pandemic that society's values were arse about face. Lockdown showed people that socially essential jobs were poorly paid, often on the bottom rung, while inessential jobs got the cream. Books were written showing that that unequal societies make for poorer health outcomes. The USA was a case in point, with the highest GDP in the world but much lower life expectancy – by five years or so – than other more equal countries. The States have still not cut that Gordian knot. Not entirely achieved here either, though we are well on the way.'

Sacha paused, then went on: 'If people are forced to live away from family and friends that can lead to isolation and loneliness. Being car-dependent means less active travel – walking and cycling – therefore less healthy exercise and casual street socialising. And all that traffic in your day made the streets unfriendly, noisy and polluted anyway – kids not allowed out as they would have been in earlier generations, women perceiving the streets as dangerous. One study of England showed that health inequalities led to a million people dying early in just one decade. Of course, there were good things going on, especially in the arts and the voluntary sector. I'm sure you could point to some of them. But governments of all colours were generally getting it wrong, believing in central control or believing the markets would sort things out – emasculating communities and local authorities. Well, the markets didn't! And central diktats are often costly, misjudged and inefficient. It was entirely predictable that health and wellbeing would suffer.'

She paused. We sipped tea. I reflected that Sacha did not seem aware of the irony that the people outside were protesting about centralised diktats. I could not work out where this society really was – how it balanced freedom and order. I wanted to understand how Britain got from the doldrums of the twenties to the present apparently happier state.

Edith intuited my need. 'So the question is, how did we turn all this around? Because, as I hope you can see, we have! Two-thirds of a century is a long time. We've been to rock bottom and back again. Now we have a lower GDP per capita, allowing for inflation, but far better human outcomes. I'm going to tell you about three things: education, fiscal policy and decentralisation.'

'Just thinking about schooling. What was it the Jesuits used to say? Give us a child up to the age of seven, and we have her for life. Actually, I suppose they said 'him'! In any case, quite authoritarian. None of this kowtowing to the child, asking them to decide what to eat, what to wear, what to do, when to play on their phones. I'm a bit of a stickler for clear boundaries myself – giving youngsters maximum freedom, opportunity and responsibility within very clear boundaries. Schools, now, as I think you saw, are open, community centres, drawing parents and guardians into the education process. We also have technical ways of training young minds, so kids with learning difficulties can be helped to realise their full potential. Though playing with minds chemically or electronically can be risky, can be expensive, so it's not often done. Personally, I'm against it. Most of what we do today is not so radical. Just very wide-ranging and socially inclusive.'

'Now I want to talk about older children. Ironically the very project that was supposed to make teenagers grow up – mass higher education – was in some ways counter-productive. They were being spoon-fed, especially by module websites, the internet and artificial intelligence. Almost kept as academic pets, with a kind of extended adolescence, their bad behaviour indulged. Contrast that with kids in the Middle Ages, expected to take adult responsibilities from puberty. And they did. Of course, that went along with awful conditions – like girls leaving home and married to older men at 14. Boys training for battle or sent up chimneys or down mines. But the point is, by their mid-teens young people are quite capable of tackling many adult activities – and are often more on the ball than their elders. And your society, Robyn, had systematically reduced teenage choice, except for academic study, which for the less academically inclined was demotivating and even demoralising.

'Anyway, early mid-century, across Britain, we ensured that secondary education gave a more varied diet: in terms of skills, cultures, social and intellectual perspectives. We introduced the Bacca – the Baccalaureate – a replacement for A-levels. Learning subject matter for exams had become less necessary as IT systems were so advanced. Even foreign language teaching had been taken over by robots and instant translation too. I have very mixed feelings about that. I believe you can only really understand another culture, like the French or the Japanese, if you can understand the language of the people. Putting that aside, the other big innovation was that we introduced the system of National Community Service, compulsory for every young person, earning their keep, a basic wage. It's very flexible, responding to personal wishes and attributes, providing incredibly useful social and environmental services, including military service for those who wish it. It's a real training in discipline and caring for others, caring for the earth, not just yourself. Responsibility and learning! That's what it gives! Treating young people as pre-adults. This went along with having earlier lowered the age of majority from eighteen to sixteen – giving them the vote, then later sexual freedom and financial rights. Childhood stops at sixteen now. It's worked wonders for young people's mental wellbeing, and physical wellbeing too. It was a real revolution in thinking – so overdue!'

'Yes' said Rufus, 'Robyn and I saw something of Community Service when we toured the countryside. Part of the Water and Wildlife project.' Edith nodded approval. I added, 'I was really impressed, it was lovely.'

Edith was on a roll – not to be deflected. She moved on to fiscal policy, explaining how change started in the thirties and was really still work in progress, as the overwhelming weight of evidence gradually shamed recalcitrant governments into action. It was a revolution in tax and benefits. The tax regime moved from VAT – Value Added Tax – which hit the poor more than the rich, to a carbon and pollution tax, which forced producers to change tactics. Apparently there were some painful transitions as that change occurred. Also a wealth tax was introduced and National Insurance amalgamated with income tax. Internationally there was growing instability during the Bad Times and governments moved to safeguard national security in energy and food and technology, so a nationalist motive combined with an environment motive to increase local self-sufficiency. Then she told me about the Life Grant, first introduced in the sixties. Everyone gets a basic income or grant. Edith told me that it has simplified administration, abolished the poverty trap, and helped people to feel more equal, working wonders for morale and wellbeing.

I was incredulous. 'You don't mean to tell me that people get paid just to live? No need to work?! Doesn't that induce idleness and boredom? And who on earth pays?' 'Good questions,' said Edith. Rufus responded: 'Robyn, if you can hold fire, the best person to explain all that is Able. He knows the background to the Life Grant, and so much else. We'll arrange a meeting for you in a day or two.'

Edith went on: 'OK, that's fine Rufus. So, the third, critical thing: decentralisation. We at last had a series of governments that believed in local democracy. Districts and provinces were given power and responsibility and financial muscle, more on the continental model. That has worked a treat! Services are more responsive to local problems and opportunities. You know, there were studies even last century which proved that if you were trying to create local jobs the last thing to do was rely on central government initiatives – many times more expensive per job than local agencies. Governments hadn't wanted to know. It was a question of accepting that with localisation there would be what used to be called a postcode lottery, and central government could say, you decide how to do this. If you manage to overcome local resistance to change, then the benefits accrue. Lower taxes. Profits from exporting energy and water to less well-endowed communities. Local authorities learn from each other how to do things better. Co-ordination and efficiency increased, inequality reduced, health improved, communities flourished. Housing and transport were big learning areas. They were transformed, and as a direct result the effective incomes of poorer households were increased, eventually much higher, because the cost of the right dwelling in the right place was much less. You should ask others about this – it's not really my forte. There are still areas of inequity, too many in my opinion, but overall …'

An alarm rang. Edith stopped and looked at her wristy. Abruptly she got up, shook her head and apologised, saying something about the demonstration. 'Got to go and play good cop, bad cop,' she said. She shook herself down, looked at us – and made a calm, deliberate exit.

ഇൗ

14
Diktat v Democracy

We all shifted in our chairs. Rufus winked at me, as if to say, just go with the flow, don't worry. He was looking at his wristy. 'They've occupied the council chamber,' he said. 'Would you like to go and see? We can hopefully stay out of the way on the balcony. Sacha was immediately keen – she knew some of the people involved. I shrugged, not knowing what might happen. We moved to the balcony. About a hundred people were in the chamber. There was quite a level of noise. One elderly woman was addressing the crowd. From what she said she was clearly a parish councillor, and vociferously complaining about SVA – Stroud Valleys Authority – forcing households to invest in water storage and replace their stone roofs with solar collectors, and because they hadn't, they were faced with unfair bills. She went on quite a while, citing what she considered ridiculous demands. Many in the room were nodding.

When she stopped, a man who I later found out was the co-mayor, got to his feet and demanded right of reply. Some in the crowd jeered, but others quietened them down. He spoke quite conversationally, quietly, but absolutely to the point, explaining what I already knew from Wulf: the

150

local authority had no choice because of climate rules about local self-sufficiency from the British and provincial governments. SVA had devised a scheme that gave as much flexibility to parishes as possible. The higher charges reflected actual costs when parishes had to import resources and/or export pollution. It was a not-for-profit system. He illustrated the degree to which rumour could exaggerate problems – for example, solar power could be collected in many ways and so would not necessarily require the removal of stone roofs. Parishes could work together in partnership, playing to each other's resource strengths, enabling the parish cluster as a whole to be energy and water self-sufficient.'

As he went on the grumblings grew again, one guy shouting out, 'tyrants, the lot of you!' Suddenly Edith appeared at her partner's side. 'So, who should pay?' she bellowed. 'Most villages are rich. They use more water and energy per person than the towns. They can collect more too. Why should the towns subsidise them? You all support community action and private enterprise. Don't sponge off others! Get your own act together!'

The contrast in the two mayors' styles couldn't have been more marked. The Chamber had gone quiet, due to the strength of her intervention. Then debate resumed, in more muted tones. Edith's co-mayor gave chapter and verse, statistics of energy and water use and the potential of particular settlements. 'The obligation is on each parish, or group of parishes, to do their bit, combating and coping with climate change, making for a fair and sustainable society.' People started arguing amongst themselves. A man who seemed to lead the protesters took the floor, thanked the mayors, and suggested the group review the situation and decide on next steps. Some people slipped out at that point. We followed suit.

'That was fun!' said Rufus. I asked what would happen now. Sacha told me it really depended how many people felt the same way as the protesters, and whether they persisted. There might be a formal public meeting in the Sub Rooms, to air the issues. If there were enough votes online then a local Citizens Jury could be instituted, to look into the questions raised and take not just views but expert evidence. There was quite a high threshold to get one established, and a jury involved a cross-section of people, not specifically the protestors. Such juries didn't happen often. When they did, they had legal force so could change local policy.

As we sat down again I asked Rufus to explain the robo-police query about me. Apparently it was the woman in the cafe at Woodchester Town Hall – who was well known as a bit of a gossip. Rufus had alerted his boss, who had contacted the Woodchester clerk, taken her into his confidence and explained who I was. It was no longer a problem, said Rufus, so long as social media and/or journalists were not alerted. He knew that the project AI unit was monitoring electronic traffic on our behalf. It was a warning to me – and made me nervous. I agreed with Rufus that extra caution and preparation was needed before I went out alone again.

Sacha was nodding agreement too. Then she took up the health and wellbeing theme once more, telling me how policy gradually evolved from funding very expensive and sometimes ineffective cures, back in my day, to much cheaper and more empowering prevention with the new NHS.

She said, 'in the thirties we learnt an awful lot from the Japanese, because they had managed to stamp out obesity in a generation. Quite amazing! Also rather draconian. In the workplace companies combatted sedentary lifestyles with diet and exercise regimes, enforced by fines from government on companies if their employees were unhealthy. And in schools they made healthy school meals free to all pupils. Very paternalistic, but it worked, and led to dramatic falls in diseases like type 2 diabetes and strokes. The Japanese became the longest-lived people in the world. Back then we also looked in depth at why the Finns were the happiest people in the world, despite the cold and the possible threat of being embraced by the Russian bear, and why Dutch children were the happiest in Europe, while British kids were quite the opposite. There were so many lessons about social attitudes, equality and services in Finland, and about children's freedoms and the attitudes to risk in the Netherlands. It took decades, but Britain gradually changed. The revival of local powers and responsibilities had a part to play. The provincial media became much more important as more decisions were being taken locally. West Country politicians found themselves subject to more rigorous challenge.'

I chipped in, 'you know, we knew all that about Japan and the Netherlands and so on even back in my day.' I told them my experience as a student in Rotterdam. 'That's fascinating,' said Rufus, 'from our vantage point it seemed that real understanding didn't happen until much later, but you're saying that many people were aware, fully aware of the truth of things even while the country was going to the dogs.' 'Of course,' I said, 'almost all the people I knew recognised we were heading down the wrong path. It was obvious! But not to those in power. Not to those with the money. They didn't want to know. Or rather, they paid lip service to the rhetoric of levelling up and climate resilience, while making only token gestures in those directions. It was all about political posturing and corporate greed!' The others were looking at me, apparently impressed.

I took a new tack. 'There's a question I wanted to ask. You know the COVID-19 pandemic of 2020 was a huge shock to the world. The worry, once it was over, was that another plague might be just round the corner. Has that happened?'

Sacha responded: 'Not recently, but yes, there were several scares in the first half century. None quite as traumatic as Covid, thank God. They studied the nature and causes of what we call 'zoonotic' diseases – diseases that are transmitted from animal to human, like HIV, ebola, swine flu and Covid – because they were increasing, rather alarmingly. And it became clear that our farming and trade habits were not helping. At some point the vast majority of countries banned the use of live animals in international trade and local food markets, including trade in pets. It was very controversial! We became more like Aotearoa, jealous of our own distinctive flora and fauna and natural ecology. All made pretty tricky as climate changed and habitats moved latitude, but nevertheless, after the crisis years the UN and WHO were given much more authority, so now we're geared up.'

I thanked her for that, while being conscious again of the huge watershed of the Bad Times. Edith had come back into the room while Sacha was speaking and now asked what I knew about those crisis years. I told her of the very helpful historical perspective given to me by Rufus and Sam. She grunted. 'Yes, good, history it may be, but for many people it still feels ... put it this way, I lived right through it, while these two whipper-snappers here were not yet thought of ...' She clearly needed to express her angst. Rufus indicated that the floor was hers. I looked receptively at her. 'It was devastating. A perfect storm. Everything seemed to happen at once. War, flood, drought, huge migrations, unemployment, solar peak activity. Just to give one year's catastrophes. As a child I remember it all too well – 2039. My parents told me that was just after a devastating cyber-attack which had wreaked havoc with bank transfers for months, plunging parts of the world into economic chaos. Then that summer the polar arctic ice melted completely, for the first time, reducing Earth's albedo. And there was a long drought in West Asia, East Africa and the Sahel, leading to water wars in several regions, while at the same time floods devastated Bangladesh, Bengal and Pakistan and migration reached epidemic proportions. It was all portrayed graphically in programmes for primary schools, including mine. That was just the beginning. It was downhill from there, for the best part of a couple of decades. Life was incredibly tricky. The sun blasted out lethal flares which almost catapulted us back to the stone age. The internet and GPS were devastated. We had to reinvent the basic tools of life. Of civilisation. The only bright side, a miracle, there was no nuclear war.'

She paused, breathing deeply. We all sat still. I felt cold, not wanting to hear. At length she recovered a little of her usual brusqueness, chin jutting, looking me in the eye, almost aggressive. 'All in the past now though! Everything changed. Gaia – and Apollo – put us through the mill. Taught humanity respect. For nature. And for each other. We're poorer now, but happier I think, living in what many recognise is really a special time. Working together for survival. Knowing it may not last. Armageddon may come again, but we'll be better prepared to face it.'

She stopped. Her body language was eloquent. I could see that her can-do brash persona hid an inner sadness. Rufus broke in. 'Thank you Edith. That puts things in perspective. A necessary corrective, maybe, after all the good news about society and health. It seems a good place to stop. Robyn, you'll be able to get another perspective on the Bad Times when you talk to Able – he has an interesting angle on the whole thing. However, the next two days are all about seeing more of our world.' To my delight he said that tomorrow we would go to The Black Mountains and have a good walk. And the day after to Gloucester to see how the city had evolved, including visiting the cathedral for a special event.

I thanked all three of them profusely, rather too earnestly no doubt. My mind was packed full of information and emotion. While the final outburst from Edith had put a damper on my spirit, underneath that I had a kind of inner glow. I'd got the sense of a humane, caring society, almost utopian, emerging out of horror.

*****

At supper that evening with Sam and Rufus I expressed my honest amazement at way things seemed to work, before succumbing later, amid the idle chatter, to a more pensive mood, returning to the issues of power and freedom, wondering whether this apparently maternalistic society had got the balance right between government diktat and individual or community choice. Then pondering the catastrophic mistakes of my own time. The Bad Times had not come out of the blue, they were manmade. The others listened to my angst, recognising it reflected debates in their society now. Things were not, they argued, brushed under the carpet. The confrontation in the Council Chamber illustrated the openness of democratic processes and the willingness of decision-makers to engage. 'At least in this case,' I said. Rufus pointed to the potential of citizens' juries to change policy, and gave some examples, where policy was obliged to follow the evidence, not party political interests.

Sam walked me back to my room. She was good! She jogged me out of my gloom by describing where we were going tomorrow, and what we would do – awakening my enthusiasm. I turned in early, daydreaming about mountains.

$\wp\!\!\sim\!\!\wp$

15
Mountains and microchips

Rufus and Sam were my delightful companions as we made our way through Wales to the Black Mountains. We had to catch the 8.00 coach from Stroud Rail'n'Bus Station, so an earlyish start to the day. In fact I woke before I had to, and lay awake puzzling in my mind about the low profile of advanced technology in the 2090s. Having grown up in an era of unconstrained IT expansion, I thought people would be full of microchips to overcome disabilities and increase their abilities; that we'd be watching hologram films and living much of the time in a virtual world; food would all be artificial, manufactured by 3D printers or some such;

that the internet of things would have taken control as artificial intelligence outstripped humanity. Yet what I experienced now was a strange mixture: technological magic in some spheres, back-to-nature – of a kind – in others, a sense of déja vu in still others.

I said something along those lines when Rufus and Sam arrived at my place for breakfast. Sam forestalled, conscious of the time: 'Robyn, Rufus, let's not get drawn into all that right now, if that's OK? We've got to eat and make sure we have everything we need for our expedition. Shall we make technology a discussion point tonight?' Rufus acquiesced – we should be back in good time this evening, and he could elucidate all the tech problems then. I agreed. We tucked into a hearty breakfast and then got everything ready, preparing sandwiches for our trek. The walking boots they had bought for me after a scan of my feet fitted perfectly – to my surprise.

I love mountains. I was looking forward to the hard exercise and the sense of freedom and the open sky. The weather forecast for the mountains was mixed: sunny intervals and showers. We took a robo-coach from Stroud across the Severn over a bridge I'd not seen before, some way south of Gloucester, which accommodated trains, buses and bikes, but not cars. Then on through the Forest of Dean, picking up the old A40 dual carriageway from Monmouth to Abergavenny. The coach was very informative, if one chose to listen on the earphones, providing a very well-judged commentary, neither too busy nor too bland. We could even type a query on the pad in front of us and be answered with perspicacity.

The Forest was still the Forest, steeped in ancient mining and wool traditions, a unique community – as I knew to my cost! It is essential for any outsider working there to try from the outset to accept their time-honoured customs. According to the coach, the Forest remained conscious of its difference. While many other towns in Gloucestershire had accepted substantial refugee populations, the people of Dean, we were told, fought them off, citing heritage and ecological arguments. However, as we went through Cinderford I saw that ethnic diversity had reached the town anyway – by the normal process of housing osmosis I presumed. The coach confirmed this and one of the images on the seat screen showed that the current mayor was black. Other aspects of the Forest had changed too. There seemed to be even more of it, more trees than before, and more of them deciduous. Judging by the visible clear-felled areas, the Forest was still a vital source of wood. There was much less traffic – that's what struck me powerfully. The area had a sense of peace and timelessness.

When we got down to the Wye Valley the age-old beauty of the place overwhelmed me. I asked the others if they would mind us making a stop here. The coach then dropped us off. There was another in an hour. We wandered along the riverside and found a glade to linger in, mature oaks all round, lush green mosses and lichens, spring flowers galore, chaffinches chattering, swallows swooping. Sam studied the flora, Rufus sat quietly musing (most uncharacteristic!) while I meandered around, looking and listening, moved by the place. I tried to remember the lines written near Tintern Abbey (in the Wye Valley) by William Wordsworth about "the joy of elevated thoughts … something far more deeply interfused …" It wouldn't quite come to me, but I knew what he meant.

Then we were back on the next coach and off again. A bit uncanny, the coach's voice was identical to the last one. 'They should give a separate character to each,' said Rufus. As we travelled along the dual carriageway beyond Raglan, I noticed that all vehicles were now using a single carriageway, one lane in each direction, moving like automatons. I asked the coach about this, and was assured that they were indeed all automatons, no human drivers allowed, so 100% safe. Every vehicle travelled at the set speed, which, the coach informed us, had recently been increased back up to 120 kph as there was no longer an energy shortage. Part of the other carriageway was now dedicated to cyclists, with the rest gradually returning to nature.

When we reached Abergavenny (now only Y Fenni on the sign!) I realised the town had swollen significantly. The robo-coach explained that parts of Wales had become increasingly popular as the climate warmed. Once people could work from home again, after the breakdown mid-century, many Bristolians moved to Y Fenni. We glided into the bus station, and as we disembarked I felt I should say thank you to the coach, which was ridiculous. But the coach responded, 'No problem. It is my duty.' Then after a quick chicoffee (not as good as the real thing, I have to say!) we took a shared shuttle-taxi up the Llanthony Valley into the heart of the Black Mountains, along the single track road that I remembered so well as a liability for cyclists and walkers. We met quite a lot of cyclists now –

on e-bikes. Apparently private cars had been banned in the sixties, except for some local trips, replaced by the shared taxi services.

The landscape had evolved. There were still sheep farms in the valley, but the marginal fields and bracken hillsides were now mostly fresh young deciduous woodlands. We had a glorious walk up and around the head of the valley, over Lord Hereford's Knob (which Rufus found very funny) and Hay Bluff, as the clouds bubbled up. The tops of the hills were still open heather moorland, though trees were beginning to colonise. Sheep and horses were few and far between, apparently rationed in the interests of biodiversity. I loved it all.

Back along Offa's Dyke the thunder rumbled and crashed. The heavens opened and deluged us. All good for the soul, said Rufus. I was beginning to like him a lot. He was so positive, optimistic, thoughtful and helpful too, with a lightness of touch which I would love to emulate. I liked Sam too – her youthful beauty and feisty character. Rufus told me that thunderstorms, which used to be more in July and August, were now common in spring.

One thing happened on the way along the ridge, which I feel I must record. For a rare moment the sun broke through the heavy grey clouds, and there, glowing in golden glory, was a cluster of gorse bushes in full flower. I told the others an old saying, with a chuckle, 'when gorse is out of flower, kissing's out of season'. I said it quite innocently, rather pleased to be so relaxed, but my body was ahead of me, lurching towards Rufus as we walked. He cried, 'So what are we waiting for?' I was momentarily startled, but in fact he was eyeing up his girlfriend. She promptly leapt into his arms and they amorously embraced.

I was nonplussed by their uninhibited behaviour, and felt a bit excluded and embarrassed. But then Sam released herself and declared, 'we can't leave you out, Robyn, you must have a kiss too! As your guardian, Rufus has to behave himself.' 'Ethics,' he said, mock ruefully. 'But I don't!' laughed Sam. She came to me and I found myself kissing her on the lips – not quite with gay abandon, but warmly nonetheless. I laughed in mixed awkwardness and delight. 'Kissing is good for you!' she said. 'More another time!' We walked on steeply up. My pulse was racing. I calmed it down, telling myself not to get worked up, to accept life more casually – that I was in my thirties, not my teens.

On the way back to the Stroud Valleys by robo-coach, I saw again how Y Fenni had expanded. Rufus, Sam and I discussed the growth of towns, the growth of population. Rufus told me Gloucester had almost doubled in size over the century. To me it was surprising that Britain had allowed in so many immigrants, knowing the suspicion, and sometimes antagonism, that people of different colour or culture raised in the traditional British breast. I was remembering the battles over refugees coming across the Channel in flimsy boats.

Rufus had done his homework. 'Actually,' he said, 'the 2020s saw the biggest influx of legal migrants up to that time. The boats were just the illicit icing on the legitimate immigrant cake.' I reacted saying what a totally odd metaphor. He had to agree, going on to explain how traditional British attitudes had gradually changed. The years of global crisis had engendered the sense of an Earth-wide community – everyone in it together. The sheer scale of death and destruction, refugee movements, consequent violence in some places and brutal local wars shocked the world. The poorer countries of the global south took the brunt of climate impacts, though least able to cope with those impacts. Refugees – the upper and middle class from threatened areas, those with money – headed for more temperate climes, depleting home-country skill levels. There was a kind of knock-on effect as Africans settled in the Mediterranean zone while some Spaniards, Italians and Greeks moved north. The United Nations brokered agreements between nations, like Britain and Bangladesh, trying to maintain social balance. It was a question of either heat and drought deaths on an alarming scale, with uncontrolled migrations and vicious conflicts as nations tried to stem the tide – or manage the process. The fact of falling populations in many of the richer countries helped to open doors. Millions had come to this country, rebalancing the ageing population, often bringing valuable skills and initiative, to be settled in carefully distributed new settlements or regeneration zones, with an absolute obligation to learn and speak English and engage with their new culture, while still celebrating their old one. Sam considered the whole process, and the welcome given to climate refugees, to be amazing, unprecedented. I absolutely agreed, barely believing it was possible.

We resisted the temptation to take an hour off in a Forest of Dean pub and got back home in good time. Cylahome, which serviced all units in the Cohousing, had been instructed to get food ready. A tasty vegetarian stew was waiting for us. Once appetites were sated and we could take time to converse, Sam invited me to rehearse my puzzles about technology – especially its low profile. I was quite replete, lounging back on the settee with a half pint of ale and the smug expression of someone who has had a great day out walking the high hills. Not perhaps at my most cogent: 'Well … what's odd, you know, early in the century, things were moving so fast. But now – OK there are amazing things, but how is it my wristy can't play any music that I want? And the pad you gave me: why can't it play films and shows? Things seem to have gone into reverse. Or is it all a malign plot to shield me from the actual shock and horror of the present world and getting to know too much – like you were saying after the Greek Games?'

Rufus responded, frowning slightly: 'Ah! You've rumbled us! Yes, there is an element of protection, but it's much more than that. It's complex. Crises galore! Telecommunications crises. But don't ask me, I've got rather a jaundiced view of the whole digital world. Ask Cyla. She can't knowingly tell a lie!'

I didn't need to ask. Cyla responded to Rufus's voice as well as mine, and clearly had been listening in. She said: 'You are being protected from communication overload. The Time Travel team know from experience that travellers from an earlier age cannot grasp the full complexity of the contemporary era – the local and international news, debate, social media and artistic activity – without potentially harmful psychological trauma. The strategy is to carefully programme your introduction to this world, allowing you to absorb the new reality at a manageable rate.

'However, it is also true that the use of electronic and wireless technologies is rationed for everybody. Earlier in the century, coinciding with challenging targets for carbon reduction, there was a geometric increase in electricity demand, driven by international data centres, artificial intelligence, electric vehicles and global internet activity. Combined with some criminal activity, cyber-attacks and unexpected intensity of solar storms – this proved unsustainable and led to the catastrophic breakdowns in 2038-39 and 2047. Downloading games, films and music on the internet is now rationed in the interest of global sustainability, electromagnetic equilibrium and international equity. The UN brokered an agreement which encouraged national provision, permitted limited growth in poor countries but put constraints on internet use in medium and rich countries, depending on the level of national supply. There are penalties if countries exceed their share. Each province in England has to police its allocation of internet energy.'

'Cyla,' I asked, 'what were those catastrophic breakdowns?'

'The 2038-39 breakdown was the culmination of a series of mini-crises in the thirties. The underlying longer-term causes were twofold: the spread of smartphone capabilities, internet games and programs to the whole world population, and the huge increase in dependence on energy and wireless technologies, including electric vehicles, cryptocurrencies and, principally, artificial intelligence and data centres. The world was trapped in a highly centralised, energy intensive, interactive electronic web with its hub in the United States. The immediate causes of crises were varied, including energy shortages, especially in the USA, and cyber-attacks by certain states, companies and criminal gangs, which sometimes disabled the internet and Cloud storage system. The 2047 breakdown ...'

I said: 'Thank you Cyla, that's enough!' I noticed how she sometimes repeated points and I'd had my fill of complex, dispassionate and depressing analysis. I needed a lighter touch, so looked expectantly at the others. Rufus took up the story: '2047 ... hmmm, let's stick with '38 to '39 for a moment. Remember what Sacha told you about the 'perfect storm' in 2039? Well, the combination of the '38 cyber-attacks and the devastating climate crises of '39 was just too much. People began to realise how foolishly we had put all our eggs in one basket. The digital/wireless basket. The loss of data from the Cloud induced a worldwide recession as organisations reliant on it tried to work out what the hell they were doing. Governments were rushing round like blue-arsed flies, trying to rescue things, also playing the blame game ...' 'Who were they blaming? I asked. 'Oh, apart from the weather, it was the usual suspects – Russia, North Korea, China, Islamic State, the American Secret Service – all later proved to be wrong. It was geometrically rising demand, and a consortium of the ultra-rich from the USA and other very unequal societies, especially in the Middle East, trying to take over yet more of the world economy. Boy did we need James Bond at that point! But really, you know, the crisis was of our own making, the whole world becoming over-dependent on a fragile system.

'Then in 2047 things went from bad to worse, because the Sun caught a cold. Well, a cough, so to speak. The peak of the solar cycle was much more extreme than we've known it since radio was invented. Huge flares powering out high energy cosmic rays which burst through the Earth's electromagnetic defences and cauterised many of the radio satellites which were the basis of modern global communication, especially for phones, GPS and artificial intelligence. Many automated systems simply stopped working. Generative AI knowledge exchange, which had been slowly recovering after the partial breakdown of the Cloud, basically gave up the ghost. That was the immediate effect. Over the following decade we saw economic collapse, regional wars and dreadful health impacts, people dying much younger because of widespread poverty and the breakdown of support systems.' He paused.

I was pole-axed. Sam was looking at me in concern. 'Yeah! But don't despair,' she said. 'Since then we have partially recovered. The cataclysms were global, and required a global response. Quite amazingly, the world has come together in a way that would have been inconceivable before. You should hear Sarah's husband on psycho-history and social capital! We're poorer now, materially, but richer politically and culturally. Currently … no major wars, slow economic recovery and Gaia, the Earth, back almost on an even keel, albeit warmer than before.' 'Not to mention,' said Rufus, surprising me with his delighted smile, 'a more equal world, people living longer, living better, living happier!'

Given the mid-century breakdown of the internet and the Cloud, I was perplexed at how machines like Cyla worked at all. Rufus explained that modern AI was just as sophisticated as before, indeed in some ways more so, but did not now rely on the World Wide Web, but a national network, using buried cables with local wireless, drawing on the national 'Cave' – no longer the semi-mystical 'Cloud' – in Birmingham. This was to avoid the proven vulnerability of monopolistic, capitalist provision in the USA and satellite communication. Links between national networks had gradually been re-established, so we now had the Euronet.

I wanted to probe more deeply into how the transition had happened, what triggered the radical shift in political attitudes. Sam responded: 'Basically co-operation, then decentralisation.' 'Yes, but how did that happen?' I persisted. 'Well,' she said, 'even before 2050 many of the great tech firms had gone to the wall and been broken up into bits. Small is beautiful was the order of the day, though inevitably many big semi-monopolistic firms still haven't noticed. Of course! Then after the solar catastrophe other long-term political trends accelerated, I'm not quite sure why. I think it was because no one trusted central governments any more, or multinationals for that matter. They'd failed us! The provinces of England were created, and empowered, just like that.'

'However, the most significant change, I guess, was the way almost all the major countries of the world demanded action from the newly reformed UN, voting extraordinary powers to the UN to co-ordinate water and energy and food production and distribution. Apparently India and the EU were the main movers, both having permanent places on the Security Council. Ahh!' She raised her hand comically and made a light-bulb-moment face. 'I should have said. You know what it was that galvanised popular opinion? People's love of nature and rare animals. There were so many worries: like the loss of the last colony of orang-utans in Borneo; mining and quarrying for rare metals; the almost total loss of polar bears from the arctic; human impacts too, the Innuit camping around the new UN HQ in Addis Ababa to campaign about the destruction of their traditional way of life. Those campaigns were huge! Most countries were shamed into accepting the new UN powers, and more or less abided by the jointly worked out survival strategy. Everything came together.'

Rufus made an open-handed gesture: 'Working together is the good news out of the bad, but we know that bad habits might well return, so we have to be on our guard. Anyway, coming back to IT and AI and so on, there were many problems before that first global meltdown. People in general wanted to escape the early century tide of unsolicited adverts, fake news and social media trolling, which had got completely out of hand. It was the decision of the nations in the UN to abolish the privately run search engines and communication networks, and put an international non-profit system in its place, linking national networks, trying to recover what had been lost and move forward in a less vulnerable, less manipulable mode. The brief for the UN now is to manage overall energy, water and information supply and demand so it's fair and sustainable.' He mused for a moment. 'It's a tall order!'

We sat for a minute in companionable melancholy.

My mind turned from the artificial systems bulwarking civilisation to the natural systems. I was disturbed that the sun, which had fostered the development of humankind for a hundred thousand years, should behave so unpredictably and treacherously. It was as if Apollo, driving the solar chariot across the skies, decided to flick an incendiary device down to Earth, casual and wilful as ever. Then my mind sifted through what little I knew about the role of the sun in causing ice ages and prehistoric mass extinctions. I asked the others, did the solar emergency strike out of the blue, or was it foreseen?

They took turns to answer. Apparently solar studies were now a core part of the curriculum in many schools. Both Sam and Rufus had learnt all about it. They were adamant that despite unpredictability the risk could have been anticipated, way back in the twenties. It was wilful blindness, they thought – as in so many things when politics and profits depend on business as usual. They explained in some detail about the eleven-year solar cycle – that at solar maximum, with lots of sunspots and solar flares, there is much more radio and magnetic disturbance, causing the Northern Lights and shortening the life of low-orbit satellites. Space weather storms could lead to radio blackouts, mess with geomagnetic fields and destabilise the outer atmosphere of Earth, with its protective shield over life on Earth. Apparently the solar maximum of 2025 was more severe than predicted – 'in retrospect we can see that the trends were apparent even in your year, 2023,' said Sam. It was all part of long-term solar variation, visible across the centuries, when the peaks themselves vary over a seventy to 110 year cycle. Previous high peaks were roughly 1780, 1850 and 1960. In the period since 1960 the world had become vastly more dependent on radio communication, so when the violence of solar activity reached an alarming crescendo between '47 and '49, the damage to satellites was pretty terminal. Unfortunately, since 2040 the sun has not quietened down as much as predicted, so there are real fears about the next big peak. No-one is willing to insure new communication satellites unless they are much more robust and very expensive. Only a few satellites have been replaced

– Europe has co-operated to ensure that GPS works for driverless vehicles. Old satellite orbits decayed and gradually the amount of space junk has reduced.

I found it completely fascinating. Apart from learning about the planets in primary school, my formal education in astronomy had been sadly deficient. I'd learnt some from books, avidly absorbing the then state of knowledge, excited by the all the unexplained mysteries thrown up by observation. I'd never read about the long-term solar cycles.

It was dark when we ventured outside. The sky was beautiful and clear, the air crisp and cool. The three of us walked away from the lights of the quad to a wide clearing at the far end of the garden. The darkness seemed intense – much less of an urban glow than I was used to. Looking up I saw the spring constellations. Following the star-trail from Cassiopeia to Pegasus to Andromeda, I was delighted to find the faintly glowing heart of the Andromeda galaxy, M31, twin sister to the Milky Way, imagining its immense scale across the sky. Then as my eyes adapted further to the darkness, there was the Milky Way itself, stretching from horizon to horizon. I just gazed. In my own day one had to go far – West Wales maybe – to see this sight. The sense of an infinite universe, with a myriad known unknowns and a myriad unknown unknowns, awed me. Even our own local star held secrets, was not entirely predictable, requiring life on Earth to learn and adapt. Could humankind, the dominant Earth species, learn and adapt sufficiently?

16
The path of Ubuntu

It did seem to me that the West Country – I wasn't sure about Britain more widely – had learnt lessons and changed its practices. But I had two very conflicting images of British society. One was immensely positive, in which people, communities, enterprises and governments appeared to be working together with logic and love to tackle the intractable problems. In the other, which sent a shiver of fear through my body, this unity stemmed from a controlling, paternalistic dictatorship of the majority, with the tools and the power to force behavioural conformity. I had seen too much of autocratic regimes in my own time to trust the spiders in the web, even elected spiders. When I expressed this to Rufus at breakfast the next day, he suggested it was a matter of shared philosophy and values. He hoped that my trip that day to Gloucester might provide some insight.

I was interested to go to Gloucester to see how the built environment had evolved in the city – which now was grown to the size of Norwich or Plymouth in my day. Rufus gave me over to Sam, with her design training. We were to explore the central area, including a visit to the Cathedral, then go to a special event in the Cathedral at 16.00, celebrating the historic cultures of England and India. I was really looking forward to this, getting a glimpse of how things were in a distant country, the biggest and perhaps now the most powerful in the world. Maybe the experience would cast light on the dichotomy – co-operation v. coercion – that I was feeling.

What it actually did was more profound. There is a moral heart to this chapter. I'll let that emerge through the narrative. But first a long digression of particular interest to me and my profession: buildings and places.

I remembered Gloucester as a city of contradictions. On the one hand an amazing history and some glorious buildings. On the other a rather decaying feel in the centre, dominated by downcast people and uncouth youth. I remembered one trip I had made alone to the Gloucester Guildhall for an avant garde film. Afterwards, late in the evening, Eastgate Street was intimidating. Drunk and rowdy lads, idling around, catcalling me as I hastened by. Groups of girls too, playing around, screaming with laughter. Maybe it was all in good sport – I was not actually threatened – but never again, I said! The retail centre, post Covid, was depressing, with too many empty shops. Much of the city was dominated by roads and traffic. And I'd been puzzled that a flat city like Gloucester had practically no cyclists. All this, though, was my relatively superficial impression. In the interests of balance (one of my enduring traits!) I have to say that friends who lived there told a different tale, and an uncle visiting for the

Three Choirs Festival loved the city, its heritage and revamped docks. Sam said she aimed to surprise me this day.

We went there by train, observing the new stations en route. The Gloucester train and bus hub was not that different from my own time, nor was the street layout. But otherwise – all change! The multi-storey car parks – gone! The big national and international retailers – nowhere to be seen. Trees now along every street. Quite crowded in parts – the people hugely varied, giving a cosmopolitan feel. Many more flats and small-scale commercial activities, some quite tatty. Sam explained that the mid-century crises had killed off the chain stores as people's disposable income crumbled. There had been a time of complete doldrums. Rents were slow to come down, because property owners had mortgaged themselves up to the hilt during the earlier boom. Then they went bust as business dried up. When the local authorities were given the power, they stepped in to take over empty properties, buying at the bottom of the market, and very controversially controlled rents so that small-scale and marginal businesses could get a look in. Now, more than thirty years later, things were on an even keel, the heart of the city thriving, being the centre of robo-bus and e-bike routes. Sam told me that while there had been more affluence before the Bad Times, there had also been more abject poverty. Now there was less disparity and everybody could afford essentials. I sensed this from the feel of the city around me, and from the look of the people. There was a wealth of community initiatives: for reuse, repair and recycling, shared workshops and swap-shops, language hubs, liquor and love-shops. There was an atmosphere of positivity – almost hedonism.

Some of the large commercial buildings I remembered – from the late twentieth century – were now apartments, all with balconies added. Many more people were living in the centre. Sam said demolitions were now rare, in order to avoid wastage of materials and make good use of the embedded capital represented by existing structures, and all buildings were designed for adaptability, so different uses could occupy them as conditions evolved – just as large Victorian and Edwardian houses had proved adaptable. To my eye the new buildings were odd: orientated to capture solar power, with roofs made of panels, more surprisingly bedecked with chimneys. Contradictory, I thought. 'Oh, no!' said Sam,' they're not for coal or wood fires, they're for natural passive stack ventilation, keeping buildings cooler in summer.'

'I guess artificial air conditioning has been banned,' I said. 'Actually, it's still allowed in certain circumstances,' said Sam. I showed my surprised. She explained: 'Yes, I know that seems retrograde, but in fact the desire of businesses for AC was a big driver of solar power mid-century. The new rules meant they could only have it if they generated more than enough electricity from the sun in situ – and stored it. Clever! It had the positive effect of saving some older buildings which were difficult to keep cool in the summer.' I was impressed.

I also found myself interested in the construction materials: as expected timber was common, though not in the newest buildings – apparently timber construction was now highly restricted because of excessive demand. Cement use was limited as well – too energy intensive. So what were they using? Sam pointed out hempcrete and bamboo structures, and 'lean' buildings printed in clay and fly-ash. She said pre-fabrication was almost the rule, and on site it was robotic control and subsequently self-repair too. It was all a new world to me – one long anticipated in my day, but never realised – always just beyond the horizon. I started worrying about all the brickies, builders, carpenters, plumbers and electricians put out of a job. Sam assured me that the motivation was exactly the other way round. Earlier in the century there were simply not enough skilled builders and craftspeople around. Automation came to the rescue and building practices were adapted. And there were always plenty of odd, awkward jobs that demanded a skilled human.

The other shock – one I was actually delighted with – was the change to all the listed buildings in the city. In my day the rules were pretty intransigent. History (or conservation officers' blinkered view of history) took precedence over efficiency. The global eco-crisis was ignored. I had coined a phrase I was rather pleased with, though perhaps not original: sacrificing the future on the altar of the past. There had in fact been the first signs of easing up before I transitioned. But now … triple glazing the rule, darkening glass, internal or external shutters, solar roofs, chimneys repurposed for ventilation, even some historic buildings where external insulation was covering brickwork. Sam told me: 'the expense of keeping up all these old buildings now, in our straitened circumstances, has become a real problem. We can't tolerate energy-greedy places any more. Some have had to go. Especially unwanted chapels and churches, which seemed like sacrilege. Others have been transformed by use-change – mainly to whole-life homes, with a lot of community-led residential projects, assisted by carbon-neutral grants. All helped by the cash which was released when we abandoned new nuclear.' We passed one such adapted chapel as she spoke. It was obvious to my trained eye that a number of conservation conventions had been put to one side to facilitate renewal. I was impressed. An onset of pragmatism.

We wandered round and about. There were people everywhere, chatting, idling, waiting for the bus, walking, cycling, or pottering about on electric motorbikes, mopeds and scooters. Something was odd about the motorbikes and mopeds. One thing was their speed – a constant 25 kph. They seemed like part of a machine, a huge automated system under the thumb of a control freak. Often there were couples on them, and I noticed something else that brought a smile to my face. The girl or woman tended to be in front, steering. Never in my day! Always the man in front. Sam laughed at my surprise. 'Of course,' she said. 'It's logical. The girl is shorter, so she's at the front, and the guy can see over her.' I laughed with her. 'Wow! Equality has come a long way,' I said. 'Not sure about that!' said Sam. 'The guys were only at the front because they enjoyed being in charge, accelerating, swerving around and so on. Now everything is controlled, so they think, what's the point?' I laughed again!

*****

Later that morning, after chicoffee, we walked to the Cathedral, planning to drop in on a service there. This was a novelty. Up to now I'd heard little about either politics or religion in this future world. I'd seen a mosque and the small Christian chapel in the Woodchester town hall. But I had rather assumed that faith in God, and in organised religion, had more or less evaporated – that Christian, Islamic, Jewish, Hindu and other faiths were only present in odd corners, surviving as relics from a lost age, blown away by the Bad Times.

However, Gloucester Cathedral had always inspired me with awe. It was still by far the biggest and greatest building in the city. Just gazing at it as we approached, the sense of wonder struck me anew: the amazing beauty, daring and sheer scale of the building, so old, constructed by medieval master-builders and a host of craftsmen without any power source, just human resourcefulness and effort – and in a far poorer era. Seeing it again, still glorious in this new age, took my breath away.

Then, there in the Cathedral Close, was an unexpected friend: the Knife Angel. A peace and reconciliation angel. I'd last seen it in early 2023. Here it was, rather tarnished, though otherwise looking even more impressive than I remembered. The support system for its imposing eight metre height was no longer visible – it was now self-supported. Constructed out of 100,000 confiscated knives, designed to highlight the dangers of knife crime and violence, it originally travelled from city to city. Sam told me it had been given to Gloucester back in the thirties, as its permanent home. I loved it. Something about the empathic look on the face and the open gesture of the hands: a real angel.

I was deeply moved, just seeing the Cathedral and the sculpture, and felt quite emotional. Sam took my hand in hers, looked at me with shining eyes. I was beginning to accept the physical contact between people, but was still shy, my hand going limp at first, until I consciously decided to firm up, be a woman! 'Let's go inside,' said Sam, 'It's become the social and cultural hub for the whole county. Quite interesting.'

That was the understatement of the year! The huge nave was crowded with people, all ages and ethnicities, mostly standing. There was a kind of service going on, though it did not feel expressly religious. We sidled in and stood at the back. There was chanting, expressive gesturing by everyone, short homilies, hymns with tunes I recognised but different words. Postcards were thrust into our hands by an earnest young man, telling us how to access the words on our wristies. He reminded me slightly of a welcomer at an Evangelical service I'd once been to. The words were about the Earth and her creatures – the Earth Mother, her health, humanity's job to care for all life, to love each other. The card explained this was a non-denominational service for human unity and global sustainability.

It was also, it seemed, a remembrance service. The precentor requested that we hold all those who died or were dispossessed by the Bad Years in the light, in our hearts. A powerful drumbeat led to a long moment of utter stillness and silence. Then out of the silence a choir sang – boys' voices! Maybe mixed boys and young girls. I was surprised. The choir sang beautifully, a piece I knew well – William Byrd's Agnus Dei from the four-part mass. It was all in English, not Latin. God did not feature, but it was still a prayer. The Dona Nobis Pacem at the end – 'give us peace' – was as achingly beautiful as ever. There was no sound from the assembled congregation. I thought how extraordinary! Traditional cathedral music re-purposed. Made universal.

After another silence, pregnant with meaning, a young woman in the middle of the nave, judiciously amplified, declaimed into the silence the Wordsworth quotation that I had been trying to remember:

> And I have felt
> A presence that disturbs me with the joy
> Of elevated thoughts; a sense sublime
> Of something far more deeply interfused,
> Whose dwelling is the light of setting suns,
> And the round ocean and the living air,
> And the blue sky, and in the mind of man:
> A motion and a spirit, that impels
> All thinking things, all objects of all thought,
> And rolls through all things.

I was fascinated. This was not Christianity as I knew it. It was not even deist. More in line, maybe, with Hindu animist beliefs, or with the concept of Gaia, the sense of unity and interdependence of all creation. There was no time for reflection: a drum roll gathered momentum, joined eventually by tam-tams and gongs, and then crowning it all the Cathedral bells pealed, cascading and rippling, until the cathedral rang out with wild sound, physically intoxicating. I could sense the growing excitement of the crowd. As the tremendous sound died away, some signal made the crowd erupt with a great shout of affirmation.

There was a shaking of hands and some hugging before people started filing out, chatting and laughing. Some stayed standing, waiting. There was an explosion of sound from the organ. I recognised it too: Dieu Parmi Nous by Olivier Messiaen, the twentieth century musical magician. The movement of people was arrested. They seemed rooted to the spot. I was completely blown away. The whole event had become so dramatic, and to finish with a work that had the hair standing up on the back of my neck! I had to find a seat, breathing deeply, my mouth open. A guy in a wheelchair stopped as he passed: 'Are you alright, love?' he asked. I nodded and smiled a beatific smile. 'The music,' I said.

Sam was watching me. We stayed to the end. 'That piece has been played here before,' she said. 'It is powerful, isn't it? It's called Terra Parmi Nous. I turned to her 'That's not its proper name! Messiaen called it Dieu Parmi Nous!' 'Wow – you know the composer! Impressive! I think I can explain,' she said. 'Let's go for a drink.'

We got up to go, when a man brushed past me, rather rudely I thought, bringing me back down to earth. 'Oh sorry,' he said, then looked at me closely. 'Don't I know you? I'm sure I know you. But not from round here, I think. Where are you from?' 'Manchester,' I said briefly, not wanting to engage. 'Ah! That must be it,' he said. 'Great place, don't you think? I was just trying to place your unusual accent. Do you know …'

At that point Sam intervened. 'I'm very sorry, but I'm afraid we have to go. Please excuse us. She took me firmly by the arm. We left him talking on his wristy. 'I'm sure he's a journalist – seemed very nosy,' said Sam. 'Let's just make sure he isn't following us; no point in asking for trouble.' 'Maybe he's just inquisitive,' I said. 'Let's not take any chances,' she replied, 'and I'm messaging Rufus. Journalists have to carry identification, and he has the app that can detect it.'

We turned a few corners. No-one was following. We found a suitable hostelry. I wanted a pint of ale, despite it being only just after midday. I chose a low alcohol one, just as good; they all seemed to be rather low. I asked Sam about the loss of Latin in the Byrd, the changed name of the organ piece and more fundamentally, about religious beliefs. Sam began, rather hesitantly at first, to explain. 'We're all about inclusion now, and about drawing together all the sacred traditions represented by our oh-so-diverse population. Latin is a non-starter for people whose ancestors were from Sub-Saharan Africa or South Asia. English has become the rule, except in some arcane, historicist circles. The purists hate it of course.' 'I can understand that,' I said. 'I'm a bit of a purist myself! I love singing in the original language. However,' I paused, 'I also get what you mean by being inclusive. I remember singing Bach's St. John Passion in English a year or two ago. Seventy years ago! And actually, being in English, and with the recitatives spoken, not sung, by actors, it came across – the story and the music came across – very powerfully.'

'There are still individual faiths being practiced,' said Sam. 'Islam, Roman Catholicism, Anglican evangelicals, Hinduism, Buddhism and so on. All are welcome at the cathedral, but the main aim now is to express the shared recognition that we are all one with the Earth, those of all religions and of none. You know – that it's the only Earth we've got, it's our habitat, we have to take care of it and all the flora and fauna that share it, and if we don't … Gaia will have us on toast!'

I chuckled, spluttering over my drink at the inappropriate metaphor, and thought of another. 'So God and Gaia have, er, got together?' I queried. Sam smiled broadly in her turn. 'Well, kind of,' she said, 'What Rufus believes – he's the psychologist – is that the mid-century cataclysm left an indelible scar on our communal psyche. We can't get beyond it.' She explained how the searing awareness of humanity's folly had galvanised the emotions of people across the globe. There was a desperate desire for a sustainable, non-threatening future, for global sanity – to avoid a repeat of the mindless exploitation of the Earth's riches and to work together for survival. Apparently insuperable barriers of race and culture and political philosophy were, for a while at least, swept away. The spirit and language of Ubuntu had spread from Africa, referring to the deep belief and moral position that everyone is equal, worthy of respect, and all humanity is interdependent, that we have a collective responsibility for the global commons we share, and to make sure all people are cared for, or able to care for themselves, including the strangers and outcasts. She told me that a wise man of the twentieth century, Desmond Tutu, had explained Ubuntu by saying *my humanity is inextricably bound up with yours.*

My mind turned to Jesus's parable of the Good Samaritan. All religions, I thought, unless they were trapped by institutionalisation, nationalism or fundamentalism, said the same thing. They had a common morality. What seemed to have happened as result of crisis was that morality had reasserted itself over dogma.

Rufus joined us during our sojourn in the pub, making light of the encounter with the journalist earlier. Together we went for a refreshing walk, past the docks and out into the riverine environment. I could see the extra efforts that the authorities had made to protect the city from floods – I wondered for how long. As we walked around the island between two branches of the Severn, notices also told us how they were trying to hold salination of the land at bay. The island was quite well vegetated now, with standing water in places, alive with insects and home to birds both many and varied. The interpretation boards told us to keep our eyes peeled for colourful bee-eaters and black-winged stilts, which were now nesting there, far north of their traditional grounds. We saw a bee-eater, flashing blue and gold, catching damsel flies on the wing.

We were to return to the cathedral mid-afternoon for cultural exchange. Sam informed me that there was a programme of international exchange funded by the West Country provincial government, intended to build bridges of appreciation and understanding between different countries, different continents. It was seen as an alternative to international travel, now severely rationed because of its energy demand. Technology made it possible, she said, to feel you were actually in the theatre – or in the forest or even someone's home – in a far-flung land. The previous month had seen an exchange with Esfahan, in Iran. Rufus and Sam had been blown away by the sheer beauty of the mosques and their water gardens, shown on the big screen. Then enjoyed the hologram presentation of an ancient Persian play. This time the exchange was with South India. We would see temples and mime artists from Kerala. I had never been to India, so this was a treat in store. How far, I wondered, had people there managed to adapt to yet hotter climes?

17
Cultural exchange

The show's timing was to enable simultaneous transmission in India and Britain. The cathedral had been turned right round, rows and rows of seats now erected facing the West end, where a huge screen hung above a stage. The programme sent to our wristies telling us the emphasis of this exchange was on traditional cultures. After an introduction about Kerala we would see dance and mime artists performing. Then from

Gloucestershire there would be a folk opera based on a medieval Arthurian tale. The event was to be broadcast across the region.

The house lights dimmed. Two dark Keralan women appeared, lifesize and completely lifelike on the stage. I gasped at the precision of the technology. One was gorgeously dressed in a green and gold sari, the other a vivid red with blue trimmings. They looked so gracious and noble. They took turns to introduce their state, Kerala, at the extreme south-west of the Indian peninsular, a beautiful place of mountains, forests, tea and coconut plantations, rice paddies, lakes, canals and coastal beaches. Images irradiated the screen. The central question they addressed was how the state had adapted to climate change – apparently this was part of the purpose of the event. Change had been less pronounced there, in the tropics, than further north in India and Asia, but had still required major adaptation, triggered by the severity of the 2018 and 2032 floods. Gaining momentum in climate resilience had taken decades. The population, which boasted almost 100% literacy, numeracy and IT skills, had stopped growing mid-century, and was now just around replacement level. Earlier in the century the industrialising economy and growing middle class had led to spiralling car ownership (relying mainly on fossil fuel), resulting in urban pollution and gridlock as infrastructure failed to keep pace. The improvement in healthy lives stalled. Global economic crisis in the fifties had in a sense rescued Kerala from itself. It was driven back to age-old more sustainable practices. Villages gradually regained their lost mojo, recovering their communal farming ethos and their carbon-neutral craft skills. In parallel everyone became connected again through the revamped local internet. Towns and cities started functioning effectively as public transport, together with e-bikes and scooters, replaced private vehicles. There were new styles of buildings that ventilated naturally, and extensive tree planting for shade. While rainfall was plentiful in season it had been necessary to safeguard water resources for longer dry seasons. Increased self-sufficiency was fostered at different levels – locally, state-wide and across India as a whole. Kerala was now on an even keel.

Someone in the audience asked about health and longevity and inequality. It was uncanny, but the two women on stage responded as if they were right there in reality. They told us that life had never been so good and the children were as happy as ever. Most people reached at least seventy before suffering long-term mental or physical impairment, and longevity was now better than in the United States. This was because lifestyles had improved, diet was healthy, extended family traditions were strengthening again and there was no extreme poverty. Then the two women introduced their cultural contribution, dance and story and mime from the seventeenth century or before, interpreted for us. They waved goodbye, and faded from view, as it were, like the Cheshire cat.

Three young people materialised, dancing – a boy and two girls, accompanied by classical Indian music, though the players were invisible. I loved it. The dancing was a glorious feast for the eye, all sparkling colour and graceful movement, unfamiliar to Western eyes, and very seductive in its way. It seemed that the boy was in love with both girls, and they with each other. I was simply entranced by the beauty of the dance. Then it was all change. A large man came onto the stage wearing an extraordinary red and yellow costume with a huge wide-spread highly decorated skirt, lurid socks, a hat like a storeyed wedding cake, bangles and jangles galore. But his face was what riveted the attention. Initially I thought it was a mask. His skin was emerald green, his mouth a brilliant pillar-box red and his eyes black as soot. Then he opened his eyes with a wicked grin and winked. His image appeared magnified behind him. His eyes travelled left, then right, mischievous, enticing. He mimicked various daily actions, causing bursts of laughter in the audience. His miming was perfection. The dancers looked on entranced, adopting stylised poses.

Then the story unfolded. The big man was trying to captivate one of the girls with flamboyant movements. She played along with him, mock-alluring, and the boy was angry, stomping around. Then she rejected the big man and did a pirouette with her young lover. The man was forlorn, until he suddenly thought of the other girl. He danced a grotesque jig and she clapped and laughed with him. But when he offered his hand, she demurely and apologetically refused. He was devastated, and acted as twice betrayed, heaving great sighs of despair. It was very funny in fact! He had the audience in stitches. Then the three young people came to him, very friendly, eyes alive with affection. He instantly perked up. All four danced together – three with flirtatious finesse, one a galumphing clown. The audience roared appreciation. The actors bowed and vanished. The audience clapped enthusiastically. We could see on the screen the Kerala audience clapping as well.

There was a short interval. We rose to stretch our legs. Sam and Rufus saw friends of theirs and moved off to greet them. The guy who had accosted me earlier came over to me. He appeared innocent enough, and came straight out with it: 'Hello, I'm an independent journalist,' he said. 'Sorry if I seemed at all rude before. I'm writing about this province, the West Country, which seems to me to be the most control-freakish in the whole British Isles, and that's saying something. I was invited to listen in to the chief urbanist's lecture in Stroud a few days ago. Well – slipped in when invited by one of the participants who agrees with me. I saw you with your minder then. And you being from elsewhere, clearly a valued visitor, I would love to interview you about your perspective on local policy here. Here's my card. No time to discuss now, but do give me a call.' 'Thanks, I'll think about it,' I said, intending to add that the issue of control interested me, but I would need to consult. However, at that moment the others caught up with me, a concerned look on Rufus's face. The journalist nodded to me and sidled away.

'That man again. Was he bothering you?' asked Rufus, checking his wristy. 'He's a journalist you know. Not to be trusted!' 'Yes, he told me,' I said. 'He raised a point that really interests me.' I told them what he had said. 'Ah! So we're minders now! I think of us as guides,' Sam expostulated. 'Seriously, Robyn, you have to be terribly careful. Watchful. Guarded. Or your true origins will come out publicly and the whole thing will be jeopardised.'

My reaction was unexpected – to me anyway. 'Yes, well, maybe it's about time you trusted me. I'm quite cautious now; I'm picking up the signals much quicker. I would be careful. But … look: I need to meet people with a range a views, not just those hand-picked by you two – though they have been brilliant. I need to retain an open mind and get a rounded perspective. I'm gaining confidence. I'm ready.'

Rufus was looking at me quizzically. 'I'm so sorry we left you alone earlier. I spotted an old friend. Let's talk about all this later, they're about to start again.'

There was a change of scene. The screen scanned landscapes of southwest England and the West Country: dramatic coastlines, moorlands, water meadows, cities, Cotswolds and Severn Vale, before homing in on Gloucester Cathedral, transferring inside in real time to show the audience and stage, and on the stage, to my surprise, Wulf O'Leary, the chief urbanist. He talked directly to the audience in Kerala, setting out the situation in the West Country, how the province had responded to the series of crises, had become carbon-positive and was planning ahead with confidence. He was a natural performer, with a certain lightness of touch, including amusing anecdotes and vivid examples flashed up on the screen. I hoped that the Keralese people would appreciate his style. Apparently they would hear an almost contemporaneous translation into the classic Dravidian language of of Malayalam.

Wulf explained how much traditional culture of Gloucestershire had been lost when the internet records vanished. How Britain, unlike India, did not have much in the way of folk memories, handing down word and song from generation to generation, relying instead on written or electronic prompt. How in Gloucester there was luckily a historic archive, all on paper, which had been avidly mined over the past few decades, leading to the recovery of forgotten treasures. One of these, a short folk opera, we were to experience shortly – based on the earliest medieval English poem, written in the late fourteenth century by an unknown poet, 'Sir Gawain and the Green Knight'. The music was inspired by English folk tunes and written in the 1960s by a local composer.

I was riveted. This was uncanny. The title of the folk opera struck a chord in my memory. My wristy told me the name of the composer, Tim Porter. I'd been much too engrossed in the reality around me to look earlier. It was a work I'd seen in Stroud in 2003, when I was eleven years old. I'd even seen the composer, taking his bow at the end. I remembered barn dancing with the band, and the 'medieval feast' that followed.

The show had started. I think it had been shortened quite a bit. A troupe of wandering players all dressed in colourful tatters, came through the audience onto the stage, where on one side was a folk band with squeeze box, bass and violin, and on the other, rather hidden from view, a tiny orchestra with strings and percussion. It was New Year in King Arthur's court and the knights were playing leapfrog to a dance tune of that name, when in came a huge green knight wielding the most almighty axe. He challenged any knight present to cut off his head, there and then, so long as they were willing to submit to his return blow at the Green Chapel a year and a day hence. Gawain stepped in to forestall King Arthur risking his life, and accepted the challenge. He cut off the Green Knight's head, a clean swipe, but then to everyone's amazement the Knight picked up his head and strode out of the hall.

Suffice to say that next winter Gawain searched for the Green Chapel to keep his promise. He and his page travelled far through wild forests and moors, almost dying of cold in the snow. Eventually they stumbled upon a remote castle, where they received a warm welcome, food and rest, as the guests of the noble Bertilac and his lady. There Gawain and his host played a Christmas game – for three days. While Bertilac went hunting, Gawain rested from his travels, and at the end of each day they gave each other whatever they had caught or found. Bertilac came back with a deer, a fox and a boar. Gawain, resting abed, was seduced by Bertilac's wife (very comically acted but rather too explicit I thought for the children present), so for his part gave kisses and hugs in exchange. But on the third day the Lady gave him a magic ring which would protect him from the Knight's blow. Gawain did not feel able to reveal this – a present from Bertilac's wife – and so lost the game.

The Green Chapel was not far away. When Gawain arrived, there was the Green Knight waiting for him, head firmly in place. The tension was unbearable, with powerful drumbeats alternating with silence. The Knight toyed with Gawain, pretending to swipe off his head, and soon discovered Gawain's deceit. Gawain was crestfallen. He had failed the ultimate test. But the Green Knight had his own magic. To everyone's surprise, he revealed himself as Bertilac, forgave Gawain, celebrating instead his steadfastness and courage. Later Gawain was welcomed back to Camelot as a hero. The Green Knight reappeared at the end, a timeless figure, representing the green world and the annual reincarnation of life. The music ended in triumph and the cast in riotous dancing.

The quality of music and acting was fantastic. It carried you away. As a youngster I had just enjoyed the fun of it, the tension in the story, the lively music. Now I saw deeper mythical meanings, seeing something of the Dragon or Pan in the Green Knight. His final words had the hair rising on my neck and sweat pouring down my brow. I realised that Porter's interpretation of the tale in certain ways went beyond the marvellous original Middle English poem, which I'd read in Tolkien's translation. I wondered how the Indian audience would respond. Rufus said that the Hindu myths were full of magic and amazing godlike beings, half human, half animal. He thought they would lap it all up. We chatted about Kerala and India, about mime artists and the sumptuous costumes they wore, about any common themes linking the two performances. 'Dance,' said Rufus. 'Sexual attraction,' said Sam. 'Forgiveness,' I said. 'You know – the dancers forgave the big man, made it up to him. The Green Knight forgave Gawain his misdemeanours.' 'Courage,' said Rufus. 'The great clown did not give up trying for the girl. Gawain went off to what could have been certain death.' Sam thought a moment. 'Yes, I think they were both very human, humane stories, full of joy and love.' 'And given the purpose of the cultural exchange,' said Rufus, 'very positive, creative and enjoyable perspectives on each country's traditions.' 'Ever the diplomat!' laughed Sam.

I was quiet on the way back to the Cohousing, pensive even. Seeing this play from my youth, rescued from obscurity, was disturbing. Why had that happened? I felt a bit as if I were in a dreamworld again. Conversely, I was delighted such a joyous and exciting drama had been given new life. Rufus assured me that he had no knowledge of my past experience of the work. It was pure coincidence – pure chance as far as he could see.

Sam tried to buck me up. Not that I was sad, just reflective. She said that tomorrow was to be a rest day (Rufus nodded firmly), a time to recharge my batteries after the intensity of experience since arrival. 'You'll have an opportunity to write, draw, paint, lounge about – whatever you want. I've got to meet up with colleagues, but Rufus will be around if you want company.' Rufus added we could leave the discussion about the journalist until I was fresh, tomorrow. Their words came as a relief to me. I needed a break.

The day ended with me feeling obscurely fulfilled, rounded, as if seeing the show from my youth helped to link up past and present – to gel my sense of being the same person in the two worlds of the twenties and the nineties. And I was delighted that the next day was free. I needed time just to be – able to absorb and digest all the rich and strange experiences of the last few days.

*****

Next day, after a jovial breakfast with Rufus and Sam, laughing at the shows we'd seen the previous day, I selected pen and ink and paper and drew pictures of the Cohousing estate: the square, the gardens, playground and buildings, public rooms and workshops, especially the wilder parts of the grounds. Some images were populated with people, many were not. Then I swapped over to water colour and began to abstract the images – much more impressionistic. I lost myself in artistic activity, doing something for myself, not simply absorbing what was thrown at me. My consciousness altered. I recovered a sense of poise and balance. Lunch was forgotten.

Eventually I felt restless, my body having been pretty static for too long. I went to the Cohousing gym and worked my way through the exercises. My desire to go for a run round the town was frustrated by Rufus's insistence, after the odd incident with the journalist in the cathedral, that I don't go out alone. The physical activity did me a lot of good. I found and ate a banana – not the usual kind from the West Indies but from South India, quite different, very tasty – then, feeling relaxed, went back to my room to focus on this new world, making copious handwritten notes. Though I had no idea whether I would ever be able to use them, the fact of writing notes helped me to gel memories and reactions.

Later afternoon, I sat down with a cup of tea and my mind wandered. A random thought made me talk to Cyla. 'Hi Cyla,' I said, 'can you tell me about myself? Look up Robyn Ghorra on Google.' Cyla was very polite. 'Hi Robyn, I have to tell you that Google no longer exists. The firm went bust in 2053 after a series of electronic and wireless crises. Before that the near demise of the Cloud meant that information about you in your thirties and forties was lost. I am looking you up on the Euronet, which was only effective from about 2050. It is clear that you had a successful career as an urban designer and then an urbanist, working in England, Ireland, later in Iran and Tamil Nadu with the World Health Organization. You enjoyed many years of healthy life. As you already know from Rufus, you had no children and have no surviving close relatives. I am unable to tell you more. Some surviving records in the Cave are forbidden to me. I am told it is essential that you know very little about your own future or that future would be compromised. But it is clear that you do have a future in the past.'

Cyla stopped talking. The thought that I had a future in the past was disturbing, to say the least. I sunk back in the armchair, rather shaken though not surprised. It had been worth a try. Though I realised my desire to know my own future before it had happened was perverse. I needed to make the future. Despite the total uncertainty about how and when I would return to my own time, my mind was turning to things I would want to do. It was soon buzzing with ideas.

A little later Rufus rang. He asked me how I felt after the exchange with Cyla. Of course, I thought, he is monitoring everything. I said I was fine, and understood the reasons for the absence of any detail about my future life. I was alive with thoughts about what I would like to do on my return. He warmly praised me. Then went on to say that my stay might be shorter than he had originally been told. 'It's not just the danger of publicity here and now,' he said, 'more a matter of what's happening to your body back in the hospital – when and how you come out of your coma. So I've arranged your next day. I know you want to meet up with Sarah again, to learn all about gender politics and stuff (he grinned). We'll cycle over there tomorrow first thing. I'll be volunteering in the woods – woodland management – very good for me – while you chat to Sarah. You may meet her husband too, he's chalk to her cheese.' I was delighted. Sarah had impressed me with her feisty, humane, no-nonsense character. Something to anticipate with pleasure.

18
Identity and sexual politics

The e-bike I borrowed next day from the Cohousing store was superb – beautifully made and no heavier than my own non-electric velocipede.

The batteries had shrunk, now amazingly light – new technology altogether. Rufus and I greatly enjoyed the ride, the exercise and the varied views of the countryside, feeling completely safe on the road. Other vehicles automatically respected the space around a cyclist. I didn't allow the bike's motor to take over – I had it on low power except up the steepest of hills, arriving at Sarah's farm glistening, puffing and just delighted. We leant our bikes against a barn and Rufus went off to the woods. He'd arranged where to go.

I was greeted by a rough-hewn giant of a man in T-shirt, tough trousers and muddy boots – clearly a land worker, and of Southeast Asian extraction. He grinned at me and welcomed me warmly, in a slightly odd middle-class accent. I realised I'd instinctively categorised him wrongly – not the first occasion, so mentally berated myself. 'I've just come back from the woods,' he said. 'One of the pigs gave birth early this morning. Mother and piglets all fine. Do cool off here while I have a wash and a change.' I saw now his clothes and hands were bloodied. 'Sarah'll be here in a mo.'

I sat down gratefully on a beautifully crafted wooden bench, looking out across the farmyard. Some things don't change! Stone flags, straggly grass, hens pecking and clucking, cock strutting his stuff, tabby cat snuggled up to an alert collie, big daisies, red poppies, old weathered sheds. All very homely and reassuring. I drank it in. Then was confounded at the incongruous sight of a farm buggy sliding by, clattering on the flags, with no-one in control. A little later Sarah erupted into the farmyard, all vitality and bonhomie. 'It'd be nice to chat out here,' she said, 'but drizzle cometh. Just typical! So … do come into the kitchen, won't you? Anyway, it's time for a little something.' She gave the phrase a characterful lilt and smiled, hinting at Pooh Bear. 'Then we'll get down to business.'

She magicked flapjacks and tasty chicoffee onto the table and went straight to business, no messing around, while at the same time somehow enfolding me in her warm embrace. 'It's gender and sex, isn't it? That's what you want to know about.' It was more of a statement than a question. I looked abashed. 'Nothing more important,' she said, 'people used to fight shy of discussing them, sex in particular – except, I gather, in stag- and hen-dos, when it was all innuendo and smut. It's vital just to be straightforward and matter-of-fact, then we learn something.'

I nodded, mute with awkwardness, but nevertheless determined not to inhibit her style. I wanted to know what she thought. 'Let's start in 2023,' she said. 'I need to get an idea of where you're coming from. Your perception of what was going on in your own time. What's your take on gender politics back then?'

I found my voice, albeit rather hesitantly. 'Uh, well, quite confused really. On the one hand there was a lot of disagreement and unhappiness around the subject. My mum and her friends profoundly believed in just male and female, born that way. More widely, though, there was a move towards inclusivity and acceptance of a wide range of sexual orientations and gender identities. But feelings ran high when the issue of how trans people were defined and treated in the law was being debated in the press and social media. The idea that people could choose to present themselves as a gender at odds with their birth sex... well, some people dismissed it as woke, while others defended it vociferously, believing in freedom of choice. For young people in particular the social media pressure was pretty intense – you weren't able to question things without raising a storm. I suppose the general politically correct view was tolerance and acceptance, and in favour of facilitating sex change if a person thought they were in the wrong body. Most of my friends took the principle in their stride, though I didn't know any who had done it for real.'

'Can I interrupt a minute, please?' said Sarah. 'While I get the general drift of what you're saying, and it interests me, there was one word that puzzled me, 'woke'?'

I thought for a minute. 'I once looked this up, because the word was being bandied around a lot in the press, especially in relation to politicians. It came from African-American vernacular English, and meant being alert to racial prejudice and injustice. Then the definition seemed to broaden to any kind of social discrimination.' Sarah nodded sagely.

'But as for me, I'm a bit conflicted to be honest. I mean, it wasn't a big deal when I occasionally met trans people – if I even knew that's what they were. At one level it makes no difference, just like skin colour. But then I started to feel that it had become a fashion – quite a lot of media celebrities seemed to be trans if they weren't gay or lesbian. Some stand-ups were really milking it. Kids were picking up on all this, even at quite a young age, as they saw it was trending on social media, and wanted some of that attention; there were stories of whole groups of teenagers announcing they were lesbian, gay, bi or trans. I worried about that, and also men transitioning to women and then playing in women's sports and using women's changing rooms. It just seemed wrong to me. But at the same time I also worry about trans people becoming disenfranchised, not welcome anywhere. People started saying that changing gender didn't mean changing sex, and every now and then there were cases of people who'd transitioned, wanting to change back. All very confusing! Do you know what I mean? Sorry if I'm not making sense.'

Sarah looked at me with understanding. 'Yes, I do. Know what you mean. Though I'd express it differently. I take a more historic and biological view. In your day the law was actually relatively supportive of gender change, though it changed a bit later. All part of a widespread attitude that people should be able to decide who they are – though society was split about it. In your time there were still some hugely prejudicial views about gender roles. Very many youngsters suffered from quite fixed parental expectations, reinforced by the social culture they lived in. You know, the macho man, the pretty girl, blue for a boy, pink for a girl. And the market played to these stereotypes. Teenage social media pulled in both directions. It could make some kids really unhappy, especially if they were an effeminate boy or a boyish girl, a tomboy, or romantically attracted to the same sex. Really awful this could be. Especially when reinforced by traditional religion. So young people felt trapped … The 2020s were the high tide of gender reassignment. In some situations it's absolutely right. We should do everything we can to make people feel at one with their body, and that can on rare occasions mean surgery.'

'So what has changed?' I asked.

'Lots! Trans people trailblazed, in a way, so that even stuck-in-the-mud communities started having to accept difference, become more open. They had to! When the reaction happened against "wokeness", (she looked pleased with herself) 'under-eighteen surgical reassignment was banned; later this was reduced to under sixteen. Fundamental social change took a generation. Eventually it no longer mattered if you were a tomboy or the male equivalent. Once kids felt no need to conform to outdated stereotypes, they could just be themselves. There were new heroes too, especially for girls. Football heroes for example. The social pressure for reassignment progressively reduced.

'And you must have noticed the style changes. Men showing off their bodies. Women not having to. Mind you, the banning of fast fashion, that's been part of it. Anyway, the result is that no-one worries about social labels like they did. Labels have largely fallen out of use, because they're not needed. There's a welcoming of personal choice to be what you want. If you want to define yourself as both male and female, or intermediate, you can now use the pronoun bee. Sorry bees! The word 'they' is just plural once again, which is good. I should add that being bisexual is commonplace, while being male or female or non-binary. Not for everyone, of course. That's where we are.' She drew breath.

I realised I had been holding myself tense during Sarah's speech. I consciously relaxed my shoulders … a barely recognised internal pressure was released. 'Thanks Sarah! That's really helpful. I can see that society has sort of grown up.' I wanted to add that my own still un-resolved sexual desires had in some way been eased, my guilt assuaged – but held my peace.

Sarah was on a roll: 'Now, issues of sex and marriage: so fundamental! Let's go for it,' she cried!

I chipped in: 'Yes. Yes. I was perplexed and intrigued when you mentioned all your husbands. Er … is bigamy legal?' 'Ah, sorry,' she chuckled. 'That was just me playing with words. Bigamy is not legal. Not like that princess in Hindu mythology who had five husbands because no one man could possess all the essential qualities – though I do rather understand that. No, sexual relationships began to change when an effective male pill became available, with no unpleasant side-effects. Let me go back to square one. A question for you. What is sex for?' Surprisingly, I had an instant answer: 'Well, "procreation, pleasure and profit" is what my puritan mother would have said! But of course, she was a bit suspicious of the pleasure element and disapproved profoundly of the profit motive, while recognising it's a sad reality. Mum was thinking of harlots – that was the term she used – but I was thinking of advertising and how sex sells, demeaning women.'

'Well, OK … that's fine. My threesome is love, lust and delight. Your pleasure is my delight!' she twinkled. 'I'll come onto the other two. We've moved on those. So has the law. First, the effect of the male pill has been startling – just like the female pill in the 1960s and '70s. Men now have even less excuse. They have to accept their responsibility. It's no longer, in the heat of the moment, wondering where the bloody condoms are. Luckily, we've also just about conquered sexually transmitted diseases, releasing behaviour on that front. Sex has become so enjoyable – cost-free, risk-free and guilt-free. Which is good, given many people are poorer now than in your day, can't afford things and live in a problematic world, needing escape from the humdrum. Sex is free, offering psychological boosts.

'Then the second thing is women's control over our bodies. Not just whether and when to have babies – but also who with. Artificial insemination has become more common with women able to select their chosen father from approved donors, or past partners. Though they have to accept the resulting kids at sixteen have a right to know who their biological dad is. Actually think it's gone too far. Of course, sex for procreation is still common, as you'd expect, with the father sharing the decision and aftermath, but far from obligatory. Some women as mothers have the opportunity to be completely independent of a partner – a 1980s women's lib dream. A rather false one, in my view. In the interest of equality, England is currently debating the right to single parenthood for unattached men. Humph!

'Then the third thing is the issue of consent, which has been a vexed issue forever. Now technology has ridden to the rescue. Our wristies listen to us – they record consent or not and can be referred to by the courts. So problems are rarer now, and rape less common. While the question of power relations still worries us, rapists will get caught. This is a revolution! Really good. So that's three pretty important changes – the male pill, which is easily available, artificial insemination and recorded consent.'

Sarah smiled broadly and went on: 'now, the law is an ass, as Dogberry I think says in Much Ado, and has taken years to catch up with the changed reality – the fact that people of all persuasions have a greater sense of confidence and boldness in relationships. The law has now at last created more sexual partner options – not just married or single, which was so restricting.'

'What do you mean?' I asked. 'Ah, well, we've now got agreements you can enter into with a mate, levels of commitment if you like. The most informal, with few legal ties, is to be buddies. Civil liaisons, like marriage and civil partnerships, have a legal framework. Marriage and civil partnerships can be for life or for a specified period of at least twenty years then no need for divorce – perhaps to bring up your children together but not committed for ever. Rather more realistic! Liaisons I'll come to. It's all about trying to give lovers more choice without false expectations, and a way of redirecting the seven-year itch, and even the twenty-seven-year itch. Sexual freedom within loving relationships – all licit! Hurray!'

Her voice had become remarkably enthusiastic. Given my upbringing I was a bit non-plussed, shocked even. 'You mean that lifelong exclusive relationships are out of the window?' 'Not at all,' she said. 'Still plenty of those, if that's what people want or need. Just there are many other relationship options which can be adopted. Of course, hearts may still be broken, but less often. Lovers know what they are entering into. There's less room for misconceptions and, as I said, false hopes. Also, the thing is, I believe people are better now at understanding motives. If it's simply sensual delight they are after, with someone they fancy, but don't love, even just with a friend, then they agree to be sex buddies for a night or a week or a month, or whatever suits them. All great fun and not necessarily exclusive. So that's lust dealt with! Civil Liaisons have only been introduced recently on a kind of experimental basis. Liaisons can be for anything between one and seven years.' I was looking quizzical. 'Yes. I know,' she went on, 'the meaning of the term has evolved. But that's language for you! You can even have an agreed liaison while being married in a loving permanent relationship to someone else. A bit like the aristocracy and artists of yesteryear had a mistress on the side. It works both ways now. Women take lovers just as often as men. More often, in fact.' She paused. 'Robyn, you look a bit odd.'

I was indeed feeling 'odd'. The morality and frameworks of sexual relationships that I had for some reason assumed to be unchanging were being overturned. In retrospect I blame my straight-laced mother and Islamic father, but at the time the new arrangements seemed to be legitimising promiscuity. I was both shocked and, I must admit, fascinated. 'Surely it can't really work. Isn't it a recipe for jealousy and hurt? It feels like pandering to male egos and desires, and making the women as self-serving and selfish as the men. Also, the young girls and boys. Doesn't it give them the wrong messages about relationships? Not so much about love and mutual respect as about legitimately exploiting others to satisfy your lust. And what about religious people, what about Muslims?' I was pleasantly surprised how articulate I was about a subject largely taboo with my women friends.

Sarah looked at me quizzically, sizing me up. 'Let me tell you a story,' she said. 'When I was about 13, living in a very working class community, you know, processed food, smartphones, e-games, social media, that sort of thing, I was well into puberty already, and rather precocious. It took some courage to stand against teenage trends. But I was a bit of a rebel, as you might guess. Unusually for a teenager, I demanded real food, not the processed junk that was absolutely everywhere, after lessons about it from a teacher I'd fallen for.

'I was wild and sexually precocious too. Unsurprisingly I became one of the teenage pregnancy statistics. I chose for my child to be adopted, which was probably for the best, given that my behaviour afterwards did not change. I was taking more care but still all out for sexual adventure, with boys, and with girls too; I was just emotionally irresponsible. I even tried to seduce my favourite teacher, the one I mentioned – without success I have to say.

'I really thought I was an artist, so I went to art college. At college, for the first time, I embarked on a longer-term relationship. It was a really open relationship. We indulged each other's sexual escapades. Artists had always been allowed wayward and self-indulgent behaviour, it seemed, so art college at first seemed the right place for me. But my interest in art didn't conform to the fashion of the day. I loved drawing people, either colourfully dressed or naked, all very sensuous. But my work was frowned on because to the staff it didn't appear to have an intellectual concept – conceptual art was the buzzword at the time. People liked my pictures, but they were just too direct for the college lecturers – no enigma and puzzle requiring trite political or social explanations. So I didn't last there. And,' she looked at me, suddenly joyous, 'that led to my St. Francis moment! A blinding flash of insight, mainly into myself! I took myself in hand and decided to learn. I got onto a course which combined my interests in people and health and hedonism – psychology and food – and never looked back. I then landed a good job in the organic food industry, promoting healthy diets. I felt so strongly about it that eventually I went into politics, when they introduced democratically elected health authorities in the forties ...'

I chipped in, 'so you came good in the ...' but she carried on regardless: 'and I think I made a difference. The West Country Province – we're talking the 2050s now – became a European leader in good diet promotion.

'Now, there's another strand which needs to be woven in. What was happening over the whole period was the development of robots. Even back in the early twenties there were amazing programs which could write a speech or a thesis. In the thirties and forties there was the development of humanoid robots, realising the science fiction dream from Mary Shelley onward. By the late forties they were being mass produced. Guess what one of the early functions was?' 'Sex?' I mouthed. 'No, no, not immediately,' she chuckled, 'but massage and cuddles. The rationale being that this was for therapeutic purposes, to help lonely, isolated and mentally disturbed people. Well, you can imagine what happened. It wasn't long before the market steamrollered all the political reservations, and was developing all kinds of robotic sex aids, some humanoid, some less so! They could communicate intelligently and warmly, becoming very expert at what was called sensual massage. People got hooked on them, they became love objects, in theory providing unending masturbatory pleasure. My partner and I tried these machines, needless to say, and became aware of the downsides as well as the delights. They affected relationships, including our own – which eventually foundered, though for other reasons too. Many people were becoming addicted to machine sex. I became part of a movement calling for the banning of certain types of sex robots in the home, using my position in the West Country health authority to demand evidence and then action. In the 2050s there were a series of progressively restrictive measures regulating sexbots, as they'd become known. There are still some situations where they are permitted at home for personal and health reasons, and some provinces, including our own, where you can have carefully controlled access.'

I'd been listening with avid attention. 'Ah, yes, I think I saw one place in town,' I said, 'Called Hotbots or something. No, Hedonism!' 'Yeah, that's it,' said Sarah, 'and very controversial it is. Not so much because of their services per se, but because it's put many members of the oldest profession out of business in places like Bristol. Anyway, one long-term trend which this kind of availability has reinforced is towards sexual pleasure for its own sake, hence all the institutionalised arrangements to manage lust and desire I was describing. Having said that, long-term partnerships are natural for humans, so many exist, and there are safeguards for children too. In my own case I'm very happily married now. My man is an IT wizard, devising new systems and simplifying old ones, at least that's one of his interests, and we have an open marriage – he's younger than me and very active. I've given up on all that. No no, not that! on politicking. Had quite enough of it! You know what I do now, this radical and experimental farm – I'm married to that too.'

I looked at her with admiration. A query sprang to my mind, about how children were brought up in this world of free love and short-term contracts. Sarah explained that for a period earlier in the century there had been a movement for women to have babies independently, changing partners at will, not necessarily even knowing who the sperm donor was. The state initially allowed this, believing in freedom of choice, but then later did a U-turn, because too many single parents were struggling financially, and there was very convincing evidence that children benefit from having two parents. Things have moved on. Its complex and problematic, but shared responsibility is more the rule now. Sarah went on: 'As for myself, I had no children after that first one, partly work and politics, partly a feeling that every extra baby was a new consumer and polluter.'

At that moment a lively, slightly dishevelled, middle-aged man came into the farm kitchen, wearing purple shorts, wellies and a T-shirt announcing 'prone to mischief' on its front. He introduced himself as Solomon ('God knows why my parents called me that!'), warmly shaking my hand and looking me in the eye with smiling engagement. 'My husband,' said Sarah, with a pleased expression. 'Nine years and counting. Could be for life!'

'Oh, my God,' he said, 'trapped for life in Sarah's sexy web. I hope she doesn't eat me all up!' His wife chuckled ominously. I could see what he meant!

'Well, it's lunchtime,' she said. 'Has Cinders got it all ready?' For some while I had been conscious of activity behind my back. 'Yes, just the table to lay,' said Solomon, 'it'll be a simple meal: a ploughman's, as they say – with our own sheep's cheese, salad and home-baked bread. Plus home brew if you'd like it.' I looked round in the direction of the kitchen units, thinking Cinders … domestic slavery? There was a humanoid robot busying around quietly. She looked like a rather plain teenage girl – or maybe boy, I couldn't work it out. I found Cinders difficult to take in, clearly not human at all, though with remarkably human hands, clothed in a blue onesie, with a small control panel on her front (in case of emergency, I was told), with an unnervingly sweet smile and well-modulated voice. Cinders and Solomon busied around, laying the table, exchanging a few words quite casually as they did it. We sat down and tucked in.

Solomon explained how he and Sarah divided responsibilities – playing to each other's strengths. Sarah in charge of the farm, as well as her ongoing role as health trustee. He cooked, managed the energy and water systems, while also being part of a regional group interested in psycho-history. He didn't dwell on that but went into the farm's energy systems. Apparently they had a big field of solar panels with sheep grazing beneath them, solar roofs for all buildings, a water turbine in the stream, linked to a mini pumped storage scheme, and also hosted a group of big wind turbines on behalf of the district. And all in the Cotswold National Park! He chortled wickedly. The farm more than covered its own needs and supplied energy to the Parish storage system, while most wind power went to the District-wide system. The surplus energy created by the local cluster of parishes had enabled a successful bid for a primary school. It all seemed quite complex to me! Sarah told me how their mixed farm satisfied many local food needs courtesy of the village pub shop, while their large surplus was 'exported' to the Stroud Valleys or Gloucester wholesale markets, with some specialist foods going further afield. As I'd learnt on my previous visit, the farm workshops were independent little businesses all based on the varied produce of the farm – apparently there was a Planning obligation to that effect.

It sounded so well arranged, realising the ideal of rural autonomy, but at a cost of intrusive oversight. Apparently the Parish Council, which Sarah sat on, kept a tight rein on things with a kind of input/output balance sheet for the Parish. It needed to do this, and gain the support of residents and businesses, in order to ensure that parish activities as a whole maintained their sustainability status, which covered soil, water, wildlife habitats, energy, wood, food, transport and local services. It all sounded like a huge bureaucratic palaver to me. My hosts assured me it had become absolutely critical as the world tried to extricate itself from the disastrous overconsumption and pollution of the period from the early nineteenth century up to around 2040 – the age of coal, oil and gas. Solomon also allayed my fears about the cost of all the necessary monitoring, review and communication. The data collection and analysis were all managed by dedicated local authority AI software which automatically gave feedback to all and sundry, produced committee reports, and linked to provincial and national systems. The district had to demonstrate net absorption of greenhouse gases, and upward trend on biodiversity. The Province as a whole was carbon positive, absorbing more than it emitted, by a wide margin, which in theory allowed poor countries round the world a bit of wiggle room with their own carbon budgets.

Suffice to say I had a great time with the two of them – Sarah so warm and open, and quite a comic, Solomon engaging and lively. He seemed to have boundless energy. If something needed doing he would jump into action, sometimes even pre-empting Cinders the housebot. He took me round the workshops and the home fields of the farm, meeting some of the others in the farm community, including families in their wood-built cottages (Cotswold stone is *verboten* he told me) gaining a real sense of the richness and diversity of the place – more a hamlet than just a farm.

Back in the farmhouse, I asked Sarah what her recipe was for a happy and fulfilling life. She had clearly thought about this before, because out came an alliterative foursome, just pat. Sun, sex, smiles and soul. I was not entirely surprised – it seemed to suit her to a T. She said, 'They may sound trite, but go beyond the literal meaning. Each is shorthand for a world.' 'Go on!' I said. 'Sun represents the natural world, the stars, the Earth, land and sea, woods and birds and flowers. Contact with nature is so important. Then sex is about human relationships, friendships, lovers and enjoyment of one's own body. Smiles is about an attitude to life, being open, positive and outgoing, seeing the funny side of things. Sex and smiles go together really. Then soul is about awareness, morality, truth, integrity, respect for every person and for all living things. That's about it.'

'Which of those is the most critical?' I asked, imagining her answer – wrongly, as it happened. 'Oh, soul, of course,' she said. 'The others follow naturally. Don't you think?'

Much later, after cycling back and eating supper with Sam and Rufus, I turned over the events of the day in my mind. I could remember everything that the others had said. Sarah's explanation of contemporary sexual relationships intrigued me. So did Rufus's plan for the morrow. He'd arranged for me to have tea with Able Cranston, philosopher of the Cohousing, and in the evening we would meet up with boy Bob (as he called him) and learn about the Communiversity. Thinking about Bob, my imagination worked overtime in directions I simply cannot write about. But I was definitely looking forward to the encounter. Cyla observed and kept her own counsel.

Part IV
Synthesis and Revelation

Drawn in Stratford Park, Stroud, the Cedar of Lebanon means strength and endurance, while the olive branch represents peace and the fig means prosperity. The Yin-yang symbol means interdependence. We all live in one world.

19
Delving deeper

Next day Able rang and suggested a longer time together, including lunch. I was delighted. We were to meet for coffee in his ground floor flat. Apparently it was Make Do and Mend Day in the co-operative. Having an hour to waste before seeing Able, I went round to the work zone. The workshop doors were wide open and I was invited inside to watch for a few minutes. It was a hive of activity as resident carpenters, metal workers, electricians and engineers took time off from their normal activities to mend people's gadgets and furniture. A big 3D printer was hard at work. Cyla provided a list of jobs on a screen and monitored progress. Some tasks were being performed by dedicated AI robots. They could be instructed by voice – and it was clear they were able to tackle specific defined tasks with enviable precision. Sam was hard at work with a carpentry robot – a woodbot, she explained – making a garden seat out of 'found' wood – old worn planks and posts. She was measuring, designing and arranging while the robot sawed and cut joints – quickly and accurately! She told me her aim was to use no new timber and avoid the need for screws or nails.

Outside in the drizzly courtyard garden, other people, including Rufus, were weeding and planting out in the mixed flower/vegetable plot with the aid of a plantbot. This machine's ability to weed was amazing. It was able to tackle a metre-wide bed, de-earthing and crushing the weeds, and preserving specified plant-types, while the people followed on with the more creative process of companion planting, guided by someone who was apparently the leading co-gardener.

I watched for a while, fascinated by the harmonious collaboration of human and machine. Then, still having some time, I wandered out of the Cohousing estate and down the road to the square, conscious that Rufus would be following my every move. I wanted to see if there was a daily newspaper for sale. I felt a bit wicked, breaking bounds. There was no paper in the general store. There was a real person – which was quite surprising, I thought – of Indian extraction – which was not. Her sari was gorgeous in emerald and blood-orange. When I enquired about papers she looked at me in a curious way. 'Just ask your house system. It'll help with more news and views than you could ever read. We do have some books, if you crave the printed word.' I examined the book shelves, thinking I needed some distraction from the remorseless learning curve I was on. I chose a whodunnit from a 'new' author, which appeared to be set in Iran, my second country, thinking that would be very interesting. It had clearly been read by someone else before me. I flashed my wristy at the shopkeeper, and saw a terrifying price recorded – inflation! I realised. But still in pounds not dollars or euros. She said, 'you'll get most of that back when you return the book.' As I was making my way back to the Cohousing, my wristy beeped and a message from Rufus popped up: 'good choice. Unputdownable!!'

A little later than intended, I rang the bell at Able's front door. He welcomed me in genially. I felt very comfortable in his presence and immediately shared my purchase with him, and my disappointment at the lack of newspapers. 'Can't say I've read that,' he said, looking at the book. 'As regards papers, which I remember with a lot of affection, even though they were all full of blarney and baloney, we can't afford them now. They use much too much wood-pulp, even with recycling. Trees are precious and grow slowly.' I grasped the point immediately, and moved on to my very positive impressions of the Make Do and Mend Day. 'But Able,' I said, 'I'm puzzled by the different priorities there seem to be. Here your friends are reusing and maintaining things conscientiously, and you've got a clockwork bell, but there are the robots helping – and using energy galore.'

Able chortled. 'Yes! Yes! Quite right. Illogical I suppose. It just shows how we are all capable of double-think. Though there are mitigations. We generate and store enough solar electricity on site to power the bots as well as other general uses. And those machines are part of the repair mentality. They self-diagnose any faults and can even mend some themselves. We bought them years ago. No built-in obsolescence like you will remember, when IT firms mercilessly exploited consumers' desire for novelty, especially in phones, and stopped supporting computers after ten years or less, phones in just five years. So much waste! It was appalling. It took forever for governments to escape from the malign clutches of international tech firms (and big pharma for that matter) to legislate for durability and health. And for standardisation where appropriate. It's much better in Europe and these Sceptred Isles now. But America is still compromised. Their whole political system, their party funding regime, remains based on vested interests. Money talks. Thank god some big-money interests are pulling in the right direction now.'

'Anyway, all that's no excuse! We are duly chastised by you – a visitor from the profligate past. How ironic. It's just those bots are so convenient and efficient. We're busy people. At least the rest of them are. I claim immunity. From employment, that is. I think and write and make coffee. Would you like some?'

I was smiling as Able talked. His style and body language were infectious. 'What? Real coffee?' I asked. 'Hmm ... can't afford that. You'll have to pretend.' I nodded yes. 'Good! Because I've made it for you. Chicoffee, of course. The milk is real, though, from our own goats. Do you take milk? Sugar? That's from English beet.' I was trying not to laugh out loud. He was playing to the gallery. I managed a sequential nod and shake of the head. 'Nice and strong, please, Able, so I can cope with you!'

He smiled broadly at that, standing in the kitchen area, and suddenly gave me a great bear hug. 'You'll do!' he said. I was taken by surprise, still shy of the level of physical contact society seemed to take for granted. As he released me, realising this, he said: 'Talk to Rufus about hugging. He's the social psychologist. He says hugging is really good for you, releases healthy bodily reactions. Good for emotions and relaxation. And it's nice and friendly, don't you think? The people from India have taught us that.'

It was warm outside. The sun had come out now. Able and I settled down comfortably, facing each other in the sun-trap patio at the back of his flat, chicoffee in hand. In the moment of silence I reflected that he had once been a woman. I looked at him, thinking now was the moment, before going into politics and economics, to ask him about that. 'Able, I hope you don't mind me asking – could you tell me something about your transition, and why you did it?' 'Not much to tell,' he said dismissively. 'It was a long time ago – I transitioned when I was a student, nineteen I was. I'd been an unhappy teenager, not at all comfortable in my own body. My parents couldn't cope with me. I wasn't interested in wearing pink or playing with dolls and other girly toys when I was young – and couldn't cope with the obsession with hair, face, figure and fashion of my teenage peer group. I left home, lived wild in the city, pretending to keep my studies going. When I changed gender, which took a while, many of my peer relationships at last fell into place, I found new friends, became highly motivated and studied voraciously, and I discovered my poetic self, it was marvellous! My parents cut me off, though. Why do you ask?'

I explained that yesterday I'd seen Sarah, and she had been rather dismissive of gender transitioning, explaining it more as youngsters' response to unhappiness and a social media fad, so I was very interested in his experience. Able chuckled: 'Yes, she would say that! And there's some truth in it. People have to be careful about switching something so fundamental, if really the problems lie elsewhere. There are safeguards now against transitioning prematurely. But there are still people who really were born into the 'wrong' body, and now we have the techniques for enabling and supporting change, physical and psychological, it would be churlish to forbid it.'

I nodded: 'Thank you, Able. That's very helpful. It chimes with my own instinct.' 'Then let's move on,' he said. 'Tell me what you would like to discuss.' I had come prepared and said: 'I've made a little list!' My inflection spontaneously mimicked Pooh Bah. Abel burst into laughter. 'Oh what fun! Who's first for the chop then – he never will be missed, he never will be missed!'

I laughed with him, 'that was completely accidental! I'd even forgotten where it came from.' 'The Mikado!' said Able. 'Of course!' I volunteered. 'I must have seen that way back, when I was about fifteen – 2007 I think. Mum was always saying a *little list*.' 'That is a long time ago,' said Abel, matter-of-factly. I paused, collecting my thoughts. 'Anyway, first on the list, I'd like to know more about the Life Wage – or is it Life Grant? – it does sound rather improbable, not to mention expensive. Then, second, housing. Wulf set the spatial framework very clearly, but I don't understand the financial side, especially how it's apparently so cheap. Then maybe something on the general economy and the wider political system – and please tell me whether we are back in Europe – the EU. Also more worldwide, what changed in the forties to make the UN so universal and apparently effective. It was just a talking shop and aid provider in my day, and also …'

'Hey, stop, that's more than enough to be going on with! You have an insatiable appetite for knowledge!' Able was grimacing with mock alarm. 'Yes, starting at the beginning, Rufus told me you were astonished when he mentioned the Life Grant. So it's my job to explain it to you. It's a good indicator of where we are as a society, stemming from quite fundamental values, like equality and freedom. Robyn, silly question I know, but how far do you believe in those?' 'All the way, Able!' I said, thinking that I should be careful not to be overawed by his age and experience, adding: 'Though in my own time we seemed to have lost sight of both.'

'Quite so!' said Able. 'Earlier this century, freedom was the watchword of those who believed in letting the market work things out, and this attitude prevailed in most countries of the world, but the result was great inequalities of wealth and the poorest finding they had very little freedom indeed. Now consider the benefits of a basic income that more or less covers essential needs of shelter, food and warmth. It offers a real level of freedom to those who are poor and less able to work, or to find work – a tremendous bonus in an age when AI is ubiquitous. No need to apply to anyone for grants. No need to accept the sense of being a failure. Most people top it up in various ways of course, with some kind of work. But it's enabled the reduction of that social inequality which got so bad in the teens and twenties. We talk about that period as the doldrums – the worst time for British society since the Second World War – never to be repeated! Simply paying a basic income to every adult, plus allowances for children, gets rid of a whole raft of bureaucratic evaluation procedures at a stroke – social security, child benefit, unemployment benefit, housing benefit, many disability allowances and so on. It cuts the cost to the state!'

'So you mean,' I said, almost laughing, 'that it's a right wing policy?' 'In political terms, neither left nor right, but right. Wise! Heavens, the English language gets itself in a pickle sometimes! Look, everyone now thinks it common sense. It works, it's practical, indeed … elementary, my dear Watson!' His grey eyes twinkled.

'Before you object on some other spurious account, let me tell you a tale. The conventional wisdom used to be that if you give poor people money, they become indolent, won't bother to work, spend it all on drink and drugs. So governments around the world tied income support to work, or looking for work, and employed loads of minions to assess and test applicants. But when those same people managed to find part-time work, they could become caught in the poverty trap because they had extra costs but had lost some benefits. There were dreadful failures of the system, costing the state dear and individuals dearer. The dire period of austerity starting in 2010 was supposed to save money but actually had exactly the opposite effect, so that by the mid-twenties the country had the highest level of taxes since the Second World War. Quite extraordinary, when we also had the highest levels of homelessness, the highest dependence on food banks, and the highest rate of working age inactivity. What had happened was that austerity had compromised many of the essential community services for children and adults, things like youth clubs, training, libraries, mental health services and primary care, failing to recognise that many people would flounder as a result, so that the state was obliged to spend more and more on social support – like disability benefit and housing benefit, and hospitals too. Building up a combined social deficit and a financial deficit which it took decades to correct. Completely bonkers! The result of false logic, false perceptions, an inability to look dispassionately at the evidence – and that's being generous!'

I was nodding my head vociferously. It all made sense. Abel went on: 'If you haven't already, watch the films of that heroic director from back then – Ken Loach. He gives such powerful perspectives on these issues. One bungling inefficiency was the support for disability. The way it was rolled out meant most applicants were refused by the system initially – the privatised system if I remember rightly – but then those with sufficient nous and energy would appeal, and most of them won. Altogether a huge waste of taxpayer cash and human effort – and highly demeaning and stressful for applicants. The unspoken agenda, even unspoken by those who created the system I suspect – the unconscious agenda was to keep the poor in their place. Inequality in the UK, and even more in the USA, spiralled. A wicked system. And this was in the face of mounting evidence that the best way to tackle poverty was to give the poorest money. No strings attached!'

I was listening closely, holding my own council, but chipped in: 'I've got reservations, well, uncertainties, about that. But first, you were going to tell a story ...' 'Oh, sorry! Yes! You got me up on my soapbox! I'll give you one story among many, which already offered fascinating evidence early in the century. In an impoverished village in Western Kenya each family group was given a one-off payment of $500 by a western charity. This was in the noughties, and $500 was as much as some families earnt in a year. Far from spending it on over-indulgence, the village was transformed: homes repaired or rebuilt, many more people owning their own home and their own livestock, more children going to school. Overall earnings went up and stayed up, so the village community became more self-sustaining. The point being that the people themselves made the decisions about how to spend the bonanza, it wasn't tied to specific targets, and the money was highly productive by any standards. However, there's a rider. It's critical to get the cash into the hands of the people themselves, not a government or national body that wastes it on bureaucracy and bribes. It can be a bit tricky!'

I was interested but still sceptical about the value of one experiment: 'Yes, sounds very impressive, but what about more generally, like the poor in rich countries?' 'Ahh ... well, yes. There have been experiments in rich countries too, luckily recorded on paper. In Canada, for example, and the City of London, supporting down-and-outs. The same basic rule applies: the people best placed to help poor people are the poor themselves. Give them respect. Give them credit. And hard cash to do what they want.' 'So they won't simply buy cigarettes, drugs and booze?' 'If you give peanuts, they may well do that, but if you give enough, unconditionally, most (not all, of course) will seize the chance to better themselves. What's more, a bit of a diversion, in relation to drugs, as you may have gathered, we've legalised them, following the lead a long time ago of the Netherlands. Access to drugs is via health services, and rationed, and it goes along with therapies to wean people off them. That has significantly reduced long-term sickness and thieving and put drug barons out of business.'

I grasped the point, but wasn't entirely convinced. 'OK. I can see what you mean. However, that is a long way from handing out a living wage to everyone.' 'Is it?' he said. 'Once upon a time – in the twentieth century – all undergraduate students received a grant which was not directly linked to their hours of study, or to their results, so long as they progressed year on year. Wages and work were essentially divorced. Your income was one thing, allowing you to live. Your work was another, which you undertook for its own sake. That is the ideal we are striving for. Work should not be a chore, done under duress, but a delight. No more wage-slavery, please! And Robyn, you must remember how it was. Early this century there was an epidemic of overwork. Any kind of work/life balance was sacrificed by so many people, and this work-stress peaked in about 2030. Britain was stuck in a long-hours, low-productivity time-warp, when in spite of all that automation, working hours were longer than at any time in the previous century. Unless of course you lived in France!'

I guffawed involuntarily. 'With their two-hour wine-fuelled lunches and retirement at sixty-three, you mean?' Able laughed with me. 'Maybe we have a cartoon view of the French, even today, but they had it right! Their productivity hour for hour was higher. Here people worked all the hours God gave them, often holding down several part-time, insecure jobs. Basic pay for critical, stressful jobs like social care was pitiful, so there was an underclass of poorly paid, hard-working people who could not afford escalating housing, energy and food costs and the rising tax bill, and a swelling number of people unable to work, stressed out, highly dependent on the NHS and social services which had been slashed by austerity politics. It didn't make any sense. The system was crap. It had to break. Though so ingrained that correction took decades.'

I was still thinking about the universal wage for living. 'I suppose ...' I said tentatively, 'your guaranteed Life Grant is not very different in essence from providing free education and health services. Just a more generalised form of support.'

Able smiled genially, telling me the results of introducing the Life Grant had been remarkable: severe poverty abolished; no beggars on the street – mind you, they are forbidden; parents having more of an option to care for young children at home if they chose, not forced to work; no-one feeling hard done by, as everyone gets the same; whole layers of bureaucratic nanny state controls removed ... He might have gone on, but I broke in, leaning forward with sudden inspiration, and not willing to be steamrollered by his enthusiasm: 'Hey, wait a minute Able! Wait a minute. The problem is not just the income, but the costs. The costs of shelter, food, energy, water, transport, services. Thinking just about housing, that's the biggest thing: renting or buying a flat in places like Oxford or Bristol, let alone London ... even here in Stroud, it's crippling. Rents go up to reflect what some people can pay, and the scarcity value in a crowded country. The market will see to that.'

'Ah-ha, that's another story,' said Able. He suddenly relaxed, laid back in his chair, spread his arms along the back, a look of pleasure suffusing his face. 'Which you are obviously going to tell me,' I said. I couldn't quite interpret his manner. 'Yes, of course. After all, why are you here? But first, how about another drink?' I wagged my head in surprise, and it turned into a nod: 'A drink would be lovely. Just water please. As to why I'm here, God knows!' 'She probably does,' said Able.

20
Housing and habit

Able went back into the kitchen. I looked around the flagstone patio with its flower pots, and up the steps to the shared lawn above, with trees beyond. A very pleasant atmosphere. Then I saw a plumptious young fox, a rich orange-brown in the sunlight, stroll onto the raised lawn not ten metres away, rolling and stretching out on the grass, really loving it. Gorgeous! A moment later I was aware of movement behind one of the bushes on the slope. It was a black and white cat, crouching in attack mode, focussed on the fox, tail snaking in anger. Suddenly he rushed at the fox, fangs bared, and the fox, three or four times his weight, righted himself in confusion and fled! The cat didn't chase, stood for a moment proudly aggressive – MY territory! Then sat down and washed.

Size and strength, I reflected, are not everything. Passion and determination had triumphed. Able, standing silently in the doorway, had seen the confrontation. 'That's Domino,' he said, adding rather unnecessarily, 'because of his colouring. Quite young still but so feisty. I lost my old cat a couple of years ago; she had me exactly where she wanted me – obeying her obsequiously. I was determined to be the master of this one, using bribery of course, but failing again! ' 'Well, that was a very bold and beautiful fox, coming down to your lawn,' I said, 'but an even bolder cat! Fearless!'

Domino was now sprawled out on the grass, still washing, legs sticking out in all directions. 'He's employed as community mouse and rat catcher,' said Able. 'He is a remarkable cat! Nothing frightens him. But he hasn't learnt to share space. Not like us! We share that lawn between half a dozen households, it's really social, ideal for kids. We share it perforce with all the animals too, though we could do without the badger digging chunks out of it. If the fox, a friend of ours, had chosen a spot just along the way, Domino wouldn't be bothered.' 'Wow, what a feline, So territorial!!' I said.

'Well, it relates directly to the topic of housing. It's not just cats. Everybody needs someplace to call home – their own territory – and will fight to defend it. To contextualise this absolutely fundamental issue, I need to go into a little bit of housing history. Sorry about this, you may know it all already of course,' said Able. 'There have essentially been three phases of policy since the Second World War – a period of nearly 150 years. The first phase was when the concept of planning for housing need was dominant. We can date that as 1945 to 1980. The second was from 1980 to around 2035, when housing as a commodity was the ruling concept. The final date there can be argued over, some people put it earlier, others later. The third phase was from 2035 until today, when housing is considered a basic human right. In the early twenties – your time – it was really the high watermark of the commodity principle. I'm wondering, was it obvious to you and colleagues at the time? How did you see it?' He smiled in anticipation.

'Let me think a bit,' I said. Yes … yes, the market was king. Much of the social housing had been sold off over many decades under the 'right to buy' policy. The original intention was well-meaning – council tenants had the opportunity to own their homes and this was seen as a route to a better life – but the policy was formulated in such a way that local authorities could not easily replace lost housing. At the same time my impression is that government subsidised the private rented sector by giving subsidies to first time buyers and paying landlords the housing benefit of poorer renters, effectively allowing rents to spiral up by increasing affordability and therefore demand.

Able interrupted: 'yes, well, fine, though not quite as simple as that. The relationship between local authorities and private landlords could be quite fractious. The exploitation was not all one way, so that small landlords could feel obliged to leave the sector altogether, or feel forced to raise rents. At the same time, of course, rental housing had become an investment because of rising prices, bolstering retirement incomes for some, making millions for the big boys who exploited the situation. It's altogether quite a knotty problem.'

I was thinking of my own experience. 'My friends and I couldn't get onto the housing ladder, owning our own place, unless we were supported by what people called the bank of mum and dad. Many were still living with parents into their thirties – which is a mixed blessing! And I am very much aware from my work on another issue. We weren't building enough houses. Everyone wanted more housing, but not in their back yard – NIMBYs, you know. And there was just a handful of major house builders with their eyes firmly on the bottom line, not on housing need. Governments stimulated demand, giving help to first time buyers, falsely imagining that would stimulate market supply. It didn't! My design firm often worked for big housebuilders, so I became very aware of what was happening, with developers restricting their building rate to force prices up, maximise profits. I read that profits per house after the financial crash in 2008, rose from £6k per house, which is not enough I guess, given the risks, to ten times that in 2017! Which is ridiculous. Also, in pretty places half the houses were bought up for second homes, or for holiday lets, like down in Cornwall, so local families hadn't a cat in hell's chance of buying their own homes and were screwed by high rents. It's – it was – an abject disaster, and the politicians never seemed to have a clue. In fact housing ministers changed all the time. Immediately they began to understand the mess they'd created, they were moved on!'

'Sorry Able, I'm a bit jaundiced about this, it's all too close to home. And work. I guess there were a few signs of hope. Like Community Land Trusts. Real local initiatives. But they were really small fry, creating housing in the interstices of the system. Meanwhile the social housing stock was lost through the 'right to buy', which gave a leg-up to some but overall the poor got poorer and the rich got richer. All part of your freedom principle, preached by right-wing political parties. Freedom for money, if you have it, to make money.' I paused, looking at Able, and calmed my voice. 'Sorry to be so cynical. Comes quite naturally to me now! So, yes, housing was very much a commodity.'

Able was looking at me with appraising eyes. Maybe even with an expression of quiet satisfaction. 'Ah! That's very interesting,' he said. 'The trouble back then, no government was prepared to tackle the basics. As you say, freedom of the market was the mantra, kow-towed to by the powers that be, despite the fact that the market was being highly manipulated by oligarchic commercial interests, while being confused by short-lived meddling ministers, not to mention the courts huge backlog. And the planners found it much easier to work with a few big firms rather than loads of small fry. So in a way there was an unholy alliance of planning and developer interests. Anyway, local authorities were effectively just agents of central government, with little power to change things.'

'Now, quite surprisingly, a real shift began to happen in the early thirties, not long before the Bad Years. A new government gained power, wielding the banner 'Freedom for ALL, not the few', stealing the neo-liberal mantra. Very simple! Very clever! Impossible to argue against. Several big things happened. First, the measure of overall success changed to reflect the rhetoric around Quality of life. It ceased to be GDP, i.e. financial growth, and became growth of wellbeing for all – and I really mean for all. Radical, that was! And about time too! Successive governments had failed miserably on GDP anyway, so the change incentivised politicians to show their worth by improving people's lot, rather than national turnover.

'That played into housing: the idea of housing as a basic human right took hold. 'Fair rents!' became the cry, yet again! Central government gave powers to certain cities and counties to experiment with housing policy and finance. London followed Scotland and Wales in abolishing the Right to Buy – which had created so much homelessness because social housing was not replaced. It proved popular – much to everyone's surprise. They used the money thus saved to implement a 'fair rents for fair housing' policy. It couldn't be all at once, of course. London learnt from bad experience of rent control in Scotland and good experience in some continental cities like Vienna, so as not to destroy the rental market. They took a calculated, softly, softly approach, punishing the rogue landlords first – those who were obliging young people to live in squalid shoeboxes at grossly inflated rents. Good, popular stuff. As a result they saved money on housing benefit, which had become a quite ridiculous drain on the public purse. They also required any new property buyers to have lived in the UK for at least five years. That was a gamechanger! Freeing up property for use, not kept empty for overseas billionaires to drop into occasionally, or even worse, just left empty year on year as an appreciating asset. All this moderated house price rises. The GLA used the savings in housing benefit to invest in land and property for social housing and social provision.'

'Cornwall was another of the counties allowed to experiment. They generally followed the London lead, and also took the second and holiday homes issue by the scruff of the neck, making sure that locals could afford housing while also encouraging the visitors that kept the economy going. After the experiment's success, eventually all local authorities were allowed the same freedoms.'

'All sounds good!' I said. 'And the chief urbanist also told me how they ensure that lots of small developers and individual households can get in on the act of building or renovating houses, while the big firms are rationed. But all so late in the day! It should have happened decades earlier.
'

'Yes,' rejoined Able. 'Tony Blair had the chance. PM for a decade! His government had power over the turn of the century, and kept things ticking along. In fact he managed to reduce inequality, increase longevity – and increase years of healthy life. But he would not tackle fundamentals, like the housing market, because things were generally going well. Then we had the catastrophic banking failure, which drained the exchequer of cash, and was itself worsened by the freedoms given the City by Gordon Brown, thinking that markets know best. Which led to austerity and cumulative problems. All water under the bridge now!'

I was very interested in the process of change, so our conversation became rather extended. Able was a mine of information. He broadened out the discussion to the economy and politics as eco-crises hit, to the impact on people, and the development of the current overarching English strategy which, he claimed, combined climate and economic resilience, biodiversity, social fairness and rising quality of life.

I picked up the occasional reference to England, not Britain, not the UK. I asked, rather wide-eyed, whether the UK still existed. 'Good heavens, no!' he said. 'Wasn't the writing on the wall even back in the twenties?' I shrugged, not wanting to waste breath on my untutored perceptions. 'No? Well, it was only a matter of time. Northern Ireland and Eire both had Sinn Féin governments for quite a while, so were able to plot and wheel and deal. You might guess what one critical factor was? Yes! The cock-up over Brexit – never satisfactorily sorted as far as Northern Ireland was concerned. It wasn't long before the Northern Ireland voting public were edging towards 50/50, staying in the UK or uniting with Ireland. There were some difficult times, risking a return to the Troubles. But reunion with Ireland happened eventually.

'And Scotland? And Wales?' I asked. 'Ah! They took longer. Especially Wales. It's still not fully divorced from England. Ironically it was English nationalism that triggered change. The UK government, dominated by England, greatly reduced the subsidy England paid to both countries. Scotland decided it would be better off in the EU, and seceded. It was actually all rather confusing. Because the EU at much the same time decided to institute two kinds of membership: political and economic. Every country had trade, environmental and cultural ties, but only the inner group were joined at the hip. Meaning, being in the Eurozone, with one central bank and agreed foreign policy. Norway, Switzerland, Turkey, some Eastern European countries and then Scotland became economic members. A bit later, when the first global crisis blew up, England and Wales joined as well. Quite a change, but the country had been edging that way for some time. In a way a bigger shift happened a year or two later. There was widespread recognition that big government had failed miserably, that taxes were going down the drain because of the inefficiencies and vacillation of central government. As a result, newly created provinces, like the West Country, East Anglia, Yorkshire and so on, were given much greater powers, as of right, very similar to Wales. A revolution! It has made a real difference, much to some politicians' surprise. It's meant that the old 'postcode lottery' argument, which the media always home in on, is used now by voters to castigate their own province, not Westminster. However, it left the Welsh feeling they were no longer being recognised as a separate country, but just a province of England. Now they're trying to become Political members of the EU. That vote, the plebiscite, is in the autumn. Mind you, it has to be a two-thirds majority now, for a constitutional change like that, so it's difficult to predict.'

I had been concentrating hard, frowning slightly as I tried to take it all in. 'Sorry!' said Able, 'that's a very condensed summary. Did you follow?' 'Yes. I think so. Does it mean the NHS is now a regional responsibility? Likewise major infrastructure? And policing?' 'Yes, mostly. Energy and biodiversity too. Though water is a special case, because that has to be planned by river catchment. It can get complex! The English government is just left with things like foreign policy, defence, personal taxation and benefits; again, more or less. Quite enough to be going on with. Some major taxes are controlled by the provincial assemblies.'

'Thank you, Able. That's fantastic,' I said. At that moment Domino, on the lawn, stood up and stretched luxuriously. I stood up and stretched in imitation, conscious that Able was looking at me with appreciation. 'Shall we take a stroll,' he said, 'I need to exercise my legs, find some lunch and pop round to the library – the History Centre.'

We were there in seven or eight minutes. Able was surprisingly quick on his feet, though carried a walking stick reminiscent of the Edwardian style, which he handled with casual aplomb, 'to ward off all the feisty old ladies who want a piece of me!' he said, raising his stick in a possibly suggestive fashion to a tall old biddy across the street. She waived, smiling. 'Though sometimes I let them have me!' he said, chortling. I tensed slightly, the comment seemed so inappropriate from an elderly man to a young woman. He looked open-faced at me and I saw he didn't mean it. It was his little joke. 'To tea,' he said. I thought I saw an edge of sadness in his demeanour.

We arrived at the one-time church, Woodchester Town Hall. Able was into twentieth century classical music. He went to the History Centre and picked up an old manuscript, music from a Welsh composer I'd never heard of. 'This is a rarity,' said Able, 'a mid-twentieth century woman composer who had vanished without trace. She was totally out of fashion when she was writing. Back then it all had to be atonal and hers wasn't. I'm studying her oeuvre, quite unique, all handwritten. This has come from the Gloucestershire Archive, courtesy of the library network. What a service! There are threats to curtail it drastically, as part of an economy drive. But I think it is a real sign of civilisation.'

While he studied the manuscript, I wandered back into the main space. A man I recognised was coming out of the refreshment area. His eyes lit up when he spied me, holding out his hand in greeting. I knew who he was: the journalist, last seen in the cathedral. 'How fortuitous, how delightful,' he said, as we shook hands, myself rather coolly, not smiling. 'You know, I was just talking about you with the woman at the drinks bar. Do you mind if we have a brief chat? I've being doing some background research.' My instinctive defences were alerted, but at the same time I was really interested. Here was someone not selected by my guides, my 'jailors', but outside the system, an independent voice who seemed sincere and nice enough. My wrist band flashed and caught my eye. I read: 'Do not reveal your origin.' Rufus was on the ball, but also more trusting, I thought.

'OK,' I said, 'just while my colleague is busy. It may not be for long, and I'm at his beck and call, really.' The guy gave a meaningful nod, as if he understood my situation. We sat down comfortably in the body of the church. I wondered if this was my chance to get the inside story about this autocratic society, recognising that his motivation was to get the inside story about me! My heart was in my mouth, but my head was clear. We started talking. In retrospect, a fateful encounter.

 လက်ာ

21
Can you hear the future weeping?

'Let me introduce myself,' said the journalist. 'My name is Frank Melia, though I'm sometimes called Frankenstein because I did a lot work on manipulative robots and the people behind them. You may have seen my Frankenstein blog. Now I'm trying to investigate secret government projects which explore psycho-history and societal change. I just wondered if you were tied up with all of that, and wanted to ask you a few questions.'

'Well, Frank,' I said, suddenly professional, 'I'm very interested in the idea of psycho-history, but haven't yet really investigated it. Tell me more.' He obliged: 'There's quite a lot written in the open-access library: you know, historical analysis of cultural and political change, how politicians often misjudge the effects of their actions, making crass decisions which have the opposite societal reaction. Some of the great precursors of the theories have got it wrong too, like Karl Marx. He thought communism would lead to the withering away of the state, while actually it was quite the reverse. The scientific evidence from different cultures and times has been analysed by this new science of psycho-history, and that's all in the public domain. Some phrases were commonplace early in the century – like 'nudge theory'. But, and it's a big but, the application of the theories now, the way current societies might evolve and what could trigger desirable change, that's all kept under wraps. The researchers and the key decision-makers fear that if such information and predictions got out it would alter people's behaviour and undermine their strategies. My belief is that secrecy is always risky, feeding suspicion of illegal activity. Things are often hidden from view to avoid embarrassment. My fear is that the powers that be are manipulating us almost subliminally, possibly for ulterior motives. Even if the motives are entirely noble, I don't like hidden agendas.'

Frank paused. I nodded, signalling to him that I got his message. His inquiries put me on my guard, but also – given my own lack of knowledge about what had happened to me – it excited me. He went on: 'Hence my interest in you. There are things that don't add up, and it might be that you can put my mind at rest. This isn't personal. You strike me as an honest and straightforward person. But I've found out you are not who you say you are. There is information about you on the Euronet – an urban designer from Manchester, and all that – but I've contacted various Mancunian firms and organisations, and you are not known up there. I'd become suspicious originally because your accent is odd. Certainly not northern, but neither southern English nor American, Kiwi or any other accent I know. Though in fact it reminds me of very old radio broadcasts. And the way you are being treated, with kid gloves, is not normal. Where is your minder, anyway? Have you given him the slip?! Maybe you can illuminate the situation?'

I was really surprised – and impressed – how cool I was under Frank's interrogation. Also, I decided that where possible I would tell him the truth, but not the whole truth, nor nothing but the truth. 'Well, very interesting,' I said, 'and I agree with what you say about secrecy, though sometimes it may be necessary. My minder, as you call him – I call him my guide – is actually listening in to everything you say. Now, Manchester. OK – you've rumbled me. I'm not there now. It was years ago I was there. And my accent – probably affected by the fact my Dad comes from Iran, and I've spent time out there living with him.'

Frank interposed: 'So why all the mystery? Why the lies? Or half-truth, if you prefer?' 'I'm not really sure,' I said, 'I am involved, like a kind of guinea-pig, in a big research project, and having been rather catapulted into this part of the country – into the West Country, which is so far ahead of the game – my job is to see things with fresh eyes and to analyse and evaluate and report back.' 'Ahh!' said Frank. 'Is that because they, whoever they are, hope to undermine the progress made, or to find reasons to compromise the reputation of the province, for their own interests?' 'Not at all!' I declared. 'Quite the opposite. They want to learn how such rapid progress has been possible. How has it been possible that all the different institutional and commercial and community stakeholders are singing from the same hymn-sheet. Sorry to use such a hackneyed phrase!'

'It's not hackneyed at all,' said my interrogator, 'It's a new one on me. Anyway, this leads me back to psycho-history … I wonder if your project is related to that? I know there's a big and rather secret Anglo-German research programme on that – much too secret for comfort in my view. And the suspicion in my circles is they are trying to work out how to manipulate the future. Whoever 'they' are! Am I close to the truth?'

'I really don't know. And that is the truth. I'm just a pawn, not a player.' I was rather pleased to be able to tell the whole truth for a change, and as I answered, I saw Able coming out of the History Centre. My rescuer! But no! He turned to chat to someone in the coffee gallery. A different deflection tactic occurred to me.

'Frank, can I ask you a question? Imagine that I am someone from a another time.' 'Maybe you are,' said Frank under his breath. 'And this is my first time here, trying to get to grips with what goes on. I'm finding a real dichotomy in this society: on one hand it seems open, well run, quite egalitarian, and people seem happy; on the other hand it appears authoritarian, very top-down, with identity chips, car ownership forbidden, rigid rules governing the market, and communities too, all anti-freedom.'

Frank was beaming. 'I think you've just admitted something. You are an interloper, maybe not a spy, but you are spying on us! And you are so right. This is a controlled society. I'm very suspicious of the motives of those in power. I think they've pulled the wool over the electorate's eyes. It's my job to try and allow everyone to see clearly again. As an aside, and just in the interests of accuracy, it's not that private cars are completely forbidden. Rather that they are taxed so heavily that most people can't afford them, and anyway can do without them, the alternatives being so cheap and available. There! That is to prove my objectivity! So now, come clean … where are you from?' He paused. 'Or when are you from? You're not from another time, another age, are you? There've been all these articles in the New Scientist exploring the possibility of time travel. Difficult to believe, but some out there do.'

'Yes, I've seen those articles, I said, 'quite extraordinary and very mysterious.' I was playing for time, seeing Able making his way towards us. 'It really puzzles me … while I can just about conceive that minds could bridge across time, I can't imagine how bodies could. It just doesn't make …'

At that moment Able came up behind Frank and without ceremony plonked hands on his shoulders. Frank whisked round and almost shouted, 'Cranston, how good to see you. My old sparring partner! Are you well?' 'Not so much of the old, you rascal. So you are still trying to bend the minds of impressionable young women, are you?' 'Enlighten, illuminate and discreetly question, is what you mean of course. But you know, this one, Robyn Ghorra, she is not very bendable at all. She has retained her Mona Lisa enigma right through our discussion.'

I wasn't quite sure whether to be flattered by his comment or affronted by his presumption in talking about me as if not there. Able responded: 'Good for her. Good for you, Robyn, don't let this man bamboozle you. I wouldn't trust him further than I could throw him. Which is no distance at all! He's a good reporter, but such warped views. I've spent blog after blog trying to educate him.' 'A complete waste of time!' said Frank. 'But you have to admit, Able, I've given you pause for thought on many occasions.' 'True enough, my friend.'

I broke into their exchange. 'Actually, I've enjoyed conversing with you, Frank Melia. And you have given me pause for thought too. But now I think …' 'Yes, look at the time,' said Able. 'We must be getting on or we'll miss lunch. Great to bump into you, Frank, let's meet for a chat another time. Give me a ring.' 'I'll be in touch,' replied Frank. 'With both of you.'

Almost as an afterthought, he thanked me, then swivelled on his feet and went off as if he had another mission to fulfil. Able and I started walking, more leisurely, towards the main square. I looked at my wristy. A message from Rufus: Brilliantly done! You are a natural. I rang him immediately, saying I was pleased that ordeal was over, but I had quite enjoyed it. He told me I had passed with flying colours, and how, in only a few days since seeing the guy the first time, I had gained enviable poise and self-possession. Much better, he said, to let me handle awkward situations myself rather than have him, Rufus, intervene and arouse suspicions. I felt chuffed!

*****

Able and I had very welcome glass of Woodchester Red with our lunch in the cafe on the square. I rehashed my conversation with the journalist with him. He said not to worry, he was sure that soon enough I would be told all about the project in which I was a pawn. He told me about his own musical researches in the library, in some detail. To distract him, and me, I posed him a linguistic question: 'Able, you mentioned people who are impaired. Is 'impairment' the same as disability?' 'Ah, yes!' he responded, 'but we don't use that term now. It eventually was seen as presumptuous and a bit of an insult. People said, we aren't disabled, we're still doing things, better than some, despite it all. So government looked for another term. Toyed with the term 'handicapped', which seemed slightly less pejorative, but ended up with 'impairment'. Nothing's perfect! Why are you laughing?'

I was rather pleased to be suddenly taken over by the giggles. Very relaxing! 'Well, it's funny! I had to study design for disability. Apparently the term way back in last century was 'handicapped'. When people mocked the notion of handicap, being rude by gesture and expression, they decided to change the term to 'disabled'. People did seem to become more considerate and inclusive in their attitudes. Now that word is contaminated, and you've adopted another!' 'Plus ça change!' said Able, with a smile.

'However, you'll have other issues on your mind. Let me guess one of them. You might like to hear first-hand about the Bad Times, because so far you've mostly been hearing from Rufus and Sam, who did not live through them. Am I right?'

'Yes, thank you Able. I'd like to hear it from you. Something happened back then that revolutionised attitudes. Rufus gave me a vivid outline, much better than Cyla in my room. She was just dry as dust. Edith, the mayor, has also given me her impressions from when she was young, and I heard from Sacha too, if you know her – an awful experience. But yes, I'd love to hear more, and how it affected you personally. You must have been in the prime of life.'

'Robyn … it's quite a painful subject. It affected me, and my family, quite profoundly. I'm not sure how to approach it. I lost my job, then our house, my adopted daughter went out to Africa and got herself killed. The world was turned upside down. You know, we were very lucky not to have burned the whole globe into a radioactive desert, everything destroyed. North Korea actually fired a lethal nuclear rocket, but it backfired on their own country, luckily not a city. We avoided nuclear holocaust by the skin of our teeth. It was absolutely awful. Many people now middle-aged were kids then; it's affected their psychology, their values – they make the decisions now. I was working on projects in the global south. I was a 'collaboration facilitator'. You've heard of the IT disaster? Yes? Well, I was in India at the time. Luckily India had developed a semi-independent system, so we weathered that, just about. Though of course America and Europe and elsewhere were very hard hit, because they were so tied up together through globalisation, and that meant huge delays and confusion. Then very soon after, there were storm surges, rough weather in many places around the world, compounded by raised sea levels when part of the West Antarctic Ice Sheet collapsed, flooding coasts, including some cities. After the huge solar storm, which happened not long after, electricity became the biggest problem. Everything depended on it, so when it went off nothing would work. No financial transfers, no computers, no bots, no vehicles, no water pumps – no energy. I may be exaggerating a bit, but that is what it felt like. It seemed like divine retribution for our wicked practices. The Earth, the global ecosystem, wreaking vengeance for the way we had despoiled the biosphere in the mad chase for profit. Maybe Gaia was forcing us to change. Places which had acclimatised to dry seasons were drowned. Places used to regular rainfall had none and starved. Some coastal cities were inundated. My daughter was a trainee nurse.' His voice slowed. 'She was caught up in violence in central Africa as whole populations tried to escape starvation and/or flood. When, once in a while, internet communication was working, her phone was turned on, she was recording events. I saw and heard the moment when she was 'arrested' and summarily executed. Beheaded.'

Able stopped talking, clearly distressed. I was weeping, barely able to see through the tears, agonised by his tale, unable really to grasp the enormity of what had happened – of what the world had been through, and this man in particular. Able leant forward towards me and I felt a surge of fellow feeling. We ended up shoulder to shoulder, head to head, wet with tears, holding each other. Words seemed completely inadequate. After a while, once I came back into myself, we sat back on our chairs. Able looked kind of smaller, deflated. We sat quietly for a while, gazing into space.

Able recovered his poise, speaking quietly. 'The scale of population displacement and migration was unimaginably huge, with an impossible humanitarian situation and many deaths in transit. The economic fall-out was dire, the ecological disaster compounded by the technological one. People were thrown back on their own resources. Some countries, some communities, had prepared for the event, building up food and water reserves, developing local energy and wood resources – though then in some parts of the world they could be vulnerable to neighbours with less foresight. When the next solar maximum proved as destructive as the previous one, it completely downed the internet. Communication almost died. We had become so reliant on it, it seemed like the end. Hell on Earth!'

Eventually I asked, gingerly: 'What happened here then, in Britain, and what were you doing?'

'Well, England weathered the storm better than some, in terms of physical infrastructure. People were becoming frightened. Unpredictable events and the long-term effects of earlier austerity increased social unrest. Poor policies, the tech and eco crises, were leading to poor health, reduced incomes, shorter life spans, unhappy lives for many. However, buildings were being retrofitted for much better energy and water efficiency – especially to abolish the need for cooling in summer – and strengthened to withstand bigger storms. Then there had been a carefully managed coastal retreat in some areas, like the Wash and the Somerset Levels. Saltwater marshes! I was involved in tortuous negotiations in Somerset. Eventually it was nature that forced our hand. Most of Gloucester City survived, though tides were sweeping further up the Severn. Not at all sure about the future of the city, though, as the sea rises. Then in relation to IT, in the forties and fifties the West Country and other provinces invested heavily in new ground- and sea-based fibre links with Europe, and the Euronet was gradually established. Caused a huge amount of aggro, 'cos it was steamrollered through by government.

'And then migration caused riots! Really violent on occasion. The military were involved. It took a long time for the sheer scale of movement from hotter climes – the inevitability of relocation – to be recognised here, let alone acted upon. Initially it was chaos. There was no plan. Then the new UN treaty in '45 began to change perspectives, with the rocket booster of subsequent solar and climate crises at the end of that decade giving momentum towards the worldwide agreement which led to the planned exodus and resettlement of whole communities. That was my job for years: facilitating agreement between tropical and temperate states.

'Able,' I said, 'that is so amazing. It must have been difficult.' 'Yes. Of course. It was the most testing time of my career, of my life's work. As though everything before had been preparation for it. It was at times very frustrating, agonising even, but as agreements started to be made, and got the ball rolling, others were either inspired or shamed into action, you know, and it became kind of exhilarating. One felt part of a great slow movement of humanity from tribalism and conflict towards co-operation and harmony. It makes me weep to think of it. You may know three times in the late twentieth century, when the same feeling of release and joy happened: the Berlin Wall coming down, South Africa abolishing Apartheid, and the Good Friday agreement being signed in Northern Ireland. But this time it was on a vastly greater scale. It felt like humankind coming of age. I hope to God we don't backslide.'

Pain and joy mingled in my blood. Able's phrase, the 'great slow movement of humanity', made me feel faint. I felt the tide of history, profound shifts in human civilisation, nudged by Gaia, by forces beyond our ken, towards a new testament. Then I laughed ironically at myself, realising that history works in cycles, in a spiral. We both sat in companionable silence for a minute. Then I asked Able to give more detail about his work.

He told me of his time in India. Within Southern Asia, he said, probably the worst affected areas were Bangladesh, West Bengal, Gujarat and the southern Indus valley, mainly due to the increased heat, sea level rise and bigger river floods as the Himalaya glaciers retreated to expose rock and faster run-off. Some parts of the vast and fertile Ganges-Brahmaputra delta area, for example, suffering repeated saltwater invasions and flooded homes, until farming and survival ceased to be possible. There were in-country migrations on a scale never seen before, putting impossible pressure on the more viable settled areas. India and Bangladesh were already densely populated. While the overall population had stopped growing, in fact was falling in places, the carrying capacity of the land was also falling. There was no way that all the internal migrants could be accommodated, indeed both governments were driven to levels of taxation that people and businesses were not used to. Able was in India working for the UNHCR. Initially he was a backroom boy providing objective data for discussions between countries and states in the Subcontinent. But reaching consensus was an impossible task. Negotiations failed. There was nowhere for destitute families to go. There was intercommunity violence. Vigilante groups sprang up, determined to defend what they had. The situation was dreadful. When the UN and governments around the world agreed to work together, Able's task was to help manage a programme of international migration. He was negotiating with several northern

European countries, including the constituent parts of the British Isles, and later Canada as well. Wars in South Asia were averted.

He went on: 'I want to tell you, at least give you an impression, of how the global community pulled itself gradually and progressively out of hell. It's actually quite a surprising and inspiring story, and I'm proud of my part in it, so I'm going to give you a personal take on what happened. After India, I'd moved to Addis Ababa, which had become the new headquarters of the United Nations. Still working on partnerships – joint working between countries, building bridges. The biggest thing, of course, was how to begin to cope with economic collapse, millions of climate refugees, all compounded by starvation, water loss, civil wars and violence. The robotic intelligences which had managed so many mundane elements of life were out of their depth and the Cloud, which had been the prime source of knowledge and exchange, was on life support. The basic infrastructure of civilisation was essentially kaput.

'As well as huge grief at the human catastrophe, a concern for nature and for iconic mammal species being lost were key motivators in the West for bringing people together. The wildlife lobby is immensely influential. And with good reason of course, given the ongoing mass extinction which humankind has been responsible for. The sense that we only have one Earth, so we'd better take care of it for the sake of nature and humanity, gained traction. To say that was and is challenging is an understatement. In essence we had to overcome the instinctive competitive assumptions, either/or assumptions, and search for creative, integrated solutions. For example, as peoples moved to new areas they risked totally disrupting the cultural traditions and the identity of indigenous human communities, long established in their geographical settings. There were some very nasty wars, within and between countries, but I won't dwell on them. Nevertheless, at long last, recalcitrant economic and political interests came round to the idea that all was connected. After the eco-crises, everyone realised deep in their hearts that humanity is part of nature, part of the Earth system, sisters and brothers to all other creatures, and we live or die together. At last there was really powerful international support for action by the UN.

'Government in many places reacted against the overweening power of big international firms. Globalisation had allowed a kind of commercial plutocracy early in the century to rule the world. In the UK and USA and other countries, democracy only reasserted itself when the mid-century catastrophe occurred, challenging rule by the elite, by the rich and by vested interests which had been wearing democratic procedures like fig leaves to hide the nakedness of their self-interest.

'It took a few years, but somehow phone communication was re-established between main cities, all relying on land and sea lines, while locally, wireless connections were re-established. A few countries sent up communication satellites to replace those lost, but the private sector wouldn't play ball because no insurance company would touch them, so the momentum evaporated. Technologically we were going back a century! The UN General Council managed to meet in person, in Addis Ababa. It was a bit like the original launch of the UN after the Second World War. The Security Council was renamed the Cabinet and its membership no longer reflected the winners of a war waged over a century before, but rotating members from different world regions. There was a surprising shared determination and idealism, wanting, needing, to make the world new. The agenda for action was immense, from the urgent, urgent need to manage migration, to feed the billions, to rehouse and re-establish communities and to the urgent, urgent necessity of cutting carbon emissions and enabling the revival of nature. And somehow we had to make the world and all the communities that make it up, human and non-human, much more resilient to future shock.

'Finance was a crucial issue. By that time so much was in private hands, and in banks. The UN Cabinet announced that the only way to achieve revival and resilience was to release this capital, and they did it through draconian taxes on capital, worldwide, enforced by most countries. Then it was allocated according to level of need, where possible down to provincial or county-type levels – to speed delivery and reduce centralised bureaucratic delays and nepotism. Some countries refused to play ball. Then they got nothing until, (mixing metaphors, I know!) they changed their tune. It was quite remarkable!

'At the same time all industries using fossil fuels – which still accounted for 50% worldwide (80% in your day), were told they had five years to stop. Technology was not the problem. Vested interest was. The price of sustainable technologies had already plummeted as demand soared. If countries didn't adapt, then when the five years were up they could not import any fossil fuel, and were deterred from exporting anything that still relied on fossil fuels by international tariffs. OK, there were black markets, but market forces in general worked for the new economy. The degree of international consensus was incredible. Stick-in-the-mud plutocrats and autocrats and elected governments fell like ninepins, swept away by their own people if they did not reform. It was like the peoples of the world took power. They, we, had no intention of becoming extinct, like the dinosaurs.'

I was enraptured by his enthusiasm, at the same time needing to come up for air. There was so much to take in! But Able was unstoppable.

He emphasised that when needs must, humans are capable of incredible invention. The rate of technical innovation mid-to-late century beggared comparison. Technologies which had been considered impractical got off the drawing board, were tested, improved, implemented. The examples he gave which particularly interested me were about batteries and energy storage, and about plastic: all those cartons, bottles, bags, clothes and so on. 100% recycling became possible, with 80% efficiency in re-use. Longevity in use also became the norm, so people and businesses still used plastic, but much less of it, and oil is no longer used for this. On another level, industrial food production, and much of the excessive food processing, was swept away by regulation and fiscal manipulation of market forces. All countries, and regions within countries, worked towards much greater self-sufficiency and resilience, in energy, water, and food.

Able told me more about the post-crisis rejuvenation of England. Water had become a big issue, so the rule became local rainwater tanks and rooftop storage to flush loos and water gardens. In some areas, like the east of the country, there were now 'three-tap' supplies, the extra tap being drinking water. The increase in woodland, and changes to farming practices, meant storm runoff in the countryside was moderated, with more rain absorbed into aquifers. In built-up areas storm water had to be managed in situ, buildings, gardens and hard surfaces had to absorb all precipitation. Not exactly new ideas, I thought, but good to see them actually put into practice, at scale.

Able elaborated things I'd been told by Rufus, explaining how the temperate rainforests in the west of England and Wales – and Ireland too

– had been revived and extended. How the island of Britain was now being treated as one huge nature reserve, with imports of live animals and exotic plants forbidden – albeit with only some success, because natural migration of insects and birds was being driven by warmer climes.

At last he ran out of steam. And we had long run out of chicoffee. He apologised for going on so. I said how grateful I was. His story had both depressed and impressed me. I realised he had been an important cog in the machinery of international change, perhaps driven by the tragedy of his daughter's death.

ᏬᎧ ᎧᏬ

22
Beer and Bristol

We ambled back to the Cohousing. Time for his post-prandial snooze, said Able. Rufus came down from his flat to meet us. 'I gather you've given Robyn the full Cranston story,' he said to Able, who replied, smiling at me, 'Oh no! I spared her that!' 'It was very moving, Rufus.' I said. 'I'm glad to have heard it. What next?' Rufus's reply was untypically circumspect. 'It rather depends. But first things first. The time is your own until we have supper together at 19.00. After that we'll go to the pub.' My eyes lit up. Were pubs still pubs I wondered? Rufus went on: 'At least, you and Sam will. And let me warn you. One of your wishes is coming true!' I looked quizzically. 'You'll meet up with Bob – you know, the athlete.' I had an immediate image of the beautiful boy with the prosaic name, and my knees metaphorically gave way beneath me. 'You asked him to tell you about the Communiversity, which he studies at, so I've arranged an informal gathering for you.' 'Oh! My goodness. I did too! Well, that'll be lovely – thank you! Though I might need a chaperone.'

'Rufus laughed. 'Oh, Sam will be there. She'll keep you on the straight and narrow. I'm afraid I've got a meeting, a video conference with the Time

Team – the group responsible for managing your visit.' 'The psycho-historians?' I asked. 'Kind of. Partly. We've got big decisions to make.'

'Yes?' I queried. He looked seriously at me. 'Like how and when we send you back.'

I felt a mental bolt hit me. 'Of course,' I said, slowly. 'And do I have a say in it?' Rufus was frank: 'I don't know. It depends. On lots of things. I hope so. I'm afraid I can't say much more at this stage. However, some choice I can give you right now. What would you like to do tomorrow? Provisionally. The world's your oyster. Well, the local world, anyway.'

I had already thought what I wanted: 'I'd just love to explore around Stroud a bit more and see how things have changed. See the Roman Pavement. Go down to the canal, on beyond the Ocean pond at Stonehouse. See some of the new housing neighbourhoods in Greater Stonehouse.' 'That's great. You're on,' said Rufus. 'I'll take you on a guided tour of Stroud Valleys treasures and blemishes, including ones you don't know about yet.'

I spent the rest of the afternoon exercising in the gym, taking a dip in the freezing cold swimming pond – in so doing successfully deflecting my mind from my future – and writing notes on my experiences and impressions (quite the travel journalist, I thought!). Later, after a delightful social meal, during which we completely avoided the issue of my transition back, Sam and I walked round to the Old Fleece. Bob arrived on his e-bike, bright-eyed and bushy-tailed. He and I had some very tasty Stroud ale. When I instinctively felt for a debit card, my wristy flashed up the cost, and the sum left in my personal account. Sam had a glass of local red. I sensed real affection between the other two, and Bob was casually direct towards me. While he moved with the lithe grace of an athletic boy, his conversation was that of a man.

Obviously forewarned, he dived almost straightaway into the historic changes in further and higher education. It was as if he knew that I was from early in the century, though Rufus had assured me he was not in that privileged group. My offhand request to him after the Greek Games, that I wanted to know more about the Communiversity – stimulated as much by his magnetism as my interest – had come back to bite me!

Apparently, way back in the thirties, there had been a wholesale revolt by academic staff. The problem was universities had become creatures of capitalism. Promotion was largely determined by how much money you drew into the coffers – in terms of student fees and research projects. Also the only publications considered prestigious were research articles for 'learned' journals (often formulaic and read by the few). Books and articles for professions and the public (read by the many) did not count. The educational process was increasingly online. Personal exchanges and free student debate were considered by some to be dangerous – too uncontrolled! Staff felt disenfranchised. Academic freedom was a myth. Originality counted for little – except, Bob pointed out, in the visual arts, where originality of concept counted for everything, never mind the quality or beauty of the product!

The crunch came, apparently, when government launched a new programme that dictated and limited higher education content to an unacceptable degree. The lecturers declared the whole system sclerotic. The sidelining of creative thought had led to the 'experts' on whom government relied, being stuck in obligatory grooves of conventional thinking. While I thought Bob was quite possibly over-egging the point (the privilege of youth!), I was generally nodding in agreement with all this. Two of my best friends had remained in university as researchers and felt trapped by the top-down business logic that prevailed – not knowledge logic, not wisdom. One had contributed to a radical review of land use policy, paid for by a government quango. But the conclusions were not to official liking and the report was supressed. The university was not willing to fight its corner, i.e. publish and be damned.

A fresh national administration responded positively to the lecturers' campaign. One result was the reinvention of polytechnics – now called 'technical universities' – geared to creativity, technological innovation and societal collaboration. Another was the invention of 'communiversities'. As the name implies, they were locally based, often absorbing the local tech, allowing students to live at home and thus avoid huge debts, responding very directly to local concerns and opportunities. Stroud Communiversity was linked to the West of England Technical University. It boasted about its 'woolly' thinking! In other words it had developed a specialism in sheep farming, both as historical study and devoted to all the ways sheep products could be developed to support modern life.

Bob was not a woolly thinker. After his French language degree, he was studying for an MA in French literature. 'It's so much less inhibited,' he said, with a winning smile, 'than German or English or Russian literature.' I asked if he had read Fifty Shades of Grey. 'My god! That was complete trash!' he said. 'I picked it up in an alternative bookshop and squirmed with embarrassment. It was so badly written! I put it straight back. How come it was so popular?' 'I haven't a clue,' I said. 'I actually bought a second-hand copy because my mother said I must not read it. I'm sure she hadn't! After one chapter I put it straight into recycling – to prevent anyone else suffering the same fate.' 'All it was fit for, then,' said Sam, who knew it only by reputation. 'Maybe all those repressed English housewives back in the past found escapist excitement. We don't need that kind of garbage now, do we, in the emancipated present!'

'Hey!' I said, 'it's my time you're denigrating! We thought ourselves pretty emancipated.' Sam gave me a sharp kick on the shin under the table, and a hard stare. Bob did not seem to notice. 'Your study period?' he said, lightly. 'Well, maybe we just have better taste now.'

We moved to some couches, swigging our second drinks. Bob disported himself like a Greek god across the length of his couch, facing us. He was so relaxed. Given my faux pas and his animal presence, I was quite surprised how cool I was. 'You know,' I said, 'having studied the twenty-teens, something surprises me. I think the difference in attitudes, then and now, is easily exaggerated. The similarities are equally striking.' The others both looked unconvinced. Sam tried to be helpful: 'Do you mean in terms of lifestyle, behaviour, beliefs, beauty, bias or (searching for another 'b' word) bigotry?' 'I think I mean how people related to each other. How they were. How we are.' Covering my tracks quite neatly, I thought. Bob looked reflective. 'I don't know much about that period – your period. Literature often gives a rather distorted picture. But, nevertheless, I take your point. I think it's amazing how people of completely different centuries, let alone decades, can have attitudes we recognise now. Even back in the Middle Ages. I just love Chaucer and his tales. Especially the saucy ones. His pilgrims are so real, so human, so like us, enjoying the same kind of stories,' 'Yes, yes, absolutely!' I said enthusiastically. 'My strict old mum didn't seem to mind me reading thoroughly dissolute tales, like the Miller's and the Reeve's, because they were written in olden time and part of a set book. I'm sure she hadn't read them either!' Bob chipped in, 'And did you enjoy them?' 'I might have!' I returned. 'I had to read the Knight's tale many times, 'cos that was for the exam. Thinking about it, his characters, like Arcite and Palamon, do seem to live in another world.' 'Hey, they were just characters in the Knight's story, not the travellers themselves,' said Bob. I was on a roll, and looked Bob straight in the eyes: 'Hey! I can still recite bits of the Prologue ....

> "A knight ther was, and that a worthy man,
> That fro the tyme that he first bigan
> To ryden out, he loved chivalrye,
> Trouthe and honour, freedom and curteisye."

'Well, there's a high bar to leap o'er!' said Bob, with a broad smile. 'And fall on the other side. I'll go for one of the less noble people, if that's OK.'

'Hey guys, you're losing me,' said Sam, butting in. 'Tell me more about Chaucer's book. The Canterbury Tales, isn't it? And what makes you think that life in the Middle Ages was not nasty, brutish and short?' Bob and I, enthusiasts both, launched into it – such a huge, confusing canvas. With great glee, Bob recounted one of the more disreputable stories in the book – all much cause for laughter – and I described by contrast the agony and ecstasy of the Knight's tale. Then the conversation became intense as we all dragged up what knowledge we had gleaned about medieval life – safely clear of my own era, I thought. We talked about jealous and violent kings, French rivalry and civil wars, Magna Carta and Robin Hood, barons and serfs, then eventually got onto more cultural matters, marvelling at the achievement of cathedral building in the midst of conflict, at the creative power of some feisty women – such as the poet, composer and philosopher Hildegard of Bingen. Maybe it was a woman who was the unknown author of Sir Gawain and the Green Knight – why else the secrecy? And at the amazing development of music and the way towns evolved. This last was getting onto home territory for Sam and me. Sam set out the remarkable planning principles which structured medieval towns, and which we try to conserve even now. I enthused about my favourite urban space in all the world, one that completely gobsmacked me when first I entered it: the shell-shaped Campo in Siena.

After all that we moved on to more trivial matters. It was late in the evening before we decided to call time. I had not enjoyed a conversation so much, or felt so at ease with any companions, for ages. Those I'd left behind in 2023 seemed stolid and predictable by comparison – and nothing like so beautiful. Tones of grey as opposed to glorious colour.

Saying goodbye was hard. Bob was off on his bike in a different direction to us. Sam and Bob kissed, a deliciously lingering, almost lascivious kiss, which made me wonder ... When he turned to me, gently laying his hand on my arm, he asked 'may I?' Puritan training could not conceal desire. We kissed beautifully, sensuous but not sustained, just lightly holding each other's waists. Sam and I walked home in silence. She held my hand, as I'd seen other friends doing in public, fondly, not flirtatious. I felt accepted, warm, in this world. I was already beginning to think of it as my adopted home.

*****

Rufus met us in the flat, warm drinks ready prepared. He was looking serious. 'We had our conference,' he said. 'There have been developments which have caused us to review your future. I'm afraid we are going to have to let you go. Go back.' He saw sudden alarm on my face. 'It's alright, not immediately. But it will be soon. If you don't mind, I think it would be best to leave any detailed discussion to the morning.' I assented, non-verbal, not quite taking it in. He went on: 'I would like if I can, to put your mind a bit at rest. It's nothing you have done that's led to this conclusion. It's factors outside our control. I was able to report to the others that you've shown quite remarkable ability to adapt to this extraordinary situation, and to absorb the way things are. And your confidence in dealing with people and in being yourself has been impressive. At least, that's my feeling. I hope you feel it too. Now I'm waiting to hear if you and I can meet up, in person, with some directors of the project, maybe tomorrow, maybe in Bristol.'

My buoyant, effervescent mood, after the lovely social evening, was gone. My face and body language showed it. Rufus said he was really sorry to be the bringer of bad news. Sam took my hand again and led me across to my room, sat with me for a while, talking it through, playing up the positives, the range of experiences I'd had, giving me some comfort and food for thought. After she left, I went to bed and mulled it all over, putting everything in context. I distracted myself rehearsing the exchanges of the evening, the warmth that I felt for my two companions. Bob no longer being so much a 'beautiful boy' as a perceptive and shrewd young man, with alluring sensuality. I wondered if he had rumbled me, suspected my origins; I realised now that I might never have the chance to confirm his suspicions. However, despite these thoughts and the existential threat hanging over me, the next thing I remember was waking in the morning light. After a quick shower I was alert and ready for the challenge to come.

At breakfast Rufus gave me the timetable for the day: a relaxed start – though no time for another walk in Stroud, then the tram-train to Bristol at 11.30. A short walk to the office, where we would meet up with Rufus's boss, Professor McCanlis, together with a European minister and Sacha. In retrospect Rufus was being less than candid, or perhaps liking to give me a pleasant surprise, revealing nothing about his boss (or the minister for that matter), deflecting my attention by mentioning Sacha.

'Sacha?!' I said, surprised. 'Yes, Sacha! We need to observe and record your reactions, while, we hope, respecting your autonomy. She's been monitoring your health and wellbeing, on behalf of the project. All part of the service.' I found the night's sleep had restored my equilibrium. 'Is that why I keep on bumping into her?' 'Partly, but of course she has other more discreet means of watching you as well. Like I do.' 'Does she indeed! It's lucky I like her, or I'd be planning to give her a piece of my mind!' Rufus and Sam laughed out loud. Sam said: 'You'll do! No-one's going to mess with you! ' 'Huh!' I said, though without rancour, 'I've already been totally messed with. What degree of autonomy do I really have?'

'Fair question,' said Rufus, 'but actually Sacha's told me that she has been just amazed at you, your independence of mind, your ability to cope, your good humour and growing confidence. That's what she said! She's at the meeting to provide an assessment of your readiness for return. I hope the minister will vanish at that point, though I doubt it! We don't want politics distorting the decision process. Now also, I can tell you that my boss, who as I said is a top psycho-historian, is going to explain the whole context of the project and your role in it, set things out for you in a way that has not been appropriate until now without compromising the experiment. Incidentally, Sacha was involved in your selection, so that'll be interesting too. We won't be able to go very deeply into the mechanics of transfer, of time travel that is. It's somewhat mysterious even to us. In fact, mechanics is completely the wrong word. It is fascinating.' 'Terrifying, might be another word for it,' I said. 'Mysterious and baffling and unfathomable might be others,' said Sam.

I did not really take in the journey - tram to the main Greater Stonehouse station, then fast train to Bristol Temple Meads - or the walk at the other end, or the nature of the place in Bristol. Nerves, I guess. But when we arrived at the meeting room, which was festooned with sweet smelling roses and beautiful lilies, I was all there, alert and ready. Sacha welcomed me and Rufus warmly, shaking my hands clasped by both of hers. She introduced me to Professor McCanlis, and I did a double take. I'd met him before! The Professor was elegantly dressed in maroon suit and flamboyant tie. Quite different from the farm-husband I'd seen before. He immediately said, 'Solomon to you, Robyn – of course – and I'm just delighted to see you. This is a very important moment, a very significant meeting. May I introduce our international sponsor, who arrived specially from Brussels yesterday, Madame Wenzel, a minister in the European Science and Technology Department.' Madame Wenzel smiled – a slightly condescending smile, I thought. She was dressed in rather a dark, formal fashion. Her voice with its German twang was quiet though with a dry and laconic turn of phrase. 'I'm Madame,' she explained, 'from my long time in Paris.' She spoke always to the point, her eyes sharp, missing nothing, clearly not to be bamboozled by the exuberant professor or warm-hearted Sacha. Or by me!

We acclimatised to each other over a relaxed lunch, in the meeting room, with excellent local alcohol-free beer if you wanted it. I did! For me it has just the same effect as if it were laced with alcohol, so I finished up the meal with a smile on my face and openness to what might transpire. Solomon started proceedings with a short reading and a silence. After jokes and light-heartedness through lunch he was suddenly a very serious person. He said: 'I'd like to read you four lines from T.S. Eliot's Four Quartets, the very beginning in fact, which got me first thinking about time travel twenty-five years ago, and inspired my work; and after that I'd like us to take a minute's silence to help focus our minds:

"Time present and time past
Are both perhaps present in time future
And time future contained in time past.
If all time were eternally present …"

He left the sentence unfinished – a question. The five of us sat in silence for a minute, maybe pondering the mysteries of the universe. Though in my case suddenly reminded of a Quaker gathering I'd once been to. I closed my eyes … then awoke a moment later as shuffling signified the end of silence. To my surprise Madame Wenzel indicated we should take hands round the circle, establishing some kind of unity of purpose. She looked at each of us rather meaningfully. 'Profound,' she said, 'not for the frivolous. One person's future hangs in the balance.' I was taken aback. 'I profoundly hope not,' I said quietly. Solomon added gently, 'as of course do we, and I do believe all will be well. We have prior experience – earlier transfers. But in one sense your future, back in your own time, does hang in the balance, because you will have been deeply affected by your experience now, here, and that will alter the way you are and the way you behave in your own time.'

He looked at me very seriously, with tenderness, I thought. 'We have interrupted the course of your life, Robyn, without consultation or permission. In the selfish interest of our own historical research, which we hope will assist productive thinking about the future. You had no choice. At one level this is immoral, certainly highly presumptuous. I am interested to know your feelings on this matter. Whether you would appreciate a sincere apology?'

I looked at him, then speaking slowly: 'Given your actions, I'm really not sure whether an apology could be sincere. Anyway, an apology is not what I want. I would not have missed this experience for the world. What I need is explanation.'

The others nodded in understanding. Madame Wensel spoke, looking meaningfully round the table, 'and that is what we must endeavour to give you.'

Professor McCanlis nodded assertively. 'Thank you Minister, and thank you Robyn, that is very helpful, very much appreciated. There is so much to talk about, to help you understand, to illuminate for us as well. Before we get enmeshed in the mysteries of time travel, I'll set out a rough agenda for the meeting, which we have discussed. See what you think, Robyn. First there might be some issues important to you, that need resolving in order to free you for the second stage, when we could ask you, with support from Rufus, to reflect on this new age you unwittingly found yourself in, and what initial implications, if any, you draw from it for your own time. We'll give maybe an hour for that. Then after a break, we will talk about the broader issues, the nature of time, of time travel, and about psycho-history, and come at last to the crucial question of your return: the reasons why we feel it is right, now, to return you, Robyn, to your own time, and what that means. How does that seem?'

23
If all time is eternally present

To my surprise I felt quite relaxed, confident even, and that surprise triggered my response: 'Thank you Solomon. That's fine. There are two things puzzling me I need to understand before we embark on the main agenda you set out. The first is how it was I came to be selected at all? Or was it just an accident? Could it have been anybody? Or did you have a time travelling spy in the 2020s? Then secondly, something that's been puzzling me almost from the start of my trip. I've always had a good memory, but since arriving here it seems miraculously enhanced. I can recall everything. At least that's my impression. And my capacity to adapt emotionally to this extraordinary change also seems untypical for me, given my rather staid, unchallenging upbringing. I'm sure part of that is due to the friendship of Rufus and Sam; and the other people I've met,' I glanced at Sacha, 'but still I remain surprised – not to mention rather pleased – at my enhanced abilities.'

Madame Wensel looked rather stern (or was it concerned?) but Solomon smiled and said, 'yes indeed, it is time we came clean about these questions. I'll take the second one first. It was only in the late seventies that we understood and successfully managed this remarkable process of personal realisation. Previous attempts were inspired by the need to help people with mental and emotional disabilities. Those efforts sometimes had undesirable side effects. But now, through precisely targeted impulses, we can safely enhance innate human capacities which have atrophied, or been supressed or distorted over the generations of armchair, desk and internet lives. They were probably more evident when we all lived closer to nature. We've begun to see evidence of that, among some humans from way back, through previous time travellers. Anyway, be that as it may, we treated you on your arrival, before you were awake, releasing your dormant memory capacity and enhancing your already strong emotional stability.'

'All under my care and supervision,' added Sacha. 'You would be amazed, Robyn, at the degree to which we can now read the fabric of a mind – anyone's mind. Not the content but the abilities. And pinpoint needs or opportunities for discreet intervention. I was very happy at the way the whole thing went in your case.'

I looked from one to the other. 'It sounds really alarming to me. It opens the door to all kinds of wickedness, tampering with people's minds, creating the bionic human!' Madame Wensel chipped in 'Worry not, woman from the past! Very few institutes in the world have the capacity, and the process is centrally controlled by the UN within a very strict ethical framework. It's expensive too. Mostly used to correct imbalances in the mind that have led to fatal behaviours including violence. There was one country which broke the taboo, trying to create men and women who felt no pain and could physically fight on regardless – like in old Irish and Welsh legends. That ended very badly. So, no. What we do now is open the door to your full abilities. We allowed it, in your case, to help you cope and to increase the potential value of the time travel experiment.'

I had suspected for some days that they had tampered with me, so it came as no great surprise – though I hoped to challenge the ethics of it later.

Solomon went on. 'Now, our reasons for choosing you and how that was possible. No, we did not have a spy in the camp. We are forbidden from sending today's people back.' 'For very good reason,' said Wensel, with slight asperity. I could sense some friction between her and Solomon. Sacha added that the risks were too great, given the political and technological situations in the past. 'Indeed,' said Solomon, 'and we know there are still many mysteries about the whole process, and no doubt some things way beyond our current grasp. We have to be ultra-cautious. The way we gain insight into the past is through people, like yourself, trapped in a coma. It's an extraordinary thing that when people appear dead to the world, their minds are somehow released from the shackles of space and time, almost like spirits. We have the technology to link back to a particular time and find the free floaters and engage with their subconscious minds. We found you and were hopeful. As far as we could judge, though it's a bit of a lottery, you were just the right age and character. And so it has proved. You have been brilliant! Excellent for us and we hope valuable for you.'

Rufus and Sacha were nodding vigorously. I felt a bit out of my depth, and out of myself. The fact that I was there at all proved the efficacy of the system, but my mind was jumping all over the place. A line from Shakespeare was insisting on being let out, and in a sing-song Welsh accent, I said to myself, *I can call spirits from the vasty deep ...*

I must have said it out loud, though, because the others reacted with surprise. Rufus laughed, and in a strong northern accent continued the quote:

"Why, so can I, or so can any man;
But will they come when you do call for them?"

'Henry IV Part 1,' he said. 'Glendower and Hotspur.' Sacha laughed in delight. Wensel looked supercilious, and spoke to Solomon, with a nod, 'She's ready.' Solomon looked quizzically at her, then said to me: 'Thank you, Robyn, very appropriate. And Rufus, you never cease to amaze me! However, back to business. If you don't mind, we'll leave further discussion of the mysteries of time travel for later. What I'd like to turn to now is your impression, Robyn, of this society, what you feel you may have learnt, or any insights you would like to share with us. To help organise initially, Rufus has some cues, for you to respond to. Rufus?'

There was a wall-screen to one side of our meeting table. Rufus said: 'Ah yes, thanks, here is something I prepared earlier.' He displayed a timetable of my days in his time, specifying where I had been and who I'd met, including when I was alone and off the leash. It was actually quite impressive, the range and scope of activity, even though all of it was simply in Gloucestershire, and over little more than a week. Looking at me, Rufus said, 'where would you like to start?'

Every day had brought new and sometimes startling insights about the contemporary age. I dwelt on each day in turn, highlighting those insights and surprises, initially being quite selective in what I said, but as time went on and I warmed to the task, I became more and more demonstrative and detailed, expressing my emotional and aesthetic as well as intellectual responses – all I hope reflected in my story – encouraged by the close attention paid by the others to everything I said. They asked pointed questions when they wanted more precision or explanation. At some point Wensel suggested that I speed up, which I thought was entirely in order, having experienced undisciplined conference speakers in the past, but to my surprise, Solomon waived her scruples aside, saying my thoughts were the most insightful and valuable thing about our meeting – he was riveted by them! Nevertheless, I did focus a bit more, eventually coming to conclusion.

Solomon simply said, 'that's great. Now, are there any overarching issues you'd like to share? About our society, or about your situation? That will help shape the agenda for the period after tea.' I'd done some prior thinking about this. 'Well, I have to admit that I've rather fallen in love with this place – and the people. There is a warmth and dynamism, a can-do attitude, and both the towns and the countryside are just amazing. But to me it seems there is also a dark side: central control. Despite all the explanations that Sam, Rufus and Able have given me – and clearly they believe them – the diktats from on high seem to determine how things are, what decisions people and organisations can make and what they can't. People are watched. I was watched all the time! Journalists are controlled. Freedom seems to be sacrificed!'

Wensel leant back in her chair, and said laconically: 'And, dear girl, all that is necessary.' I looked sharply at her, then the others, expecting some debate. But Solomon moved us on: 'Thank you Madame Wensel. If you don't mind, Robyn, we won't explore that now – we'll tackle it after tea. Do you have other worries you want to share?' 'Yes, indeed I do. Everything seems hunky-dory now, in the aftermath of all those huge existential crises. But how long will this unity of purpose survive? Several people have said that there will be a counter-reaction in due course. So how do you hope to maintain your current momentum?'

Solomon nodded. I paused, as a new thought occurred to me. 'Then also,' I felt the incredulity rising in my voice, 'I really, deeply need to understand about my return, what does it mean? Why now? Do I have a say in it, and am I still unconscious back in my world? What will I feel? Will I be the same person? And surely, going right back in time, then forward in time again at the proper pace, everything will be different! Will I have my memory intact, of everything that's happened to me here? And what do you expect of me when I get back – if anything?' I paused, rather out of breath. 'Is that enough? To be going on with?'

Rufus was nodding at each query I raised. Wensel was looking as if she had heard it all before. Sacha was smiling in obvious pleasure. Solomon said, 'Yes – that will do very well. We will try to clarify all those points after tea. They give a good agenda. As well as tackling the vexed issue of the nature of time, and the questions around how societies evolve. In that respect, I want to contextualise your own future by explaining what we mean by psycho-history – my own intellectual angle on all this. So now – refreshments, and the opportunity to stretch our legs.'

He gave the word, and a robot brought in hot water plus a selection of fruit teas and tasty nibbles – including flapjacks, my favourite! I took what I fancied and went out with Rufus onto the balcony, enjoying the fresh air, gazing at the very urban view, trying to relax. I was grateful for the break, just wanting to disengage from the deep questions and clear my mind. Some of the buildings around were in good condition, quite colourful, others rather unkempt though obviously in use. The public realm was well maintained and attractively designed. Swifts were scudding across the sky, screaming in the joy of their dance. The bells of St. Mary Redcliffe were ringing the changes, and the 'fairest parish church in all England' was visible if I looked to one side, the steeple crystal clear.

I could hear the others talking avidly inside. I wondered what about – my future?

*****

When we reconvened, Solomon went straight to the point I'd raised about centralisation. 'It is a big and contested issue,' he said. 'The official view – and I do believe it is the correct one – is that central guidance and control is essential. Without it, given the nature of market systems, of capitalism, we would rapidly move away from a sustainable trajectory. When the motivation is profit, then social and environmental priorities take a back seat. If you think about it, in your own time, action on climate change, social inequalities, health and wellbeing, species and habitat loss, were distorted by money interests. Governments fell into the trap too, in part due to unequal lobbying powers, especially in the USA. In Britain, austerity led to public squalor and private affluence for some, while ironically the tax burden reached record levels for peacetime, and central government controlled local government almost to extinction. The rich grew richer and the poor grew poorer, and the fourth great species extinction was under way.

'What we have now is a clear distinction, written into statute, between principle and practice. Ends and means. So government pushes the problems of implementation down to the organisations at the coalface.' Solomon smiled at his outdated metaphor. He went on: I should add that one of the successes of the last forty years is that species extinction has slowed, and has almost certainly reversed, despite the climate changing. Maybe you have seen evidence of that in your brief time here. A triumph, I believe.' Then he asked Madame Wensel if she would like to add to what he had said.

In her rather clipped way, she obliged: 'Huge ecological and tech crises, like world wars, demand that everyone pulls together. Hence centralised governmental decision-making. People voted for it. The UN, the EU, the African Union and other continental groupings gained power, co-ordinating nation states. Nation states dictated policy. However, both internationally, and here in England, I know, there was awareness of the risks and inefficiencies of overweening central power: central groupthink leading to wrong analyses and inappropriate local application. Communities powerless. So the principle of subsidiarity was resurrected, and taken seriously. Meaning that decisions should be taken at the lowest appropriate scale. It was more democratic! Subsidiarity built into the constitutional framework. Here in Britain the government ceded power as of right, indelibly, to provinces – as already was the case with Scotland. Provinces delegated power to local authorities, and they to parishes and so on. Push responsibility down. But with clear goals and guidelines. Does that answer your worries?'

I smiled at her. She was very concise and clear. Then, surprising myself with my boldness: 'Thanks Madame. Very helpful. But what about civil liberties. When everyone is centrally identifiable and traceable? Identity cards were a no-go option back in my day.' It was Solomon who answered: 'There was a big political row about this some decades ago, demonstrations galore. Identity motes were approved in the teeth of significant opposition. It was in fact a citizen's jury that recommended the use of identity chips so that AI observation systems could more easily trace criminals. People wanted less crime, and were persuaded, correctly, that the robotic surveillance would deliver. So, fewer criminals, less pressure on prisons and rehab. What swung Parliament was not just the crime argument, but the cost of the old system – when every part of government had separate lists. You know: passports, employment and tax, your health number, police records – you name it, Britain had separate systems. Totally inefficient, as many other countries had found. We combined a unified approach to records while also upping the legal rights of individuals, firms, and community projects in the face of what could have been excessive bureaucratic power. That won the day. Overall, I would say that our system today is in many ways less centralised than in your day.'

I nodded in understanding. Sacha intervened: 'You're right, Solomon, but to be fair it hasn't always gone as smoothly as you imply. There were lots of problems early on. Robots acting over-zealously, or risk averse, accusing people wrongly, also unable to distinguish truth-tellers from charlatans. Agreed we have ironed out most of those difficulties, but they almost led to the abandonment of the policy back in the sixties.' 'True enough, Sacha, thanks,' said Solomon.

He looked round at everybody. 'Now, if you are agreed, I'd like to move on to the fundamental reason we are here. First, to explain to you, Robyn, how you got here. OK?' There was general assent. 'So, something on time,' he continued. 'Science fiction has long played with the idea that one could travel through time like across space. H.G. Wells's The Time Machine was the trailblazer – a brilliant book! In a way the cosmological theories of Einstein give oblique backing for the possibility of time travel, though Einstein himself said no way. Relativity says that the speed of light is constant for any observer, and therefore if one observer travels very fast to a different star, when they return to their home planet they will have aged less than the people who stuck at home. That sounds like time travel to me. Nevertheless, the powerful scientific consensus earlier this century was that time is an ever-flowing stream. One-way only. It is not the same as a dimension of space. However, little pinpricks of evidence began to raise questions in some people's minds, even in the 2020s. Quantum mechanics is equally mysterious as relativity, dealing with the almost infinitely small as opposed to the almost infinitely big. There was a discovery in 2023 that if two connected and identical particles, such as photons, separate and go to completely different locations, when one is altered the other one is too, identically, at the same instant, apparently beating the speed of light. Later discoveries added complexity to this initial finding. Then some years later, in the 2050s, a great puzzle in the understanding of our universe was at last solved. Up to then nobody had managed to integrate theories of the microcosm and the macrocosm – quantum theory and relativity. There was great rejoicing in the astrophysics community! I won't try to explain how they were integrated, in fact I'm not sure I could.' ('Thank god for that!' said Rufus under his breath.) 'This unified theory led to many reappraisals of the laws of physics and of our understanding of the human mind. One such reappraisal led to the conclusion that identical particles can remain identical when they separate across time as well as space. Time is not, after all, an ever-flowing stream. Another set of insights led to the controversial realisation that consciousness of mind and spirit can at the margins shape physical change, not just in a particular individual, but more broadly. Of course, that was not news to some of the world religions. They had always believed there is power in prayer. But it was a huge shock to conventional scientists. They had to come to terms with the apparent fact that Mind in some way held the universe together. Over to you, Sacha.'

Sacha praised Solomon for what she thought was a brilliantly succinct resumé. She said she had at last begun to grasp things that had completely eluded her. What, she asked, were the implications for time travel? Solomon nodded and looked at me. 'To cut to the chase, Robyn, these new theories led to the belief that time travel was possible, and in the last few decades we have been, as a world community, led in particular by India, Brazil and China, developing and refining techniques which make it feasible. We can now send time-scouts back to earlier eras, almost like outside of time – in spirit though not in body – where they may appear a bit like ghosts. When someone is in a coma, their mind floats free, almost angelic. You'll know that even when simply unconscious, people sometimes have out-of-body experiences – so it is just a development on that. Our scouts can find and engage with those floating minds, and if they are lucky, they find a mind that's like an open book, revealing its essential nature. Quite a rare occurrence. Your spirit mind was one such. The scout tries to assess how deep the coma is, what openness and flexibility there is in the mind. Suffice to say our scout recommended you for transfer. We were then able to look into the historical record, insofar as it still exists, which is not much. Births, marriages and deaths are the most reliable sources, always written down, not just electronic. You were chosen as our first twenty-first century person. Very experimental! We drew your floating mind to our own time, and from your mind we built you a body to inhabit, which to all intents and purposes is a living replica of the one comatose in 2023. A bit like 3D printing! We have to find the ingredients of life for your mind to work on. Incredible! It seems almost like a natural subconscious process. Indeed, your mind was itself asleep, unconscious, while it happened. It could only awake once it had a temporal body, fixed in time. Then there is the moment of truth. Having assessed the state of body and mind, we calculated when you would awake. We put you on the train with Rufus in Swindon. You came to, beautifully, exactly where we hoped, in the Cotswold tunnel. And the rest ... you know.'

Rufus was looking at me with real concern. I was wide-eyed with anxiety. For a moment I felt my mind running wild out of my body. Then I came to with a vengeance. 'Excuse me, but fuck! How do you propose to get me back? Back into my real body? Or is my stay here to be forever, and I die, never wake up, back home. Back home! I need to get back!' I paused, looking at each of them in desperation. Rufus had moved close. 'What have you done to me? I'm in the wrong body. Altered to suit your purpose. What is your purpose anyway? Why am I here? What do you want of me?' Tears of fright had started in my eyes.

Rufus laid a tentative hand on my arm. I shook it off. He stood up and took both my hands more firmly in his, and said: 'Robyn!' I glanced up at his eyes. He held my gaze. I saw love and tenderness in his eyes. And tears in his eyes too. I took a deep breath, and sighed. My tears began to change to those of sorrow. I determined not to cry in front of this eminent gathering. I released one of my hands, found a hanky and dabbed my eyes dry. Tried to smile. Sacha and I said the same words at the same time: 'Thank you, Rufus.'

Madame was looking severe. Solomon was quite laid back, genial, and said: 'Robyn, the questions you have asked are all vital ones. When you are ready, we will endeavour to answer them, and perhaps put your mind at rest. I hope so. Would you like a drink? The sun isn't over the yardarm yet, but this conversation, this situation, calls for something. What would you like?'

'I would like – just water please. With ice and lemon. On second thoughts, please, gin and tonic.' The others made their choices, all except Rufus chose non-alcoholic. The housebot took the order and obliged. We took a few minutes off, out on the balcony. Then it was back to work.

Solomon took the lead again. 'I'll try to explain how you will safely return to your original body. But first, I want to say why we believe it is time for you to return. While we cannot observe your body in its coma, we know from much experience what the signs are in the time traveller, that the depth of unconsciousness back in time is weakening. We begin to see those signs in you. The last thing we want is for your mind to be untimely wrenched out of this era and plummeted back to base. So pre-emptive action in good time is necessary. A supplementary reason is that your media friend Frank Melia suspects who you really are, and is beginning to spread rumours. You won't have heard them because you are not on the public circuits. We don't want them to bounce back on you in unpredictable ways. So the time has come. Probably tomorrow.'

'Tomorrow!' I exclaimed. 'But I love it here. I want to know more!' I realised my reaction was exactly counter to my previous outcry. But the shock – the immediacy of it – despite the hints in advance. Wensel spoke in a gentle, commiserating tone of voice, most unlike her, I thought: 'Well, Robyn Ghorra, I'm afraid your time here is up.' The others waited for me to take it in. Eventually I said: 'If I am to go back, which of course I do most earnestly desire, will I have my extra powers of memory? Will I remember all this here?' It was Sacha who answered: 'We believe so. Just as you have arrived here with memories of your earlier life apparently intact, you should be able to wake up with the most vivid, coherent and long-lived dream ever. When floating free of the body the mind seems to be largely inert; it can only be re-alerted by attachment to a physical brain. As far as we can tell your coma brain is still waiting for your spirit to return, and is not damaged, just on pause. There is a remote chance that your extra powers will evaporate during transfer back. Or in the weeks that follow. But we trust not.'

'Well, thank goodness, that's a huge relief. It must have been quite a tussle, accepting that mind was not the same as brain, but could float free. The question is, will I believe my dream is real?' Sacha answered, 'We can't tell for sure. I believe so. It is so detailed and coherent that it would be quite extraordinary, mystical, if it were just a dream.' I looked at her: 'I find it quite extraordinary and mystical-magical anyway!'

Solomon took up the thread: 'Robyn, we need to forewarn you what the process of transfer involves. From your point of view, we hope it will be quite straightforward. Tomorrow, or even tonight, back in Woodchester, we will put you into an induced coma. You will just feel that you are going to sleep. Your mind will float free of time. It will know where it has to go, guided back to base by your own spirit. You will re-enter your original body, but of course you won't inhabit it fully until you emerge from the coma. We cannot tell whether that will be in days, weeks or months. When fully recovered, you should remember everything. We hope and pray that you will take that memory into your future life.'

*****

They were all looking at me. I nodded in understanding. Rufus had previously told me what would happen. Solomon went on: 'Now, I'd like to turn to much more general matters – the way societies and history evolves. Have you ever read Asimov? His Foundation Trilogy? You have! Brilliant! Well, he coined the term psycho-history, meaning the study of how societies change and develop, taking into account the psychology of peoples – large groups and nations reacting to events and the emotions they generate. The Foundation was set up to try to shape the future benignly, using education, policy triggers and nudges. Many historians have played with these ideas, trying retrospectively to explain, for example, the rise and fall of the Roman Empire. Marx was a great theoretical psycho-historian, before the term was invented, but he miscalculated. Much more recently historians have been systematically looking at the evidence, and developing theories on that basis. The reaction of the

German nation after the punitive treaty following World War I, led to support for Hitler. This in marked contrast to their positive and creative reaction after losing World War II, giving much pause for thought. Likewise the British vote for Brexit in 2016. And many instances since. The theories do not work well in relation to dictatorial regimes, but remarkably well when governments have aspirations to be democratic. People's reactions can be predicted, on a probability assessment. And since the crises mid-century the discipline has often been called on by rulers to recommend policy strategies that can help lead to desired outcomes. Risky, of course, and some big reputations have been lost, while others have been made.'

I was following this quite easily. In fact, I'd been allowed onto the Euronet a couple of days earlier and had read up on psycho-history. I had a question ready: 'So Solomon, am I right in saying that your own specialism is the reactions of British society, and other nationalities too, in the aftermath of the eco and tech meltdown?'

The professor smiled: 'Yes indeed! I'm fascinated by the speed and widespread nature of social and political change since that meltdown – not just here but in most countries across the world. The world heated up and was going to hell in a handcart, but somehow society took massive and co-ordinated avoidance action. Across the globe there were still wars, mainly of words, but the world had been shocked into co-operation. Again I can draw parallels with the period after the Second World War, when for a while the rich nations of the world aspired to human rights, social justice, quality of life, before the capitalist zeitgeist re-asserted itself in around 1980. Some psycho-historians reckon this current social phase could have only a decade or so to run before it starts to break down with growing atomisation of society and market monopolies beginning to dominate again. The cliff edge is still there. We could go back and take again the primrose path to the everlasting bonfire, but the United Nations is working very hard to avert that possibility.' Wensel was looking askance, but said with a smirk, 'Thank you Solomon, very good, and that's quite enough literary references piled up on each other to be going on with. Now, please get to the point.'

Solomon took no offence. 'Our reason for searching for a potential time traveller from the 2020s was simple. Evidence! So many records and reports from earlier in the century had been lost due to solar activity and internet breakdown. We needed more evidence of how things changed, or didn't, to feed into our models and appraisals, to write history. Very chancy, to find appropriate people from that time who just happen to be in a coma. You have been brilliant! So observant, widely read, thoughtful and honest. We couldn't have asked for a better person. All those debriefing sessions with Rufus and others have bolstered our understanding. Thank you so much. We owe you a lot. Thank you!' He looked around at his colleagues. 'We'd like to show our appreciation.'

The others were smiling broadly. Each thanked and congratulated me in their own style. Then to my great surprise they all stood up and clapped. Rufus cheered me. Wensel drew a bottle out of her bag. 'The very best Woodchester wine,' she said. 'For you and your friends to enjoy together, tonight. But now, time to wrap up. I think we are done.'

I was beginning to enjoy all this approbation and praise. It went to my head a bit: 'Could I maybe save this lovely wine, a little of it, for when I wake up back in my real home?' Maybe it was the gin speaking. Rufus, Sacha and Solomon laughed out loud. 'On no account!' said Rufus, 'It would vanish! And Sam and I intend to enjoy it too. And also whoever else you invite. Sam is concocting a most extravagant repast. We'll add another bottle or two.' I realised that this was to be my leaving do, and immediately thought who I would like to be there. 'Sacha – could you join us?' I asked. 'Of course I will,' she responded warmly.

There was a pause. I looked round at them all. 'I didn't expect this, this grand goodbye, at all, you know. And I have to say that my whole stay here has been the most extraordinary experience. I've learnt one hell of a lot and it's been incredibly inspiring. Which leads me to think, and worry, perhaps I have a job to do, when I get back. Is that part of your plan?'

Solomon looked serious again. 'What you do when you get back is entirely up to you. You are a free agent. We have no influence, indeed no contact will be possible with you. What is more we have no knowledge about your immediate future beyond what Rufus has already told you. Several longterm partners, no children, a respected professional career, including work for international organisations – though even on that the records are ridiculously sketchy. It's for you to work out your own destiny. Naturally, we hope that you fully remember and value all that's happened here.'

I nodded in acceptance and agreement. In fact, I was suddenly conscious of the weight of responsibility on my shoulders. Not to my companions in this future age, but to myself, to my ideals and ethics – and to the old world I once again live in.

Rufus brought me back to the moment … joking irreverently about the holy grail of sustainability, as was his wont. The final half hour before walking back to Temple Meads Station was filled with warm words, idle banter and (from Madame in particular) scientific curiosities, including the continuing mystery of the black hole at the heart of the Milky Way. Then we caught the train and tram to Woodchester, and later enjoyed the most marvellous, celebratory feast in Sam and Rufus's flat. I'd invited Able, of course, as well as Sacha. Able's cat invited himself, too, leading his 'manservant' Able up the stairs. It was clearly a well-rehearsed tradition. After the meal, when I was curled up on the sofa, with Domino purring loudly on my lap, I was already dancing into the rainbow. He left early, plumptious and smiling, almost Cheshire cat style, with his fluffy tale proudly erect.

We drank much too much, everyone letting go for once. So sozzled was I that I barely noticed when Sacha gave me an injection, 'To help you sleep deeply.' I knew what she meant, but with all the laughter and bonhomie, I didn't care. I found that I was ready. Before being guided to my own bed by Sam, all four of them hugged me long and tight. I felt a moment of complete irresponsibility, and wanted to kiss Rufus – and Sam too – on the lips. Their love for me! So I did. Gorgeous! Though if truth be told, it was a dozy kiss.

I fell asleep almost instantly, and never again woke in that world.

Epilogue: Tiger spirit

I am only one, but still I am one. I cannot do everything, but still I can do something...
I will not refuse to do something I can do.

Helen Keller

In mid-July 2023 I returned to the land of the living, after that fateful cycling collision. I'm told that for three months my body had lain prone in a hospital bed, in a coma, more dead than alive. But my mind was elsewhere. Indeed, it was apparent to me that I was elsewhere in body as well as in mind, in another time altogether, another world, though strangely in the same place. It puzzled me that while I'd been in a coma for so long, my time in the future had been only ten days. However, in those ten days I was living life to the full, meeting people of the new age, learning more than I ever knew or could have conceived. How this was possible I cannot say. Perhaps it was nothing more nor less than an incredibly long, coherent and vivid dream. But I cannot accept that. The enhanced abilities which were realised in the 2090s have stayed with me – a crystal clear, miraculous memory of everything that happened, and much greater confidence than before – confidence in myself and in how I relate to others. Perhaps reality is not what we take it to be, and there are more things in heaven and earth than are dreamt of in our philosophies.

The strange experience has changed me. It has radicalised my understanding of what is possible for the earth, society and the individual. It has transformed my hopes and intentions for my own future.

When I woke up back in this age, the medics who had been monitoring me and keeping my body fed and watered were astonished by the speed of my recovery. So was I. My first fleeting impression was that I was waking from a good night's sleep. But when I tried to get out of bed, my body would not respond, my eyes were blurred, my brain befuddled. Someone touched me lightly on my hand and face. I tried to stretch and mumbled something like 'good morning'. Limbs and lips failed to respond appropriately. But I am told by those who had gathered round my bed that from their perspective I positively bounced into life. Mistily I saw them round me, smiling encouragement, whispering to each other. It took a while for my brain to process the situation, not realising initially what had happened, puzzled at my state, lacking orientation or focus, gradually beginning to realise that my body was helpless. Eventually I began to interpret the words that had been whispers. The words were warm, comforting, telling me not to struggle, telling me to relax, don't try speaking, not just yet. Doctors were peering at me, looking in my eyes, testing reflexes. I latched onto the words 'coma' and 'accident'. The memory of the accident was still there, in my brain. In my confused state I tried to link that memory and where I was now.

It took a while. But later that day I understood just where I was, and was beginning to string words together. Food and drink were injected into me, as must have been happening when I was dead to the world. My limbs were enfeebled, almost lifeless appendages. The medics told me that despite the three months, they had never given up hope. My physical injuries had healed. They were amazed that I could recall anything about the accident.

It took time for my body to regain strength, sufficient to stand and walk, but since at last being discharged, I've been back in my flat at the top of town, dazed, somehow otherworldly. My mum, despite her mild dementia, has been more support than I thought her capable of – simply accepting me and asking no questions as I begin to digest what to me has been the most extraordinary experience of my life. Close colleagues and some running mates have visited me; thankfully they've avoided probing too deeply into what happened, not wanting to risk disrupting my gradual recovery.

I've been walking every day in the parks, woods and fields around the town, absorbing the feeling of being in nature, luxuriating in the views across the Golden Valley and the Severn Vale. Eventually I dared to venture down to the canal, and into town, revisiting places that now have palpable new memories associated with them. I've gradually been able to bring a semblance of order to often contradictory and puzzling events. A sense of normality and acceptance has imbued my soul.

So now I have come to the point of wanting – of needing – to share my experiences, trying to find meaning, trying to understand. Initially I did consider writing a quite technical report on my travels, focussing on the issues around the built environment, health and climate change, contrasting today and the future I visited. It did not seem to flow. I think this was because my experience in the future was so multi-dimensional that I was being false to the truth, artificially confining my text so that the full societal picture did not emerge, hiding my personal responses and realisations behind a veneer of professional expertise.

So instead, this book is a kind of diary, telling day by day what happened to me, the people I met, my insights into the way society operated, based on vanished notes that I made while it was all happening, which somehow have become imprinted on my memory. I've also allowed myself to reveal how my beliefs, self-image and behaviour have been influenced, trying to give a rounded and very human story.

Lacking writing experience beyond technical reports, I needed a collaborator. I chose Hugh Barton – friend, neighbour and my professional mentor for a number of years. He was enthusiastic! Working with Hugh has been an absolute pleasure. Downloading everything from me to him has taken many discussions, recordings and interviews, with me talking nineteen to the dozen, and him trying to make sense of it. I've reviewed and commented on everything, to ensure it expresses what I know and captures something of the feelings as well as the facts. Hence my decision – inspired also by Grayson Perry's example in his ghost-written autobiography – that the book is written in the first person.

The title News from Somewhen is an explicit reminder of News from Nowhere by William Morris, which deeply impressed me when I was a student. In it he imagines a time traveller to London in the distant future, who discovers the conurbation has dissolved into self-sufficient urban villages, like the state dissolves in Marxist theory. Very utopian, appealing to youthful idealism. Not real, I said. But there is hope in the future world I found, far from utopian but not dystopian either. I feel my experience is one to counteract the many nightmare narratives in fashion: books like Brave New World, The Handmaid's Tale and The Feed; in films like The

Matrix Resurrection, Dune and The Midnight Sky. My tale does have some very dark elements but provides the vital antidote.

I can only report what I know, and you may or may not choose to believe it all. If you respond with incredulity, that's your choice! But what I crave is empathy and openness, so that the insights which I received while my body, to all appearances, lay inert, can inform awareness and actions now. I can tell you that to me all my story is real – profoundly real. There is much I found puzzling, disturbing and even shocking, but there was also much to inspire hope for the future, for a fairer society, for a sustainable world – and to inspire wonder.

*****

Responding anew to the situation now, in the twenties, it is probably not surprising that I am horrified by the social inequalities and environmental compromises apparent, and the spatial trends in our villages, towns and cities. There is a huge gulf between the apparently well-meaning words about climate change, health and wellbeing of government, local authorities and businesses, and the mundane, unsustainable, inequitable and often ugly reality. The Covid lockdown shone a light on something profound: that the people who are most essential for life and community support were those paid the least. The level of inequality was brought home to me by my volunteering in the local food hub. So many people strapped for cash, even when they have jobs. So many poor people suffering prematurely from physical or mental illness, younger people dropping out of the rat race, employment rates falling.

I hope my diary has elaborated these points effectively. OK, not everything is depressing. Britain is ahead of the game in moving from fossil fuels to renewables, though the world is not. There is real improvement to some farms and green spaces, with tree planting and rewilding. And the cultural scene in my home town of Stroud is vibrant: art, sculpture, music, theatre, poetry – all are thriving. The cafe culture has taken over the town centre. Many older people are dynamic members of voluntary organizations. Many young people are demanding change, to recognise the global crises. One can, putting on tinted spectacles, see some green shoots.

Before my unprecedented coma experience, I was losing all hope. But now I can see how some of those green shoots could eventually blossom into leaf and flower, seed sustainable growth and transform our habitat. We may very well not be able to avoid meltdown. But we can and must take actions now which will fashion a long-term future worth living for.

The urban environment is part of the problem, crippling the life chances of people in poorer households – their incomes gobbled up by high rents or big mortgages, and the necessity in many areas of owning a car, even one car per adult. The pattern of development and the rules of engagement are to blame. I know how to plan people-friendly places, with good, reliable and frequent public transport, how to manage habitats and mitigate hot weather and the changing water cycle. Nevertheless, most decisions still pull in the opposite direction: in the Stroud area business parks and other new facilities have sprung up way out of town; new 'exurbs' sprout in inconvenient locations; pedestrian connections are broken by barriers and dangerous crossings; streets and junctions that are intimidating to aspiring cyclists remain unaddressed.

The ironic thing is that we have made a commitment, set in law, to cut emissions dramatically, to net zero by 2050, and hope to restrict global heating to 1.5 degrees above pre-industrial levels, to avoid the worst case scenarios of sea-level rise and ecological disaster. If we were planning effectively for the wellbeing of people, we would also have a chance of hitting our environmental targets, creating a resilient world. What is good for people is also good for the planet. But political dogma, market pressures and bureaucratic inertia are leading us, with our eyes wide open, down the wrong track.

In this context I have vowed to be an agent of change. My work will be the vehicle. It gives opportunities for innovation in the fields of urban design and planning for the human environment, and more broadly for global ecology, albeit at a small scale. Through promotion and advocacy, it can, I hope, reach public and private sector actors and influencers. The key is a clear and consistent ethical stance. Building on that, when faced with technical problems, it is possible to find creative solutions, which work strongly for health, sustainability, beauty and economic viability.

Doctors take an oath – the Hippocratic Oath – to promote human health. From the same era, an older colleague of Hippocrates, Hippodamus, has been called the father of town planning. He established sound spatial principles for new Greek settlements round the Aegean. I believe designers and planners should adopt a Hippodamic Oath as part of their professional philosophy. I will promote this idea, which is not new, through the professional institutes. It would mean that just as doctors are committed to preserve human life and health, so urban designers and related professionals would be committed to creating sustainable healthy human environments. They would be unable to sign off projects which fail that test. Such principles will not instantly revolutionise commercial or political priorities. They need to be adopted by all the linked professions: planners, architects, engineers, surveyors, land managers and landscape architects. The hope would be that some powerful bodies, driven by the growing sense of crisis, would adopt them too. And mean it!

*****

So … I hope to be part of a movement for human survival, for nature, for the earth, a catalyst for change, inspired by everything I saw and heard in the future world.

The memory of that future world is still strong in me. The images of the people I met are still vivid. However, I can sense that the clarity of the vision could fade. Hence my desire to write up my sojourn now, while the intensity of memory remains.

Of course, the professional and political perspectives are only part of the story. What I loved about the future world was its diversity. My guides introduced me to many facets of life and society. It was a rich and riveting experience. I find myself changed. Whether it be a deeper recognition of cultural identity, a new insight into behavioural and sexual conventions, or the insights of the psycho-historians, my own inherited perspectives have been challenged, my ideas of what is possible revolutionised.

I find myself altered in a much more personal sense. Once I'd regained my strength after the coma – a process that took many months, allowing me to tell my story to my friend Hugh before returning to employment – I realised that there is more fire in my belly, more steel in my bones, more warmth in my heart. I have a level of confidence I could not have dreamed of before my remarkable transition there and back. I am seeing people more clearly, more openly, not pre-judging by habit or fashions. It is so refreshing, freed from the constraints that inhibited me before. This applies both to work and social life. In work I have found not only greater confidence, but also a level of direct engagement with colleagues and clients – much less formal – that helps me be more persuasive and build bridges. In social life I have found myself much more outgoing and empathic. I am making new friends through sporting and musical activities, and those friendships deepen quite naturally as we share confidences and enthuse each other. It is as if I have been released to be myself. I can already sense that this release will open up sexual and romantic opportunities which in my earlier existence seemed foreign to me – something other people enjoyed but where I was simply the observer. That is not to say that my emotions were not stirred before. Rather that feelings and desires had often remained hidden.

I'll put it another way. My coma, my time travel explorations, are more than incidental episodes in my life, much more. I've crossed a huge threshold. I see the world anew. Black, white and grey have transformed into vibrant colours. I take delight in everything. I take joy in everything. Despite deep awareness of all the problems in society and the existential risks to global survival, I sense, with Wordsworth, the unity of earth, nature and humankind.

This sense of the oneness of creation has given me a newfound determination to make a difference. It is my profound hope that it is not too late for the world to turn the corner: to get to grips with the crises of climate, biodiversity, inequality and health. It is in this context that I hope this account and the extraordinary story it tells has impact beyond casual interest and entertainment. I hope that you, the readers, are moved to take action in your own lives and in society. I want the story to make waves – to influence public, professional and political perceptions. I want people to wake up!

There is an old saying, that all it takes for evil to triumph is for good people to do nothing. The reverse is surely true – at least to an extent. When good people take dynamic action, evil forces will retreat. Let us fight together for humanity, for the earth.

Robyn Ghorra

Thanks

It is not conventional to include acknowledgements with a novel, even one claiming some future history reality. But I feel it is right to throw convention to the winds in this case, because of the invaluable support given to me writing the book while ill with Multiple Myeloma.

First, inestimable thanks to my wife, Val Kirby, without whose loving care for me while ill, and persistent encouragement when the odds were against it, this book would never have been completed. Second, to my two 'coffee club' friends, Liz Bavister and Leonora Rozee. who read each chapter at it emerged, and whose infectious enthusiasm and comments were so helpful. Third, to my initial publication advisor Martin Large; to Jenny Saunders, my patient and thoughtful editor; and to Rachel of the Choir Press who managed production meticulously.

Beyond that, there are a host of people who have contributed their knowledge and ideas, through their books, writings, websites and other media; also through specially arranged interviews on specific aspects of society and technology. Many thanks to all of them.

Some will recognise chapter headings that are inspired by T. S. Eliot, *Four Quartets*, or Ben Okri, *Tiger Spirit.*

Hugh Barton